Bad Eye Blues

Bad Eye Blues

Neal Barrett, Jr.

KENSINGTON BOOKS

http://www.kensingtonbooks.com

KENSINGTON BOOKS are published by

Kensington Publishing Corp.
850 Third Avenue
New York, NY 10022

Copyright © 1997 by Neal Barrett, Jr.

Library of Congress Card Catalog Number: 96-079077
ISBN 1-57566-173-X

First Printing: June, 1997
10 9 8 7 6 5 4 3 2 1

Printed in the United States of America

With love and respect,
this one's for
JOE R. LANSDALE,
MY EVIL TWIN

1

My head hurt bad.

It was clear I'd been out for some time.

You can tell you've been out when you're somewhere else, when you're not where you think you ought to be. I was not in a chic restaurant. I was not with the lovely Claire de Mer. I did not smell Coq au Vin, I did not smell Chanel. What I smelled was doughnuts and diapers, Doublemint gum. Cardboard coffee and ancient onion rings. Wet socks and winos, yesterday's tears. Chicken parts and kiddie farts, diesel and despair.

This rank and gamy scent was ripe enough to choke a goat, strong enough to bring a rhino to its knees. I didn't have to guess. I opened my eyes and saw people I didn't want to see. Where I was was on a bus. Me, and ten tons of losers in a big blue box. Me, on a goddam bus.

I never ride a bus.

I turned to the man in the seat next to mine. He had very broad features, very dark hair. Cheekbones and predatory eyes. A nose like the guy on nickels, the kind you can't find anywhere.

"Listen," I said. "This is going to sound kind of goofy, okay? Would you happen to recall how long I've been here, did you see me get on? Do you know where we're going, do you know when we left D.C.?"

"You're awake," he said, "that's good. Don't be startled or alarmed. Don't make any sudden moves. Don't cry out, don't try to get away. Don't speak to anyone. Don't try to pass a note. Anything of that nature could result in injury or harm."

I stared at the man. "What are you talking about, are you nuts? I bet you watch a lot of TV."

"I'll watch a nature show, they got an eagle or a bear. I'll watch a college game sometime. This is an abduction, Mr. Moss. You're being taken against your will. Don't do nothing real stupid, you're going to be fine."

"You're *kidnapping* me? On a bus?"

"Yes I am."

"That's ridiculous. You can't kidnap a person on a bus."

"Yes I can."

"What for?"

"That's none of your concern."

"Well I think it is, I think it's very much my concern. Who are you, anyway? You look like a Native American to me."

"*Native's* got a bad ring to it. You can thank those Tarzan movies for that. I'm an Indian of the Nez Perce tribe. The coming of the horse in the 1700s changed our lives. We're responsible for breeding the famed Appaloosa. In 1877, we fought a great war against the whites. We're a very proud people but we're nearly wiped out. Big fucking surprise. You want to hear this?"

"No I don't. Listen, friend, I don't know what this is all about, but I can tell you right now that I won't sit still for an abduction on a bus. I'm not going anywhere with you, I'm getting off right now."

A passing car lit his face. I saw his skin was hard as stone, I saw he had a bad eye. One of his pupils was white as milk.

"I'm Bobby Bad Eye," he said, "and *you* listen to me. We'll be together some time. Don't do anything dumb. Don't give me any trouble, we'll get along okay. You want an orange?"

"No thanks."

He reached down between his feet. He had a bunch of oranges in a little net sack. Two things you got to have you take a bus. You got to have a ticket, you got to have oranges in a little net sack.

Bobby Bad Eye picked up an orange. He studied it a minute and looked right at me. "You're going to do something stupid. I can see it in the way you move your mouth. You're going to try and get away. You think you're Bruce Willis, you think you're going to take me unawares."

"Yeah, and what happens if I try?"

"What happens is I gut you with my Native American knife."

Something stuck me in the ribs. Bobby Bad Eye sucked an orange.

I said, "I'll try later on, I don't guess I'll try now."

"That's cool."

"You've got to sleep sometime."

"That's true, I do. But Rocco doesn't. Rocco doesn't have to sleep at all."

"Uh-huh. And who would Rocco be?"

"That's me, Mr. Moss. I'm right back here."

Someone tapped me on the shoulder. I nearly jumped out of my skin. I turned and saw a white pumpkin head. Skin white as soap. No eyebrows, no hair. Pink eyes and a little sucker mouth, a little baby nose.

Bobby Bad Eye said, "This is Rocco, Mr. Moss. Rocco doesn't sleep. Rocco stays awake all the time."

"I haven't closed my eyes since Bong Son, February 1966. I been real jumpy ever since."

"I think I saw you in *Deliverance*. November 1972."

"No sir, now I never been there. I was in Talcum, Kentucky, in '72. We might've run across each other then."

"You play the banjo, right?"

"Shit, how'd you know that?"

2

I am having dinner in a chic restaurant with the girl who found a sandwich in Lucky Lindy's plane. The sandwich has been there since 1927. The sandwich is seventy years old. The lovely Claire de Mer is twenty-two. Ash-blonde hair, black jersey dress. Soft bare shoulders and bare nearly everything else. Her skin is this dusty olive tone that looks gold in candlelight. The name sounds French, but the eyes say Italian to me.

What happened is, Claire is on a scaffold in the National Aeronautics and Space Museum. She is doing a routine check on the Lindbergh plane. She is tightening a screw on the instrument panel and the sandwich drops out.

"This is amazing," I said. "It just drops out. You're tightening a screw, it just drops right out. This is the sandwich the guy didn't eat on his record-breaking flight."

"It's there," she said, "it just drops out. God, I thought I'd die, you know?"

"Hey, who wouldn't, something happens like that, you're tightening a screw, you make this great historical find. Your average person has got to react to that."

"It was ham and cheese, they know that. It was petrified but nearly intact."

"Whole wheat or white?"

"Oh, white. This is 1927. It was definitely white."

"New York to Paris. Up there all alone. Thunderheads and ice. He fights to stay awake all the time."

"It was worth it, though. A triumphant welcome at Le Bourget Field. He was very shy, you know. He didn't like the crowds. Wiley, two things, all right? One, I am quite attracted to you. I think you're attracted to me, you've been looking down my dress for some time. Two, I don't want to get involved. Not with anyone at all. The last thing I need is some deep emotional shit messing up my life. Can you live with that, hon? Is that enough for you?"

"Just a surface relationship, you mean. This is what you want."

"I can't give you any more than that. I simply can't right now."

"We use each other. Satisfy our physical needs."

"Yes. That's how it has to be."

"Claire?"

"Yes, Wiley?"

"I can live with that."

"Oh God, I am *so* glad." She reached out and touched my hand. I looked down her dress again.

"I was afraid it might be—messy, you know? That you might not want me this way."

"I'm not as narrow-minded as all that, Claire. I can be pretty understanding, as I think you'll come to see."

She sighed and closed her eyes. "Do you have any idea what it's like for me? Being young and lovely's not all it's cracked up to be. There are drawbacks an ordinary woman never has to think about. I date some guy, you know? He's thinking, wow, this woman is flat-out gorgeous. A stunner, and a top-flight aeronautical engineer on top of that. This girl is no roll in the hay. You even make a *move* on this person, you better have commitment in mind. It's the same crap every time. You understand this, Wiley, you know what I'm saying?"

"Oh, absolutely, I certainly do."

Jesus, I certainly did. I understood if I didn't screw up, like tell her we were meant to be one, or give her my college track pin, I had stumbled on a woman who wanted no more from me than meaningless sex, carnal enterprise, coupling on a lazy afternoon. A sexist pigette, so to speak, intent on her own base desires.

No one's that lucky, of course. Certainly not me. She had to be unstable, a psycho goddess, a leggy lunatic. A nut or a bolt just rattling about in that perfectly beautiful head, a booby on a weekend pass.

But, hey, that was okay with me. We are each of us blown by the wind, we are none of us master of our fate. And you've got to respect someone for that.

All this in a very cozy restaurant across the Potomac in Fairfax County. When senators take their wives somewhere, when they want to be seen, they dine in Georgetown. When they want to get away from it all, they come here. I didn't know about this, since my paycheck doesn't call for fancy nights out. Claire knew, though. She had obviously been there before and I didn't ask with who.

Dinner was a coronary dream. After that, we had her favorite liqueur, which was made out of unborn fruit of some kind, and tasted as good as Dimetapp. It came in a little tiny glass and cost twenty bucks a pop. It was made by Spanish monks, who had taken a vow not to ever be poor.

"My God," Claire said, when we'd had another glass, and I was hoping we could go to her place instead of mine, "can you imagine what it must have been like up there? A young mail pilot with a vision in his head. The darkness, the cold and deadly Atlantic, never far below."

"I can see it," I told her. "I can see it, Claire."

"You can, can't you? I know that now."

She looked at me with those incredible Mediterranean eyes. They were blue, they were brown. They might have been black. They were the color of smoke on a morning in Seville, though I've never been overseas before.

"I haven't flown," I said. "I mean, I've *flown* lots of times, but not like that, not in control of the aircraft itself. Now I take that back. When I was a kid, the guy next door, his dad took me up one time. Had his own Piper Cub. I believe it was an old J-3. He let me hold the stick and I put us in a dive. He wouldn't take me up after that."

"And where was this? Where was my Wiley as a child?"

She leaned close to me across our table. I could smell her skin. I could smell that drink that cost twenty bucks a whack. One of her straps slid down a golden shoulder and my stomach did a flip.

"We lived in Cincinnati at the time. My family's from Defiance County, Ohio. That's in the northwest corner of the state. Our people were into hardware there."

"A farm boy, then." She showed me a lazy smile.

"Oh, yeah. Not a very exciting start in life, I'm afraid."

"I'd love you to take me there some time."

"Where's that?"

"Five Ants County."

"Defiance."

"Whatever," Claire said.

She dipped her sharp little tongue in her liqueur. My heart skipped a beat.

"The Ryan wasn't his first choice, you know. A Bellanca was considered. And a Fokker after that."

"I know," I said. "But the Ryan won out. Wright engine, 223 horses. Maximum speed, 124."

"You know what he had? No night instruments. Not a one. And no lights. He's crossing the Atlantic, he's got a fucking *flashlight*. You want to picture that?"

"He couldn't even see out front. He had that enormous gas tank."

"I'm getting real hot, Wiley."

"Lord, Claire, so am I."

"My strap fell off. I bet you can see my whole top. Can you see it yet, hon?"

"I can see some. I can't see it all."

"You know what? I am shaking all over. I even *breathe*, everything's going to fall out."

"For God's sake, let's get out of here. I can't take any more of this."

Claire bit her lip. "I'm going to have you every way there is, Wiley Moss. Straight up, backwards and upside down."

"I like to think I'm a fairly modern guy. Anything goes with me." My throat went dry. "Where you from originally, I don't think I asked. My guess is Italy or France."

"Shawnee, Oklahoma."

"Is that right? Hey, I was pretty close."

She stood, then, uncurling like a snake. I thought I saw something but I couldn't tell for sure.

"Get the car, all right? I'll meet you out there."

I told her that I would. I told her she could count on that. I watched her as she crossed the dining room. I watched the sweet undulation, the heart-stopping motion of her hips, the *swish-swish-swish* of the black jersey dress. And so did everybody else.

And if the evening sent the folks up at Visa in a spin, if my card set off whistles and alarms, what did I care? I had the lovely Claire de Mer. And the lovely Claire de Mer had me.

I walked across the asphalt lot, searching for the car. It was summertime, and our nation's capital is a hot and sultry swamp, even at a quarter after ten. I spotted the car. Two rows down. I thought about Shawnee, Oklahoma. I wondered if she'd lied about that. And if she did, why there?

That's when someone came up behind me, stepping from the shadows of a '96 Lexus. I think it was the natty 400. It might have been blue, it was too dark to tell. Something sharp stuck me in the ass, and I don't recall a thing after that.

. . . Except for a quick, very brief insight, that told me women like Claire seldom happen to a guy named Wiley Moss. Not in real life, which is what I'm most accustomed to. And that, I'd guess, is why everything got completely screwed that night, everything except Claire de Mer and me.

3

"There's a lot of stuff I don't get, you know? I mean, I *get* it, it's not I don't get it—I'm thinking, I get it okay, but it don't look right, it isn't how it ought to be, you know? You know what I'm saying? Like *Ben Hur,* okay? This ol' boy, he's tryin' to do Charlton Heston in? He's the major asshole, is who he is. I don't recall the man's name, it's Stephen Boyd is who he is, I mean, this is who he is in real life.

"So there's—what? Fifteen, twenty bozos from all over, they're all lined up for this major chariot race. I mean, there's jokers from Africa, Greece, there's even a Jew guy there. Everybody's got a chariot, right? And everybody's chariot is pretty much alike. I mean, say one's a Ford chariot, and another one's a Dodge, you know what I mean? They got different colored horses, their chariots are pretty much alike. Everyone except for Stephen Boyd, okay? *He's* got this fuckin' *blade* on his wheels. Fuckin' thing looks like a *saw,* for Chrissakes. Boyd gets close to some guy, this thing goes *shhhrrrrik!,* somethin' like that? Chews up your spokes like a ripsaw from Sears, man. You're lyin' flat on your ass in that arena—the fall don't kill you, some horse runs over your head.

"You're drivin' next to this guy, he's goin' for your wheels, you're thinking—hey, just what is this? Nobody told me we could have a bunch of saws or anything, what's the fuckin' deal? They don't have a ref, some guy knows the rules? What is this? See, this is what I mean, this is what I don't get. Something like that isn't fair, someone oughta caught that."

"There was a lot of injustice in Rome back then," I said. "Happened all the time."

"Yeah. Well fuck that," Rocco said. "Someone shoulda caught it."

"Someone should've," I said.

Bobby Bad Eye was asleep. He didn't slump over, he didn't lean back. He sat straight up. I wondered if this was a personal habit, or something in his Indian genes. Everybody had to sit straight back then and be ready for bears. Later, they had to watch out for white guys.

It was true what Bobby said. Rocco didn't sleep. Rocco didn't close his eyes. He talked all night, and breathed on me with Milky Way breath. It wasn't too bad, because he talked in a perfect monotone, as soothing as any lullaby.

I drifted off in *Sands of Iwo Jima,* and woke up in time for *Ben Hur.* Rocco didn't look real smart. That's because Rocco was dumb. Still, Rocco knew his movies. Everything there was to know. Everything you didn't *want* to know. There were seven, maybe eight pictures he hadn't seen. Maybe nine or ten. *Deliverance* was one that he'd missed. Be grateful for small favors. Lately, that's the only kind I get.

Before I dropped off I saw a sign. We were passing through Cumberland, Maryland, a hundred and forty miles from D.C. West, on Interstate 68 which I happened to know, because I knew a guy from there. If we kept on going, the map in my head said West Virginia straight ahead. Then what? And, of more concern to me, *why?* What did these crazy mothers want with me?

They already had my wallet. I'd reached back and checked. Ten dollars, ten or twelve. My wallet and my watch, and a greatly depleted Visa card, thanks to my evening with Claire de Mer. If they tortured me for five or ten seconds, I would reveal my secret PIN code. They could stop at an automatic teller and get my entire three hundred bucks.

It didn't seem to me there could be a lot of profit in that. Take out expenses—three bus tickets, Bobby's sack of oranges, Rocco's

Milky Ways. No way. It had to be something else. Something important. Important enough to wait for me, stick me with a needle, and haul me out of a parking lot. Maybe they'd confused me with somebody else. A rich guy named Moss who ate all the time in expensive restaurants.

How likely was that? About as likely as getting kidnapped by a one-eyed Indian and an albino movie fan. Throw in a cross-country bus, and figure the odds for yourself.

"Who you think's the best lookin'—Nina Foch or Simone Signoret? Which one you think?"

"I have no idea," I said.

"Hey, there ain't no contest, boy. Nina Foch is number one." He slapped the back of my head to make a point. "Nina Foch is a fine-lookin' woman, okay? I mean, she's gotta be real old now. Shoot, I don't know, she's maybe dead. But that's the magic of motion pictures. Time stands still on the big silver screen. You're always a star up there."

"Yeah, right."

"What's that supposed to mean? She ain't attractive to you?"

"She's terrific, Rocco. What time is it?"

"What do you care? You aren't going anywhere. Gregory Peck. *The Yearling.* That little ol' deer. I love that fuckin' deer. Jane Wyman. You see her in *Johnny Belinda?* She used to be married to President what'sisname."

"Franklin Pierce."

"That's the guy."

"It's ten after twelve," Bobby Bad Eye said. "I would like you to shut up, Rocco. Cool it with the movie stars."

He turned and looked at me. His milky eye looked spooky in the dark. "Don't be asking Rocco stuff, Mr. Moss. Like about what time it is, where we are an' where we're going."

"I didn't ask him that. I asked him the time, I didn't ask him that."

"No, you were thinking on it, though. Next time you think about it, don't. You care for an orange?"

"No thanks."

He reached in his sack. "Fruit's good for you. A person ought to eat a lot of fruit. Fruit and stuff that's green."

"Where are we," I said. "Where are we going, what do you want with me?"

Bobby Bad Eye gave me that look. The last thing Custer ever saw. "You're doing it, aren't you? I told you not to do it, Mr. Moss."

"You told me not to ask him. I'm not asking him, I'm asking you."

"You probably never pissed off a full-blood Nez Perce before. It's not a real good idea."

"No it's not," Rocco said. "It sure ain't a good idea."

"Take a break, Mr. Moss."

"Okay I guess I will."

I looked out the window. A lonely little town flashed by. One service station, shut up for the night, a 20-watt bulb inside. A clapboard house with a tree and a porch, everything dark downstairs. Upstairs, the shades pulled down, and someone in there. If I could overpower Bobby, and Rocco of Hollywood, I could get off and knock on that door. Maybe a small-town beauty lived there, someone as lovely as Claire de Mer, but with simpler, cheaper tastes. Someone who was gentle and kind, and happy with grocery store beer.

I couldn't see a sign, but I figured West Virginia by now. The bus would keep to the interstate, so we'd have to cut through a little slice of Pennsylvania, back to West Virginia, then over the line. Back to Ohio, back to my native land, like anybody cared. Or maybe somewhere else. Indiana or Kentucky. Alabama or Brazil. How the hell would I know, I was just the dumb shit sitting there, I was just the kidnapee . . .

Maybe Alabama did it. I felt real hot. Like my skin was on fire. I felt like a total fucking dope, sitting there taking abuse from people I didn't even know. I hate to do what other people say.

Goddamn it, that's it—I've had enough of this!

"Okay," I said, "I've had enough of this. Do whatever you want, I don't intend to keep still. I don't think you'll do much, I don't think you'll risk it on a public bus. I don't think you'll stick me with your Native American knife. I don't think you really want a major hassle here."

Bobby Bad Eye shrugged. "Okay, you got one right. So what?"

"I've got one simple question, Mr. Eye."

"Hey, man, don't be calling me Mr. Eye."

"Fine, whoever."

"I want an answer, and I want it right now. Where are we going and what's this all about?"

"That's two questions."

"Huh-unh. It's just one question, it's got two parts."

Bobby Bad Eye gave me a weary look. "What if I said you're in no mortal danger, Mr. Moss? That it isn't that kind of a thing, and no one intends you any harm? Would you trust me on that?"

"Certainly not. Why would I want to do that?"

"See, if it was, it was something like that, we wouldn't be having this interestin' conversation right now. You yakking and keeping me up, telling me shit that I don't want to hear. Where you'd be, you'd be in a Hefty bag back in D.C., you'd be floatin' to the top somewhere."

Bobby Bad Eye stuck a finger in my face. He had a very nice ring, a rattlesnake with turquoise eyes.

"The thing is, you keep nagging at me, I'll start accumulatin' excess acid, which is something I do in times of stress. I start doing that, I'm waiting till we stop somewhere, I get me some Tums, I'm picking up a Hefty bag.

"In the interest of happy traveling, Mr. Moss, I got to tell you, doing a guy on a bus isn't any big deal. You got to do it, you do it, okay? You get where you're going, everybody else gets off. You're still sitting there, you're not gettin' off. Guy comes and cleans out the bus, he gets a big surprise.

"Keep your eye on him, Rocco. I got this spiritual vision in my head. My grandfather sees Mr. Moss here leapin' up and down, yelling at the passengers, causing great disturbance on a bus. I don't want to see that."

"You won't see it, Bobby," Rocco said. He patted me on the neck. "He ain't going to leap nowhere."

"Good. I don't want to see that."

Bobby closed his eyes. The bad one, then the good eye, too. Good posture. Straight up. Sound asleep.

"You shouldn't irritate him like that," Rocco said. "You don't want to get Bobby riled up. It's an awful thing to see."

"I can't wait."

"Don't kid about it, man. That wasn't bad at all. It was only 'bout a two."

"It was what?"

"About a two. Your native 'muricans is closer to nature than us. Sometimes they'll hark back to ancient ways. They got a breakin' point, which is a private and personal thing. Bobby calls his 'reaching nine.'"

"Nine's not good."

"Shit, I guess. I don't even want to think about it."

I thought about it.

"This grandfather stuff. What's he do, smoke some illegal plant and go into a trance?"

"He could do that. He'll mostly just get him on the phone. Mr. Badger's got a Honda dealership in Santa Fe. The family's real close."

"Santa Fe. And that's where Mr. Bad Eye's from, I'll bet."

Rocco chuckled to himself. "Shoot, you know better'n that, Mr. Moss."

He touched my neck just below the ear. "This little spot right here? You press a little harder than—*that*—you feel that right there? Do that, and you'll be with Lord Jesus 'fore you can say scat. You want a Milky Way?"

"No thanks."

Rocco took his thumb away. I took a deep breath.

"I don't think I'm talkin' out of turn, I tell you I think Bobby likes you a lot. I saw it right off."

"I must've missed that."

"No, I did. See, he don't like to get close to no one on the job. Hell, you can see why."

Rocco was fast as a trained guard dog. The instant a muscle twitched, his big hands clamped my shoulders tight.

"Just take it easy, Mr. Moss," Rocco said. "Ever'thing works out like it should, you got a two-way comin' back. Isn't everyone can say that . . ."

4

It looked like a truck stop looks.

What you've got, you got a shit load of trucks, you got pumps and bright lights. A lot of the truckers just stay inside a truck. They're asleep, they're smoking dope, they've got a sweetie in there. If they're not in a truck then they're inside the stop, drinking lots of bad coffee, eating cornstarch pie.

Nobody told me where we were. We got off the bus and the bus went away. I sneaked a look at Bobby's watch and it was something after three. We were up pretty high. The morning air was cool, and I saw a lot of pines.

I thought about Claire. By now, we would likely be asleep. Done in and played out, our lusty needs entirely satisfied. I would reek of manly sweat; Claire would exude the musky scent of womankind. I played out the evening in my head. Checked it over twice, to make sure I'd left nothing vital out. We did everything that we could do, including certain acts that required gymnastic skills.

What did she think when she found that I was gone? Did she search the restaurant, roam about the parking lot? Did Bobby Bad Eye leave my car there? No, this redskin was crafty, he was smarter than that. If the car was still there, the cops would suspect foul play. And if the car was gone? They'd take one look at Claire de Mer and decide that I was nuts, that I ought to be locked up somewhere.

We were sitting in the weeds beneath a tree. There were radiators there, and empty oil cans. Bobby wouldn't take us inside, which wasn't hard to figure out. I hadn't tried to bolt on the bus. It didn't make sense to do that, but the busy restaurant was something else. I could likely cry for help before Bobby did me in. There were thirty or forty large truckers in there, poor odds for anyone, even a man with a very long knife.

Instead, he sent a kid in and the kid came back with a sack of greasy burgers, coffee and saturated fries. The kid had found two bruised peaches and an overripe banana for Bobby Bad Eye. This seemed to suit him just fine.

I watched him bite into a peach. Juice ran down his chin.

I used to be very good at track. I figured the distance to the restaurant at forty-five yards. If I could get a good start, I could dash into the open and beat him hands down. I could, if Rocco wasn't sitting right behind me, breathing down my neck, bolting down his candy bars.

"Best thing for you to do is just take it easy, Mr. Moss," Bobby said, clearly guessing my thoughts. "I told you—behave yourself, you got nothing to worry about. Think about that pretty lady. You get back home, you can take her out to dinner again."

"Right," I said. "I'll just tell her I was kidnapped by an Indian and his paleface companion on a bus. I'm sure she'll go for that."

"I'd be more than glad to write you a note."

"Don't go to any trouble for me."

Bobby studied a peach pit and tossed it in the dark. "You're a real fortunate man, Mr. Moss. A woman like that could be a New York model or a TV star. Wouldn't have to mess with a bunch of airplanes. Wouldn't have to go out with you, far as that's concerned. I doubt you appreciate your lot. I've seldom met a white man who did."

"Hey, that burns me up," I said. "Miss de Mer and I happen to have a very close relationship, and she *likes* going out with me. As for what she does, she can— How do you know what she does?"

I stared at Bobby Bad Eye. I *knew* how he knew, and that irritated the hell out of me.

"Christ, you've been following me around. That's an invasion of my—"

Bobby shook his head. "I don't look through keyholes, friend, I just do an ID. That's your standard procedure, where a guy works, where he lives. You work at the Smith, she works at the Smith. Different building down the street."

He stood and brushed off his pants. "Breakfast is over. We're outta here."

"Where are we going now?"

Bobby didn't answer. He stuck a banana in his pocket and stalked off down the road.

Rocco, who hadn't spoken a word until now, said, "None of your beeswax, man. Do like Bobby says."

He poked me in the ribs. It hurt, and I did what Bobby said.

We walked some fifty yards up the highway. Besides the truck stop, there was a mom-and-pop grocery—closed up tight—and two or three darkened houses set back in tangled trees off the road. There were apparently people here, but it wasn't exactly a town.

"You mind me askin' you something?" Rocco said. "It's something I'd like to know."

"Yes I do," I said.

"Do what?"

"Mind you asking me something. I mind it a lot. Anything to do with you or Mr. Eye there, I don't like it, I mind it a lot."

"I know what you do, Bobby went and told me that. What I want to know is why, Mr. Moss, 'cause I never heard of anyone doing it before. Why you want to draw a bunch of bugs?"

"Because I do."

"Yeah, but *why* you want to do it, I don't get why you want to do that . . ."

I stopped. Rocco kept walking and nearly knocked me over in the dark. "It's none of your beeswax what I do, all right? Just because you're holding a person against his will, that doesn't give you any right to intrude upon that person's life, or question his professional career."

I looked at his pasty white head. His face was as bright as a tiny moon. "Why do you do what *you* do, Rocco? Does it make you feel good to push people around, to poke your finger in their back? Does this satisfy some deep-felt need?"

"No, sir. I don't guess." Rocco grinned, showing off his pumpkin teeth. "What it was, I saw a chance to better myself. I was mesmerizin' animals at Rudy's Roadside Rattlesnake Zoo, over up near Yellowstone. You know, you touch a rattler or a duck or most anything else just right the sum'bitch'll drop off. Just pass right out. The kids really go for that. You get 'em all turned on, they'll wart their folks to death to buy a bunch of souvenirs.

"So Bobby drops by one time to sell Rudy some snakes? He sees me put a badger under in about a second flat, he says, 'I can use a man's got magic in his hands. You want to work for me?' I says, 'Yeah, I guess.' He settles up with Rudy, and we been together ever since."

"What a lucky break for you."

"I'll say. Happenstance don't strike you every day."

"Rocco, button it up back there." Bobby turned on us in the dark. "Mr. Moss doesn't need to hear your life story, and I already heard it a couple of hundred times."

"Don't see how it hurts no one . . ."

Rocco mumbled under his breath, but Bobby had ancient tribal genes, genes that could hear a buffalo fart at three miles. He looked hard at Rocco, and Rocco looked contrite.

Bobby turned away, stopped, hesitated, as a semi whined up the grade, catching us all in a searing cone of white, shaking the earth with trucker pride, headlights sweeping past a sign that read BILLY'S GAS & AUTO REPAIR, a ruined, barely legible sign punched with rusty cratered holes by marksmen passing by.

We stood and watched the truck disappear, watched the shrinking square of lights. Bobby walked off the road, and we followed him down past the sign to a building made of corrugated tin. There were dead transmissions in the tall dry grass, engines gutted belly-up. A hand-painted sign on the building said CLOSED. Bobby doubled up his fist and started banging on the door.

"They might be closed," I said.

"They might well be," Bobby said.

"What are we doing, anyway? What are we doing here?"

"Shut up," Bobby said.

"Yeah, shut up," Rocco said, and poked me in the back.

Bobby continued to hammer on the door, a steady and irritating beat. A dog began to bark nearby. Another, then another took up the cry. Soon, the silent countryside was alive with doggie howls.

A light came on inside, framing the cracks around the door.

An unfriendly voice said, "We're closed. Open up at eight A.M."

Bobby didn't stop, didn't break the rhythm of his blows.

"Listen, it's four in the morning," someone said. "I'd suggest you stop that right now."

Bobby kept on, Bobby didn't stop.

"He won't stop," Rocco said. "I could tell that joker, Bobby isn't goin' to stop."

"That'd be my guess," I said. "I don't think he's going to stop."

"*Okay*, you fuckers, stop it right now or I'm firing through the door!"

"I hope you'll reconsider that," Bobby said.

"What for?"

"You could injure someone out here."

"That's just what I intend."

"What are you using, you don't mind I ask."

"Parker double barrel. Walnut stock with the checkered pistol grip."

"Why, that's an antique weapon," Bobby said.

"It'll still make mincemeat out of you."

"Is that a 16-gauge or a 12? I'll make you a handsome offer if it's a 12."

"I don't want to sell."

"Let me take a look. You might change your mind."

"God*damn*, I am gettin' tired of you."

"Think it over. I got lots of time."

Bobby kept knocking, Bobby didn't stop.

The door jerked open. The man standing there was bigger than Rocco or Bobby, either one. Thick-neck, shoulders wider than the door, a gorilla stuffed in Sears overalls. Hair sprouting from his shoulders, hair on his toes. A wild array of hair on his head and a heavy beard to match, the beard full of tangles and mats, full of unseemly clots, full of gobs of this and that, meals that hadn't made it to his mouth.

"Shit." He blinked at Bobby with little red eyes. "It's you. How come I didn't figure that?"

Bobby looked right at him. He didn't look at the weapon aimed at his private parts.

"I've got a Lincoln Town Car here," Bobby said. "I left it with you to get it fixed."

"I know you did." He glanced past Bobby to Rocco, then to me, then back to Bobby again. "It's all done. Four-hundred seventeen-fifty, as I recall."

"Sounds reasonable to me."

"Good. We open up at eight."

"I'll go ahead and get it right now."

"I don't guess you will."

"And why's that, sir?"

"It's the middle of the night. I was sleeping real fine. I was having my way with Vanessa Redgrave, you went and woke me up."

"Isadora," Rocco said, "1968."

"Mary, Queen of Scots. I'm a sucker for a costume picture of any sort."

Bobby turned a milky eye on Rocco, then faced the man again.

"I apologize for waking you up. I don't mean to be inconsiderate, friend, and I'm willing to pay a small bonus for your time. But I've got to have that car."

"That right, you got have your car? You got to have it right now?"

The man showed Bobby a nasty grin. "No fucking way, you reading me, *friend?* Even if you was white, Tonto, we still open up at eight o'cl—"

It gets a little hazy right here. I think it might've gone the way it did, with or without that ethnic affront, but there's no way to tell about that. What happened was something like a blur, like a trick of the eye, like something didn't happen but it did. Bobby Bad Eye had the shotgun now, and the man had a moment of wonder, of doubt and disbelief, a moment very brief before the butt of the weapon struck his crotch, and the barrel smashed him hard in the mouth.

He staggered back and shook his head, surprised to find his mouth full of blood, surprised to find his beard a bright red. Bobby didn't give him time to think. Something winked, something flashed, something in his hand went *slik-slik-slik!* like a painter slashing bold strokes of color in the air. The man made a noise, like a squeak, like a mouse, and then everything began to come apart, like you're taking out the garbage and the bottom drops out . . .

Something started coming up, something tasted awful bad. Rocco got me quickly outside. I threw up my burger and my coffee and my fries.

"I'm sorry you had to see that, Mr. Moss. Bobby's goin' to take offense sometimes, you never do know when."

"Uh-huh." I wiped my mouth on my sleeve. The dogs had stopped barking, everything was quiet.

"What is it you called it, he starts going nutso like that? Stretching nine?"

Rocco grinned. "Shoot, that wasn't a nine, Mr. Moss. That was 'bout a five."

"A five."

"Yes, sir. It was edgin' up to six, but I'm going to say a five. Listen, you want to roll your sleeve up for me, now? Bobby'll want to get moving, so you better get your shot."

"Huh?" I stared at the needle that suddenly appeared in his hand. Jesus, where did *that* come from? "No, now you guys don't have to do that, you already did that—"

I backed off a step. Rocco reached out and grabbed my neck. He said, "Night-night, Mr. Moss," and pressed his thumb somewhere behind my ear.

I looked at his Pillsbury head, at his little rabbit eyes, at his Halloween teeth. I said, "Aw shit, man," and then something hurt bad and then everything went black and then nothing hurt at all . . .

5

What it feels like is when you don't feel good and you don't feel bad, you feel stuck there in between. Which is how I used to feel when Giselle and I and Phil and one of Phil's leggy friends used to do drug abuse all the time. Phil's friends were from the gene pool at Parks and Wildlife. His friends were named Heather, Beth or Anne.

Phil Greenburg, my very best friend, works at the Department of Agriculture, and so did Giselle at the time. Giselle worked in Grasses and Grains, and knew all there was to know about wheat. Phil has something on someone on high, and hardly ever works at all.

Phil got our drugs free, because Ag was doing stuff like "Effects of Cocaine on the Arctic Wolverine," and what pot will do to pigs. The only trouble was, some of these drugs didn't have any names, and weren't meant for us higher forms of life. We learned about this when Giselle announced she was a soft-shell clam, and wouldn't come out of the tub. This frightened us a lot and we didn't do drugs after that.

Drugs weren't a good idea for Giselle anyway, she had faulty connections in her head, neurons not entirely intact. Sometimes we'd make love and she'd ask me who I was. Sometimes she'd go off to Haiku kwan do Tuesday nights, and show up on Thursday afternoon.

All of which has nothing to do with my semi-conscious state in the back of a Lincoln Town Car except it does, because that goofy albino has shot me full of paralyzing drugs which reminds me of incoherent times with Phil and his leggy friends from Parks and Wildlife, and especially it reminds me of Giselle. Oh God, those China-blue eyes and that black-black hair! Those lovely moving parts, and that faraway, dysfunctional smile.

At least I *think* that's Giselle . . .

I get her mixed up with a brown-sugar woman named Grace, with a redhead named Mary Elaine. I get her mixed up with Claire de Mer. I get her mixed up with crazy Annie in cutoffs short enough to make you cry. The sun's making stripes on her honey-colored skin in the Underseas Wonders Museum, which is down in Galveston. Jesus, how I hate that town.

Everything's confused. Everything is perfectly clear. I'm floating in blackstrap molasses somewhere and I'm. . . . Oh shit, I'm falling somewhere and a car's not supposed to be high—!

"Mr. Moss, you sit down and shut up or I'll be forced to hit you in the head. Rocco, I thought you strapped the son of a bitch down, I told you, you didn't strap him down."

"I strapped him down, Bobby."

"No, goddamn it, he's up, he's jerkin' around, you didn't strap him down. Will you kindly hold on to him, he's kicking me in the nuts. I don't like it, somebody's ki—"

"I got him, Bobby, I—oh, man, he's throwin' up. Oh, shit, man."

"Good. That's because you didn't strap him down. He's throwing up 'cause you didn't strap him down."

"Let me out of here right now we're all going to die!"

"Shut up, Mr. Moss, sit *down.*"

I hit Rocco in the face. That was a bad idea. Rocco grabbed me under the chin and slammed my head against the glass. I could feel my eyes rattle in my head. I looked down and saw tiny little people, tiny little cars. My stomach dropped down in my socks. Something went *bump!* then something went *clup!* then Rocco did something with his thumb, and everything started going black . . .

The girl said, "You feeling better, hon, you like a little ice cream?"

I said, "No, I wouldn't like some ice cream. Where am I and who the hell are you?"

I was sort of sitting up. Heat rose off the hot concrete. A little red airplane farted by. I smelled a lot of gasoline.

"Listen, you'll feel okay. Have a little ice cream. It'll settle your stomach some."

She stuck a cone down in my face. It was dripping on the bright cement. I took a bite and spat it out.

"Jesus, what *is* that? It tastes like mashed potatoes!"

The girl laughed. "Well it's supposed to, silly. It's potato ice cream."

I looked at her. She might've been cute, I couldn't see her in the sun. "Listen, where am I? I think our car might've hit a plane. Did anyone else get out alive?"

The girl licked her ice cream. "Nobody's dead, everyone's fine. You're in Killcreek, Idaho, man."

"Aw, shit," I said, and threw up again.

6

The girl was named Daisy McCall. We bounced in the back of a very black car, grinding over boulders, rattling over ruts, whining uphill without a four-wheel drive, climbing straight up, maybe eighty-five or ninety degrees. Rocco said it was a state highway but I didn't fall for that.

I said, "This car could use some new shocks. I'd get heavy duty if I were you."

Rocco said, "Shut the fuck up, Mr. Moss."

Throwing up on him had put a wedge between us, and this was his standard answer now.

Rocco sat in front. Bobby Bad Eye hadn't come along. In deference to his pink bunny eyes and his dead white skin, Rocco wore heavy sunshades and a broad Stetson hat. Bela Lugosi out West.

The driver's name was Nix. Someone had hit him in the face with a shovel. His features were flat, and his neck was as wide as his head. He might have been the Steeler front line. Nix didn't say and I didn't want to ask.

I watched a lot of nature go by. There was a ragged line of mountains far away, blurred by a veil of blue clouds. I didn't look down. I'd tried that once. I wasn't about to do it twice. I was still off-center from Rocco's last shot, semi-stunned and only partially intact. Not so goofy I couldn't recall Billy's Gas & Auto Repair, and what had happened there. Conscious enough to remember Claire's strap sliding down, to wonder what the *hell* I was doing in the state of Idaho.

"You want a san'wich or something?" Daisy said. "I got a cooler in the back. We got beer and assorted soft drinks."

"No thanks," I said.

"There might be a slice of cold pie."

My stomach took a lurch. "I don't think so, Daisy. I'm a little unsettled right now."

"You need anything, you just ask."

"I'll do that."

"I'll be right here. I mean, anything'll make the trip more comfortable, all right?"

"That's very nice. How long a trip are we talking about here, anyway?"

"Don't ask her a bunch of questions," Rocco said. "You want something, don't be askin' her, ask me."

"Good. How long a trip are we talking about?"

"None of your fuckin' bidness, Mr. Moss."

"Okay. Fine. Thank you very much."

I looked at Daisy McCall. Daisy smiled and gave a helpless little shrug. The road had straightened out for the last few miles, but it was still full of bounce. Daisy bounced good. A full-bodied woman, eighteen or thirty-five, depending on the light. Blue jeans and T-shirt. Blonde hair in tight ringlets, hazel-brown eyes. Pouty lips she kept in motion all the time. I was sure she had a picture of Marilyn Monroe, and practiced every night.

I think we were up pretty high. Sheer granite slopes loomed over the narrow road. The trees were real tall. I think I saw a fir.

A bug landed on the hood. Lost its grip and slipped off to the ground. Oversized head, iridescent eyes. *Tabanus atratus,* the black horsefly.

"Say what, Mr. Moss?"

"Nothing," I said. I didn't know I'd spoken out loud. Rocco turned and gave me a curious look.

"Idaho is the forty-third state," Daisy said.

"Is that right."

"Admitted to the union in 1890. Lana Turner was born here in Wallace. 1920. Wallace is in Shoshone County, off Interstate 90 up north."

"You know a lot of state facts."

Daisy looked pleased. "I like to keep track of where I am. Helps pass the time, you know? Ezra Pound was born here too. He wrote a lot of poems but they're real hard to read. Ernest Hemingway took his own life. He's buried in Ketchum, that's kinda south of here. Down near Sun Valley where they ski? Mr. Moss, we still got quite a ways to go. If you want me to like—*do* anything, you know? You just ask, okay?"

Something did a flip inside, something right below the belt.

"Uh, Daisy, Miss McCall, you don't mind if I call you Miss McCall—"

Daisy caught my look and grinned. "Why, you are turnin' all red, Mr. Moss. I do believe I've embarrassed you."

"No, now you didn't at all. I'm just—I'm not used to the height, heat—I'm not used to either one."

"I tend to be forward sometimes. I guess it's a natural bent."

"Well that's not true. I don't think you are at all. I think you're a very nice person with an—extraordinary knowledge of the forty-third state."

"You do?"

"I certainly do."

I risked a look at Rocco and Nix. They didn't seem aware of us at all. Maybe they were used to Daisy's natural bent. Maybe they knew all about Idaho.

"Listen, what you said, that's nice of you to ask. And I'd like nothing better than us—you and me—doing something together sometime, something like what you're talking about, possibly in the privacy of, possibly by ourselves somewhere. I think, what I think, I think the events of the past, of the past few hours, I think I'm emotionally off the track right now."

Daisy sighed at that. "Rocco don't care, if that's what you're worried about."

"I don't care," Rocco said.

"How about those sandwiches," I said. "I could use a sandwich right now."

"You got your trout and mayo, you got salami and cheese. I still got that pie."

"What kind of pie is that?"

"Potato peach."

Rocco said, "I'll take the fuckin' pie."
I said, "I'll take a cold drink."

We came to a semi-paved road. Steep rock walls plunged straight
into whitewater rapids down below. The river disappeared now and
then, lost behind a curve in the road, hidden by a thick stand of
trees. I thought I saw a horse. Daisy said it was a white-tailed deer.
She told me there used to be grizzlies and black bear and cougars
but there weren't anymore. I told her it was the same everywhere.
I told her there were over a million species of insects that we'd
discovered so far. That this was only a small percentage of those
we'd yet to find. That many had already disappeared before they
could even be identified.

Daisy said this was fascinating and squeezed my leg in a very
suggestive way.

Rocco said, "Who the fuck cares?"

Daisy said, *"Rocco,* now that's not nice at all."

Rocco, of course, didn't care.

Daisy fluffed up her hair the way women like to do. Her T-shirt
said: SOUVENIR OF SALMON RIVER, but the peaks and the valleys on
this very topographical girl left nothing but a puzzling group of letters

OU   IR
AL   ER

unless you got up real close.

I looked at the scenery with Daisy and I looked at Daisy herself.
She smelled fresh and clean, with just a touch of cheap perfume, the
kind they still sell in dime stores. Her hand still rested on my leg.
Now and then she'd tap me with her finger, tap-tap-tap, like she was
singing something to herself.

I saw a lake off to the north, the sun and the mountains reflected
on the water, which looked awfully cold to me. I saw an eagle or
something up high.

And then, just ahead, an enormous billboard read:

TURN IN NOW FOR

MT. VINCENT HIGH COUNTRY LODGE AND WHITEWATER RESORT

FAMOUS SCENIC VIEW

MAMMA DEMARCO'S IDAHO PASTA CAFE

GAS & EATS, SOUVENIRS
FREE BALLOONS FOR THE KIDS
ANGELO'S MOOSE INSEMINATION RANCH AND RESTAURANT

"Hey, we're here," Daisy said, and bounced up and down with delight.

"Where's here?" I said.

Nobody answered. Nix turned off the semi-paved highway onto a white gravel road. We wound through various trees. I saw another deer.

"White-tailed," I said.

"Mule deer," Daisy said. "You can tell by the white-patched ears."

"I knew that," I said.

Everything was made of logs. The bark was stripped off and the logs had been varnished that raw, yellowy color you see in phony shitkicker bars. I like it when they leave the bark on. A log ought to have some bark on, you ought to leave the bark alone. You can bet Daniel Boone built a house, he didn't take off the bark, he left the bark alone.

We passed Mamma DeMarco's Idaho Pasta Cafe. There were red and white curtains, but no one was there. There was also no one at the souvenir shop next door.

I looked for a tourist. An old guy with varicose veins and baggy shorts. I didn't see anyone at all. Off through the trees, I could see a sprawling structure that had to be the lodge and resort, but Nix turned off before that. A sign said EMPLOYEES ONLY, the gravel road turned to rocks and ruts, and Daisy started bouncing again.

There were weeds and tangled brush, all kinds of crap like rusty motor parts, wood from a torn-down shed. A dead dishwasher and a stove. Empty beer bottles, broken aluminum chairs. This was clearly not the FAMOUS SCENIC VIEW promised on the sign.

We passed a clapboard barn, sagging and silver gray. A tack shed and a corral, with a bunch of shaggy horses inside. We have barns and corrals in Defiance County, Ohio, where I was born and raised. Contrary to the movies and paperback books, the West is *not* the only place they've got a horse. We've got horses in other places, too.

Nix stopped the car. Rocco turned and squinted behind his shades.

"You'll be staying over there, Mr. Moss. Nix'll show you where."

I looked where Rocco was looking and I didn't see anything at all.

"Huh-unh, I'm not going anywhere," I said, "that's it, that's all. I've had enough of this. I want to see whoever's in charge of this parade, I want to see him right now. You, and everyone concerned with this affair are in a lot of trouble, Rocco. I expect you know that. I ought to bring charges, I've got every legal right. Christ, there are plenty of offenses, I wouldn't know where to start. But if we can get this straightened out now, if we can work this out before I suffer any more inconvenience or bodily harm, I might be willing to go easy on everyone involved. I might be willing to walk away and forget the whole thing. And I said *might*, all right? A great deal depends on you, on your actions right now."

Rocco said, "You finished now?"

"Yes I am."

"Fine. Get out of the fuckin' car."

"Did you hear me? Am I getting through to you or not?"

"Nix, get Mr. Moss out of the car."

"You can do whatever you like, I'm not getting out of this car."

"Nix, get him out," Rocco said.

Nix opened the driver's door. He was bigger than I thought. Bigger than a rhino.

"Okay, all *right.*" I got out fast. "Maybe we can talk. I'm out of the car, that doesn't mean we can't talk."

Daisy stuck her head out the window and smiled. "I'm getting out here too. I'll walk up with you, Mr. Moss."

"No you're not," Rocco said. "You're staying here."

"What for?"

"What you think, what you think for?"

"I don't want to." Daisy showed him her famous Daisy pout. "I don't want to, Rocco, I got a lot of stuff to do."

"Yeah, right."

Rocco slid his bulk into the driver's seat. The car took off with a jolt, leaving a plume of dust in the air. Daisy said something I couldn't hear.

Nix said, "Come on, I ain't got all day."

It was the first time he'd spoken a word. His voice was like gravel in a can. He took off in a quick, jerky start, like someone had wound up his key. He walked like the guy in *Frankenstein*.

I caught up with him, keeping some distance between us in case he fell.

"You don't mind me asking, who were you with? I bet I've seen you play sometime."

Nix looked straight ahead. "Don't be talkin', don't be sayin' stuff to me, I don't want you sayin' stuff to me."

"Right. That'll be fine."

"I'm just takin' you there. Don't be sayin' stuff to me."

Plain enough. A man who knows his mind. Nix walked on and I didn't say any stuff at all.

Past a little clearing, past a pile of building stones someone had dumped there sometime. Past something dead. I remember the smell from growing up on a farm. You walk outside, in the fields or in the woods, there's dead things there all the time.

Nix lurched to a stop and I lurched to one, too.

"Up there." He raised his arm and aimed it at the woods. "Number Seven. That's you."

Nix's arm dropped to his side, as if someone had suddenly cut his string. He found the right gear and stomped off across the field.

I turned back to the woods. At first glance, all I saw were trees. Then, the afternoon shadows played tricks upon my eyes. There, hidden among the pines, I thought I saw a covey or a pride, a herd of aluminum trailers, a flock of silver shells. They were scattered about, one here and one there, as if God had stalked across Montana on his way to Las Vegas, on his way to L.A., stumbled, tripped and nearly fell, and spilled bright suppositories down on Idaho.

Making my way across the soft pine needles, I found Number Three. No one seemed at home. I found a five and then a four. Number Six tilted off its concrete blocks. Vines grew up the metal walls. There were empty Del Monte cans, empty cans of Spam. Moldy girlie magazines. A K mart smoker with a fossilized burger on the grill.

I found Number Seven in the shade of two very tall trees. I stepped inside. Everything was neat and clean. Someone had stocked the little fridge with the basic food groups: lunch meat, mustard and beer. There were fresh towels and Irish Spring soap. No hairs in the shower stall at all. Clean pillowcases, clean sheets.

I don't like RVs or trailers, never did. I don't care to sleep in what I drive. That's what Jesus made motels for. Still, for what it was, it

was fine, and anyway I didn't intend to stay. Rocco, Nix and Bobby
Bad Eye were merely hired hands here. There was someone else in
charge. And whoever that was, it was clear he had made a big mistake
abducting me. He had the right name but he had the wrong guy.
Nothing else made a bit of sense. No one would go to all this trouble
just for me. I didn't have money, and didn't know anyone who did.
Even under torture, I had no secrets I could spill. I could tell who
did what to who at the Smithsonian Christmas bash. I could tell
who was straight at Interior, and who was gay at Ag. I could, but I
didn't think anyone would care.

I looked through the closets and the drawers. There were blue
jeans, T-shirts and checkered flannel shirts. A sheepskin jacket, a
black Western hat. Nikes and socks. Toothbrush, razor and clean
underwear. Not a good sign. Somebody thought I'd be staying for
a while, and everything looked my size.

I wanted to take a shower and fall into bed, but I wanted a beer
more than that. It tasted real fine. I got a sack of Fritos from the
pantry and walked back outside. It was late afternoon, and the sun
looked golden through the trees. There was a very slight chill in the
air. If it gets any cooler, I thought, I can put on my cowboy suit.

I heard somebody laugh, I heard somebody shout. I stood there
and listened a while, then walked behind the trailer and down through
the pines. The pines gave way to a clearing. I stood there in the trees
and drank my beer. I saw something land on a branch beside my
head. It might have been *Chrysopa aculata*, I really didn't care. Thirty
yards away, there were three big trailers parked around a portable
pool. The laughter came from the pool, and the fourteen naked girls
frolicking inside.

Fourteen. I know, because I took the time to count. Just to make
sure, I took the time to count them twice . . .

7

I watched naked girls for some time. Then I took a nap. I dreamed about watching naked girls. Rocco kicked the bed and I woke up with a start. That's what you do when the first thing you see is Rocco in the dark. Wake up and there's a great white head, a disembodied loony, a Halloween horror with a grin and bunny eyes.

Rocco said, "Get up, take a shower, get dressed."

"What for?" I said.

"You're going out to dinner. Put on somethin' nice."

"You people have my wallet and my watch. I'd like to have them back."

"I'll be outside," Rocco said. "Take a shower, get dressed. Don't screw around in there."

I put on some Levi's pre-washed jeans and a blue flannel shirt, Nike shoes and white socks. I took along my sheepskin jacket. It might get cold in Idaho.

Like I thought, everything fit just fine. What did these bozos do, go through my stuff in D.C.? What else did they find besides my size? My Spike Jones records? The underwear Giselle left behind? If anyone messed with my Sally Field tie, I'd make these mothers pay.

Rocco had a flash. He shined it in my face, whirled it around, looked me up and down.

"Watch your step," he said. "There's lots of rattlers out this year."

"Thanks a lot," I said, "where'd you park the car?"

"Enjoy. This is the great fuckin' outdoors, pal."

I followed him back the way we'd come. Past the rock pile and the rusty auto parts. It was pleasantly cool and the jacket felt fine. Rocco didn't bother with a wrap. He wore a red and white checkered shirt, the sleeves rolled up and the tail hanging out. An overweight sack of Purina Dog Chow.

The air was crisp and pure, a dizzy, intoxicating mix, a shock for the system if you came from the summertime swamps of D.C. A night like this, a million ACs would be pumping cold air.

A friendly glow of light appeared ahead. Along with the heady scent of pine, I smelled a wood-burning fire.

"You like your place okay, Mr. Moss? Those trailers are pretty nice. You got about anything you need."

"No I don't like it, I don't like it at all."

Rocco looked hurt. "Why not?"

I stopped on the path. "Why do you think, why do you think I don't like it, Rocco? I don't *live* here. I live in our nation's capital. I don't live in a trailer in Idaho. You remember that, you remember bringing me here?"

Rocco growled like a dog. "You don't like nothing, man. Number Seven's the best we got. You ought to see Number Six. A guy had the trots in there."

"Mayo and trout. Potato peach pie."

"You little shit." He turned on me and glared. "I bet you didn't even serve, I bet you hid out somewhere."

"Serve what, what are we talking about here?"

"What I bet, I bet you was a hippie stayed home while guys was dyin' in 'Nam. Shoot, you'd of been with us at Bong Son in '66, you'd of been happy with any kinda trailer you could get."

"Sixty-six."

"You got a hearin' problem, man?"

"I was four."

"Four what?"

"Nineteen sixty-six. I was four. I tried to get in. I told them I was eight. I said, I may be small but I'm tough. I beat up a girl in the sandpile just the other day—"

Rocco shook his head. A gesture of disgust. Guys like me, we'd say anything to weasel out of a war.

"You'd of been in it, you'd of been plenty scared. I bet you'd done it in your pants you'd been there."

"I bet I would too."

"You see *Platoon?* Oliver Stone. The guy in it, I forget . . ."

"I saw it. Where's Daisy, Rocco? And who are those girls out in back?"

"None of your fuckin' bidness," Rocco said.

The Mount Vincent High Country Lodge and Whitewater Resort rambled up the side of a rocky, tree-covered slope. There was a large main building with a sign that read CHUCK WAGON & OFFICE. Behind it, nineteen or twenty log cabins were scattered artfully up the hill. I saw a light in one cabin. Three cars. That didn't seem like a lot for the peak of the tourist season.

Up the hill and off by itself was a two-story house, hidden in a grove of dark trees. It was built like the cabins down below, but on a much grander scale. Shutters, floor-to-ceiling windows, shake shingles, stonework everywhere. At least three chimneys I could see.

"Nice place," I said.

"North by Northwest," Rocco said. "Cary Grant."

"So what?"

"Go up and knock. I ain't going in."

"Why not?"

" 'Cause they don't eat supper with the help, that's why."

"Hey, imagine that?"

Rocco gave me a look and stalked off.

I didn't have to knock. The moment I climbed the steps, Bobby opened up.

"Come on," he said, "you're letting skeeters in."

Bobby didn't look good. He looked sour and mean. Puffy in the face, constipation of the skin. He wore a Western-cut suit that nearly fit. White shirt with the collar too tight. A turquoise thing on a string that's supposed to be a tie.

"In there, straight ahead," he said, and raked me with his milky agate eye.

"Who's there, who am I going to see?"

"What do you care?"

"You've got a lot of anger inside, you know that? It might be that fruit, too much fruit'll cause you stress. You ought to try a little pork. No offense, but a lot of your minorities don't eat a balanced diet."

"Shut the fuck up, Mr. Moss."

"I knew you'd say that."

I followed Bobby Bad Eye down the narrow hall. Flagstone floor, cactus in a pot. Indian rugs, Indian artifacts. The hall turned abruptly to the right. Bobby stepped aside. I took one step and stopped, staggered at the sight.

I was suddenly thrust into a great, enormous room, a cavernous chamber that swallowed me whole, a room much smaller than the Great Pyramid, smaller than New York, a room that was crammed, jammed, packed—every inch of the ceiling and the walls and the floor, with assorted Western crap. There were signs from Wells Fargo and Railway Express. Pictures of Indians and Buffalo Bill.

Spurs, saddles, branding irons and ropes. Badges, bowie knives and belts. Spears and rusty axes, crosscut saws. Chaps, maps, bludgeons and saps. Every shotgun, rifle and revolver ever made. Real bad paintings of the West. A photo of the Daltons dead in Coffeeville. Kit Carson and the young Jesse James. General Custer, looking slightly sick. Red Cloud looking like he might be related to Bobby somehow. There were chairs made of antlers, sofas made of cows, chandeliers made of wagon wheels.

And, if it wasn't a gun or a saddle or a belt it was a head. There were wolves, bears and shaggy buffalo. An eagle and an elk. Bighorn sheep and a big-nosed moose. A whole herd of deer. There were animals I knew, animals I'd never seen before, and each and every one looked wide-eyed and surprised, stupefied and stunned, totally bewildered to find themselves dead, hanging on somebody's wall.

Jesus, I thought, I'm in John Wayne's house. He isn't gone at all, he's been living right here.

The guy popped up from a cowhide chair. It wasn't John Wayne, it was somebody else.

"Vinnie DeMarco," he said. "You can call me Spuds, everybody calls me Spuds. Have a drink and sit down."

I said, "Kidnapping's a federal offense. I think it's twenty to life, I forget."

The guy grinned. "Hey, I like that. You get right to it, you don't screw around, Wiley Moss. What do you want to drink?"

"Scotch and water's fine."

"Nix." The man snapped his fingers. "Scotch and water for Mr. Moss."

Nix lurched out of nowhere, mumbled to himself and staggered off. Black pants, white shirt, black bow tie. He was either a waiter or a boxing referee.

"What I want to do, is arrange to get out of here," I said. "There's been a big mistake. I'm not who you think, that's somebody else. Everybody makes mistakes, I can overlook that. Like I told your man Bobby, we can work something out."

"We'll talk about it, right? I think you oughta sit, I think you oughta have a drink."

He touched me on the arm and led me through the Western maze. Worn blue jeans, an old red shirt and scruffy boots. He was maybe five-two, maybe one-twenty-six. Flat broken nose, buck teeth and a squirrely little mouth. His head sloped back like an egg. Salt and pepper hair combed flat, straight back, the comb lines still there. Fifty, fifty-five. A sad little guy that might have been a bellhop in a fleabag hotel, except for his black lizard eyes. Black with no whites, shiny and wet. I hate lizard eyes. Lizard eyes give me the creeps.

He perched in a chair. I sat on the sofa nearby. A fireplace crackled at my back. It was big enough to cook a Volkswagen on a spit.

Vinnie Spuds said, "You're not happy, you don't want to be here, okay? I unnerstan' that. Try and enjoy yourself, Mr. Moss. Don't get all excited, don't get pissed off. That don't do you any good, it don't do anything for me."

I took a deep breath. "How many times I have to tell you people? You don't want me, there's been a *mistake*, Mr. DeMarco, I'm supposed to be somebody else."

"Spuds. Everybody calls me Spuds."

"Spuds. There's been a mistake, Spuds."

"There isn't no mistake."

"There's been a mistake, there's a real big mistake. I'm not supposed to be here, I'm supposed to be in D.C."

"You're supposed to be here. You're Wiley Moss. You're the Wiley Moss draws bugs, that's the Wiley Moss I got here."

I stared. "So I draw bugs, what—what the hell's that got to do with anything?"

Spuds reached down beside his chair. He handed me a stack of magazines. A *National Geographic*, three *Smithsonians*, a *Scientific*

American. My stomach did a queasy flip. Every magazine was clipped open to a page of my work. Illustrations for the piece on wood nymph butterflies. The two-parter on mayflies, *Ephemeroptera,* and the thing on aphids where they got the green wrong.

I looked up at Spuds. "I don't get it. I mean, this is my work, this is what I do. So what do you care?"

Spuds grinned. He showed me his scary little teeth. "I love the way you draw stuff, Wiley Moss. Christ, I don't know how you do that, you know? I couldn't do that, I couldn't draw a straight line, you draw lines all the time, you draw stuff's got a whole lot of curves it don't even have a line. I don't know how you do that, I couldn't do that if I tried. I mean, I'm sittin' here, I got what'sisname, I got Rembrandt, I got the guy draws *Batman* holdin' my hand, I couldn't do that, I'm sittin' here a couple million years, I couldn't do that if I tried."

"Mr. DeMarco, Spuds—"

"Your bugs, they aren't just bugs, Wiley Moss, your bugs got character, you know?"

"Character."

"Yeah, they're not just pictures, they're something else, they like pop out of the page, you know what I'm saying? You got your dung beetle, you got your eastern hercules here. That little son of a bitch is lookin' right at me, he's coming right off the fucking page."

"You think so?"

"Right off the fucking page."

Nix arrived with drinks. I grabbed mine off the tray and drank it down. I tried not to let my hand shake. Spuds caught me with his little lizard eyes.

"Get Mr. Moss another drink," he said. "Get the guy a drink, Nix."

Nix walked off. I looked around for Bobby Bad Eye. It occurred to me I hadn't seen him since Spuds DeMarco appeared. Maybe he was eating a mango somewhere.

"You're a little confused, you're a little shook up, Mr. Moss. I'm going to straighten that out, I'm going to lay it on the line, okay?"

He reached down and tweaked the creases on his jeans. His jeans were old but they were ironed, the creases were as sharp as razor blades.

"I like your art, I like your stuff real good. You got a God-given talent's what you got. You oughta be grateful for that. You got a mother and a father still living, Mr. Moss?"

"My father's dead," I said. "My mother lives in Mexico."

I didn't tell him she lived with a boy named Paco who made her piña coladas all day.

"Your mother, she's gotta be proud."

"Oh, she is."

She couldn't care less.

"You see her a lot?"

"Whenever I can."

I wouldn't go down there on a bet.

"That's good. Show your mother respect. A mother, you gotta show a mother respect. A man, he's a real man, Mr. Moss, he's got respect for his mother, he's got respect for womanhood. How you like your trailer, everything okay? I told 'em, I said, Bobby, give him Number Seven, give this guy the best."

"The trailer's just fine. There's everything you need in there, you wouldn't ever have to go outside."

"Hey, great." He finished his drink and set it down. "You do art good, Wiley, I can call you Wiley, okay? I want you to do some art for me."

I sat up straight. "You want me to—draw bugs? You brought me out here, to goddamn Idaho to draw bugs?"

Spuds made a face. "No, I don't want you drawin' me a bug, you already drew a bug, why the fuck I want to do that? Babes, Wiley. I want you to draw me some *babes.*"

A blink and a stare. "Babes. You mean women. Girls."

"Girls, broads, whatever. Babes."

Vacant, nothing in the head. Then, two little neurons went *ping!*

"Babes. Like maybe fourteen. They're naked, they got a nice pool, they live in the trailers out back."

"Seventeen." Spuds gave me a manly grin. "There's three outta town you ain't even seen yet . . ."

8

I had another drink. I had a double after that. I was tired of Vinnie Spuds and I wasn't feeling great. I didn't need a drink, I was weak and underfed. The last real thing I'd eaten was a truck-stop burger and some very bad fries. I threw that up in another time zone, I don't even know when. There was a moose above the mantel. Someone had stuck a cigarette in its mouth, someone always does that. He tried to make eye contact and I looked away fast.

"Listen," I said, "let me spell it out again, let me try and get it right. I don't do women, I don't do girls. What I do, I do insect life. A bug is not a girl. Your bug, your average everyday bug's an invertebrate, it doesn't have a spine. Thorax, six legs, compound eyes. A girl's hardly ever like that. A bug and a girl, that's a whole different thing."

"Hey. Wiley Moss . . ." Spuds held up a hand that said "stop." "I know that, okay? Do not insult me like I don't know a broad from a bug. Do not do something like that."

"Fine, right. No offense—"

"A guy says no offense, a guy says somethin' like that, what the guy's saying, he's maybe saying, hey, you fuck, I spit in your eye. That's what the guy's saying to me."

"Now I never said that. There wasn't anything about spitting in an eye."

"Hey, I didn't say there was, I didn't say you were spittin' in an eye. What I said, I said, a guy, he's maybe saying something like that."

He gave me a grin like it hurt to move his mouth. "I didn't say *you* were saying somethin' like that. A guy like you, I don't think so, I don't figure you for that. I don't see Wiley Moss, he's sayin' something like that."

A little shiver down the back, a little picture in the head: A lizard on a rock, he's smiling at a fly.

"I'm no good at personal skills," I said. "I'm working on that."

"Personal skills are good. A guy knows how to get along, he's going to do fine."

I glanced up at the moose. The moose was looking somewhere else.

"You can do girls. You can do girls real good."

"I don't think so," I said.

"I'm saying you can. I'm saying, what—five K. Five K a babe."

"What?"

"Five big ones, five K. You got this problem, you don't hear nothing, what? You draw a babe, I give you the bread. Cash free and clear. No tax. You got a trailer, you got a lot of trees, you got fresh mountain air. You got a free vacation in the West. What's so fuckin' bad about that?"

There had to be something, but I couldn't think what. Five thousand times fourteen—seventeen girls. I did it in my head. I ran through it twice. It came out every time to eighty-five grand.

Vinnie Spuds caught my eye. Vinnie Spuds showed me a toothy smile. Vinnie knew greed when he saw it, Vinnie was a greedy man himself.

"Wiley, come here. I want to show you somethin', somethin' you gotta see."

He stood, grabbed my arm and helped me up. He was wiry for his size. He had a little scar above his eye. I could smell his hair oil. Lucky Tiger, 1943. He came up to my chest, and that was in his Idaho boots.

I wobbled a little, the floor had tricky waves. Vinnie had matched me drink for drink, and Vinnie walked perfectly straight. He led me to a very large window that took up one entire wall.

"This is terrific country, Wiley Moss. Christ, you got the rivers, you got the mountains, you got the fuckin' fruited plain." He swept a broad vista with his hand. "You got peace, you got an eagle up there, sometimes you got a bear. You see a bear just turn and walk away, don't mess with the bear, the bear don't mess with you. Who's got a better deal than that? Bidness is good, I got my health, I got the scenery besides. You ever see something prettier than that? Tell me you seen somethin' prettier than that."

"No," I said, "I don't think I ever have."

It was dark and I couldn't see a thing. I could see our reflections in the window, a Vinnie and a Wiley in reverse. A mirror image of a moose. I could see something else that I hadn't seen before. Just behind Vinnie, half hidden by a chair. I could see it in the mirror, I hadn't even seen it straight on.

It was a hundred-gallon tank, lit by a soft blue light. The tank was full of trout. It was night and they didn't move around.

"Nix is fixing dinner," Vinnie said. "Nix puts on a good feed. Jesus, I hope you like elk, we got elk meat comin' out the walls. Nix, get us another drink."

"Nothing for me," I said.

"Two more," Vinnie said, and walked back to the fire.

I stopped to see the fish. Most of them were rainbows or browns. Trout like a mayfly, they're nuts about *Cercyonis pegala,* the common wood nymph. Maybe I could catch a fish. Daisy could take me way off in the woods and show me how.

I turned away, then something caught my eye. Most of the fish were stark naked. One of them wore a red shirt. Its fins stuck out the short sleeves. Its tail stuck out of little jeans. It was dressed like Vinnie Spuds. It didn't swim with its friends, it didn't swim at all. It lay on the bottom and tried to breathe, gasping with its little fish mouth.

I blinked and rubbed my eyes. The trout was still there. I stood by the window like a stone. It was clear they'd put something in my drink. The thought of that scared me half to death. These people had me in their power. I was helpless, I couldn't do a thing.

"Hey, Wiley Moss. Get over here, I got your drink."

"No more for me," I said.

My heart settled down and I walked back to my chair. The drink tasted great. Little *hors d'oeuvres* had appeared from somewhere. They looked like rabbit shit perched on tiny bits of toast. If Nix made these, I thought, and I'm certain that he did, that's exactly what they are . . .

"What I'm thinking, what I'm thinking, see, what I got in mind, I'm thinkin' pictures with class. I mean, you got your T and A, that's fine, but I'm talkin' taste, right? Nobody's hangin' upside down, no acrobats, nothin' like that. And no crotch shots, okay? We're not looking for that."

"No crotch."

"No crotch. We're doing art, we're not doing a peep show, here. These aren't floozies, Wiley, these are sweet little gals, I can't emphasize that too much. They're young and they're clean. You won't find an unsightly rash somewhere, like a broad she's from the city, she's maybe got a pimple, she's maybe got a zit, she's got a private part that you wouldn't want to see. These girls eat right, they got fresh air, they got the outdoor life.

"Okay, bottom line, we're not talkin' angels here, right? We're talkin' the girl next door but she's got a little spice. You got your kinky shit, you got your carnal enterprise, but her skin's real nice, she's got healthy-lookin' eyes, you know what I mean?"

"Womanhood."

Vinnie grinned and gave me a buddy punch. *Anchors Aweigh,* 1945. "Yeah, that's it. I like that. Womanhood. That's the Spudettes, it suits 'em to a 'T'."

"The Spudettes."

"What d'ya think?"

"I bet you named them after you."

"You're quick, Wiley Moss. I like a guy's quick, a guy don't stand there with his finger up his nose. A guy like that, he's goin' to make it fine with me."

Being quick like I am, I didn't have to ask what the Spudettes did. Vinnie Spud's ideals of womanhood made it pretty clear. Daisy McCall and her warm-hearted, giving attitude was another good clue. What this slick little gecko had going was a backwoods brothel, a whole herd of Idaho tarts, chippies with the sweet, whole-grain goodness of the great outdoors.

And I draw their pictures when the ladies aren't busy, when they don't have something else to do. Sort of like the guy plays whorehouse piano downstairs; after a while, you don't even notice that he's there. A cowboy buys me a drink. Everybody calls me Jake.

And they said I'd never amount to anything at Defiance County High. Hey, Miz Brogan, Chemistry I, take a look at Wiley Moss now.

"What you want to do, you're not drawin' sometime, you got nothing else to do, you want to get out and see the sights. I'll get a guy, you don't have to do nothing, this guy, he's gonna drive you around. You go down to Blackfoot, okay? They got a big exhibit, they got the Potato Exposition down there. What they got, they got this potato chip, you never saw nothin' like it anywhere. This is no ordinary chip, you see in the store somewhere, this fucker is big, this fucker is two feet long.

"Listen, you think I'm shittin' you? God is my witness, they got it right there. I'm lying, I'm dyin', man, they got it on exhibit right there. You got tourists from everywhere, you got busloads of kids, they're comin' to see this fuckin' chip. You go through the place, you see the other stuff, you get a free baked potato on your way out. It's free, don't cost you a thing. This place, it's got anything you want. Long as it's potatoes they got anything you want. You want something else, you don't want to go there.

"You want to go to the balancin' rock, that's just outside of Buhl, you don't got to know where, this guy, this guy I'm going to get, he'll take you there. This rock, what it's doing is balancing there, I mean, how's it do that? Nobody knows, it's just sitting there. You need to go see it before it falls off.

"You need to go over to the—hey, babe, Bobby said you wasn't going to make it, glad to see you, hon . . ."

I'd drifted off a while, talking to the moose. I drifted back because Vinnie stood, and I thought I better stand too.

There she was and something fluttered, something shook, something came alive below my hunger line. She was slick and she was tall. Soft as a bunny foot, hard as rusty nails. Midnight hair hanging loose about her shoulders, red-red lips and a sharp and foxy nose. Red-rimmed glasses and glacier-blue eyes.

"My sister, Angel," Vinnie said. "Wiley Moss from D.C. He's the art guy."

"Angela," she said. "Don't ever call me Angel, Moss, I won't put up with that."

I said, "Don't ever call me Moss. Mr. Moss is kind of formal, Wiley's just fine."

Not a blink, not a smile. She wasn't even looking, she was looking right past me like a cat. She sat, sort of flowed and sort of slid, into a cowhide chair. Black, form-fitting jeans, black turtleneck.

"I'm telling Wiley here, I'm tellin' him the stuff he's gotta see, I'm telling him about that chip. Hey, you remember that? You and me, we went and saw the chip. I'm tellin' him—I tell you this or not?—I'm telling him he's got to see where what'sisname, that Evil Neevil guy, tied a rocket to his motorcycle, tried to jump the Snake. Guy doesn't make it, what's goin' through his head? He's halfway there, he knows he can't make the other side. He's thinking, hey, what am I doing out here, why did I go and do this? He's thinking— Jesus, Nix, you a cripple or what, we need a drink over here."

Vinnie popped up like a squirrel, talking to himself, and vanished through the Western maze. I'd been sitting there quietly, watching Angela's eyes. People have to blink. You don't blink, your eyes get dry. Angela didn't blink. Her frosty blue eyes moved up and moved down, moved this way and that, but Angela didn't blink.

"Don't look at me, Moss. I don't care for that."

"I'm not looking," I said. "I'm not looking at you at all."

"You're looking, all right. You're looking, I don't like you doing that."

"Fine. I'm not looking now. I'm looking at something else. You live here too? I mean, around here someplace? Somewhere nearby? Close to Idaho?"

Angela didn't blink again.

"You're the art person."

"Yes I am. What I'm saying is, that's what he *thinks* I am. I tell him I'm not, I can't make him understand. I'm not right for this, it isn't what I do, I can't make him understand."

"Don't."

"Don't what?"

"Don't try to make Vinnie understand. Vinnie knows what he wants to know. That's what's in his head. He doesn't hear anything else. Everything else he tunes out."

"Like you," I said.

"I beg your pardon."

"You hear what you want, like him. I ask you a question, I ask you where you live, you don't even answer, you ask me something else."

No comment. Another arctic stare. She crossed her long legs in a whisper, a sound not at all like denim, a sound like satin and silk. She caught me watching her again, and I pretended I was doing something else. I pretended I was sniffing the air and I smelled something awful when I did.

"Is that elk?" I said. "I never had elk, I don't know how it smells, does it smell okay to you?"

"I think Nix burned the elk. Nix burns nearly everything. I think that's marmot you smell."

"*Marmot?* I know nature, I know what a marmot is. A marmot is a rodent. Like a great big—"

"I never stay for dinner," Angela said. "I come by for the drinks. If I were you, I'd try and eat somewhere else."

Ever since she'd arrived, I'd been trying to place the voice. Sort of whiskey-soft, like there's maybe a piano in the background, like she's maybe a singer in a club. If the singer doesn't like you very much, if she's cranky, ill-mannered, gorgeous and mean.

"You met Bobby. Bobby brought you here."

Questions again. But never with a proper question mark.

"Right," I said. "Bobby Bad Eye and Rocco."

"Bobby's all right. He's been with Vinnie some time. He's fair, but I wouldn't cross him if I were you. Rocco is totally unstable. Rocco's not right in the head."

But Bobby's *all right?* Did this iceberg know about Billy's Gas & Auto Repair?

"Thanks," I said. "I appreciate the advice. As long as I'm here, which I hope isn't long, I'll try to get by."

"Wrong, Moss."

"Wrong what?"

"Don't start doing that ego thing, don't start getting vainglory in your head. This is for me. It was not my intention to be of any help to you, that would never cross my mind. I like it peaceful and reasonably sane around here. I don't like conflict, I don't like noise. I will not put up with that."

"Nobody says 'vainglory' anymore."

"Is that right."

"See? A question and no question mark. What do you think those little things are for? You just raise your voice on the end, you get a question mark. It's like baked potatoes, you go through the sentence, you get one free."

"I need another fucking drink."

"If I knew where to get one I would. Do I go by the picture of Billy the Kid, or the authentic arrowheads? See, I'm new here, I don't know, but I'll be happy to give it a try."

And that's when I picked up Angela's glass and mine, when I looked past Angela, past the sausage stuffer, 1899, past the tacky antler chair, looked up in time to see Vinnie and Nix by the dark picture window, Nix with a bottle and some glasses on a tray, Vinnie giving Nix hell.

And, just as Vinnie shifted on his tiny Western feet, turned to one side, made a broad gesture with his hands, a hole appeared in the window, a frosty little star, followed by a very loud sound, followed by a second, much darker hole in the side of Nix's head.

Vinnie hit the deck.

Angela gasped and brought her hands up to her face.

Nix staggered back, like he'd maybe hit a train, staggered and flailed his arms about, scarcely less clumsy, I decided, than he was in better times. His body struck the tank with a force of nearly three hundred pounds, with a load of hard muscle and fat. Tray, bottle and tumblers, flew off in a manner that the laws of physics provide. The aquarium shattered, trout took wing and glass flew everywhere, water gushed forth like a special effect. Nix went through the tank and out the back. His feet flew up and he slammed to the floor, sodden and pale, his bow tie partially intact, a little jerk, a little spasm here and there, like the biggest fish of all . . .

Jesus, I thought, this is *déjà vu* all over again, how can that be? For it was hardly a year to the day that I'd found myself in another state I didn't like at all, found myself in the web of criminal enterprise, in the midst of killers and thieves. And all because my daddy had suffered a fatal aquarium accident, that was certainly no accident at all, but foul murder plain as day, and here it was happening again.

Now what, I wondered, are the odds against that?

9

Everything happened at once.

Okay, it didn't but it did. Something like that, you got your chaos and your clamor, fish flopping all about, you got people getting dead. Nobody knows what, everybody runs amok, everybody goes nuts.

Vinnie got a chamber pot, 1846, started picking up fish.

Rocco charged in with a sawed-off ten, held it at his hip and blew the window all to hell.

Bobby appeared with a big .45. Took one look, turned around and ran out.

Angela set her mouth in stern displeasure and stalked out of the room. There was noise and confusion in there, disorder and discontent. Angela wasn't happy, she would not put up with that.

No one looked at Nix, no one remembered Nix was there. I tried to think about him, but mostly I thought how I wouldn't have to dine on marmot that night. A selfish attitude, I guess, but I can't help that. I don't feel Julia Child, on her very best day, could make a dead rodent look nice.

"Let's go, Mr. Moss," Bobby said, and we went.

He led me out the way we'd come in. He had a walkie-talkie clipped onto his belt and he'd worked up quite a sweat. It was easy to guess where he'd been. There were men all over the place, flashlights stabbing through the dark. A few down the road and near the lodge, but mostly up the slope, past Vinnie's where the shot had come from.

Bobby walked a few steps behind, his flash picking out the path ahead. He didn't say a word. Past the rusty auto parts, past the rock pile. His silence was ominous at best. We both knew what we weren't talking about, and what happened back there.

We passed ghostly trailers in the dark. Number Seven had a 40-watt light outside which I hadn't left on. Bobby fished a key out and opened the aluminum door. I didn't even know I had a lock. He flipped on the lights inside, quickly looked around and walked out.

"Stay inside. Lock up. Don't be wandering off somewhere." He dropped the key in my hand. His bad eye looked soapy in the bulb above the door.

"One thing you want to do, Mr. Moss. You want to forget you were up at the house tonight. You want to remember that you stayed right here."

"I can do that," I said.

"There you go." A half-smile slid off his face.

Bobby looked tired, sleepy, ragged and alert. He walked off into the night. Far down the path, he met another light. They talked for a minute, then went their own ways.

I went inside and sat. My heart slammed hard against my chest. My hands began to shake and I couldn't make them stop.

Okay, dumb shit, you're doomed, I told myself. There's no use pretending there's a way out of this because there's not. You have witnessed two murders now. Maybe they can overlook the first—which doesn't make any sense at all—but why would they overlook two?

The answer was no, they would not. There was no real reason why they should. They'd keep me around until I finished drawing girls. Waste not, want not, Vinnie would think of that. As soon as I was done, I would quietly disappear. I would not pass GO, I would not collect eighty-five grand. These people, whoever they were, were into illegal affairs, shady deals of every sort, you could bet your ass on that. I was sure the Spudettes were just the tip of the iceberg here.

And if Vinnie DeMarco was a native of Idaho, I was from the South Pole. Jersey, maybe. South Philly or Queens. But not from Idaho.

I choked down some crackers and cheese. Drank a glass of water from the sink. Spit it out at once. I think there was a marmot in the line somewhere. I got a cold beer, and another after that. Bobby said don't go out, but I was getting the creeps inside. Your bottom-of-the-line mini-trailer is a little bigger than your suit. It fits just fine if you don't thrash around a whole lot.

I turned off the lights inside and the one above the door. Outside, there were hawk moths and tigers, moths of every sort, frantic to discover why the light had gone out. *Anopheles* was out there, cutting the night with its irritating whine, unaware that the air was too cold for its kind. Idaho skeeters have no more regard for rules and regulations than skeeters anywhere.

What I could do, everyone looking for the shooter, everyone occupied, I could slip through the woods, stay close to the gravel entry road until I got to the main highway. Walk down a mile, wait till a car comes by and get a ride. I get out at a town, any town will do. There's got to be a sheriff or the highway patrol. I tell them what's happened up here. I haven't got any ID, but I call Phil Greenburg, someone in D.C. Hey, I could talk to Claire de Mer.

It won't take long to verify who I am. The F.B.I. will jump in with both feet. Kidnapping's a federal offense and they'll lock those bozos up for life. I hate to do the Spudettes any harm, but they chose the strumpet path, and I can't be responsible for that.

I thought, I better take my sheepskin coat, it's sure to get colder out there. I better take some crackers and some cheese. An extra shirt won't hurt, I'll take some more socks.

I turned to go back, to go back inside, then something caught my eye. Someone glowed down the trail, someone sucked a cigarette. The glow disappeared, but not before I saw a face. I felt my heart sink. The Plan fell apart before my eyes. I was doomed just like I thought. Bobby hadn't forgotten me at all. Rocco was out there, watching over me in the dark.

I drank a lot of beer. I dropped off quicker than I thought. Fear and apprehension can rob you of your sleep. Alcohol can help you pass out.

I dreamed about Angela DeMarco and me. We were riding on a bus. The driver was Rocco and so was everybody else. Men, women, winos and little kids. Everybody had candy-corn teeth, everybody had a Pillsbury face.

We tried to get off. I said, "Stop right here."

All the Roccos said, "Best picture, 1949."

"All the King's Men."

"Best director?"

"Robert Rossen."

"Best actor?"

"Broderick Crawford."

"Best actress?"

"Susan Hayward."

"Wrong!" all the Roccos said, and the bus rolled on.

Angela turned into Claire de Mer. We were making love on the table in a classy restaurant. The other patrons were too polite to watch. The waiters didn't care, as long as the tip was over fifty percent.

Dreams can go anywhere they want. The restaurant was gone and we were in the trailer now. She stretched silken arms about my neck, kissed me soft and long. Duck feathers tickled up my leg. Hot breath puffed along my chest. I caught the magic scent of girl, lipstick, toothpaste, lemon-fresh shampoo. Red wine and Fritos, ferrets in heat. She twisted and she turned, moving this way and that. Friction is the secret, friction is the key. Nothing glides, nothing slides, like a midnight girl.

I looked through a mist of spider hair, saw moonspots on her breasts, on a creamy collarbone. I looked up in somebody's eyes.

"Hey, who are you?" I said.

"Hey," she said, "what do you care?"

I woke to the sizzle of bacon, to the lovely mix of coffee, orange juice, blueberry muffins, scrambled eggs with cheddar cheese. None of these items, I knew, were in my fridge the night before.

I pulled on jeans and walked into the kitchen, not a big trip in a trailer, no great effort at all.

"Well, hi there," she said, and gave me a happy smile. "You sleep pretty fine?"

"I slept real good."

"I'm Laurel. We're kinda neighbors now."

"I'll bet you know Daisy McCall."

"I bet I do too. Daisy's my very best friend. Daisy sends her kind regards. Daisy says you're kinda shy. I don't think so at all."

"Daisy caught me at a real awkward time. I'm not much fun in a car. Hey, I'm sure glad you dropped by."

"Nice of you to have me, Wiley Moss." A little wink in case I didn't get that, in case I was slow as well as shy.

I wasn't that close, but I knew she'd come up to my chin. Cornsilk hair and intense blue eyes. Olive skin with a touch of Western gold. Nose a little thin, mouth a little wide. There's a lot of things you see in the dark, in the fever of romance, and a lot of things you don't.

She was wearing one of my new flannel shirts, the sleeves rolled up, the tail hanging just above her thighs. I prayed for a yawn, a little stretch, the need for something on a shelf.

"Laurel what?" I said, "what comes after that?"

"Laurel Mae Dean. But that's my *nom de guerre*. All the Spudettes are flowers or plants of some kind. Daisy, me, Fern, Lily, Columbine, Poppy, Buttercup . . ."

"I can't wait to meet Buttercup."

She was spooning scrambled eggs in a dish. She stopped, paused in mid-spoon, and gave me a funny look.

"You don't approve of me, right? I mean, I know you do in the bodily sense, I guess I know that. I'm talking profession-wise, okay? Respect for my calling, for my chosen career."

"What?" I put my coffee down. "Now what on earth makes you say that?"

"The way your eyes went, you know, sorta shifting off somewhere? You said, 'I can't *wait* to meet Buttercup,' the way you said that? Like I sense a little mockery there? Perhaps a little scorn for her field of endeavor, for the service she provides?"

"Hey, now you're wrong about that."

Laurel shrugged, a gesture which gave me a collarbone shot.

"Hell, forget it, let's eat. Daisy says I'm real touchy sometimes. She says being a student of human nature's just fine as long as people don't take offense. That's what I'll do sometimes. Some guy'll say, 'Nice afternoon,' and I'll say, 'What the shit you mean by that?' I still say I know an accent when I see it, I'm not backing down on that."

She put some scrambled eggs on my plate. Set three strips of bacon in a line. Two muffins next to that. I got a kick out of watching, she was like a little kid. Everything tidy and neat. A party with toy food and toy cups.

She caught me looking, gave me a little frown.

"Don't do that."

"Don't what?"

"Don't go laughing at me."

"I can't help it. You're a lot of fun to watch."

She closed one eye. "You mean that?"

"Yes I do."

"Then that's okay."

"Good. I think a person ought to say what they mean. They shouldn't all the time, but most of the time that's the thing they ought to do. Sometimes you can't do that, you do that, it's the worse thing you can do, you wish you hadn't said anything at all . . ."

"My mother used to call that the 'wellums.'"

"The what?"

"Well uh, this, well uh, that. Your mouth starts going and you don't know how to stop."

"Guilty. I do it all the time."

Laurel grinned. "Everything taste all right?"

"Everything's fine."

She bit off a tiny crumb of bacon, two or three molecules of pig, her fingers raised in a dainty arc.

"Like I said, I am prone to irritation, Wiley Moss, my outlook on life is out of whack. The way folks see me is not the way I am. This is an everyday problem a girl like me has to face. It's a well-known fact, a guy, he'll do a whore on one end, that's fine, he doesn't much like it when the other end starts talking back."

I choked on my coffee. It ran out my nose and I grabbed for a napkin which had fallen on the floor somewhere.

"Hey, you all right?" Laurel looked concerned.

"I'll be just fine."

"You don't like the word, huh?"

"It's not that at all."

"Yeah, it is, too. What do you like? Doxy, harlot, wench? Tart, floozy, trull?"

"I don't guess I've heard 'trull' before."

"It's obsolete, pretty much out of usage now."

"I'd say it is."

"It comes from the German, *trolle,* or *trulle.*"

"Who told you that?"

"See?" Blue eyes fade to black. "Goddamn it, that is what I am talking about. Nobody told me that, *I* told me that. I went to a respected Eastern college, I got a degree. I'm a real person, Moss, just like you!"

"Laurel, for Christ's sake . . ."

Laurel set her chin on her elbows and looked me in the eye.

"Which don't you like most? The profession or the word? I'm not angry with you, Wiley, I would like to get this across. What we've got, we've got a confusion of values is what we got here. People think they're saying one thing, but they're not. That's what people do. The average person can't help how he'll react, that's what he's going to do. Take *glue.* You hear glue, you get a picture in your head. You think sticky and gummy, tacky and yuck, you think glue. Doesn't matter what you *want* to think, you think glue.

"*Dogshit.* Now that's something else, you got a dogshit image in your head. You can't help that, that's what you're going to do. Someone in Poland, they maybe got a word *sounds* like that. Sounds like dogshit, okay? You go over there, guy hands you a double fudge ice cream cone, says, 'Here, have some of this dogshit, Wiley, this is really good.' You're never going to eat that cone. I don't care if it's the finest chocolate in the world, you're never going to touch that cone."

"You're right," I said. "I don't think I would."

"I know you wouldn't. You wouldn't touch it. You wouldn't eat that cone. You've been raised in a wholly different way, you got different verbs and nouns. Dogshit's got a different meaning for you, you're never going to cross that line."

Laurel filled my cup, got me a brand new saucer because I'd spilled a drop. I said to myself, this girl is really neat. This lovely person is the tidiest girl I ever saw.

"Laurel . . ."

"What? Something else you need, you okay?"

"No, I'm just fine. Laurel, before you came over last night—I don't know when it was because I haven't got a watch anymore, somebody took my wallet and my watch, I haven't got anything at all. . . . Anyway, before that. Maybe, what? Maybe ten o'clock. I was up at Vinnie DeMarco's house, you maybe know about that. If you don't, I know you heard the shots, saw everybody running around. Something happened up there. What it was—hell, I don't know what it was. An unfortunate incident in which someone got—"

Laurel's face went pasty white. The lights behind her eyes went out. I reached out and took her hand. "Laurel, there are things I've got to know. I am in a real spot and there's no one I can trust, I've *got* to know what's going on here—"

She jerked her hand away fast, looked the other way.

"I don't know what you're talking about, Wiley, any—incident or anything else except what we were doing, you and me, which I thought was awfully nice. All that other stuff, that doesn't make a *bit* of sense to me."

"Laurel, I've got to talk to you."

" 'Scuse me, I got things I've got to do . . ."

She was up and she was out. One hand brushed the coffee pot. It shattered on the floor. The trailer door swung open, letting in the harsh morning light. She still wore my new flannel shirt. Her bare legs fairly flew. The door slammed shut and she was gone.

10

What I wanted to do was run and get her, grab her and bring her back. I hardly knew Laurel and I liked her a lot. I liked the way she looked. I sure liked the way nearly everything showed when she wore my new shirt. And it wasn't just that, just your physical appeal, the way she frolicked in the dark. She was fun to be with, fun to talk to. A little too touchy, and a real smart mouth, but it was maybe like she said—the business she was in, you might tend to act that way yourself. I probably would, if I was in her shoes, if I was lovely and desirable, if people would pay me for sex—which so far hasn't come up.

You don't run after somebody when they're scared. Even if you catch them, it won't do any good. I stayed right there and cleaned up. Breakfast was terrific, but she'd really made a mess. My small kitchenette didn't have a lot of dishes, cups and pots and pans, but Laurel had used up every one.

While I stood at the sink, I felt a funny itch right between my shoulder blades. I turned and looked back now and then. Even walked to the door once or twice and looked out. I knew what it was. Laurel had left an aura of fear behind and I'd caught a dose myself. I couldn't forget the way her eyes went blank, the way her mouth kind of twisted out of shape. You get scared, that happens. You try to say something and the muscles won't work, the words won't come out.

Was it Vinnie, or bozos like Rocco and Bobby, the late and terrifying Nix, who struck fear in her heart? Or was it simply that girls in "the life," as they called it on the TV shows, were frightened, on edge, wary all the time? Maybe it was both. You didn't have to be a Spudette to know something was fishy at the Mount Vincent High Country Lodge and Whitewater Resort. All you had to do was take a long look at Vinnie Spuds himself.

I was making my bed, enjoying the memories of carnal enterprise, the lingering aroma of delight. I inspected the clothes she'd left behind. Just a routine check, nothing kinky at all, nothing special in mind. Tiny black panties, plain T-shirt, ordinary jeans. Inside each garment were labels like Chanel, Ralph Lauren, Anne Klein. Stores like Lord & Taylor, Neiman Marcus, Bloomingdale's. Only, the labels weren't real. They weren't even cloth, they were paper labels, cut out of fashion magazines.

Bless your heart, Laurel, I thought, you've got a K mart budget and a weakness for the latest Paris trends. You're wishing you were somebody, somewhere else, instead of where you are. No big surprise there. It happens all the time, it happens to nearly everyone. Still, it was a sweet, childish and kind of sad gesture, and those labels got to me somehow.

This is what I was doing, taking an undue interest in women's outer- and underwear, when Bobby Bad Eye rapped on the door. I stuck Laurel's clothes beneath my pillow and walked to the front to let him in.

Bobby said, "Step out here a minute, I got to talk to you, Mr. Moss."

I didn't ask him in, I didn't offer him a beer. We hadn't bonded yet, and I didn't think we would.

I stepped outside. Bobby looked a little better than he had the night before. He'd had a little sleep. His good eye was healthy, and the wrinkles on his face were freshly pressed.

"I thought you'd like to know what happened last night," Bobby said. "Something like that, a guy gets curious, he's sitting around, something of an unusual nature occurs, he's gotta wonder what."

"No, not really," I said, "not at all."

Bobby let me know I'd scored about a two on that.

"We found out what happened. What happened, it's something you'd figure, one of those tragic events it's gonna happen sometimes. Some kids was hunting out in the woods, they were twelve, maybe thirteen years old, just a couple of kids, they were huntin' possum at night, they didn't have any business up here. What it was was a hunting accident. One of the kids, his gun went off. He wasn't even near the house, his gun went off like a gun's going to do sometimes. We didn't tell 'em anyone was hurt or anybody got croaked. Vinnie, Mr. DeMarco, he doesn't see how ruining a couple of kids' lives, how that's going to bring Nix back. Mr. DeMarco, he doesn't have any kids of his own, but he likes kids a lot. So what he's going to do, he's going to let it go, he's not going to make a fuss."

"No fuss."

"Huh-unh. No fuss, he's going to let it go."

"That's a nice thing to do. Mr. DeMarco's got a good heart."

Bobby thought about that. He looked at me a minute and decided to let it pass.

"What Mr. DeMarco's doing, he's asking everyone, staff and guests alike, out of respect for Nix, and the fact that Mr. DeMarco had a high regard for the guy even if he didn't have a whole lot of smarts and couldn't cook worth a shit. What he's asking is, that everybody forget about this as quick as they can and get on with our respective tasks and lives. This is what he'd like, this is what he wants us to do."

"That's what Vinnie wants, then that's what I'd like, too."

"That's good. That's what he wants you to do."

"There's nothing we can do," I said, "for Nix or for anyone else. The river of life flows on its way, and every man is swept up in its path. Only the Great Boatman Himself can say when you and I will be caught in the current as well, Bobby. Anything can happen, any time."

"Yeah, right. Mr. DeMarco, he says he's sorry about the dinner, some other time."

"I'll sure look forward to that."

"Rocco says, Rocco tells me last night, you don't like the trailer. He says you were complaining a lot."

"Rocco must've misunderstood."

"Rocco understands pretty good."

"Well he didn't this time."

"Fine. I am relieved to hear this. Mr. DeMarco, he's going to be glad to hear it too."

A gnat flew in Bobby's dead eye. Bobby didn't notice it was there. The gnat settled down, giving the illusion of a tiny, black demonic pupil, before it flew away.

"You need anything, let somebody know. Mr. DeMarco says he'll be down to take a look, see how you're doing on your art."

I stared. "I don't have any art. I haven't even *started* yet."

"Start," Bobby said.

I watched him walk away. The gnats followed him down the path, a black veil swarming about his head. It occurred to me that I'd never drawn a gnat, that no one had ever asked me to. Even in the very intense, specialized field of the small invertebrate, the gnat doesn't get a big play.

Bobby, in his way, had told me something that I already knew. That Vinnie Spuds DeMarco would keep me in beer and blue jeans, would keep me intact, until I finished my portraits of the lovely Spudettes. After that—what? I didn't care to think about that.

I tried to remember the story I read as a kid. This woman's knitting something, that's what she's got to do. Only, the people in charge, they don't know she's stalling, that she's knitting all day, she's unraveling everything at night. They're not too bright, and they don't see this. I thought, if I could draw all day, and *un*draw the stuff at night . . . how long would it be before they caught onto that?

A little after one I fixed a sandwich and opened up a beer and walked out under the trees behind the trailer. Everything smelled fresh, everything smelled fine. A woodpecker drummed overhead. It was early afternoon, but the ferns underfoot were still wet from the night before. Crows made a racket somewhere. A fly whined around my head and I slapped it away.

At once, I got a picture from the past—Wiley Moss younger, Wiley somewhere else. Just like that, and because of that fly. Nothing takes you back like the lazy buzz of flies. It might've been the city, or out in the country somewhere, a fly's going to take you there, a fly'll take you back. A fly'll take you back somewhere.

When I was growing up in Cincinnati, the flies came in through the screen. Mother tried to patch the holes. A fly doesn't care, a fly's going to find a way in. Mother fixed the holes because Daddy wasn't there. Daddy was on the road, working on a deal somewhere. A "deal" was what we called it at the time. What Daddy was doing, he was screwing someone in a scam of some kind. This is what my Daddy did.

On October 8, 1978, I turned sixteen. Daddy gave me a stolen racing bike. On October 9, he left Mother and me for good. He went to the store for mayo and bread and he never came back. It was eighteen years before he showed up again, only this time he was dead. He was murdered in Galveston, Texas, tossed down a number of stairs. Before he was cold in the ground, the killer nearly did me in as well.

I can't say I cared for my stay on the Gulf of Mexico. Those were not pleasant moments in my life. An overweight stripper tried to smother me under her ponderous mass of flesh. I was forced to steal a number of dogs. I threw up a lot of seafood. It was summer, and unbearably hot, and the flies were bad, too.

Returning from my trip down memory lane, I was startled to find I had come to the break in the trees. Past the sunlit clearing, I could see the silver trailers and the Spudettes' swimming pool. No one was naked, no one was there.

This was not a conscious act. I hadn't meant to come, I hadn't meant to peek. You're walking along and your head's somewhere, you might go anywhere at all.

Something flittered through the brush, a streak of bright orange. *Danaus plexippus*, the common monarch butterfly. A few years before, we thought they'd all frozen down in Mexico. Everyone at the Smith was quite worried at the time.

Something else flittered, this time to my right, off in the shadow of the trees. Not a butterfly. Something like an oversized onion, something like a weather balloon. Rocco, who else? When I looked up again he was gone. The cold beer was good and the day was real fine, and then I felt terrible again. I'd forgotten, for a moment, that I wasn't a guest at the Mount Vincent High Country Lodge and

Whitewater Resort. What I was was a prisoner of Vinnie DeMarco, a captive in a trailer, forced to do exotic girlie art.

Who could have guessed something like this would happen to me?

Everyone in Defiance County, Ohio.

Everyone but Uncle Wally Stutt, who dreamed I'd die in a thresher accident before I ever reached fifteen . . .

11

There were sounds coming out of my trailer. A van had pulled up outside. Two hefty men were hauling boxes from the van through my doorway.

"Hold it," I said, "this is my trailer, what's all that stuff and what are you doing here?"

The men didn't answer. One of them was short. Dark, curly hair and a broken nose. One of them was tall. Dark, curly hair and his nose looked fine.

I sat down under a tree. The men finished up, got in the van and drove away. I walked to my trailer and took a look inside. I could hardly squeeze through the door. My tiny living room was gone. Boxes were packed from the ceiling to the floor. Boxes flowed out into the hall.

I didn't have to open up a thing. The labels made everything clear. I was inundated with brushes, canvases and paints, drowning in art supplies. I had every tube of oils and acrylics ever made. I had phthalo blue and titanium white. Burnt sienna and azo yellow light. I had gessos and water jars, turpentine and linseed oil. Oil pastels and soft pastels, several jars of gels. Twenty or thirty kinds of brushes—sables and synthetics, bristle filberts and mongoose flats. Wide fan brushes and floppy Japanese. Brushes fine enough to do the lashes on a gnat, brushes big enough to paint a house. Watercolors, pens and colored inks. Canvas, hardboard, papers of every sort. Staplers, hammers, stretchers and palette knives.

I had enough shit to start my own art school. The Wiley Moss Idaho Academy of Arts. I could paint the Sistine Chapel several times. Do it until I got it right. I could cover the pyramids with shapely Spudettes. I could do most anything, except walk into the living room.

Most of these supplies were from a Boise art store. They were all good, too, first rate. Professional brands, no artsycraftsy hobby shop stuff. Someone picked it out who knew what he was doing. Probably the guy who ran the store. He had closed up early, picked up his wife, picked up a case of champagne.

Okay, I told myself. With all these materials, I can stretch out the job for twenty years. The Spudettes will be too old to work. Vinnie will be in a home and I can walk out of here.

I could still get to the kitchen and the bathroom and the bed. I had already searched the place for books and magazines. There was nothing there to read. I could walk down to the lodge, there might be something there.

What would Vinnie Spuds and Rocco and Bobby Bad Eye read?

Vinnie and Bobby had me stumped. Rocco was a snap. The man had the soul of a poet. No question in my mind about that. You could see it in his jack-o'-lantern mouth, in his pink bunny eyes.

Mother liked William Basse, some bozo who lived in the sixteen hundreds sometime. This guy was so famous, they don't know exactly when he lived, they don't know when he died. Nobody seemed to care. Basse was one of Mother's weapons in her ongoing battle with old Dad. If Daddy wasn't ready to take off on a scam, he'd leave pretty quick when Mother started spouting William Basse.

Mortality, behold and fear!
What a change of flesh is here!

Mother liked Basse because no one else had ever heard of him before. These were the people Mother liked. Anyone completely undefined, anyone obscure. She was very fond of Victoria Woodhull, who ran against Grant for President in 1872. Woodhull was for free love, short skirts, magnetic healing and birth control. Mother had a lot of respect for sports immortal Colonel John Bodine, who cinched the Great International Rifle Match of 1874 for the U.S. team.

I don't know why Mother cherished such people, except that I'm certain she felt obscure herself. Or maybe it was simply to irritate Daddy. Something she could truly call her own—a talent, a power, something that would always piss him off, get him on the road. For no matter how much she complained when he was gone, she really didn't want this man around the house.

I thought about a shower. Instead, I changed my socks. I read the labels on my shirts. I read the fat and fiber content on a saltine cracker box. Squeezing through the hall, I edged a case of cerulean blue aside, and retreated outside.

There was no sign of Rocco anywhere.

If he was there, he was skulking in the trees. I thought I might walk through the woods, try and find Laurel, meet some Spudettes. I sensed Rocco wouldn't go for that. Second choice was amble on down to the lodge, try and find something to read. Try and spot a phone somewhere. Set fire to something, draw everybody out, call in the F.B.I.

Rocco didn't appear. I passed the rock pile. Someone had dumped some more rocks, or stirred the old familiar rocks around. One rock looks like another, so I couldn't tell which.

I reached the gravel road that wound up through the pines to the Mount Vincent High Country Lodge and Whitewater Resort. The wind sighed nicely through the trees. The day was diamond bright, and I could see a line of faraway peaks. An eagle or a hawk, something very large, circled in the sky overhead. I never cared for birds. Birds prey on the insect population, and I think I resented them for that.

While I was peering at the sky, tires crunched on the gravel and a Jeep pulled up by my side. A guy got out and walked around the hood. He had broad, chunky features and hardly any hair. He wore a pinstripe suit, white shirt, blue polka-dot tie. He didn't look at all like Idaho.

He stopped a foot away and poked a finger in my chest. He said, "I know who you are. You're the art guy."

"Yes, I am," I said, "don't do that again."

"Do what?"

"Do what you did."

"Like that? That what you're talkin' about?" He poked at me again, pulled up short and showed me a crooked grin.

"Turkey buzzard."

"What?"

"Turkey buzzard. That's what you were looking at."

"Fine."

"You want to see a moose?"

"No thank you. Not right now."

"I'm Angelo. Vinnie Spuds's brother." He took off his shades. They were the yellow kind that make everything look like Mars. Without the yellow shades, I could see the family trait, the familiar lizard eyes.

"Get in," he said, "you and me got to talk."

"What for?"

"Jesus, what's the matter with you?" He looked weary and distressed, like he'd known me some time. "Get in the Jeep, we'll see a moose. We'll talk, we'll get somethin' to eat, get in the fucking car, man."

I got in the fucking car. Angelo got in the other side. He was big all over, built like a heavyweight. Still pretty solid, just shy of getting out of shape. His nose was too small, his mouth too big for his face. Not an ugly guy, but ugly wasn't too far away. Except for the cue-ball head and the frigid reptile eyes—and twenty years off of Vinnie Spuds—the two looked nothing at all alike.

"You ever see a moose? You ever see a moose before?"

"I don't think so," I said. "I saw one on *Northern Exposure*. I saw one maybe in a zoo."

Angelo gripped the wheel as we left the gravel road and took off in an unfamiliar gear. We were driving through knee-high brush, racing downhill with the hot wind whipping through our hair. If there were boulders or great enormous holes up ahead, Angelo didn't care.

"You ever see a moose, you'd remember. You'd remember, you seen a moose. A moose is real unique in your animal kingdom world. There isn't nothing like a moose. You tell me there's something like a moose, I'm saying, you don't know what you're talkin' about, you haven't ever seen a moose. How come you draw bugs, why you want to do that?"

"How come you like meece, why you want to do that?"

Angelo made a face. "That's tired, man, I heard that a thousand times. There isn't any meece, it's just moose. All you say is moose.

Period. You say, 'There goes a moose.' You say, 'Hey, there goes a
whole bunch of moose.' Same thing. You met my sister up at Vinnie's
place. Angela. Me and her are twins."

"No you're not."

Angelo laughed. "So she's better looking, so what?"

He was looking at me and we nearly hit a tree. He jerked the
wheel in time and we swerved off to the right. A branch hit the
windshield and pinecones rattled in my lap.

I thought about Angelo and Angela. Big brother Vinnie, and the
DeMarco twins. A lovely family, right out of *Godfather II.* So what
the hell were they doing out here?

We continued down the grassy hill. There were more trees ahead.
I don't know all my trees, but I know a cottonwood. We've got
cottonwoods all over Ohio, too.

Angelo stopped. I could see the bright flash of water through the
trees. A river or a lake.

"We get out here, and walk the rest of the way." Angelo's voice
was a whisper. "Most of these animals are pretty tame, they been
around a while. But I got a new bull I traded a female for, guy up
in British Columbia, coupla weeks ago. He's still kinda spooky, he
isn't settled in."

I said I'd be quiet. I told him the last thing I wanted to do was upset
a bull moose. One that wasn't settled in. I said this was something I
tried to avoid at all times.

Angelo went first, walking through the grass toward the trees. I
was right. The trees were indeed cottonwoods, and I was pleased
about that. The water I'd seen was a small blue lake, the surface so
clear the reflection of the mountains and the trees was a still and
perfect image, only upside down.

Angelo held up a hand. To the right, a path wound down to the
lake. Just above the shoreline was a wooden shack maybe twenty by
ten. A painted sign above the door read:

ANGELO'S MOOSE INSEMINATION RANCH & RESTAURANT
MOOSE TACOS * COLD DRINKS * SOUVENIRS

The door of the shack was closed, everything locked up tight. Just
like the lodge, and everything else in Vinnie's empire. Two or three

cars, a couple of people staying overnight. Nobody buying souvenirs, nobody looking at a moose.

The afternoon was still and hot. I could clearly smell Angelo's hair. Lucky Tiger, just like his brother used. If I ever got close to Angela, I knew she wouldn't smell like that.

Angelo stopped, pointed past the shack.

"There. Down by the shore. There they are, right there."

There they were, just like Angelo said. A whole herd of great, clumsy animals, impossible to miss. A dozen or maybe more. Large, ungainly creatures with long stalky legs. The legs didn't fit. The legs were too long. Tall, awkward meeces with their bodies too short. Enormous, oversized heads and a sad, droopy moose nose. You can see a moose a long way off, you're not going to miss that nose.

All except two of them were females, Angelo explained. The ones with the antlers were males. Only the males had antlers, that's how you could tell.

"The males, they shed their antlers in the winter and then they grow some new ones in the spring. The antlers are palmate. That means they spread out like a hand. Like the palm of your hand, okay?"

"Just like your hand."

"You got it," Angelo said.

I learned that the moose is the largest member of the deer family. That they only mate in the fall. That they aren't very social in the wild until then, but this bunch was pretty tame. In the fall, the males might weigh well over a thousand pounds, and top out at the shoulders more than six feet tall, and what did I think of that? I said that was big. Big and really tall.

Angelo had a lot of moose lore. Most of it I forgot. Unless you're a real zoo nut, you can't stand and look at an animal very long. An animal just sits there, it doesn't do a lot. You look at a bear, you move along. You see a kangaroo, you look at that awhile. It doesn't take long to see a moose. About a minute and a half. You watch a moose longer than that, you haven't got very much to do.

"So what do you think?" Angelo asked me again. "You ever see that many moose before? All in one place? In their fuckin' natural habitat?"

"Not ever," I said.

"Goddamn right."

"So which is the new one," I asked to be polite. "The big guy, the one you got from Canada?"

Angelo smiled. I was showing the right attitude. "He's up there in the trees, he's kinda shy. It's going to take a while. The other males, they're young. They won't go near that son of a bitch."

"Probably the smart thing to do."

"It is, no shit. And those clowns know it. The new bull won't mess with the females till fall, but the other males, they'll keep out of his way. It's a instinct thing, you know? What it is, it's built in your moose genes. One of those chromowhats they got, it says, 'Hey, leave that mother alone, don't fuck with the biggest moose in town.'"

"Words to live by," I said. "We can all learn a lesson from that."

Angelo had an ant on his neck. I didn't bother to point it out. "The insemination thing, where do you do that? You got a place here or what?"

Angelo slapped his ant. "That's technical stuff. You don't want to hear about that."

"Yeah, I do too."

"What, you into mammals having sex? You like that shit?"

"Just the technical stuff. Not the actual sex itself."

He seemed to think about that. That or something else. He was looking at the meece, he didn't look at me.

"Listen, Moss . . . okay I call you Moss? I don't like to call a guy his first name, I'm going to call you Moss. You and me, we got to talk."

I didn't answer. He checked to see if I was paying attention, that I hadn't wandered off.

"What I'm telling you is, I'm telling you coming up here, this is not a good time. You shouldn't ought to be up here."

"What?" I stared at Angelo. "You think this was my idea? This is my idea, I'm up in Idaho?"

"I *know* it's not your idea, you think I don't know that? I know that. It's my fucking brother's idea is what it is. Vinnie gets a wild hair, that's what he's gotta do. You seen that room of his? You been up there. All the Western shit? He's got an ordinary room, he's got sofas and chairs. He's got a TV and a bar. You can sit up there and watch a game, you can have a beer and see a sport. Any kind of sport you like. The room, it looks like anywhere else.

"This is what pisses Vinnie off. Vinnie ain't happy with that.

Vinnie says, 'This place looks like my goddamn house in Chicago, it don't look like Idaho.' I tell him, 'Vinnie, it looks like Chicago, it looks like Chicago because that's what it's supposed to look like. It's your stuff, from your goddamn house. What do you expect it to look like?' 'I know what it looks like,' Vinnie says, 'it don't look like Idaho.'

"Two days. Am I lyin' or what? All that shit he's got up there, he picks up a phone, all the shit's there in two days. Two days it looks like that, all the stuff from Chicago, he's giving it away.

"Jesus . . ." Angelo looked for help from the sky. "Why am I tellin' you this, what do you care? You want to know why? I'm telling you this because you are Vinnie's latest wild hair. He's sittin' there, he's watching a sport, he jumps up and says, 'I need an art guy. I gotta get a guy to draw the Spudettes.'

"This is you. This is what you're doing here. This is why you're here, you shouldn't be up here at all."

"That's about the way I figured it," I said. "I didn't feel a great deal of thought went into this."

"Vinnie don't bother with the thinking part. That's the part he don't like. There wasn't any thinking here at all."

Angelo turned away. I noticed he was wearing, with the pinstripe suit, two-tone black-and-white wingtip shoes. Lace-up shoes, with the little tiny holes on top. You don't see that much anymore, but they were very natty shoes. Adolphe Menjou, 1942.

"What it is, Moss, what I'm saying is, this is not a good time for you being up here. You're an art guy, okay? No offense, but you're maybe not into bidness talk. There's nothing wrong with that. An art guy, he don't have to know that. What I'm telling you is, what we're going through, we're going through a changeable shift. We got an oscillation of the current bidness clime. We got holes in our structure, we got lousy personnel. Our corporate posture's like afflicted with various kinds of shit. You getting what I mean?"

"These are troubled times?"

"That's exactly what I'm saying. We got troubled fuckin' times."

Angelo took off his shades and rubbed his nose. The sun had heated up his hair oil, and a droplet was running down his neck.

"Just talking like this, I am putting myself in a risky situation, Moss. I don't know you, I'm making a call on this, we're standing here awhile, I'm thinking you're a stand-up guy. I figure you got some smarts. A guy he can draw real good, even if it's bugs, you're not some dummy off the street."

Angelo looked right at me, stabbed me with his blue lizard eyes. "You're not so stupid you think Nix got it in a hunting accident. You're sittin' there, you got to be a moron, you're going to swallow that. You know something happened, you don't know what. What I'm thinking is, I'm thinking, a guy like you, if he had a way of getting out of here, he'd just go. Like that. He wouldn't stir up nothing, he'd go home and keep his mouth shut. He'd forget all about Idaho. Am I right, am I on track with this or what?"

"You're absolutely right," I said, "you are right on track, this is exactly how I feel." I tried to look cool. I tried not to look like cardiac arrest.

Angelo didn't move. A gecko on a rock, thinking hard about a fly.

"I know what you're thinking, Moss. You're thinking, this guy, why's he doing this? What does Angelo DeMarco get out of helping me?"

"It might have crossed my mind," I said. "It absolutely did. Too be perfectly honest, I really don't care. I absolutely mean that."

Too late, I realized I'd said "absolutely" three times. Did he notice, would he read any meaning into that?

Angelo ran a hand through his hair. Looked across the lake. Looked at a greasy hand. Looked back at me.

"What I am saying to you, I am saying, you and me never talked about this, okay? We never even came down here, we never talked about a moose. You got that?"

"I got it. We never talked about a moose."

"Right. We didn't talk about nothing, because we wasn't here." He started to poke me again, remembered I didn't care for that.

"You do your art stuff, you look at the rocks and the trees. You don't say anything to anybody else. What I'm doing, I'm figuring a way to get you out of here. You'll hear from me, I got it figured out."

"I really appreciate this. What you're doing for me. It's a really pretty state but I don't like it here."

"Hey. Nobody's doing *nothin'* for you." Angelo looked pained. "What I'm doing, that's family bidness, that's personal to me."

"Okay. That's fine too."

"Good. I'm glad that's fine with you. And when I say nobody, I'm talking about the bimbo too. And don't get shook up, I'm saying that, it's my bidness to know who's doing who."

"I don't think I'm shook up," I said. "I mean, I don't feel shook up at all. If I was I think I'd know."

"You look shook up to me. You look shook up and you got no reason to. A guy needs care and understandin', fine. That's a natural bodily function, that's a manly thing to do."

"Yes, it is."

"You get a chance, you get to know a gal named Buttercup. Buttercup's a real nice kid."

"I've heard the name before."

"Buttercup's okay, she's got a good attitude. She isn't like a lot of your bimbos who—*ho-ly shit!*"

Angelo stared. His mouth dropped open and the shades fell off his nose. I turned, looked, saw where he was looking. Saw what he saw, or at least I thought I did. A first impression will fool you every time. What I thought I saw, I saw Rocco running toward us, running toward us past the meece down by the lake. Not really running, sort of stumbling and falling, jerking and thrashing, in an awkward and uncertain gait. He had both hands around his throat. What he wanted to do was get rid of that long red tie. He didn't want to wear that tie, he didn't like that tie at all.

This is what I thought, this is what I thought in a second and a half. Right before I wondered why the red tie was running through his hands and down his shirt, down his belly and his pants. That wasn't right at all. That is not what happens with your ordinary tie.

Rocco plowed through the herd of frightened meece. The meece scattered and bolted for the trees. Rocco had his mouth open wide but he couldn't make a sound, he couldn't say anything at all . . .

All of which happened in a flash, in the blink of an eye, before the new, imported bull moose, still unsettled, still unsure of his surroundings, of his strange environment, for a reason known only to himself, became extremely pissed off. Maybe he didn't like people with pink eyes and jack-o'-lantern teeth. Maybe guys with red ties don't smell good to meece. Whatever the reason, this great, ungainly beast with knobby knees and fury in his eyes, charged out of the woods, kicking up stones and snapping off young trees, snoring and wheezing, honking like a '57 Caddie, head down low and big ugly nose to the ground, came down the slope with a vengeance, with a Rocco on his small and furry mind . . .

The moose hit Rocco like a truck, like an angry Tiger Tank, struck him with a sickening jolt that made orthopedic hash, made a sack of scrambled bones, lifted Rocco on his broad and massive antlers, on his sharp and fearsome prongs, the moose making up for all the tacky hat-racks, all the disembodied heads, all the meece mal-treatment dating back to ancient times.

Rocco sailed toward the lake, a doughboy in flight, a Rocco doll with all the stuffing coming out, everything askew, very little left intact. We watched as he hit, a flat, ungraceful splash. The moose watched too. Pulled up a mouthful of grass and stalked back to the woods.

"Jee-sus Christ," Angelo said.

"From Here to Eternity," I said, hoping that Rocco might hear. "Burt Lancaster, Frank Sinatra, Donna Reed. 1953."

12

What happens is, you don't think for yourself, then someone else will.

The Rocco horror show flat scared the shit out of me. I wasn't myself at the time. I suspended all rational thought, I listened to Angelo instead. Angelo said, "Stay in your trailer, pretend you weren't there, pretend you weren't with me!" We whined up the hill at half the speed of sound, Rocco said "Jump!" and I ran like hell, got in my trailer and hid.

This is what I did. I didn't stop to think that Angelo was looking out for *his* ass, and not mine. He didn't want anyone to know that he was there, he didn't really care about me.

Which, by the way, says Angelo wasn't thinking real straight either at the time. It seems very likely that Rocco followed me down to meeceland when Angelo picked me up. Stayed on my trail like they'd told him to do. Clearly, someone followed *him*. Which is how he wound up with a bloody red tie. Did the killer find Rocco before, or after, Rocco found Angelo and me? Angelo didn't think of that, and neither did I . . .

I squeezed my way through the hall past Art Supply Hill. Stripped to my shorts and fell down on the bed, snapped on my reading light, picked up my paper and read. The paper I was reading was the lining from my bathroom shelf. March 22, 1982. Chopped steak at Claude's was on sale. Willie B. Spencer, 11, was bitten by a great horned owl. Deputy Danny Murk said the boy should have left the owl alone.

Fuck this. I got up and got my clothes on again. Put on my jacket and walked outside. The day was nearly gone. As they used to say in *Woolly Western Tales,* night comes quick up in the high country, and it sure gets mighty still.

I didn't have my watch. I figured it was nine. Down by the lodge, flashlights stabbed at the dark and men shouted in the trees. A real familiar scene. Much like the Nix Incident the night before. Was this an old Idaho custom? Something to do in the summer, when nothing's any good on TV?

Cold air swept down from the mountains and I stepped back inside. Locked the door twice, like that would keep anyone out. Heated a can of soup, couldn't get it down and threw it out. I lay down on the bed. I knew I couldn't sleep. I'd be up all night, haunted by Rocco's silent screams, the fear in his little pink eyes. This is what I thought I'd do, but I dozed off instead.

Woke up in a sweat from an awful meece dream. The worst meece dream I ever had. I put on my shoes and stepped outside again. I looked up at the stars. When I was a kid in Ohio, I knew the constellations by heart: Leo the Lion, Murray the Marmot, Taurus the Bull. If you know how to do it, you can always tell time by the stars. If you don't, then you'd better get a watch.

It felt like early morning, maybe three or four. The posse had given up the chase, and no one was up and about. If a new guard had taken Rocco's place, he was keeping out of sight.

Maybe, I thought, with all the other crap going on, they've forgotten all about me. What I should've done instead of take Angelo's advice was haul ass when I had the chance. Vanish in the woods. Live on berries and nuts. It was better than hanging around the trailer park, waiting for someone to—

"Wiley, that you?"

"*Shit!*" I leaped half a foot. Laurel was right there beside me in the dark. "Listen, try not to do that. I'm not good at that at all."

"You sure are jumpy, man."

"That's what I said, isn't that what I said? I said, 'I'm not good at that.' People come up in the dark that's what I'm going to do. Laurel, what are you doing out here? I'm glad to see you and all, but it's not a good night to be walking around. I don't know if you're aware what's going on . . ."

"Am I aware? Yes, I'm aware, Wiley Moss. I am so fucking *aware* I cannot tell you how *aware* I am right now. I am so *aware* if you ask me another dumb question I'll—oh, for Christ's sake, just leave me *alone,* all right?"

Before I could stop her, she turned and sprinted off through the dark, back into the trees. In school I got a letter in track. Laurel ran like a girl and I caught her pretty quick.

She didn't try to get away. She grabbed her arms and hugged herself tight. Her hair smelled clean and fine. I took her in my arms, a manly gesture women really like.

"Goddamn it, don't you *do* that!" She jerked away quick and backed off. "Don't you dare try and comfort me, Moss, I won't put up with that."

"Okay," I said, "I won't."

"Good. Make sure you don't."

"Just what are you up to, Laurel? Tell me if I'm wrong, what it looked like to me when you took off in a huff, it looked like you were headed for the lodge."

"I wasn't in a huff."

"You were pretty much in a huff. That's the way somebody looks, they're in a huff."

Laurel looked cold. She had on jeans and a jacket but she trembled anyway. If I offered her my coat she'd hit me in the crotch.

"That's where I'm going," she said, "if it's any concern of yours. Just run on back to your trailer. Please. No offense, Wiley, but I'm not looking for a date right now."

"You're going down there."

"Yes I am."

"What for?"

She looked tired, tense, uptight and out of sorts. "Don't do this anymore. *Please* just leave me alone, okay?"

I wondered if I could pick her up and take her off. She was small, but she was very athletic, agile and pretty strong. I had learned all this under ideal conditions the night before. She was not in the throes of passion right now, but she could probably handle herself.

"The thing is, Laurel, there's stuff going on here I don't know about. I think there's a lot of stuff I don't know and you do."

"So?"

"See, you see that? Now that's what I mean. You're making it clear that you're not going to help. You're saying, what you're telling me is, I'm not going to get any answers out of you. This is how you're coming across, okay? I'd like to know why that is. I am in desperate need and there's people getting killed around here and I am not used to that. That is not my lifestyle, I am not real happy here."

Laurel looked away. "You don't want to know, Wiley. Trust me on this, you really *don't* want to know."

"Huh-unh. That's not good enough for me, I won't go for that."

"Maybe you'll just have to, hon."

"Damn it, Laurel . . ."

I grabbed her shoulders and turned her around. This time she didn't jerk away. "I've got a better idea than you going down there, which is not any place you ought to be. Let's stop all this shit. Let's both get out of here. Right now."

"What?" Laurel blinked, Laurel looked confused. "What are we talking about? Are we talking what I think we're talking about?"

"Yes we are. I thought about it earlier. When everyone was busy, after the—after the tragedy occurred down there. Everyone was distracted. I think I could've pulled it off, I think I could've made it out of here."

"You do, huh?"

"Yes I do. I think it was a very good time."

"You run off in the woods."

"That's a good start."

"And go where?"

"I don't know where, Laurel, anywhere. Out to the highway. Maybe throw them off, go the other way. I know there's a river down there. I haven't been to it but it's there. We could possibly build a raft. Float downstream until we came to a settlement or a town. You're going to ask me if I've built a raft before and the answer is no. I saw some guys do it on a PBS show. We had a raft exhibit at the Smith, okay? *Rafts Through the Ages.* I remember that."

Laurel stepped up close and laid a hand on my chest. "You're a real nice guy, Wiley Moss. I mean that. You're very sweet, and you're a sport in the love department, too. I ought to know, I'm a lady's got mucho degrees in deviant behavior and pleasure in the sack.

You're good at that, babe—but you don't know shit about the game around here. You're going to do this and you're going to do that, and you don't have the foggiest what you're talkin' about. You don't see a guard, you figure he isn't there. That's your ostrich outlook, that's your linear thinking, hon. The guards, they're there, okay? They're wandering around. Out in the woods, down by the river. *Every*where."

Laurel paused and rested her hands on my neck. She looked very thoughtful and sincere. Maybe if she used small words I could possibly understand.

"The kind of place this is, no one gets in or out of here unless Vinnie wants 'em to. This place is what you call *secure*. That's what it's all *for*."

"You don't have to pronounce everything. I can keep up just fine."

"Can you? Good. Then I guess you've already noticed this isn't your ordinary summer paradise. Like, there isn't hardly anyone here? I imagine you can tell we don't have a whole lot of tourists flocking in."

"Who are they, then?"

"Who's what?"

"The guys that stay here. You've got about two cabins rented, a couple of cars. How did they get in?"

Laurel sighed. "Let's talk about this some other time, sweetie, all right? I'm real worn out, and I've got a lot to do."

"Like what? Like spooking around down there? Jesus, Laurel, you're not still thinking of doing that."

"Am I talking slow enough for you?"

I looked up at the stars. Bob the Badger, Gemini the Twins.

"What about the guards? The guards are everywhere, I remember that."

"I've been out here for a while. Freezing my lovely ass while you were sawing logs in there. I live here, too, you recall that? Those boys aren't original thinkers, I know about where they are."

I looked into the dark. I could see my own hand, I could see Laurel's face. I couldn't see a lot beyond that. It was chilly enough when you breathed you could make a little cloud. All the summer bugs were quiet. Your invertebrate life doesn't care for cold nights.

"Okay," I said, "you got to do something dumb, you're not going to do it by yourself. You're going, I'm going too."

Laurel rolled her eyes. "And do what? You going to take care of me, Wiley? Hey, I can't wait for that."

"I just might. I've taken care of someone before."

"Good. Go back to your trailer. Leave me alone, take care of yourself. Oh hell, hon . . ." She closed her eyes and made a face. "I'm sorry, okay? I didn't mean that. I am not exactly myself."

"That's what I said, right? I said I'm sorry, you hear me say that?" She gave me a peck on the cheek. Cold lips, warm heart. "Go back to your trailer, please? I'll be just fine."

"I'm going with you."

"No you're not."

"Yeah, I am, too."

"Don't you follow me. Don't even think about it, hear?"

"You're not my real mother. I don't have to listen to you."

Laurel let out a breath. Showed me a proud, defiant chin. "I'm leaving, Wiley Moss. And you'd better stay right here."

"Fine. Good-bye," I said.

She turned and walked off. I counted to six. Six is a good head start.

I suddenly had a thought. This can happen any time. Why were we going down to spy on the Mount Vincent High Country Lodge and Whitewater Resort? What for? I wished I'd thought to ask.

13

Woodcraft is an art.
    It's something that you start real early, and it's best if you do it all the time. Your people of the Native American persuasion can look at twigs and grass, they can tell you if someone's been by. They can even tell you when. If it's a man or a woman or a child. They can tell you how tall a person is, they can tell you what he weighs. They can tell if he's a Baptist or a dentist or some other kind of faith. They can tell you what a person had for lunch, but I don't care to think about that.

Six was too long a head start. When I passed the first tree, Laurel was already out of sight. I stood there a moment, hoping for a scent. Fritos, lipstick, a whiff of womanhood, the tang of Maybelline. I couldn't smell a thing. I couldn't see a twig or any grass.

Laurel stepped from behind a tall fir and said, "I bet you were raised in the city. I'll bet you never saw a tree before you came here."

"I've seen a lot of trees," I said. "They're different kinds of trees than this. You've got a different place, you've got different kinds of trees."

"Fine. Watch where you're going. Don't talk. Don't make any noise again."

"Okay, I won't. I'll be real quiet. I won't say anything at all."

"Shut *up*, Wiley . . ."

She walked on ahead. Except for her very dim shape against the greater dark of night, I could hardly tell that she was there. I didn't step on very much at all. When my eyes got used to the light, I scarcely made a sound.

The few times I'd walked toward the lodge, I had always taken the open path. It was longer through the trees. Still, in just a few minutes, we could see lights ahead—the yellow squares of windows with the blinds drawn down. I knew where we were. To our right was the large main building. In the daytime, a sign said CHUCK WAGON & OFFICE. From what I'd come to know, I doubted if either one was there.

Just behind the office were the first of the cabins. The third one was where the light was coming from.

Laurel stopped and raised a hand. I walked up behind her and she motioned me to wait. She took a deep breath, let it out, went down on her hands and knees. She crawled through the sparse underbrush and disappeared.

I waited. She was gone a long time, or that's how it seemed to me. There are always noises in the woods. Night birds, mice, little critters scuttering about. Everything sounds like something it isn't when you're out there by yourself.

Laurel made a noise. A sharp intake of breath, nearly a little cry, stifled almost at once. Hair climbed up my neck. Someone had spotted her. She tried to call for help. Someone clapped a hand across her mouth and cut her off.

I went to the ground. Felt around and grabbed a broken branch. It seemed very light. I felt it with my other hand. It was five, maybe six inches long. I could hit somebody if they came in real close.

The sound of pine needles scraping on the ground. Laurel backed out of the brush. I crawled to her side. Even in the faint light I could see she was frightened—something had shaken her, something had drawn all the color from her face.

"What is it, what happened up there, you okay?"

She reached out and squeezed my hand. Her fingers were cold as death.

"Michael. Michael's here . . ."

"Who's Michael?"

She was trying to breathe, trying to level out.

"I was . . . standing past your trailer, I was there a long time. I saw the two cars pull in the drive. Two big Lincolns. I knew it was Michael. That's what he drives, he won't drive anything else."

Laurel paused, looked off somewhere in the dark. "What I was doing, Wiley, I was trying to get the nerve to do what we're doing now. Come down here. Get that—*close* to the man."

A very slight shiver, a tired and very weary smile. "How about me? Laurel Boone, frontier hooker. Somethin' else, huh?"

"Now don't start that."

"I was scared, hon. I got a little braver, taking it out on you."

"That's okay. Using somebody else, it's the natural thing to do."

"No it's not." The words came out in a soft explosion of sound. "Not for me it's not. I don't *like* doin' that!"

"Who is he, Laurel? Who's Michael?"

"Michael is—Michael is Michael. Michael Galiano. Chicago, Las Vegas, L.A. I guess wherever he wants to be. Michael is Vinnie's boss. He put Vinnie out here. Set him up in Idaho, set up the whole operation out here. Vinnie's father worked for Michael's father. That was a long time ago, back in Chicago, when the two old men were both still alive. Michael's a whole lot younger than Vinnie, he came along late. Vinnie's father was Sal DeMarco. He did—he did things for Vinnie's father, John Galiano."

"What kind of things?"

"Jesus, Wiley . . ."

"Yeah, okay. Things. I think I got your meaning. I just thought— *things* could be anything, right?"

Laurel's look said *wrong*. It said don't be a jerk, I mean exactly what I said.

She peered at the light through the trees. A patch of yellow fell across her cheek.

"Michael being here, that's not good. Michael shows up, it's never good news. With Michael, it's always something bad."

"Like Rocco and Nix."

"Like that . . ."

"And?"

"I didn't say *and*."

"You didn't say *and*, you were going to say *and*. You almost said an *and*."

"You could get on my nerves, Wiley, you know that? It wouldn't take a whole lot, you got a real good start."

"Okay. Fine."

"I am really on edge, all right?"

"Fine."

"Don't say that again, you already said it twice."

Shit, here we go again . . .

I looked away a minute. Laurel slipped past me and crawled off through the trees.

"Laurel—!"

Laurel didn't answer. I left my deadly club behind, and followed her shapely self. It was easy, now, I didn't have to look for twigs. The trees were thick and tall, lodgepole pines, and they grew right up to the lodge itself. I felt we were reasonably safe. Not as safe as, say, France, or up in Norway somewhere, but fairly safe for Vinnie's place in Idaho.

Laurel was right. Two Lincoln cars, one of them black. The other one was babyshit brown. I don't think they call it that, I think they maybe call it something else.

The driver of the lighter car was standing by the hood. Black suit, black shirt. Built like a side of beef. Club fighter's face—nose squashed flat, fungoid ears, a silly little chauffer's cap perched on top his head. He didn't move, he didn't breathe. He stood with his arms folded over his massive chest.

"I know *him*," Laurel said. A catch in her voice, a little shiver by my side. "That's Carl. Carl's unbelievably bad, a real fucking freak."

"I wonder how I guessed."

Laurel squinted into the dark. "Two guys in the black car. One in the front, one in the back. I can't see 'em from here."

"I can," I told her. I could see this one coming. "I can see them just fine."

"Stay right here, I'm going to move up some."

"No you're not."

"Who's going to stop me? You?"

"Yes I am."

"Bullshit, Moss. I won't put up with that."

She gave me a look and crawled off. I stuck my hand down her jeans, grabbed a handful of denim and lifted her butt off the ground.

"Let go of me, Moss." A very calm, a very patient threat. "Do it right now."

"I don't think so. We've got one rhino upright out there, I don't see waking the other two."

"Will you get your hand out of my pants?"

"Will you sit still?"

I took my hand away. She made a big deal out of tugging her jeans up tight.

"You're pathetic, Wiley Moss, you know that?"

"You've mentioned this before."

"You keep acting like you do, I'm likely to mention it again."

"Boy, your skin's nice. You sure feel good."

"Everybody says so, man."

That really hurt. A girl feels good to touch, your romance gene it's going to take off, it's going to slip right into gear. You forget that the lady's slinging fries, she's a teller at a bank, she's a famous movie star. She's maybe like Laurel, she's gone into business for herself. A man crazed with beauty and desire is a man who doesn't care.

I thought about something to say. I don't know what it was, it was something sincere. Instead, the door to Cabin Three opened wide and flooded the ground with light.

I hunched down quick. Laurel held her breath. Vinnie came out, holding a drink in one hand. The man beside him was tall, loose, wiry and cool as glacier ice. Three-piece suit, maybe raw Italian silk. Late thirties, forty, forty-two. A guy like that you couldn't tell. He moved with the grace and assurance of a trained athlete, a man who knows his body will always do him right.

When his face caught the light, Laurel gave a start, squeezed my hand tight. A quick glimpse of dark and lazy eyes, a lopsided smile. Bold and striking features, a Greek marble statue with a Palm Springs tan. Michael Galiano. I didn't have to ask.

Laurel's nails were digging holes in my palm. Laurel couldn't make up her mind. I was either Elmer Fudd or Lancelot.

Michael stepped outside the square of light. He leaned down to Vinnie, spoke to him softly, gave him a manly embrace and stepped back. Both men laughed. Michael's laugh came from somewhere in his gut, a deep and pleasant sound. Vinnie's like someone had goosed him. Pee Wee Herman, early Don Knotts.

Vinnie stood by the door as Michael walked back to the cars. Michael waved over his shoulder without looking back. I looked back at Vinnie, past him to the door. Angela was standing there, leaning against the frame. Arms crossed, one hip out of joint. Her hair was a shadow, a spidery veil across her breasts, a frame about her angular face. Bandanna halter, hollow tummy. Deep belly button to match. High-fashion cutoffs, hugging her thighs just right.

Laurel poked me in the ribs. A little disapproving brow. I felt a happy chill, delighted to know she cared.

Just outside of Cabin Three, Vinnie turned to Angela, said something to her I couldn't hear. Whatever it was, Angela didn't like it at all. She spat an answer back, glared at her brother and stalked off up the hill.

Vinnie muttered to himself. Took a few steps, and snapped off the light in Cabin Three. I watched him as he stood there in the dark. He seemed to sway a little, unsteady on his feet. I wondered how much he'd put away. The booze hadn't fazed him at all the night Nix fell in the trout, and we missed out on Marmot Surprise.

I wondered where Angelo was. Two of the DeMarcos on hand to greet Michael, why not all three? I suddenly remembered, with a queasy little lurch, that someone else was missing too. Bobby Bad Eye was always around, but he wasn't around right now. I never missed Bobby, unless I didn't know where Bobby was.

"Listen," I whispered, "I am not feeling comfortable here. What I think we ought to do, I think we ought to—"

I reached out for Laurel. Laurel wasn't there and I touched a tree instead. Jesus, I thought, that honey's slick as a snake. How did she manage that?

I took a deep breath, checked out Vinnie once more. Vinnie was crocked. Vinnie wouldn't notice if a herd of meece ran by.

Run, said Elmer Fudd, get us the hell out of here.

Hold it, Lancelot said, what about the girl?

She'll be all right, I said, but we all knew better than that . . .

I crawled on my belly toward the cars. Michael was talking to the Rhino. The Rhino listened real hard. He mouthed Michael's words. He looked Michael straight in the eye. He wanted to make sure and get it right. It was too dark to see the black car. I assumed the other guys were still there.

The leaves were cold and wet. It was dark, but I could clearly see the fight scars on Rhino's prehistoric brow. I could see the rubber tits on the new Pirelli tires. I couldn't see Laurel anywhere.

My family in Defiance County, Ohio, was not at all pleased when I told them I wanted to pursue an art career. They wanted me to get in hardware. "That's what our people do," they told me, "we've done it for over a hundred and fifty years. What's wrong with you, boy?" "I've got to draw," I said. "I've got this fire, and it's burning inside." "What you've got is a brain full of shit," said Aunt Lil. Lil liked to skip the niceties and get to the heart of things.

I couldn't find Laurel, and I couldn't get closer than I was. If I got any closer, we'd all be best friends. Michael slapped Rhino on the shoulder, walked past the babyshit Lincoln and stopped at the car in back. He spoke to the driver, opened the back door and slipped inside.

At first I couldn't see the other guy. The door light didn't work or someone had taped it shut. A few seconds later, a flash went on. Michael had something in his hand. He was showing it to the man. The man looked nervous, like he didn't want to see it, like he didn't want to look. His face had gone to fat, his head was nearly bald. Slate-colored eyes and bad teeth. It wasn't hot out but his face was slick with sweat, sweating so hard that he—

Laurel popped up out of nowhere and scared me half to death. She wasn't two feet away, I hadn't seen her there at all. I reached out to grab her and missed. A little cry stuck in her throat; she tore at the underbrush, swept it aside, stepped on my head, and she was gone.

Rhino went berserk. He went *"Huk! Huk! Huk!"* Lowered his head and charged past me through the trees. I could smell his body odor, his socks and his cologne. *Obsession for Men,* what else? A car door flew open. Michael Galiano said something—something *fuck!* Ripped off his coat and joined the chase.

I didn't know what to do next. Whatever it was, the best thing to do was very likely something else. I wondered how Aunt Lil had known. How could she guess how my life would turn out? How could she tell, when I was only nine at the time?

14

Fear and indecision can often save your life.

You got a good reaction time, you're going to act fast. You're going to bolt, you're going to dash. You're going to jump, you're going to run, then someone's going to shoot you in the ass. This happens to rabbits all the time.

I didn't act fast. I didn't act at all. I hugged the ground, stunned and paralyzed. Rhino and Michael passed me by. I could hear them to my left, thrashing through the trees for lower ground. I stood up and listened for a second, then ran off to the right. Left is okay if you're not in the trees. The path in the open runs straight as an arrow from the trailers to the road, and up to the lodge itself. In the woods, though, you've got to go right, you've to go up instead of down.

Your practiced woodsman gets to know these things. We can pick up a scent, we can follow the faintest track. It doesn't matter if it's noon or the murky black of night. Besides, Laurel was running like a gut-shot grizzly, flattening everything in sight. Your neophyte tracker could tell where Laurel had been. Stevie Wonder could follow Laurel's trail.

Very soon, I picked her up myself. She was tearing up the wilderness twenty feet away.

I called out, "Laurel!" as softly as I could. Laurel stopped at once, frozen in her tracks. She jerked around and stared. Saw it was me, took a deep breath and clutched her breasts. I went to her at once, opened my arms to take her in. She doubled up her fists and hit me in the face.

"It's me," I told her, "stop doing that."

"You son of a bitch, I could've had a fatal stroke, you come on me like that!"

She hit me in the eye.

"Laurel," I said, "there are people in pursuit. We don't have time for this."

She pummeled me again. I grabbed both her wrists, ducked and put my shoulder to her waist. Picked her up in the fireman's carry they taught us in Eagle Scouts. Laurel called me several names, struggled and pounded me on the back. Off in the woods, someone called out to someone else. Someone answered back. I could drop her and run. Get out of there fast. Listen, guys, I slept with her once, but I can't recall her name . . .

Lightning blinked far off to the north. A quick flash of silver through the trees. I stopped for a second and stared. I could scarcely believe my eyes. There it was—my trailer right ahead! I was filled with confidence and joy. It had to be an omen, it couldn't be anything else. God knew where I was, even in Idaho.

As I sprinted for the trailer, the thunder came grumbling through the valley, rolling off the peaks. A fresh wind sighed above the trees. The first, swollen drops of rain crackled on the soft forest floor.

I got us through the door with a good half second to spare. Lightning ripped the night apart. Thunder shook the trailer and rain drummed on the roof.

What more can you ask? I told myself. Nature's run amuck, and God's on your side. You're high and dry, and those assholes are out there in the rain. If you left any tracks, they're surely gone by now.

"Goddamn it, put me down!" Laurel started pounding again, bit me on the shoulder, kicked me in the chest.

"Shut up," I said, "I'm thinking. I can't think straight, you're doing that."

Tracks. Tracks inside and tracks out. Think about that.

I stooped through the hallway and dumped Laurel down on the bed.

"Strip, undress. Get out of those clothes."

"Do what?"

"Just *do* it, Laurel. Do it right now."

I found a box of matches in the bathroom drawer. Laurel continued a litany of abuse—four-letter words without sentence structure of any sort. I went down to my knees, checked the hallway floor. A few drops of water, mud here and there. I backed toward the bedroom, wiping my way with a dirty towel.

Okay, what else? Nothing I could think of, nothing but the clothes. We'd gotten in fast, but there'd still be a few little drops, a wet spot here and there.

I started taking everything off. Lightning struck again. Laurel was sitting on the bed, watching me with a cold and wary eye.

"I told you, get everything off. Let's not go over this again."

I kicked off my shoes, stood on one foot, peeled off my pants and shorts. Laurel didn't move. She looked like a badger who might put up a fight.

"You got real bad timing, Moss. I am not in a carnal frame of mind, I am not up for this."

I tossed my shirt on the floor. "This isn't a true violation, don't think it is. This is just pretend."

"I guess I've heard that before."

"Laurel, I'm not going to talk about this. You're going to get your stuff off, you're going to get in that bed."

"Hah!" Laurel said.

Reason can waste a lot of time. I didn't ask again. Laurel saw me coming. She kicked at me and yelled as I stripped off her jeans and the micro-panties under that. Kamikaze-red. Big enough to cover up a dime, if you happened to keep one down there.

I pulled off her T-shirt, threw it across the room. Gathered up her clothes and mine. Dropped a few at random from the bedroom to the bath. One night only, The Hansel and Gretel Show. Dumped what was left on the bathroom floor. I turned on the shower for a second, got the towel wet, dropped it on the clothes. Ran back to the bed. Pulled the covers over Laurel, and jumped in myself.

Laurel gave me that painful look again. "I'm the little camper, you're the kindly troop leader, right?"

Lightning split a tree nearby. The trailer shook. The walls turned an alien green. Laurel grabbed my hand, remembered she didn't want to, and quit.

"Listen, I don't care for this. I like a guy to act nice. You could've said it nice."

"Said what?"

"Like, 'Laurel I'd like to screw you now. Would it be all right if I removed your garments, hon?' "

"I told you. That isn't what it's all about."

"Yeah, it is. That's what it's always about."

"No it's not."

"Well, tell me about it, friend. I never been in love before."

She sat up in bed and crossed her legs. "Jesus, Moss, I thought better of you. I am scared half out of my wits, you're dragging me off, you're playing let's-get-naked again. I don't go for that caveperson crap, that doesn't work for me."

"Laurel. That isn't it."

"Don't you say that again."

"That isn't it."

"What the fuck is it, then?"

Someone kicked in the trailer door.

"That's it," I said.

Laurel went blank. She said, "Shit-shit-shit!" and covered up her head.

Bobby Bad Eye stepped through the hallway and flipped on the light.

"Goddamn it," I said, embarrassed, indignant, truly pissed off, anything I could think of that applied.

Bobby looked at me. He looked at the lump beside me in the bed.

"Got company, huh?"

"Yes, I do. I believe you broke my door."

"Who is it?"

"I don't see that's any of your concern."

"Let's see who's in there."

"This is a clear invasion of my rights. I won't stand for that."

"Shut the fuck up, Mr. Moss."

Laurel poked her head out and glared. "It's me, Bobby. That okay with you?"

"Hi, Laurel."

"Hi, Bobby. What the hell you doing in here?"

Bobby ran a hand across his face. He was soaked to the skin, his hair was plastered flat. Rain trickled past his milky eye. He took a step closer to the bed.

"Pull the covers back."

"No I won't," I said.

"Do it," Bobby said.

"Forget it, he's seen it all before." Laurel flipped the covers back, twirled one foot in the air, pulled them down again.

"Wow," I said, "was that exciting or what? You get off on that, your motor running good?"

"Wiley, leave it *alone*," Laurel said.

Bobby didn't seem to take offense. That was the trouble with Bobby, you couldn't ever tell. He didn't seem real upset at Billy's Gas & Auto Repair.

"How long you two been here," he said. "How long you been in bed?"

"I don't know," I said. "Joy lifts me up, and I lose all sense of time."

"We been here 'bout an hour and a half," Laurel told him. "The boy here isn't any rookie. He can lift that joy of his real fine."

Bobby muttered something to himself. His good eye took in the floor, followed the trail of clothes. Wandered into the bathroom, stayed there a second, and walked back out. He looked at us both. Chewed on his lips for some time. It was hard to hold his gaze. Bobby's gaze was something fierce. I think he saw a fort, I think he saw a wagon train. He wanted to find something there in that trailer, he wanted to find it bad. He couldn't, and he was burning inside about that.

He didn't say another word. He turned around and left. There was a good-size puddle where he'd stood. I waited a minute, got up and padded naked down the hall. Cold rain pelted me in the face. I tugged on the broken door, shut it as best I could. Maybe the rain would leak in and ruin my art supplies. What would Vinnie Spuds think of that?

Laurel drew the covers back, wrapped her arms around me, covered me up again. Drew her body close.

"Hey," I said, "you're as hot as you can be."

"I'm a ragin' furnace, I got a real fever for you, hon."

It was a terrible line, and someone must have said it, probably in 1942. Laurel and I laughed together. Maybe a little too much, maybe strung up a little tight.

Laurel let me go, fell on her back and sighed.

"God, Moss, I guess you think I'm pretty dense. I wasn't thinking straight, I thought you were just coming on real strong, you know? When I heard that door give in . . ."

"You were scared, Laurel. I know that."

"Damn right I was."

"You were so scared of what you saw down there, you forgot about everything else. Like somebody coming up here."

I felt her stiffen up. She was silent too long, she didn't answer quick enough.

"I told you, I got kind of spooked down there. Michael's a heavy dude, and Carl, Carl's as freaky as they come. Carl flat gives me the chills . . ."

I leaned up and looked down in her face. The storm was moving off, and the distant lightning flickered on her skin.

"I know what scared you. I saw what happened down there. Nothing happened till you saw that guy in the back of Michael's car. Michael turned the flash on, you saw the guy's face. That's when you lost it and ran. Who was he, Laurel? Why did the fat guy scare you more than Michael or Carl?"

Laurel shook her head. "You missed the boat on that one, babe. I saw him and he's fat, but I don't know the man."

She smiled up at me, and touched a finger to my lips. The smile was just right. The smile, and the sleepy look in her eyes. I might have believed her except for the tic—a funny little twitch at the corner of her mouth.

"You don't know him."

"I never saw the clown before. I told you, I got spooked, is all."

I settled down beside her again. She felt real good, satiny and slick. The sweet deviations of our previous encounter were vivid in my head. The feelings, the scents, everything was there.

"You want to do something?" Laurel said. "We can if you like." She knew what I was thinking, she didn't have to ask.

"No," I lied, "I don't. I want you to tell me what you know about the guy in the car. I want to know the things you know that I don't. I want you to tell me what the hell is going on, why people tend to get killed around here."

A nervous little laugh, a finger on my lips again. "You're asking me that, you think I know that? Jesus, Moss, I don't *want* to know that. If I did, I'd keep my stupid mouth shut for once."

"Okay."

"Okay what, what's that?"

"Okay, you don't want to tell me what's happening here, you don't know the guy in the car, you don't know shit. Meanwhile, I am stuck in this dump, and I've seen a lot of stuff I am not supposed to see. I am not a moron, Laurel, I strongly doubt if anyone intends to let me leave. But you don't know a thing, right? My ass is on the line, and you couldn't possibly be of any help."

"*Wiley—*"

"Forget it, Laurel."

"If there's maybe things I know, and I'm not saying there is, okay? But if there were and I did, and I didn't say anything because it wouldn't do you any good, would you be—would you be mad if I didn't, if I knew and I didn't do that?"

"I think I'm still with you. If I am, I guess I'd say no, I wouldn't be mad at that. What I'd like, I'd like you to tell me what you know about this goddamn zoo and let me decide myself."

She turned and nuzzled up beside me, scooting out a little nest. "There's something I'll tell you. But you won't like it much."

"Uh-huh, what's that?"

"Vinnie told me to stay with you. Before you got here. I'm your live-in delight. Sorta like a complimentary drink?"

"I knew that, that's no surprise," I said.

I didn't, but I'd guessed. Like a number of things I didn't want to know, I'd conveniently set it aside.

"You're supposed to tell him what I'm doing, what I'm saying, right?"

"I *was.* I decided not to, though. Right from the start."

"And why'd you do that?"

"Because I figured you and me were different, that's why. You weren't a John and I wasn't what I am. The minute I hopped in your bed, I sensed there was something more lasting than sweat between us. Something that might be part of a grand design."

"No offense," I said, "I think I've seen this picture before."

"Shoot, so have I, hon. But what if it's real? What if we're under a spell?"

"That'd be fine, Laurel. It's been some time since I even thought about a spell."

"Well, you might just try and *believe* me, okay? Whatever we got, we got a little trust, Wiley Moss. Shit, if I haven't blabbed to Vinnie before, I'm sure not likely to now. In light of tonight's disturbing events."

"There's that," I said.

"Well there certainly is."

Laurel laid her head on my arm. Her long hair tickled my face. Her hand brushed my chest, and she slid one leg across mine. Something else tickled my thigh, and I felt electrified. Nothing could disarm me quite as quick as that. If I had any more searching questions, they vanished like smoke from my head. I kissed her cheek, I kissed her mouth. I placed my hand gently on her breast. Laurel made a happy little sound.

"It's true as it can be what you said," I whispered into honey-colored hair. "We'd all like to think there's some magic out there, that tomorrow's the day fate'll hit us with a spell. I've thought more than once that I'd found the real thing. I'd say maybe seventeen times.

"Once it was Giselle, who I don't think I've told you about. We lived together once in D.C. She had a few neurons out of whack, and wasn't always fully there, but she was really awful sweet. She went away with Stirling LaFrance, the Chicken Man, who's big in poultry parts. There was a woman on a plane who had beautiful feet. That lady had skin like cream, and arches that wouldn't quit. There was a girl in college, Amy something, I don't recall her name. She looked a little French. And Jesus, there's the lovely and haunting Claire de Mer. We might've had magic of a personal kind if Bobby and Rocco hadn't come along.

"How many's that, I lost count. Anyway, it's been a whole lot, and I'm not counting the unrequited kind, like the girl who does the news on TV, or a nurse you maybe see on a bus. I wonder if there's any way a man and a woman can help breaking each other's heart? How can people be together, without pissing each other off? We want to believe it's going to last—on the other hand, we're terrified it might.

"Time is the enemy of love. Time makes assholes of us all. My friend Phil Greenburg, who works at the Department of Ag, Phil says commitment is another way of getting laid twice. Now that's an awful thing to say, and I've thought about it some, and I hope he isn't right. I hope two people can like each other without stimulation of their parts, though there's nothing wrong with that and I certainly wouldn't want to rule it out. Laurel? Laurel, are you asleep or what?"

It looked like Laurel was. She was breathing pretty deep. It was quite outside except for the rain still dripping off the trees. Tapping on the roof like a faucet you can't ever fix, even if you put a washer in.

I looked up at the ceiling, and listened to Laurel breathe. I lay very still and watched floaters for a while. If a person's got weird enough floaters in his eyes, he doesn't need a TV.

I dropped off just before daylight. My arm was dead under Laurel's neck. I hated to move it, but I read a lot of Patrick O'Brian and his tales of the sea. Two things that worry me are scurvy and gangrene.

Laurel moaned a little when I moved. I tried to turn over but she burrowed in my chest.

"Wiley . . . you okay?"

"I'm just fine."

"I was having an awful science dream."

"I've had 'em myself. I really hate that."

"I was dreaming about the universe. How ninety percent is made up of dark matter, stuff we can't see?"

"Yes, it is."

"Dark matter scares me, hon."

"I think it scares us all. Go on back to sleep."

I couldn't get to sleep myself for some time. I watched the day creep along the shades. I listened to the blue jays squawking in the trees. The squirrels jumped on the roof, and ran about like maniacs. I finally dropped off. When I woke up again, Laurel was gone. That woman's always gone in daylight. It's real irritating sometimes.

There wasn't anything to eat. I pulled on my jeans and walked barefoot outside. The air was washed clean. If I stood there a while, coffee might appear.

I walked into the field beyond the trees. In the distance were the rusty auto parts. Closer, the familiar pile of rocks. I looked at them again. They didn't look all that familiar this time. They looked like they had the day before, the morning after Nix was shot. They didn't and they did. It suddenly struck me why the rock pile looked a little different every day, why it wasn't always the same. It always looked different, I decided, because they had to dig it up at night. And they wouldn't do that, if they didn't have something that they had to put in . . .

15

When Bobby showed up I wasn't looking at the rocks. I was sitting on the steps of my trailer, looking at an ant. This was a small red pharaoh, a *Monomorium pharaonis*. He had found a little something for breakfast, which was more than I had managed for myself. There are well over 2,500 species of ants that we know of so far. I expect there are many more than that.

Bobby walked up and said, "What are you doing, Mr. Moss, what're you looking at?"

I said, "I'm looking at an ant."

"You had any breakfast yet?"

"No, I haven't."

"Me neither. Listen, there's a couple things we need to clear up. What we got, we got a current event. I take that back, we got two. You're aware we had an accident the night before last, you were sitting right there. This is Nix I'm referring to, the victim of a hunting accident. Last afternoon, tragedy reached out an' struck us again. Rocco was fishing by the lake. He hooked him a pretty big rainbow, and suffered a fatal heart attack."

"My God," I said, apparently stunned at this news. "That's terrible. How did it happen?"

"You didn't hear me, you didn't hear me say Rocco was fishing by the lake, he had a fatal heart attack, you didn't hear that?"

"Well of course I did, I'm just stunned. I mean it's hard to believe. That bell tolls, that could be for you or me, it could be for anyone."

"You didn't know this, you haven't heard this before."

"Huh? Hear what?"

"Hear what we're talking about, that Rocco is dead."

"No, I didn't know Rocco was dead, who's going to tell me that he's dead?"

Bobby nailed me with his single evil eye. I tried for bewildered, agog and mystified. Bobby squatted and plucked a blade of grass. He poked it at my ant.

"You were here in the trailer all night, is that right? You were screwin' with the whore."

"Laurel and I sought each other's companionship during the evening. You may be referring to that. Anyway, I don't see the point to all this. If you'll think back, Bobby, you'll recall that you broke down my door. You walked in and jerked our covers off and I guess you maybe saw that we were there. I was the guy. The one that was acting real effeminate was Laurel."

Bobby kept looking. Once they start looking, nothing's going to stop a person of the Indian persuasion. They can stand in the woods or on a mountain somewhere, they can stand there and look all day.

Still, I went ahead and said it, because it was the normal thing to do, he'd figure it was something that I'd do.

"You mind me asking, you mind telling me why you busted in last night, what you came up here for? What do you care if I was up here or not? Is this about Rocco or what?"

"Yeah, I do."

"Yeah, you do what?"

"Mind explaining stuff to you. I don't have to fuck with that, explaining stuff to you."

"Okay, fine."

"You say that's fine?"

"That's fine."

"Good. Because if it's not, I can go over it again."

"No, that's fine."

Bobby Bad Eye stood. "You don't mind, I'd like to go in and use your john."

"You got to use mine?"

Bobby gave me a look.

"Watch yourself," I said, "the door won't work anymore."

Bobby kicked the broken door and stepped inside. I was hoping he only had to pee. You live in a trailer, someone comes in, you're hoping that all they'll do is pee.

I let myself relax, let a little tension out. I felt like I'd passed Miss Proulow's Eighth Grade algebra test. Bobby had a single ball bearing eye, and Miss Proulow had two.

Okay. So nobody knew I'd been down there with Angelo when Rocco got slashed and moosified. For some happy reason, Angelo didn't want it known that he was there as well. I didn't care why. Whatever the reason, it was good enough for me.

Another thing Bobby didn't know was that Laurel and I had been out on a spree, lurking in the trees, spying on people that we shouldn't ought to see. If Vinnie, and Michael Galiano, knew we'd been there . . . If I hadn't found Laurel in the woods . . . If Jesus hadn't cued the rain at the absolute ideal time . . .

That's two lucky breaks, two sly winks from the Fates. I gave a little shudder, and hoped I wouldn't have to try for three.

Bobby came back. Bobby said, "All that art shit, it's still just sittin' there in boxes, Mr. Moss, it isn't even unpacked."

"What?" I stared. "What's with *unpacked?* What do you suggest I do with it, stack it in the yard? You know what happens when a squirrel gets hold of art supplies? It's something you don't want to see, I'll tell you that."

Bobby looked disgusted. "I don't care what the fuck you do with it, Moss. It's 7:30 now. Get your ass in gear, get over to the Spudettes, you're drawing up Zinnia at nine."

I stood up fast. "You mean *today?* Huh-unh, no way. I'm not ready yet, I am not prepared for that."

"Nine," Bobby said. He turned and walked away.

"Listen, what'd you do in the john?"

"Nothing you'll regret," Bobby said. He didn't stop, he didn't turn around.

She had skin like Chinese ivory, black-black hair and toasted almond eyes. Thighs soft as kittens, breasts hard as hand-packed ice cream. She was five feet of absolutely lovely California-Hong Kong-

Hawaiian womanhood. Most of her growth had gone into her legs, which started at Shanghai, and wandered clear up to Peking.

At the moment, she was lazing stark naked on a fake-fur leopard-skin couch, sort of twisty in the middle, sort of halfway on her side. Up on one elbow, chin in her hand, tiny little waist flaring up to a jaunty swell of hip, down to the endless legs below.

I was sitting in a turquoise beanbag chair, one of the exotic artifacts like tie-dyed curtains, beads on the door, gold-sprayed Buddhas, multicolored saints, Mickeys, Minnies and Donald Ducks, which Zinnia had collected from roadside stands across the West.

The ghetto blaster played the Top Forty hits out of Taiwan, a pirate CD. The sound shook the Jackie Chan posters on the wall. *Rumble in the Bronx, Drunken Master II.* And Zinnia's favorite, *Fists of Fury,* 1972.

What I was trying to do was get Zinnia on the page. I was working with the warms, using Rowney soft pastels on a charcoal-gray paper. Burnt sienna, yellow ochre and cadmium orange, accenting with a little sap green. What Zinnia was doing was distracting me any way she could. A sigh, a pout, a thrust of a collarbone or hip. A little muscle in the thigh, a little hollow in the tummy that would suddenly appear. All of this unposed and subtle, small accidents, all designed to rattle the artist who had been drawing bugs for several years. A man who was easily inflamed by a Wonderbra ad on TV.

"Zinnia," I said, "you're going to have to calm down. It's real hard to draw someone, they won't keep their parts still."

A throaty little laugh, a pout that she'd seen in a movie somewhere.

"I always have trouble with my parts. Can't seem to hold 'em down."

"Well you give it a try."

She was drinking wine with a straw. It sucked in her cheeks and made her eyes bug out.

"I don't want to make the artist mad. He might make me ugly. Might make me look like a insect or a fly."

"I don't think I'll do that. You don't look at all like a fly."

"What you think I look like, then? You think I'm kinda cute, Moss?"

"Let's just stop that, Zinnia. Cute is not an issue here."

"I make you nervous, huh?"

"I'm a professional artist. You don't make me nervous at all, you've just got to keep still."

"Can I see what you're doing?"

"No you can't."

"Why not?"

"Because you can't. It's a work in progress, a preliminary sketch. It's not finished yet."

"I just want a little peek."

"You can see it when I'm done."

"Laurel said you were fun."

"I am, I'm just not fun now. I might be fun later on."

"When'll that be?"

"Zinnia, be still."

"Does it bother you if I do this?"

Zinnia wiggled her pretty toes. Zinnia twirled one leg in a graceful little arc, one of Zinnia's petals looked at me and winked.

I snapped a pastel in two. The box fell off my lap. Cadmiums and purples and cobalts rolled across the floor. Zinnia got hysterical and choked on her drink.

"Okay, twenty-minute break," I said, and bolted for the door. The A/C worked fine, but it was always hot inside.

What we did, we did serious art for maybe three or four minutes, followed by a twenty-minute break that lasted for an hour and a half. Starting in the morning, we did this all day. I ate chicken sandwiches and drank a lot of wine. I got to meet Rosemary, Poppy, Bluebell and Fern. Marigold, Violet, Lily and Columbine. Gardenia and Orchid and the famous Buttercup, and some I can't recall. Buttercup was cute as she could be. Pink baby skin and baby fat. She wore a pink swimsuit and liked to splash around in the pool. Poppy was mocha-brown and tall. The water beaded up on her skin and she didn't wear any suit at all. Columbine was stunning to behold. A little like Laurel, only Laurel had blue eyes and Columbine's were green.

Laurel had a system. I could talk to any girl I liked until my eyes began to glaze, and then I'd have to quit. Daisy didn't count. Daisy was Laurel's best friend, and I could talk to Daisy all I liked. You could look at these two and know they were close. They had that special air, that unspoken ease that says you're lifetime buddies, you're more than just friends.

I was glad to see Daisy again. She was friendly as a puppy, healthy and tan, and I'd liked her from the start. I thought she'd be upset because I'd turned down her very lovely self driving up here in the car.

"Shoot, don't you give it another thought," Daisy said. "A turn-down's kinda refreshing now and then. Like, a guy's maybe thinking we could talk or maybe do something else."

"Hah!" Laurel said, "not likely, babe, you're talking about Wiley Moss. You don't have to wonder what *he's* got on his mind."

"Hey, that isn't so at all." I tried to look hurt, and it came up goofy instead. "You and me, we've talked lots of times."

"Excuse me?" Laurel rolled her eyes. "That part you're always talking to? That's not an *ear,* hon, it doesn't hear that good."

Laurel laughed like a horse. Laurel had a fit. It wasn't that funny, but Laurel wouldn't stop. When you're drinking lots of wine, you're your own best fan.

"Now you just quit," Daisy said. "I think Wiley's real nice."

"Oh, yeah?"

"I think he's cute as he can be."

"You do, huh?"

"I certainly do." Daisy gave me a sassy grin. "If you and me weren't *friends,* Laurel . . ."

The warning lights blinked. Hell, they nearly screamed aloud in Laurel's eyes. Daisy didn't catch it, Daisy was having fun.

"You want him, take him. *What the fuck do I care!"*

"Laurel . . ." Daisy didn't miss that. That one nearly cut her in half.

"Uh, hey," I said. "I'm on a break here," but no one was listening to me.

"You take that back," Daisy said. "You ought to be 'shamed of yourself."

"I should, huh?" Laurel gave her a nasty, lopsided grin.

"You certainly should!"

"But you don't think I *could,* right? Goddamn . . . gah'dam hooker couldn't be . . . 'shamed of anything, right? Hooker hasn't got a decent thought in her—in her fucking head."

"Jesus," I said, "will you stop?" I reached out for her glass. Bad idea. She jerked it back and tossed it in my face. Daisy stared and backed off.

"Well I can, bitch. I can be as 'shamed—as 'shamed as anyone, aw'right? I been ashamed a whole lot! I been 'shamed *plenty* of times. I been—I been . . ."

Her face screwed up in a terrible hurt. Her eyes shut and her mouth twisted wide. The anger there suddenly exploded into tears.

"Oh, Lord. Laurel, hon . . ."

Daisy reached out and held her. Laurel buried her face in Daisy's breast. Her whole body shook.

"She's real uptight right now," Daisy said. "I know that and I don't take offense."

"Did I do that? I don't think I did—"

"You didn't do a thing, Wiley. She'll be all right in a while."

"You sure?"

"She'll be just fine."

"Okay," I said, but she didn't look all right to me.

I left them alone and walked back around the pool, back to Zinnia's place. Spudettes lolled in the sun. Spudettes spoke politely as I passed.

"Bye," said Lily, and "See ya," Poppy said. But no one looked at me. No one really saw me, they were looking at Laurel instead.

Sometimes it takes me a while. Sometimes, something gets through.

It struck me that maybe if I hadn't been stupefied with Asters and Orchids and Marigolds and such, tipsy on girl sweat and drugstore wine, I might well have noticed it wasn't just Laurel who was slightly on edge, who was screwed up tight—it was *everyone* in Spudetteland. Every blossom in this lovely habitat was trying too hard to have fun. Everyone had glassy eyes, everyone had a Halloween smile. They were touchy, they were scared. People were getting dead. Bad shit was happening down at the lodge, and no one had bothered to tell them why.

This is ever the way it is. No one tells the help. No one tells the maids the hotel is on fire. Everyone can hear the sirens, everyone can smell the smoke. For the Spudettes, it had to be worse than that. Your average working girl is not a self starter. Doesn't know what to do, doesn't know where to go. Fear is a natural state of mind. Like a deer caught in the lights, she is likely to freeze, stand on the highway while the pickup runs her down.

I can't let this happen to Laurel, I thought. I've got to get her out of here before things get any worse. And Daisy, of course . . . and Zinnia and Poppy and Buttercup . . .

For a moment I was dazzled, elated by this daring concept. I could see it in my head. Smithsonian employee brings down criminal empire. Bug artist saves the strumpets of Idaho.

Jesus, I wondered, what was I thinking about? I was trapped by an Indian and a Mafia dwarf. How did I imagine I could rescue a herd of Spudettes, when I couldn't unkidnap myself?

16

My session with Zinnia continued downhill.

When she posed, Zinnia drank. When we stopped for a break, Zinnia drank some more. The more she drank, the more she squirmed. That girl had a lot of moving parts. For a very small person, she could squirm a great deal.

My impulse was to jump her right there. Squirming's going to do that, squirming's going to stir some basic needs. I could take care of that, maybe try and slow her down, and who'd blame me if I did? Who'd fault me for helping both me and Zinnia out? Laurel would, for one, and she could walk in the trailer any time. A woman has a real uncanny sense of timing when she knows it's just you and a very naked person inside.

I worried a lot about Laurel. She'd just about lost it out there. If it hadn't been for Daisy, Laurel would've likely come apart. I wondered how much she'd told the Spudettes, how much was still bottled up inside. They knew about Rocco and Nix, she didn't have to tell them that. I had an idea, though, she'd kept our adventure with Michael to herself, I didn't think she'd told them that. I think she was too scared to share that with anyone else. Hell, she wouldn't tell me, and I was there.

The fat guy, whoever he was, the fat guy shook her up a lot. Something got to her, something heavy, something grim, and she was keeping it locked up in her head. How scary could it be? I wondered, a fat guy in a car, you see him in the light for a second and he's gone. For Laurel, a second was clearly long enough. Something happened sometime, something bad that she couldn't forget.

"I looked at your picture," Zinnia said. "You were outside some, I took a peek. I mean, I didn't look a lot, I did it pretty quick."

"I asked you not to do that," I said. "That's an artistic courtesy, Zinnia. An artist isn't finished, you're not supposed to look."

"It isn't too bad."

"I appreciate that."

"The legs aren't right."

"What do you mean, they're not right?"

"They're not right."

"The legs are fine, the legs are just right."

"The legs are too long. What you got, you got your basic male fantasy there. You got your prehysterical desires, you got your primal wet dreams."

"Is that right. I don't know how to draw a leg, I got a primal dream."

"A primal *wet* dream. It isn't like a ordinary dream, it's a—"

"I know what it is and it isn't what I've got. The legs are just fine."

"They might be fine if I was white, I'm a supermodel and I'm seven feet tall. What I am is your ethnic Asian type. You're not going to find any Oriental chick's got legs as long as that, she didn't run away from a circus somewhere."

"What I think you are, I think you're—I think you're a very lovely exception to the rule. I draw a leg like I see it, and I think yours are quite extraordinary, I don't have to make 'em up."

"You mean that?"

"Yes I do."

"Moss?"

"What?"

"Does it bother you if I do *this?*"

"Jesus, Zinnia . . . !"

I snapped off another pastel. Crimson lake pinged off the trailer wall. Zinnia laughed and took a drink. A ribbon of wine made a lazy circle down her breast. I followed its happy trail.

"You sure do break a lot of chalk," Zinnia said. "Mr. Sparks used to do it all the time. He'd write this formula for salt on the board? Some kinda shit like that? I'd cross my legs and *snap!* there goes another piece of chalk. I got an 'A,' in there. Maybelline Chang, who could do an entire valence in her head, Maybelline got an 'F.'"

"Life's not fair," I said. "You want to try and be still?"

"You got it, man."

"It's pastel. We call it pastel."

"We do what?"

"If it's art, we don't call it chalk. We call it pastel."

"What's the difference?"

"Just be still, Zinnia, okay?"

She was still for a second and a half. One toe started to twitch, then another after that. She sat up quickly, swept her hair aside, and touched her feet to the floor.

"You want to tell me something, Moss?" She gave me this funny little sideways look. "You going to stick around till you're dead, or you figure on moving your ass out of here?"

She got my attention with that. It isn't that the subject hadn't come up from time to time, but with Zinnia it wasn't quite the same. She had this ability to look both naked and sincere.

"Listen," I said, "I appreciate your concern. There is nothing I would much rather do than get out of Idaho. I think about it all the time."

"You do, huh?"

"I certainly do."

"Shit, man." Zinnia rolled her eyes. "I was you, I'd give it more thought than that. What I'd do, I'd put in some overtime. I think you're a pretty nice guy, and I don't think you understand the situation here."

"I bet I do, too. I know guys are getting killed, I know—"

"Yeah, right. Everybody knows that." Zinnia waved off these minor incidents. She drew her knees up under her chin and wrapped her arms around her legs.

"Something you *don't* know, Moss, is last night. Something happened last night, okay? Iris saw it and so did Poppy and Poppy told me. They were out in the woods, they got a thing for each other which is none of your business, I am simply telling you what they were doing there, right?"

She leaned in close and let out a little breath. "Michael Galiano was here last night. He was down at the lodge with Vinnie and his sister and they talked a long time. You don't know who I'm talking about, you don't know Michael from a duck, so I'll try and make it quick. Any time Michael shows up is bad news. Michael shows up in a Santa Claus suit, he's tossin' hundred-dollar bills, this is fucking bad news.

"Michael's old man was Johnny 'Thumbs' Galiano which you probably heard about. You see a gangster picture, that isn't Marlon Brando, that's Michael's old man. Only Michael's not a greaseball, Michael's not Johnny 'Thumbs' at all. What Michael is is worse. Michael's been to school. He's been to Harvard or Yale or somewhere, shit, he's maybe been to both. He's got a bunch of degrees, he's got your GED, he's got a PhD. He's got your MBA, which is Mob Boss Asshole, okay? Michael's smart and Michael's mean. Michael looks at a guy on the street, the guy's dog has a stroke, the guy's potted *plants* are going to die. Michael Galiano is one bad mother. This guy is real. This guy is no Vinnie DeMarco, he is no potatohead."

"Potatohead . . ."

Zinnia laughed. "Local joke, Moss. You're not with it, man, which is where you want to be."

She took another drink. The wine had a squirming effect. Aside from that, it didn't seem to bother her at all. I noticed that we weren't doing Chinese rock, we were doing Jerry Vale. Jerry sang a few old hits and we faded into Bach.

"Potatoheads are the clowns who work for Michael," Zinnia said. "You know, Vinnie, Bobby, the late Rocco and Nix. Bozos, dummies, fucking potatoheads. We made it up. The Spudettes. Moss, don't you *ever* say potatohead to anyone else, okay? What I ought to do, I ought to keep my mouth shut."

"Idaho. Potatoes. I'm working on this, I think I'm getting close."

"You are fast, man." Zinnia waved a pretty foot. "You screw up, *zap!*— you're off to Idaho. This is Galiano Gulag, Moss, the Family garbage can. Rocco . . . that stupid son of a bitch, Rocco got sent on a hit. The job was supposed to be in North Carolina, only Rocco shows up in Fargo, North Dakota. Offs some guy nobody ever heard of before. Nix . . . shit, Nix was just Nix. Someone got tired of looking at him and sent him down here."

"And Vinnie? Vinnie and the twins?"

"Vinnie fucked up big. Misplaced a couple *tons* of coke some-where. Vinnie's old man was close to Johnny 'Thumbs' so Michael didn't kill him, he dumped him out here. He probably would've whacked him, only Michael knows Vinnie is too dumb to steal.

"Angel*o* and Angel*a*? Angela's the only smart DeMarco in the bunch. Angela can do long division in her head. She's also a klepto. Steals shit from stores. Ashtrays, diamonds, mink coats, two-dollar earrings, Angela doesn't care. Michael had to get her out of town. Angelo's here because he won't let Angela out of sight. Angela isn't there for lunch, Angelo starves. Angelo doesn't know what to eat. The guy's a real zero, he's funny in the head."

Zinnia made a face. "You know what he does, you know about that? The clown hangs around a bunch of moose. The guy's a grown man, he wears a suit, he's hanging around a fucking moose."

"Hard to believe," I said.

"Yeah? Don't get me started. Don't get me started on the lovely fucking twins. You ever go to a Jackie Chan flick? The man's terrific. He does his own stunts."

"I heard that somewhere."

"They call him *Dai Goh* in Hong Kong. That mean's 'big brother.' That's the kind of respect the guy's got. What do you think of that?"

"Wonderful," I said, "what about Bobby? Bobby doesn't look real dumb to me."

Zinnia gave a good imitation of a shiver. We heard Stan Kenton do "Artistry in Rhythm" and "Tampico," followed by "Me and Jesus," Tom T. Hall.

"Bobby is *dumb*. He's dumb, and he doesn't know he's dumb, all right? Bobby thinks he's smart, and that's the worst kinda dumb there is. He'll sit and he'll think for a real long time, then he'll do whatever's wrong."

Zinnia sighed, lifted her knee up to her chin and inspected her toes. From where I sat, this was a disconcerting sight.

"I don't know why I'm telling you," Zinnia said. "You got to see the man firsthand. Orchid overheard most of this, so it's true. Vinnie sends Bobby up to get you, Bobby wants to fly. Vinnie's too cheap, so he sends him and Rocco up there in a car. From Idaho to D.C., right? A real pretty drive. Somewhere on the way, the car goes bad. Bobby and Rocco leave it to get it fixed. They steal somebody's van, they get into D.C. That's where you come in. Only you wouldn't know, I understand. Daisy says you were under heavy drugs."

"I was kind of sedated from time to time."

"It's a wonder you weren't kinda dead. Rocco doesn't know what a 'cc' is, he mostly knows gallons and quarts.

"So they snatch a guy, which is a federal offense. The van has a flat. Bobby and Rocco, neither one of 'em ever fixed a flat. They dump the van and catch a bus. Is this brilliant or what? They find the car, the car's fixed. Rocco runs out of gas in the boonies somewhere. They're both out of money by now. Vinnie's not that stupid, he's not going to give these clowns a credit card. So Bobby calls Vinnie. Vinnie says he'll wire some cash. Bobby says 'no way,' he's tired of riding cars. He's still pissed at Vinnie for making them drive, he tells Vinnie to send the company plane.

"Vinnie nearly has a stroke. The plane belongs to Michael, no one's supposed to use the plane without Michael's okay. He says, 'Fuck you, Bobby,' and Bobby says, 'Fine. Me an' Rocco, we're here in Coldwater, Kansas. We're going to whack the artist. We're going to get jobs and settle down, we're going to live right here.'

"Vinnie doesn't know what to do, he goes ahead and sends the plane. Bobby left you at the airport, right? You rode up with Daisy and Nix."

"Yeah," I said, "in a Lincoln that's falling apart. I get to look at Daisy, which is fine. I don't have to look at the back of Nix's head."

"Michael drives his Lincolns a year, gives 'em to the potatoheads. The potatoheads drive them until they fall apart. Bobby got drunk. He didn't want to face Vinnie, so he went and got drunk." Zinnia leaned down and found her bottle on the floor. "You know what I'm telling you, Moss? Bobby's dumb, but he's *dangerous* dumb, nobody knows what the hell he'll do next."

I didn't tell her she was wrong, that I'd seen Bobby Bad Eye in action at BILLY'S GAS & AUTO REPAIR—a graphic example, I felt, of what the man might do next.

Tom T. Hall finished up with "The Year That Clayton Delaney Died," and we went into "Old Deuteronomy" from *Cats.* I looked at Zinnia, and looked down at my pad. In spite of everything, I thought the sketch was doing fine. I felt real good about that. It had been some time since I'd loosened up and let myself go. You don't loosen up a whole lot when you're into invertebrate life. Absolute realism here is the key. A girl is not a bug. You want to give a girl long legs, that's fine. Try and do that with a damselfly, you'll hear from a guy in Poland, a guy with ten degrees and not a vowel to call his own.

"Moss?"

"What, Zinnia?"

"Moss, you mind coming over here?"

"Ah, what for, Zinnia?"

A naked girl is lying on a couch. She looks at you with lazy China eyes, and you ask her what for. It's one of those rhetorical questions they're always talking about.

I said, "You think that's a good idea?"

"Don't you?"

"Well yeah, I do. I think it's a great idea."

"So let's do it, huh?" She scooted back and patted me a place on the couch. Just in case I didn't know where.

My mouth was dry as chalk. Dry as pastel.

"Someone might object to this." I tossed my sketch pad on the floor.

"Someone might. But someone's not here."

Laurel walked in the trailer door and said, "Hi, kids, how's Mr. Art and Miss Model this lovely afternoon?"

"Shit," Zinnia said.

Laurel gave me an understanding smile. The smile said she understood exactly what was going on here.

"I guess we better go, hon. You've likely worn Zinnia out, lyin' there with everything showin' all day."

"Huang lo wan chi," Zinnia said.

"Chou sa tche," said Laurel, and gave me a gentle shove out the door. I heard the last airs of *Lohengrin, Act I,* the start of *Favorite Shepherd Songs of Pakistan.*

"How did you know?" I said.

"I know her, for one. And I know about how much resistance *you've* got, Moss. Add 'em together, divide by four and carry your two." Laurel shook her head. "You're better off, babe. That woman knows Oriental secrets Western man is not ready for."

I am, I thought.

"I heard that," she said.

17

On the short walk back to my trailer, we didn't say anything at all. Laurel had stuff for me to carry which helped a great deal. When you carry stuff, you don't have to talk. If the woman you're with is pissed off, pick up a rock, pick up an empty box. A woman thinks a guy he's carrying something, this takes a lot of thought.

I knew how Laurel was feeling, I didn't have to ask. She was better than she was when I'd watched her fall apart. She was still unraveled and she smiled too much, but Daisy had managed to bring her back. Not all the way, but she was functional and partially intact. Considering the day-to-day pressures in Vinnie's hoodlum hideaway, who could ask for more than that?

The packages I'd carried turned out to be food. Through Laurel's magic touch, peculiar shapes in aluminum foil filled Trailer Number Seven with heavenly smells. Idaho salmon filets in wine butter, with tangy almondine sauce. New potatoes the size of baby plums, lightly sizzled in parsley, garlic and olive oil. Very small tomatoes with sprouts, dandelions and other weeds Daddy made me pull out of the lawn.

"This is terrific," I said. "This is really fine."

"Yes it is," she said, "and good for you as well."

Laurel was wearing cutoffs and an oversized T-shirt that left one shoulder bare. The shirt was full of holes and the color was faded out. Laurel looked great. Laurel could wear a dustrag and a Safeway sack, she'd look like a woman in a fashion magazine.

"Moss?" Laurel paused with a bite halfway to her mouth. "Moss, if you like the salad that much, why don't you go ahead and eat it? It gets even better when you put it in your mouth."

"Hey, I'm saving it," I said, "I always do that, I did that when I was a kid. You didn't do that, save your salad when you were a kid? You eat it right off it's all gone. You save it, you can think about it all through the meal, how good it's going to be. A lot of people don't even know that nature provides a variety of greens in the wild. I'll bet a lot of this stuff grows right around here. I bet you could walk out there and pick a whole basket for yourself. I might try it in the morning. Get me a basket, see what I can find . . ."

"If I hadn't walked in, you'd of jumped her, you'd have jumped her right there. Don't tell me you wouldn't, don't bother to make up a lie. You son of a bitch, I hadn't come in, you'd have nailed her right there."

Now how did we get onto this, and what did it have to do with greens?

"Okay. I found Zinnia to be a very nice person. It'd be untrue if I said there wasn't some degree of carnal attraction there."

"I'll say."

"Which doesn't mean a thing, because in spite of what you think, nothing would have happened at all. An artist and a model, there's professional respect between the two. You're looking at a naked girl's personal parts, you're looking and she *knows* you are, see, so you both got to have an objective attitude, you got to be impartial in your head. That's where the professional respect comes in. You respect what you're looking at, and she—"

"Is there much more of this?"

"No, I think that's it."

"It bothers you, doesn't it? It worries you a lot."

"What does?"

"Why I should give a shit who you stick it in or not? I'm a hooker, I'm a *professional*, right? What difference does it make, what do I care?"

"Laurel, let's not do this."

"You guys always have it figured out. You can feel anything you want, whatever's in your head. You're fucking your secretary, you're fucking a movie star. A whore's whatever you want her to be."

She picked up a fork in her fist and squashed a potato flat. The potato caught it, but her eyes were on me.

"Who do you want me to be, Wiley? Zinnia, Poppy, Iris, Columbine? You want to do the Nazi and the nun? It doesn't matter, right, because a whore doesn't have any feelings, she's just lyin' there— shit, shit, shit, I *hate* this!"

She closed her eyes, squeezed them tight. Took a deep breath and let it out.

"Listen, I'm sorry, okay? I'm not blaming you, you're a man, that's what you got to be. It's not you, it's me." She gave me a desperate, sorrowful look and a single bright tear. "Goddamn it, Wiley, I am not havin' fun anymore. I am not a happy person and I do not like it here . . ."

I started to reach out for her hand. Instead, I got up and put the coffee water on. The afternoon sun slanted off the imitation walnut counter. A golden stripe touched Laurel's bare neck. I leaned down and kissed the sunny part.

"Thank you," she said, "that was very nice."

"Laurel, you'd be a certifiable nut if you weren't upset, all you been through. I mean, not even counting The Rocco and Nix Show, last night in the woods was enough to shake up anyone."

"Yeah, there's that."

I stood behind her and watched the water boil. "I know how you must be feeling. I know a little more than I did. Zinnia told me quite a bit. No offense, Laurel, but you've got this habit of leaving things out."

"Yeah, well. I didn't want to spoil your summer fun."

"Hey, come on. She told me a lot about Michael Galiano and Michael's old man and the kind of clout Michael's got, and what Vinnie and the others are doing here. She told me about the potatoheads."

"Zinnia's got a big mouth. Zinnia talks too much."

"She knows about last night, by the way. Poppy and her friend were out cavorting in the woods. The funny thing is, Zinnia doesn't know *you* know."

"Damn." Laurel gave a helpless little laugh and dropped her head in her hands. "If this wasn't so awful it'd be a circus, hon." She turned and looked over her shoulder at me. "You know why I don't blab everything I know? Because being *dumb* in this place is the smartest thing to do."

"It didn't help Rocco and Nix."

"You *know* what I'm talking about, Moss. Don't pretend you don't."

I dumped the coffee in the filter and poured the water in, watched it turn to mud.

"I know what you're saying, and I don't believe that at all. Being in the dark doesn't make you any safer. What you *don't* know's likely to sneak up and bite you on the ass."

Laurel stuck out her chin. A defiant, but very fetching look. "And you think that's what I'm doing? I'm keeping you in the dark so something'll happen to you? Well shit, Moss . . ."

"No, I don't think that. What I think, what I think, Laurel, after all you and me have been through, you could maybe trust me some. It isn't like I just dropped in, okay? Christ, I got to see the whole show. I had a front row seat when Nix did his diving act. I was with you thrashin' through the woods, and I was down there with Angelo's goddamn meece when Rocco got his throat cut—"

Laurel stared. "You did what?" She gripped the arms of her chair. "Wiley Moss, you didn't tell me that, you *never* told me that!"

"Well see, that's it. There's plenty of stuff you don't tell me. Now you know how I feel. Besides, I thought I did."

"My God . . ." Laurel stood, squeezed her hands on the sides of her head and made little circles on the floor. She didn't know what to do next or she was going in a trance.

"You were with Angelo. You were *there?*"

"Yes I was."

"And Angelo hasn't told anyone you were there. If he had . . ."

"I don't think he has. I got the very strong impression he didn't want anyone to know he was in the neighborhood."

Laurel bit her lip. She wasn't looking at me, she wasn't looking anywhere. I poured her a cup of coffee. She brushed it aside. Like, don't irritate me, man, I'm having a really big thought.

"Stop it," I said, "don't do that to me. I am in this up to my neck and I think I've got a right to know why. Someone's knocking off dumb guys. Is that what's behind all this? They're working their way up the IQ scale? Nix, then Rocco. Who's next?"

I reached out and grabbed her shoulders. "Only what is real peculiar here is that Rocco and Nix getting whacked doesn't bother you half as much as a fat guy in Michael Galiano's car. I just can't figure that, can you figure that? What the hell's going on here, Laurel? If you don't exactly know, you've got a damn good idea."

"You're wrong. I don't know a thing."

"Look right at me and tell me that, Laurel. Do that."

"I don't know, I don't know a thing."

"You're not looking at me, you're looking the other way."

"Wiley, leave me the fuck alone."

She shook off my hands and walked out of the kitchenette. Stopped at the bathroom, looked inside and walked out. Started for the trailer door. Forgot about the avalanche of art supplies and stomped back in.

"I'll take that coffee now, you don't mind."

"I'll heat it up, I think it's cold."

"That's how I like it. Don't you try and heat it up, I like it cold."

"Will you just relax?"

"No I won't."

"Fine, then don't."

She poured a cup and took a sip. Curled up her lips in disgust. "Any damn fool can make a decent cup of coffee. How many spoons you put in?"

"Thirty-six and one for the pot. You and Zinnia were saying stuff in Chinese? What'd that mean?"

"It doesn't mean a thing. She doesn't speak Chinese and neither do I. We just make it up."

"What for?"

" 'Cause we like to, okay?"

"Uh-huh."

"Uh-huh what?"

"I didn't think you two were close."

Laurel gave me a puzzled look. "Why the hell you think that? Zinnia and me are second-best friends. Daisy's first, but Zinnia comes right after that. I just don't want you fucking her. That doesn't mean we aren't friends. You got any more dumb questions, hon?"

"Yes I do. If Michael Galiano's such a big shot mobster, why is he wasting his time on guys like Vinnie and this Mickey Mouse vacation spot? What, he's living off the Spudettes? He's making a killing in moose tacos? The guy could make more money in coke in half an hour than he could in this hole in twenty years. What's the big deal here, what's the point?"

Laurel shrugged. "I don't know, ask him."

"Well now, there's a good idea. Hey, I could ask the fat man. I'll bet the fat man knows."

Laurel turned white. "Don't you say that. That is not funny, don't you ever say that again."

"Say what?"

"What you were—what you were saying."

"Fat guy."

"*Wiley*—"

"Fat-guy fat-guy fat-guy—"

"You stop that!" Laurel pounded me in the face. I grabbed her by the shoulders and pulled her to my chest. She tried to keep pounding but you can't do that if you're standing real close. She gave up in a minute and buried her face in my neck. I think I heard a sniff. I think she sniffed twice.

"I'm not crying or anything. Don't you think for a second that I am."

"I didn't say you were."

"Well I'm not."

"I don't want you to cry. I'm not trying to make you cry, I'm trying to make you talk to me, Laurel. We've shared danger and intimate relations so far. I think we like each other too."

"I think we do, Wiley."

"Fine. Then don't treat me like I'm a—a foreign spy, instead of someone who's seen you without your clothes on."

Laurel rolled her eyes. "For God's sake, I do not think you're a foreign spy. That is a totally bizarre thing to say."

"Well you treat me like one."

"I don't do any such thing."

"Good. Okay. Then tell me who the fat guy is. Tell me who he is right now."

Silence.

"Laurel?"

"Okay, Wiley."

"Okay what?"

"Okay, I *will!*"

She pushed away and sniffed. Wiped her nose on a paper napkin. Picked up her coffee and drank it down. Set the cup on the counter. Moved it an inch to the right. Folded her arms and looked the other way.

"You're not going to tell me."

"Yes I am."

"When?"

"Don't start pushing me, Wiley. I am real uptight right now and I won't put up with that."

"You're scared of the fat guy," I said, "I understand that, there's nothing wrong with that. Just get it out, Laurel. Tell me and you'll feel a lot better. Everyone feels a lot better, they get something out."

"I don't think I will. I think I'll feel worse."

"Laurel . . . Laurel will you look at me?"

She turned real quick and tried to get past. I wouldn't let her by.

"Get out of my way, I got to pee."

"Huh-unh. You don't got to pee, you got to talk to me. We've got to share stuff, Laurel, or all we've got is a shallow relationship based on bodily needs. Okay, there's nothing wrong with that. I can live with that. Correct me if I'm wrong, it was you who said I ought to do deep. This is what I'm thinking, we share stuff together, this is going to help a lot, this'll get us into deep—"

"Goddamn it, I have to pee right now!"

Laurel squeezed by, caught me off guard, shoved me up against the narrow hall. Our bodies were as one. Any other time this might have been fun. It wasn't fun now. Laurel was beating on my head. She was screaming quite a lot. Her eyes showed apprehension and alarm. I wrote this off to bladder irritation, then I saw she wasn't looking right at me. She was looking past my shoulder at the former living room, at the overstocked warehouse of costly art supplies. I turned to take a look. A big hand wrapped around my chin, jerked me off my feet and tossed me down the hall.

I landed real hard, ripped through a stack of canvas frames, heard the sound of breaking glass. Linseed oil began to drip down my back. A carton split open and paint tubes tumbled in my lap. Winsor and Newton, a very fine brand. Raw umber and titanium white. I take that back, it was ivory black.

I tried to get up. Slipped on something and went down again. Bobby Bad Eye grabbed a handful of hair, hefted me up and threw me out the door. I skidded on my face, rolled over twice and blinked up at the sky. Vinnie looked down at me and grinned.

"You doing all right, Mr. Moss? You enjoyin' yourself up here?"

"No I'm not," I said. "What the hell do you think you're doing, I won't stand for treatment like this."

Vinnie kicked me in the ribs. I yanked my knees up to my chest, grabbed my legs and howled. Vinnie found the other side and kicked at me again.

The pain did me in. Vinnie was a blur and I couldn't get a breath.

"Don't even think about passin' out, asshole," Vinnie said. "You and me are going to have a conversation. You and me got a lot to talk about."

"Whafer . . . wha'for?" My voice didn't sound good at all, it sounded like a moose, it sounded like a duck.

Vinnie shook his head like this was very sad, like this was a day I would come to regret. He was wearing a Western outfit. White Stetson, red silk shirt, pre-washed jeans. Tiny little boots with wicked little toes. A jockey in a John Wayne suit.

"What it is," Vinnie said, "I am disappointed in you, Mr. Moss, I ain't happy with you at all."

"I wasn't sure about the pastels. We can try watercolors, we can do some acrylics or some oils."

Vinnie kicked me again. Not too hard, just a little teaser, just a tap in the head.

"What I did, I had Bobby here put a bug in Zinnia's trailer. It isn't any trouble, you run it right up through the floor. I done it lots of times, you know? It's employee relations is what it is. It's my way of keeping in touch."

"Use of an illegal listening device. There's a heavy penalty for that."

Vinnie shook his head. "Bobby used a cheap wire and there's a lot we didn't get. That hooker spilled a lot of wine and the mother shorted out. Bobby had to call on his low-tech skills. We wasted an hour getting Zinnia to recall your fucking happy afternoon."

Oh, God, I thought, and something cold reached out and clutched my heart. Vinnie saw I read him loud and clear, Vinnie grinned and squatted down.

"Jesus, Moss, you are a nosey son of a bitch. You know what you're supposed to be doing up here, you remember what I brought you here for? You're supposed to be doing fuckin' art. Anybody tell you to do something else, anybody say, 'hey, poke your nose in Vinnie DeMarco's affairs, mess around with stuff that isn't none of your business, that don't have nothing to do with you.' Anybody tell you that? Nobody said that, nobody come and told you that.

"You try and be nice to people, what do they do? They betray the trust you give 'em, they stab you in the back. You got a guy here he's drawing art, is he drawing any art? Fuck he's drawing art, he's playing with colored chalk, he's sitting in a trailer, he's watching a whore, the whore is drinkin' drugstore wine."

Vinnie stood. He shook his head in disgust. "You're a guy I held in respect, you know what? I thought, you gotta respect this guy, there isn't no one can draw a bug like Wiley Moss. The guy's terrific, the guy works at the Smith, the guy's been in your major science magazines. You see a Wiley Moss bug, the little bastard's real enough to squash. You look at that bug, you're thinking, that little sucker's going to sit right up and take off. Christ, I was going to have you come up to the house, I got some Mexican beer. I was going to tell you Bobby was bringing down a color TV. Well fuck that, pal. You got no respect for Vinnie, Vinnie says hey, fuck you."

Vinnie stalked off. I didn't care about the TV. I thought about the Mexican beer. Bobby's shadow appeared and blotted out the sun. Bobby reached down and dragged me to my feet. I saw a black van nearby. I hadn't seen anything before except the hair in Vinnie's nose and the Idaho sky.

"Mr. DeMarco, he wants you should see something," Bobby said. "He wants you to take a good look, okay?"

He held me up straight, and marched me to the van. He opened the door and there was Zinnia, Zinnia huddled on the floor, Zinnia looking very small, Zinnia trembling in a blanket, though it wasn't very cold. It took me a second, I didn't know who it was. I knew it was Zinnia because of the long black hair. The hair was wet and tangled, clinging to her skin, covering her face. Her skin looked fevered, like someone who'd been sick a while. I searched her face for bruises, but there was nothing there at all. There was pain and there was fear, but Bobby had done his job well and hardly anything showed. No unsightly cuts or abrasions, nothing that would even leave a scar. There was nothing there to see unless you looked into her eyes . . .

Oh Jesus, oh Christ, Zinnia!

"You son of a bitch," I yelled at Bobby, "you lousy son of a bitch!"

"Yeah, right."

Laurel started screaming somewhere and I knew she'd seen Zinnia, and Bobby said, "Get on back inside, Laurel. This isn't none of your affair. Get on in, do it now."

I couldn't see if she did or not. Bobby shoved me roughly away, doubled up his fists and grinned. I looked in his face and in his one good eye. He looked content and satisfied, pleased with the prospect of dishing out some pain.

"What I got to do, I got to work you over, Mr. Moss. It's going to hurt some, but it isn't going to be real bad. I mean, it's your ordinary beatin', it isn't nothing serious, nothing like that."

"Fuck you," I said.

"There you go with that attitude, man . . ."

He hit me in the gut. I doubled up and rolled on the ground. Came to my knees and threw up between my hands. I thought about fighting after school in Cincinnati. We'd get a bunch of guys and go down to the dump and meet the kids from the other side of town. You couldn't just hit somebody, that wasn't enough, you had to get a mark yourself. A split lip, a black eye. A broken tooth was best. If your folks didn't have a lot of money, a broken tooth would last a long time.

I thought about Zinnia, and what that bastard had done to bring a look like that to her lovely, fragile face. I thought about what Laurel had said: *Being dumb here is the smart thing to do.* Very sound advice. A little too late, but prudent all the same.

I got one foot on the ground, pushed myself up with my hands. I was wobbly as hell, but I was there.

"You don't want to do that, Mr. Moss," Bobby said. "That's a real bad idea."

I didn't answer that. There wasn't much to say. I put one foot before the other, held my hands close to my chest, watched Bobby's eyes. Bobby wasn't overly concerned. He came right at me like I wasn't even there. My choice, I could move and get out of the way or he could plow me in the ground. When I saw it in his eyes, in the muscles in his neck, I took half a step and kicked him in the crotch.

Bobby went *"whuuuuh!"* and looked surprised. He was the hunter and I was the prey. The victim gets hit, the victim's not supposed to hit back. I came in fast, followed through with a right to the head, a left that caught him on the ear. He stumbled and caught himself, held up his hands and backed away. I wasn't dumb enough to follow, he was too good for that. I stood back and waited. Bobby wiped a hand across his mouth, looked at the little smear of blood. He circled to my right, came in again, chopped at me with a left. I ducked and hit him hard in the chest. He shook his head and grinned, let me know he wasn't impressed.

"I liked you some," he said. "That was right off at the start. It wore off pretty quick."

I swung at him again. I should've known better. I did, but once you get started with this kind of shit, there's no way to stop. I'd gotten in a couple of blows because he didn't think I could. I was totally overmatched, and we both knew that, and I wouldn't get close to him again.

He took his time, then knew exactly what to do. He walked in and caught me with a jab, slammed me in the chest, shook me with a vicious right to the head. I took a few blows on my arms, tried to fight him off, and he came in like a tank. One step at a time, a little flat-footed stomp, and I held him for a minute, a minute and a half. A left to the belly and a half-ass right that never made it anywhere. That was all I had. My knees turned to water and I sank to the ground.

Bobby stood above me, barely out of breath.

"My people treated Lewis and Clark real nice. I realize that was a big mistake."

"I just got in town," I said. "I wasn't here for that."

Bobby kicked me in the head.

"Break his fuckin' hands," Vinnie said from somewhere. "The son of a bitch wants to draw, he can draw with his fuckin' feet . . ."

18

I woke up and blinked, tried to sit up. Pain zapped me hard and I fell back on my head.

"Hey, what happened, where am I?" I said, like they do on TV.

"We are locked up in your trailer," Laurel said. "I am sitting up, you are lyin' on the floor."

"Am I hurt real bad? What'd he do, did he hit me on the head? I don't remember that, I—oh, my God!"

I remembered something else. My heart leaped up in my throat. I didn't want to look but I did. It was dark and I could hardly see my hands. I wriggled my fingers, held them up close to my face. Eight . . . nine . . . ten . . . just like everybody else. I nearly cried out with relief.

"Laurel, he didn't do it, my hands are okay. Vinnie told him to mess up my hands, but my hands are okay!"

"Bobby and Vinnie 'bout got in a fight over that," Laurel said. "Bobby said it didn't seem right, ruining your career and burning you to death on top of that. Bobby said it smacked of undue excess."

"He said *what?*" I decided I'd better sit up. "I don't think he said that, Laurel, I think you misheard that. The word *burn*, that's got a bad connotation, I think he maybe said something else."

Laurel sighed. "It's a terrible thing to wake up to, hon, I know that. But Vinnie's not a reasonable person. Your people of the mob persuasion, they're going to take a slight real hard."

"Well to hell with that. If that clown thinks I intend to get fried in a trailer that doesn't even have A/C, he better think twice."

I looked at Laurel. Her face was a blur in the light from outside. "When's all this supposed to happen? This is tonight, right after breakfast or what?"

"I think what it is, Bobby's gone to find some gasoline."

"Oh, shit, Laurel, I don't like to hear that. Gasoline's another word I don't like at all."

I reached out and touched her, ran my hands past her cheeks and through her hair. "Listen. Don't be frightened, just get hold of yourself. I'll get us out of this."

"Okay, hon."

"I'm proud of you, Laurel, I want to tell you that. You're doing real fine. You're handling yourself real well."

"I brought a fifth of scotch for us to drink after supper. I've drunk a lot of that. I think I'm pretty crocked."

"Good. I better have some too."

"There's not a lot left," she said, and handed me the bottle in the dark.

I downed a healthy slug, felt it warm me to my toes. I pulled myself up. My head didn't care for that.

"What we've got to do is get out of here," I said. "This place is jam-packed with solvents and paints. We're talking highly flammable goods. We'll have a full-blown holocaust here. This place'll go up like an art supply store."

I moved past Laurel down the hall. I guessed it was maybe nine or ten. Laurel had a Mickey Mouse watch, but I didn't even look. Those little yellow gloves don't mean a thing to me.

No use trying the broken door, Bobby would've taken care of that. I tried anyway. He'd jammed it up tight. I peered out a window. There was nothing there to see, nothing that would do us any good, nothing but the dark . . .

Sure there is, dummy, what are you thinking about?

It hit me like a brick. "Windows," I yelled back to Laurel, "we got windows, babe. We'll break a damn window and haul out of here!"

"Burglar bars."

"What?" I jumped half a foot. She was standing right behind me in the dark.

"Burglar bars, Wiley, you can't get in or out. How come you didn't notiz—notish that?"

"I just didn't, that's all." I looked at her close.

"Notish? Are you all right?"

"I'm drunk, Wiley, I thought I mentioned that."

"Yeah, I guess you did. I think you better sit."

"I'm just—I'm just fine, okay?"

"No you're not." I led her to a kitchen chair and eased her down. Her body turned to syrup and she slid off on the floor. The floor seemed a good idea. Gravity is a physical force of some repute. Drunks try to fight it but they come up losers every time.

I laid her out nicely by the fridge. She mumbled something I didn't hear. I checked the burglar bars. Something like that, they're just there, it doesn't even cross your mind. There were three horizontal and three vertical bars, woven together in a pseudo-Spanish twist. I went down the hall and got the shaggy bathroom rug. Holding it to the window, I hit it half a dozen times with a skillet from the stove. Glass went everywhere.

"Jesus, whash'at?" Laurel came halfway alive, then drifted off again.

I set the rug and the skillet aside, grabbed the burglar bars and tugged. They were bolted in solid, they didn't give an inch. Fine. There's no use paying for protection if it isn't any good. I dragged the kitchen table to the window, crawled up on it, turned over on my back. Got a hold on the window and kicked the bars as hard as I could. The dishes rattled, the trailer shook like it was coming apart. I kicked until my feet couldn't take it anymore.

"Got to take a break," I said to no one at all, "got to catch my breath."

A sudden vision, Bobby Bad Eye, lugging a five-gallon can back up the hill. You can hear the liquid sloshing in the can, you can always hear it sloshing when you walk. The smell drifts up, and there's no smell like it, nothing like it anywhere.

I didn't take a break, I started kicking hard again. I kicked until my feet went numb. I kicked and I tried to get my breath and the fucking bars didn't give at all.

"We are going to fruh-fry like franchise bacon," Laurel said. "You know what I'm saying? They cook it so hard it crupper-crummels in your mouth . . ."

"Shut up, Laurel, we don't need that."

I got off the table and started pulling out drawers. Nothing. I looked beneath the sink. There was a dried-up bar of soap, a plastic bucket for leaks. And over in the corner—thank you, God—a real nice hammer from Ace Hardware.

I pushed the table aside and crooked my hand out the window. I could get the hammer under the bars, but the angle was bad, awkward from inside. If I was outside it'd work a lot better, but if I was out there, why would I want to do that?

Laurel started crying. One minute she was stiff as a zombie, the next she was bawling up a storm.

"Laurel, now don't take offense," I told her, "but you're going to have to stop doing that."

"I am *real* scared, hon. I mean I am scared awful bad."

"I am too. And if crying helps, there's nothing wrong with that."

"I don't mean about—about us." She suddenly appeared. She was leaning against the fridge, wiping her eyes with the edge of the tablecloth. "I'm worried about Daisy, Wiley. I am real concerned."

I turned and looked at her. "We're locked up in this barbecue pit and you're worried about *Daisy?* You mind telling me why?"

Laurel sniffed. "I can't go into that."

"Why not?"

"I just can't, is all. Goddamn it, quit nagging me, Moss, I won't put up with that."

I put my hammer down. "Laurel, you do this to me every time. You talk about something that you can't talk about and you can't say why and that drives me absolutely nuts. You know what? I bet anything you want this has something to do with that fat guy. The fat guy's mixed up in this, right?"

"Don't be ridiculous." Laurel looked the other way. "I don't know why you'd say that. I cannot imagine why you'd say that."

I dropped down beside her. Her eyes were too bright in the dark. She looked like a petrified owl. "You can't imagine? *I* can imagine. I imagine it's because about *everything* you can't talk about has something to do with the fat guy you saw in Michael's car. You think that's maybe it? Is that why you're suddenly concerned about Daisy, she's got something to do with this guy?"

"It isn't that sudden."

"What?"

"I said it isn't a sudden kind of worry, it's—longer than that."

"How long you think it is?"

"Long enough."

"And it's the fat guy, right? I'm right about that."

Laurel rolled her eyes. "I want you to stop that, Wiley, that is real irritating. Jesus, try and get your mind on something else."

"You twitch."

"I do what?"

"Twitch. Any time you think about the fat guy, you twitch. You didn't say Daisy had anything to do with the fat guy, you didn't have to. You didn't have to because you twitched."

"Shouldn't you be working on that window instead of sitting here? It isn't going to mean shit, I'm squatting here talking 'bout fat guys, my lovely ass is on fire."

"Forget about it," I said. I tossed the hammer in the corner. " 'Fate having writ its spidery hand, the long cold night approacheth quick. The boatman slides across the dark water, and silently beckons us hence.' "

"Say what?"

"We are pretty well fucked, as near as I can tell. There isn't any way out. That hammer isn't working at all."

Laurel stared. "Well try something *else*, Moss. Get me out of here!"

"I thought you were swacked."

"Well I'm not anymore. Give me that hammer. I'll rip this mother apart."

She started up. I reached over and pulled her back. "Sit down," I said. "You think I'm through, you think I'm going to quit? I'm going to try the other windows. Those bars have been in a long time, they've got to be weak somewhere."

"Did you think about digging through the floor?"

"This is a quality recreational trailer, Laurel. I doubt if they're going to build it so anyone can hack through the floor with an ordinary hammer from a hardware store."

"Well excuse me, Mr. Home Improvement. It wouldn't hurt to fuckin' try."

"There. *Wham-wham-wham.* I gave it a try, okay?"

Laurel gave me the evil eye. I broke another window and tried the bars there. I broke all the windows in the trailer except the ones in the living room, lost behind a ton of art supplies. It seemed a lot easier to fry than try to plow through all that. Screw it, I thought, who wants to do that?

What that is, it's primal human nature kicking in, it's just the way we are. It wasn't like I didn't take Bobby seriously, it wasn't that at all. I'd seen that loony in action at Billy's Gas & Auto Repair, and, worse than that, I'd seen what was left of Billy, and that was good enough for me.

Still, even if you know, if you know what a guy like that is going to do, you don't *know*, right? A guy says, "Hey, I'm going to cook you medium rare, get back to you soon," someone says that, you believe it and you don't. Maybe in the movies, maybe on a TV show. Maybe somebody else, but not me. You can tie up your belly in a knot and you can think about how it's going to feel when it's your fat dripping in the fire, but there's *no* way your head's going to conjure that up, there's no way you're going to make it real.

If there was, you'd have people dropping dead, people having strokes because they just learned exactly how it feels to get squashed in a car, or go screaming to the ground in a plane. You can get pretty scared, you can just about scare yourself to death, but you can't get anywhere *close* to scared as that . . .

Which is why I finally dropped my hammer in exhaustion and disgust, and Laurel wrapped my hand where I'd cut it on a piece of window glass. We sat on the floor and drank cold coffee and nibbled on hard dinner rolls. My hands were numb but my head was full of bright ideas. When your body gives out, that's when your head starts working overtime. That's when desperation comes to life.

I appeal to Bobby's native soul. I tell him that I'm one-quarter Sioux, that we need to put our differences aside and bring the white man to his knees. He doesn't go for that so I whip out my hammer and whack him in the head. He staggers back, stunned and surprised that I am swift as an eagle, strong as a grizzly bear. In his very last moments, he calls me his brother and names me *Asaka-ke-pa*, which translates roughly as Drawer-of-Bugs-with-a -Mighty-Big-Hammer-in-His-Hand . . .

"What would you do," Laurel said, "if you were to get out of this? Would you go on back to D.C., would you keep on doing what you do?"

"Let's not get started," I said. "I don't want to do this."

"I was thinking once about quitting the life and getting into dental hygiene school. I read this survey said a dentist would ditch his first wife and marry whoever in the office was close to sixteen. They said it wouldn't hurt if you had good legs and an ample pair of tits. It occurred to me then that it isn't much different whatever you want to be, a wife or a hooker or a big movie star, there's going to be a guy says 'lie down, honey, let's check your job skills.'"

"There's a lot of that going around," I said, "there isn't any doubt about that. But things are getting better for women all the time."

"Uh-huh." Laurel gave me a look. "You'd be surprised the people I run into now and then. I know a big lady judge, I know a woman's got three hundred tankers full of oil. There's a woman back East knows all there is to know about quarks. Woman's got a brain the size of a basketball. You think a man cares about that? Shit. Every one of those ladies gets hit on all the time. A woman goes to college, all she's going to do is meet a higher class of pricks."

"I went to college," I said.

"You came out better than some."

"Well thank you very much."

"Don't go looking hurt, Moss, I won't put up with that."

"I wasn't looking hurt. I wasn't looking anything at all, I was— Christ, what's that!"

Headlights cut through the dark, swept across Laurel's startled face and out of sight. Taillights blinked in the trees. A car skidded off to the left; the lights disappeared in a cloud of road dust. Two, maybe three seconds after that, gunfire echoed through the woods. Three quick shots, *snip-snip-snip!* like a cranky little dog. A shotgun answered back, a deep and throaty roar that ripped the night apart. I clearly heard the sound of broken glass. Someone cried out, the voice cut off by the chatter of an automatic weapon, a serious weapon you could take to any war.

"Shit-shit-shit!" Laurel said, and dug her nails in my arm.

"It's down at the lodge, the shooting's down at the lodge some-where. I saw a flash from the guns."

"Wiley, I want to get out of here, I want to get out of here *now.*"

"Good. So do I. I wish I knew how."

"Don't you say that, don't you say that to me."

"I'm doing the best I can."

"No you're not, you're just—*sitting* there. Get up, Moss. Get up and act like a man."

"Laurel—"

"Hey, is everyone all right in there?"

Laurel screamed. I jerked her away from the window and pulled her to the floor.

"I want you to know I don't like this business at all," Bobby said, from somewhere in the dark. "I said, 'Vinnie, you want to burn 'em, fine, but you ought to shoot 'em first,' and Vinnie said, 'What's the point in that?'"

"Bobby, you are not going to do this," I said. "You know it's not right."

"I'm drawing wages, Mr. Moss. You take a man's wages, you got a responsibility for that."

"I don't think I ever mentioned this, hell, I know I didn't, we haven't had a lot of time to talk, and I wish we'd done that. What I'm saying is, we might be related, my people settled in Defiance County, Ohio, real early, I've got a lot of Indian blood."

"Me too," Bobby said.

More noise from the lodge. The shotgun again, a heavy burst of automatic fire.

"Bobby, what's happening, what's going on down there?"

"Nothing that's going to bother you."

"I have always been as nice and courteous to you as a person possibly could to someone of your crude and savage ways," Laurel said. "This is no way to repay a kindness, I'll tell you that."

"Bobby," I said, "talk to me." I clutched the burglar bars. I couldn't see Bobby, but I smelled the gasoline. "Damn it, we can talk, what's it going to hurt to talk?"

"What you two want to do is sit down and be still. I watched a similar event in Reno, Nevada, and it didn't last any time at all. Well, hell, I don't think I got a match."

"I hope you're not asking me."

" 'Course I'm not. What do you take me for, Mr. Moss? Okay, I got it, we're all right now."

"BOBBY, GOD'LL GET YOU FOR THIS!" Laurel screamed.

"I think he's likely already settled that," Bobby said.

I couldn't see Bobby but I saw the match flare and I saw it arc off to the left and I heard that awful *WHUUUSH!* like it does when Bruce Willis barely gets away, then everything around us turned bright, turned hot, turned incandescent white, and the whole fucking world was on fire . . .

19

When disaster strikes, when your life is measured in seconds, there's no time to reason, no time to think. Nothing you have ever done before has prepared you for this, for the knowledge that a heartbeat stands between you and a final moment of terror, of white and searing pain, and then—What? Darkness, the end, a happy afterlife? Or maybe a world filled with greater horrors than the one you left behind?

And in that instant, it happens. A miracle of the spirit occurs, and you reach down deep into your soul, you call upon an inner strength you never dreamed you had. You are suddenly filled with a strange sense of calm, and you know that you're not going to die, that you'll do the right thing, that your newfound strength will see you through, that God is on your side—

Okay, that's one thing you can do.

The other thing is you can scream and you can yell, you can howl like dog. You can fill up your pants, you can climb up the walls. You can totally lose it, flip completely out, foam at the mouth, go crazy, go berserk, go ape-shit fucking nuts.

I don't recall reaching down deep, so I must have been doing something else. I remember I did not feel this was the movie of the week. I would not break free, I would not get out, I would not win the girl. I would not break free, because this was a real life holocaust trailer, this was not on TV. I would not win the girl because the girl was real too, and she would turn into a real crispy critter like me.

From the moment, from the *WHUUUSH!*—two seconds, maybe three . . .

Flames scorch the sides of the trailer, blaze through the windows I've conveniently broken out. Terrible heat, dense and roiling smoke fills the room . . . fire roars up the walls, curls up to the ceiling, licks off the paint and turns everything black.

We hit the floor quick and this doesn't help a lot. Bobby doesn't want us to suffer, so he dumps gasoline right under the kitchenette.

Five seconds, six . . .

On our hands and our knees, and I push Laurel blindly down the hall. I can no longer see her for the smoke and the fire's right behind me, burning up my soles and heating up my pants.

Nine seconds, ten . . .

We can't get out and there's nowhere to go, nothing ahead but a solid wall of pens, pencils, paper and palettes, pastels, primers and paint. Sap and sienna, purple and pink, our ammo dump that will burn very hot and very colorful and bright, which I won't get to see because I'm not going to be around for that. I'm not going to make it for another sweep of Mickey's yellow glove because it's

Thirteen, fourteen seconds . . .

and I can't see Laurel anymore and the fire is a hot and hungry beast, angry and alive and howling straight at me down the hall—

"*Shithead!*"

"*Moss!*"

Two distinct sounds. A "shithead" and a "Moss." Clearly not the same. I suck in a breath to call back and I fill my lungs with smoke. Gag and choke and gag again. Draw another breath and this doesn't help at all.

I throw up my hand to ward the raging monster off. Feel the flame, feel the pain, smell the awful scent of burning hair and I know the smell is mine. I wonder if Claire de Mer and I could find happiness and bliss, go on a funny-honeymoon, settle down and make puppies somewhere.

Twenty seconds, twenty-one . . .

God picks me up and jerks me through the fires of hell, slams me down hard and rolls me on the ground. Slaps me and pounds me, makes me hack the smoke out and suck in the air.

"Wiley, Wiley Moss. You okay?"

Angela . . . The fire is bright on her cheeks, it's dancing in her eyes.

"Yeah. I think so."

"Good. Get up. We've got to get out of here."

"Are my eyebrows all right?"

"One of them is, the other's not."

"One's fine. I'll settle for that."

Angela helped me to my feet. Her shirtfront was open and I couldn't help looking down that. Someone else was behind me, lifting me from there. I turned and saw it was Angelo.

"Hi," I said, "good to see you again."

Angelo said, "I don't know you, shithead, I never seen you before in my life."

Angela gave her brother a funny look. Angelo waddled off, leaving the scent of Lucky Tiger Hair Oil, 1942, maybe 1945. One of the vintage company Lincolns and a Jeep were nearby. Angelo got in the Lincoln, threw up dirt and took off without any lights.

"Where's he going? Someone tell me what's going on here," I said.

"Forget it," Angela said, "get in the Jeep, Moss. Now."

"Just a minute. I asked you a question, I don't believe I got an answer yet—"

Laurel cut me off. She squeezed past Angela, wrapped her arms around me and held me tight.

"Oh Lord, hon, you all right?"

"I'm okay. I'm still a little hot."

"One of your eyebrows is gone."

"I heard about that."

"Knock it off," Angela said, "get in the *car.*"

"We're talking right now."

"I don't have time for this, friend." Angela pulled a silver-plated revolver from the back of her jeans and pointed it at my head.

"You are flat-out stupid, Moss. I am trying to get you out of here, I am trying to save your life."

"What for?"

"I'm a fucking humanitarian, all right?"

"That's good enough for me. Laurel, is that okay with you?"

"I guess."

"Let's go, goddamn it!"

Angela waved her pistol in a threatening manner and we trotted toward the Jeep. I looked back at the trailer. It was totally engulfed. We were twenty yards away but the heat was intense. The flames leaped high, catching the lower branches of the trees. Pine needles popped and snapped, loosing little parachutes of flame into the air. The gaping hole where the door should've been was howling like a furnace, spewing out long tongues of fire. I didn't see the door. Angela and Angelo had pried it off and tossed it somewhere.

I nearly stumbled over Bobby Bad Eye. He was laid out on his back, arms stretched up above his head. Whoever had shot him, knocked him out cold, struck him with a nuclear device, had dragged him free of the fire. A very nice gesture on somebody's part. As a recent survivor of Bobby's little prank, I wondered if I would have left him there to fry.

The Jeep was parked under a stand of trees, near the familiar rock pile. Angela said, "Let's go!" She threw herself in the driver's seat and I jumped in the back.

"No!" Laurel stopped in her tracks. "Zinnia . . . If Bobby was after us, he went after her too. We got to go and see."

"Are you out of your mind?" Angela turned her weapon on Laurel. "Get in—the—*car!*"

"Huh-unh, Zinnia's my second-best friend. You want to shoot me, Angela, go right ahead."

"Fine. Okay. You got it, babe . . ."

I didn't like the spark in Angela's eyes, it wasn't all the fire. She had that ominous family trait, the DeMarco lizard stare. I stood up in the Jeep, grabbed Laurel by the waist, lifted her off the ground and plopped her in my lap.

"Moss, you bastard, you son of a bitch!" She kicked at the windshield and beat on my arms but I wouldn't let go. Angela didn't care for this at all. Angela rolled her eyes, grabbed at a gear and we took off with a jerk.

"Listen," I said, "there is no fire over there. The only fire is my fire, Laurel, if he'd set another fire I'd see it, okay? I don't see another fire."

"Well *that* makes sense. That's the only way you can off somebody, you set 'em on fire. You don't set 'em on fire they're not dead!"

"See, I think Bobby would. I think Bobby, he gets an idea in his head, that's what he's going to do. If Bobby's thinking 'fire' I believe he's going to follow through."

Laurel kicked me in the shins. "You don't know that, you don't know what that crazy redskin's going to do. Your full-blood savage doesn't think like you and me, they still got a bunch of primal genes."

"Now that's a racial myth," I said, "that's exactly what it is. You can't condemn a whole people for what a single person's done."

"I can do whatever the fuck I want to," Laurel screamed, "let me go, you—Midwestern shit!"

"My, what a lovely couple," Angela said.

"This is between her and me," I said, "you keep out of this."

"Fine. I'm pretty sure I will."

"Good. Just mind your own—hey, you're driving without any lights, you're going to hit something, you're driving in the dark!"

"You shut up. I'd rather hit something than something hit me."

"What? What are you talking abou—"

Something went *SNANG!* or something similar to that. A small branch fell into my lap. I heard the sudden chatter of gunfire from the darkness down the hill. Jesus—everything had happened so fast I'd forgotten we weren't the only feature that night, we were on a double bill. That's what happens when all you do is think about yourself.

I said, "We're not going down there, are we? I think we ought to do something else, I don't think we ought to do that."

"I do," Angela said. "Who asked you?" She hunched over the wheel like they do at the big-time tracks. We raced down the hill, dodging enormous pine trees in the dark.

"This is not a good idea," I said again. "There's major trouble down there."

"Vinnie."

"What?"

"Vinnie. It's Vinnie and Michael down there. Those two assholes are shooting up the place. They're trying to kill each other is what they're trying to do."

What's wrong with that? I thought. Angela gave me a look like I'd said it out loud.

"The stupid fuck's my brother. I've got to try and help."

"Oh God," Laurel said.

"You keep quiet, you just shut up." She gave Laurel the evil reptile eye. "Just shut—the—fuck—up. Both of you." She slammed her fist hard on the wheel. "I am *real* uptight. I do not need any comments, I do *not* need any help."

It wasn't like Laurel to plan far ahead, to imagine what she might say next. This time, she made the right decision, and shut the fuck up like Angela said.

I heard a loud explosion, looked back and saw a gout of multicolored flame rise up into the sky. Cobalt, I thought, a touch of raw sienna, a lot of gasoline. And, not to be outdone, the rattle of automatic fire, the tubercular cough of a shotgun echoing up from the lodge. We were much too close to those hooligans, and I didn't care for that.

"Keep those lights off," I said, "don't turn them on. We're safer in the dark."

Angela didn't answer. Bullets whined off a tree. She yanked the wheel abruptly to the right, tore through a stand of brush and skidded to a stop. There were dark fir trees all around. We were sitting behind a small building but I didn't know where.

"Get out," Angela said, "over there."

She pointed the way with her pistol, walked across dead grass and unlocked a metal door.

"Okay, in there."

"No thanks," I said. "It's dark in there and I don't know where I am. I've decided to stop doing that, going into unfamiliar places, going somewhere I don't know. That isn't working out for me at all."

"One . . ." Angela said. She thumbed the hammer back.

"Okay, we can talk about it, we can work something out."

"Sit down and be quiet. Don't try to get away. Don't touch anything. Don't talk. I get Vinnie okay, I'll come and get you out of here."

We stepped inside. Angela slammed the door shut. I heard her key click in the lock. It sounded like a very good lock, better than the kind you can get at an ordinary store.

"Bitch," Laurel said. "You hear that, you hear what the bitch said? Vinnie sends Bobby to do us, the bitch is going to go get Vinnie, she's going to get the fucker out. That is inappropriate at best. That is really disgusting, Moss."

"He's her brother," I said. "The way I understand it, your gangster families are awful close."

"That's it, that's all you got to say?" Laurel made a noise like she'd maybe stuck her finger down her throat. "You're disgusting too, Moss. That is a dumb thing to say, I didn't think you'd say something like that. I thought you'd say something, I didn't think it'd be as dumb as that."

I had heard this sort of thing before. That's what you're going to hear when Laurel goes off on a tear. I didn't feel an answer was required. I moved along the wall, feeling the way with my hands. I came to a corner at once, and another after that. It was clear that the room was very small.

"What you're going to do now," Laurel said, "you're going to say, 'Hey, where are we, Laurel, where do you think I am?' I don't have to guess, that's what you're going to say. Where you are, Moss, is in the back of MAMMA DEMARCO'S IDAHO PASTA CAFE. I expect you saw it when they first drove you in. It's got a sign, it's got pretty little curtains out front."

"I saw it," I told her, "it looked real nice. It was closed at the time, there wasn't anybody here."

"Nobody's *ever* here. That's the point, okay? It's a front, Wiley, like everything else in this fucking place. Like, there isn't any Mount Vincent, right? There isn't any such place except in Vinnie's goofy head. You see a FAMOUS SCENIC VIEW, you see any SOUVENIRS? You don't see GAS & EATS, you don't see a moose."

"Now there's meece here, Laurel, I saw the meece."

"What you saw is some token moose, Moss. There isn't any moose insemination stuff going on, either, that's all a bunch of crap. As far as I know, they fuck when they want to, like everybody else."

"They've got a special season."

"What?"

"They've got a season when they fuck. I think it's in the fall."

Laurel didn't hear me, or didn't care to comment on that. I could hear her moving about the room, rubbing her hand across the wall.

"Come over here some," she said finally, "over toward me to your right."

"What for?"

"Yeah, there we go. That's where I thought it was."

Laurel opened a door. It was in a corner that I hadn't explored before. In a moment, I could see in the light from outside. There were curtains on the plate-glass window. Half a dozen tables with checkered tablecloths. Italian posters and plastic grapes hung on the wall. A sign above the door where we were standing said KITCHEN, and there was nothing back there at all.

"It's a fake," I said, "it's a phony. You couldn't make a bread sandwich in here."

"Well did I say that? Did I say this whole place is phony, you recall me saying that?"

"You said that, that's exactly what you said."

I walked to the front and looked out the plate-glass window. I could see the gravel road, but the lodge was too far to the left and I couldn't see that. I stood there and listened for a while. We hadn't heard shots for maybe—what? Three or four minutes, now, right after Angela locked us in.

"It's quiet out there," I said.

"Too quiet," Laurel said.

"What was that in, I don't recall. I want to say *Stagecoach*, 1939. I don't think I'm right about that. Listen, how come this Michael person just happens to show up now, you want to tell me that? He was here last night, and now he's here again."

"Shit, man, that's no big deal, that's Michael to a 'T.' You figure Michael's going to be somewhere, Michael won't be there at all. You figure he *is* going to be some—"

"Right, I get the picture. It just seems funny to me. Vinnie decides to do us in, Michael decides to do the same to him. Bobby tries to cook us, Angela lets us out. What's it all mean? There are vital pieces missing here, Laurel. Would you mind explaining that?"

Laurel moaned. "We are not starting *that* again, Wiley, I cannot handle that. Just put it right out of your head."

"Well it's not like you haven't kept stuff from me before . . ."

Laurel held up a finger, added another, and went on to three. I was glad I'd stayed awake in first grade. Laurel and Angela were testing my number skills.

"You want to know what started this shit? You want to know that? It was that tape of you and Zinnia is what. Whatever you and her said, that's what set Vinnie off."

"Zinnia did all the talking, I didn't say a thing. She knew about Michael meeting Vinnie at the lodge. Which you and I knew because we were there, too. She told me all I ever want to know about the Galiano family, and Vinnie, and Vinnie's old man. She told me why everyone's here in Idaho, because they're too dumb to be anywhere else. The name 'potatohead' was mentioned once or twice."

"Oh, well, I can't imagine why Vinnie took offense. God, Wiley, I'm surprised he did something nice as burnin' us to death—what? What are you looking at?"

"Nothing," I said, "I was just thinking. That's why Vinnie's gone crackers, I think I got that. What's Michael's problem, though? Why's he want to whack Vinnie out? You know what I think? I think it's that fat guy, I think the fat guy's got something to do with this. I'll bet you he does, and I'll bet you know why, Laurel, I'll bet you know that."

"Will you *stop?*" Laurel pressed her hands against her head. "I told you I will not put up with this, I have had about all I can take with your—with your accusations and your snide innue—innuendos and your—*Lord, hon, what the fuck is that!*"

A searing white light filled the room, so bright I could see our stark shadows on the wall. White turned to yellow then red then back to white again. The sound came half a second later—a shock you could feel down in your gut, a jolt that nearly threw you off your feet. The walls shook and the windows rattled and I grabbed Laurel's shoulders and slammed us down fast beneath a table for four, jumped on her back and covered up my head as plate glass turned into a million killer missiles at Mach ninety-six.

I didn't have to guess, I didn't have to ask. I knew, by psychic intervention, by mystic enterprise, that Vinnie's paradise had exploded, ripped itself to pieces, blown itself to bits. I could hear assorted logs, rocks, antique revolvers, Indian rugs and mummified meece begin to rain down on our roof, this, and other debris I didn't care to think about. Blood-red flames and black smoke lit the Idaho sky, and if this was an ordinary night, I wondered what the hell these people dreamed up for the Fourth of July . . .

20

She was gone before I could catch her, out through the shattered front window and into the fiery night. I yelled at her to stop. No one ever does, no one ever stops. Demi Moore in the big disaster scene, she's never going to listen, she's never going to stop. I was after her as quickly as I could, through overturned tables, over broken shards of glass. I stopped outside and stared—stunned, dazed, stupefied by the awesome special effects. The air was thick and hot, it scalded the lungs with every breath. It was snowing black ash, sooty flakes of this and that. Live cinders sparked the night. A rising breeze fed the fire, and the flames crackled up in a roiling cloud of smoke.

It was no more than twenty, thirty seconds since the explosion shook the night, but the fire was already everywhere. The tall stands of lodge-pole pine were blazing torches of red. I couldn't see a thing up the hill. If anything was left of Vinnie's charming hideaway, it was lost behind a solid wall of fire.

A few yards down the slope, the small guest cabins were swallowed up in flames. They went up like a string of grenades, bright yellow pyres of light. Fire licked at the lodge itself. A pane of glass exploded somewhere. Wires shorted with a flash. I spotted Laurel, running past the woods. There was nothing behind me anymore, nothing but a searing wall of fire. No sign of Vinnie or his minions. No sign of Michael or Angela, or anything alive.

I called out to Laurel. She couldn't hear above the roar of the flames or didn't care. I caught up with her halfway up the hill. She glanced back and saw me but didn't stop. I reached out and grabbed her, turned her around. She tried to shake me off, but I was used to this tactic by now.

"Goddamn it, will you stop doing that, Moss? You are the worst grabber I ever saw."

"We need to stop and think," I said. "In a situation like this, it's important to have a plan. We are in grave danger, Laurel. That fire is spreading fast."

"No shit? Well I didn't notice that."

She jerked away and started walking fast. "You want to help, Moss, just don't get in the way. I got to get back to the trailers before those girls do something dumb and barbecue theirselves. Christ, they'll be running around like a herd of lunatic chickens, they won't have any idea what to do. Half of 'em were raised up Baptist and they're scared to death of fire."

"I wouldn't worry," I said, "they'll all head for the pool. That's instinct, it's the natural thing to do. Your basic animal gene says go for the water, that's a primeval drive. That's how Bambi and his friends got through the fire."

"Yeah?" Laurel thought about that. "You might be right. I never met a whore hadn't seen every Disney film twice."

She ran on ahead, and we passed the rock pile and the spot where my trailer used to be. There was nothing left to see. If Bobby Bad Eye was still laid out somewhere, he was truck-stop toast by now.

The fire had burned Number Seven to the ground, but it hadn't stopped there. It had spread to the trees and charred the grass black. One small break for us—it wasn't a big fire yet, and the wind was driving the flames downhill, toward the woods and the lodge beyond that. Fine for now, I thought, but the wind could always change. Wind didn't have a lot to do besides that.

"Michael, you see him down there," Laurel said, "you see—you see anyone else?" She looked a little startled. She'd had other things on her mind and she'd just remembered that.

"No one. Anyone close when that place went up, they're still in there, they didn't get out."

Laurel didn't answer. She nodded, then cut off to the right, toward the tall firs that hid Zinnia's trailer. I ran up and stopped her, turned her around.

"I'll get her," I said, "you know where the girls are, I don't know a thing about that and you do."

She hesitated, decided I might be right for once, and headed toward the pool. I didn't want Laurel going into Zinnia's place. I was almost certain Bobby hadn't been there, but I didn't want Laurel to see her if he had.

A crimson glow lit the sky over Zinnia's trailer. I wondered how much time we had, which way we ought to go. Away from the fire seemed the logical thing to do. Only no one had told me where I was, or what the land was like I couldn't see. Maybe it was country you couldn't *get* through. If the wind turned around and we were caught somewhere . . .

I'd seen a lot of shows on TLC and I knew you couldn't outrun a fire. You could if you had a good road and a car. A fire's real fast, but it's not as fast as a Buick Park Avenue. You could outrun a fire in a '39 Ford. Michael and Vinnie and the DeMarco twins had cars. But if any one of those mothers had survived, you could bet that they were gone. Mobsters are not the Red Cross. They do not have doughnuts or coffee, they do not give a shit about hookers or Wiley Moss.

Zinnia wasn't dead.

She was thoroughly stoned, which is sort of like dead but not the same. She was passed out naked on the bed. A bottle of soda-pop wine was cradled between her breasts. A Jackie Chan comic book was open on her tummy, another had fallen to the floor. The music was "Don't Fence Me In," Shep Fields. There was a stack of CDs on the chair. Harry James, Wagner, the music from *Waterworld*. I knew I was falling in love again.

Zinnia looked fine, she looked grand. She looked a lot better than she had in Bobby's van. Being in a stupor will relax you every time.

I stood there and gazed at this unclad lovely, every peak and every hollow, every swell, every shadowy delight. With no shame at all, I looked at her lashes and her lips and her delightful collarbone. I looked for some time at her personal private parts. I wondered where the fire was, I wondered if Laurel was very close by.

Instead, I found a pair of jeans and a Batman T-shirt and some pink running shoes. I crammed the jeans and T-shirt and the shoes in the front of my pants, picked up the very limp Zinnia and carried her back outdoors. Holding her close and smelling the sleepy scent of girl did little for my knightly attitude. I stopped at the pool, kissed her on the head and dumped her in.

She came up screaming, gasping for air, having chlorinated fits. She treaded water like a dog. She didn't see me, she saw the fire and smelled the smoke and saw the dark roiling cloud against the sky. She yelled and slapped the water and I walked down in the shallow end, grabbed an arm and a foot and pulled her out. Set her on the bank by her clothes, and went off looking for Laurel and assorted Spudettes.

Laurel wasn't hard to find. She had heard Zinnia's screams and so had everyone else. Strumpets and chippies, blondes and brunettes, floozies, redheads, ladies of the night, ladies named Iris, Aster, Poppy and Fern, Bluebell and Buttercup, Orchid and Marigold, a covey of trollops, doxies and tarts, poured out of a single trailer like aggravated ants.

They were frightened, they were tense and out of breath. In the face of disaster, they had clutched their most precious possessions, held them to their ample C-cups, to their B's or their A's, or their cheerleader breasts, held on tight to the treasures they didn't want to lose. Poppy had a hat with a feather on top. Orchid grasped a tiny black dog. The dog wore shorts and a silver sequined top. Orchid wore a shabby blue robe. Aster had an Emmy and a People's Choice Award, and I'll bet there's a tale behind that. A long-legged girl I didn't know lugged the works of George Eliot, tied up in a string. All the favorite titles like *The Mill on the Floss, Silas Marner* and the zany *Adam Bede*. Tragedy brings out the best in us all.

Laurel stalked toward me, her calm exterior masking anxiety and dread, fear and alarm no deeper than drugstore makeup, panic about to break through. Behind her, the Spudettes came to a halt, stopped at an invisible line, eyes wide as terrified mice. I knew what they saw. Their happy pool was the color of dark and turgid blood, a grisly reflection of the fire above the trees.

"She's gone," Laurel said. "She's not here, I can't find her anywhere."

"Daisy," she said, before I could ask. "She's not in her trailer, nobody's seen her. Columbine's missing too. Jesus, Moss, I knew something like this was going to happen, I *knew* it, I should've *done* something, I shouldn't just—oh, goddamn, Moss, goddamn everyone!"

"What," I said, "you should've done what? I'm not with you on this."

Her mouth began to tremble, her face was a mix of fury and tears. "Something, I could have done *something* instead of—instead of just—" She looked past me at the pool. Zinnia was pulling on her jeans without any underwear.

"Wonderful, Moss, I can't leave you for a minute. Zinnia, hon, you okay? Lord, you're not killed or anything?"

"I am going to kill *him*," Zinnia yelled, "I coulda had a heart attack!"

Zinnia was fine. Laurel didn't look at her again. "Poppy thinks she maybe saw her. Daisy, I mean. She didn't see Columbine at all. It was dark but there might've been a car."

"Daisy's got a car?"

"No, she hasn't got a car, she might've got *in* a car. You listening or what? Poppy said she might've got in a car."

Laurel sniffed and wiped a hand across her face. "I am *trying* real hard not to have a breakdown right here, Wiley, but if that girl got in a car I am thinking it was Michael's car, and if he's got her I will not be able to live with myself, I will not live out my life if that son of a bitch has got her, I could not abide that . . ."

I stared at her. "I'm not following this too well, okay? Why would Michael have her, what would he want with Daisy, that's the part I don't get."

"I can't go into that."

"Oh, fine, here we go again."

"We are not going anywhere again, so don't start that. I am saying we will *not* get into that, Wiley Moss, and it is not important right now, what's important is my very best friend is abducted and likely dead and I could've stopped it if I hadn't been somewhere else, if I'd have been right here."

"I'm sure she's all right," I said, and knew right away that was not what she wanted to hear, but I didn't stop there, I said, "I'm sure she'll show up, I'm sure she's not dead."

"God*damn* it, Moss, I say my best friend's dead, she is *dead*, you hear me, you hear me say my best friend's dead!"

"This is a real defeatist outlook on life, that isn't going to help."

"Well I feel pretty fucking defeated right now, okay, that okay with you? If it's not, Moss, you can—"

Conversation came to a halt. For an instant, the sky lit up like noon, or maybe three or four, a bilious mix of copper, babyshit and liver-red. The Spudettes gave a collective gasp as the fire rose up in an awesome mushroom cloud, roasted the tops of the trees and vaporized the air. The roar of the firestorm reached us half a second after that, and with it a blistering wall of heat.

Laurel said, "Oh, shit, Wiley," her standard reply in troubling times, and we backed away from the pool, Zinnia on our heels, half in a T-shirt, one leg in her jeans.

You didn't have to be a forest ranger to know what had happened down there. The wind had driven the fire from the lodge up the hill, met the blaze from my trailer coming down. Through the magic of thermal science, the fires had joined forces, gained new strength and a bad attitude.

"Okay," I said, "we've got to clear the area, we've got to get everyone out of here and we've got to do it fast. I'm just a guest here, so what's the best direction to go?"

"The fire's coming from the west," someone said, and I looked around and saw Orchid and her dog. "That's out. South's no good and neither is east. The canyon drops a good half mile straight down to the river, there's no way out from there."

"North. North sounds good to me."

"Huh-unh." Orchid shook her head. "North's the highway, which is fine if you could make it, but the country's real rough. It's under three miles, but it'd take us half a day."

"We got any other choice?"

"Not unless you got a frequent flyer card."

"Horses . . ."

"What?" I turned to see the long-legged girl. She had a redneck mouth and sleepy eyes. I really liked those eyes.

"We got horses, man, a whole barn full. Right over there." She pointed past the trailers, vaguely to the west.

"Ohs" and "ahs" from Spudettes. A few jumped up and down.

"My Lord, Phlox, you're right, I flat forgot!"

Phlox?

Orchid handed Aster her dog, gave Phlox a hug and turned to me. "We'd never make it north on foot, but I bet we can do it on a horse. A horse can get over rugged ground that might be impassable to us. I bet a horse can do fine."

A chorus of cheers from the Spudettes. They didn't need to vote, they turned about as one, clutching their possessions, running after Aster to the west.

I took Laurel's hand. Laurel shook me off. "Huh-unh. No way. I'm not leaving Daisy, Moss."

I could see she wasn't thinking straight. Only moments before, she'd been certain Michael Galiano had whisked Daisy off in a car.

"I wouldn't leave her either," I said, "you ought to know that. What I'm thinking, I'm thinking we can find her better on a horse. With a horse we can cover more ground."

"Yeah, right . . ." Laurel gave me a slightly addled look. "You'd do that, hon? You'd put yourself in peril for Daisy and me?"

"Well what do you think? Of course I would."

"You're a sweetheart, Wiley Moss. I said so from the start."

This wasn't so, but why go into that? If a loved one isn't thinking straight, leave her alone if she seems to be leaning toward you. She kissed me and tears streamed down her cheeks and we ran past the trailers to the barn.

The Spudettes were lost in a cloud of dirty smoke. The fire was now roaring through the last grove of trees between us and the flat ground that led to the trailers and the pool. The flats would slow it some, but not much. The heat was already intense.

I'd seen the horses, too, and the sagging gray barn, my first day in Vinnieland, but I'd put the sight out of my mind. We have horses in Ohio, and one glance told me there were no big Derby winners here.

I hadn't looked nearly close enough. On a scale from "Frisky" to "Sedate," the word "Coma" came to mind. These miserable nags were shaggy and swaybacked, feeble and scabby, listless and infirm, pitiful creatures that were possibly blind, too depressed to care about impending death by fire.

What were they doing here? I wondered. I guessed they had been here all along, when the lodge was still a lodge, with tourists and happy trails, before the Galiano Family came along and filled the place with potatoheads.

The wind was still blowing from the west and the smoke was getting dense. The Spudettes were running in all directions, shouting at one another, and waving their hands about. I feared a stampede but the horses didn't care. Laurel said we'd be just fine, that Iris, in her formative years, had served as a rodeo queen.

Her leadership was clearly needed now. No one knew what to do, no one had the slightest idea. Iris kept her head. There weren't any saddles, but Iris found a rack of moldy bridles in the barn, and explained which end they fit on.

"Which do you think is Eliot's best work?" I asked the long-legged woman named Phlox. "*Silas Marner* or *Middlemarch?*"

"Are you kidding, man?"

"No I'm not."

"Forget about the popular stuff. Eliot reached her peak with *Felix Holt.*"

"I didn't know that."

"I'd be surprised if you did. Most everyone gets wrapped up in the story itself, and forgets about the fierce, moralistic tone of the writer's work."

"I'd like to discuss this with you sometime."

Phlox gave me a squint-eyed look and walked off toward the corral. Boy, that woman could walk. I could watch her walk all day if we didn't have to talk.

"Legs aren't the end-all of life," Laurel said, coming up behind me like she always did, with scarcely any warning at all. "That woman's got a heart like a stone. Physical charm doesn't ever make up for a mean spirit, Moss. I don't imagine you ever thought of that."

I had, but not much. I noticed Laurel was leading a very tall and mangy horse. The horse had something in its nose.

I said, "That's an awful-looking horse. Where's mine?"

"We're going to have to double up. Iris says some of these ponies would have a stroke if you tried to get on top. You know what they been feeding 'em here? Leftover Italian food, for Christ's sake. That's not what a horse likes to eat, a horse won't put up with that. Hon, I think Daisy and Columbine are dead. I think Michael had Carl come and drag 'em off and kill them somewhere."

I could see the fire reflected in her eyes, I could see the confusion and the sorrow and the pain. Behind her, I could see the long-legged girl riding by, holding tight to Orchid's waist.

"You don't know that, Laurel, you don't know that at all. She might be okay. She might be just fine."

"I don't know it but I'm *feeling* it," she said. "That's a family trait on mamma's side. Feeling's the same as knowing when it comes to your tragic event."

I didn't comment on that, it wouldn't do any good at all.

"You ever ride bareback before? It's not quite as easy as it looks on TV."

"I never rode any way before, and it doesn't look easy at all."

"Neither have I. I feel we better find a fence."

It went a lot better than I'd thought.

It wasn't the Bengal Lancers but it wasn't Looney Tunes. It was Captain Moss and his Bimbo Brigade the day Idaho caught on fire. We rode north and slightly west, Iris in the lead, as fast as our mounts would take us, which was nowhere fast enough for me. The fire howled at our heels less than a hundred yards away. The flames leaped thirty feet high. The heat was worse than a cheap apartment with a broken A/C.

"It's getting close," I yelled at Laurel.

"Too close," she cried out in my ear. "We're going to burn up, Wiley, we're never getting out of here."

"We're going to be fine," I said, and knew that wasn't true at all.

I choked on smoke and the horse up ahead disappeared. The smoke cleared a second and I saw a horse stumble, saw its legs collapse, saw the riders go down. Someone cried out. I gave the reins to Laurel and slid off to the ground.

It was Poppy and Iris. They were okay but scared. Orchid and Phlox appeared; they'd seen the fall and stopped to help. The fire-storm roared and we couldn't hear ourselves but there wasn't much to say. I helped Iris up behind Phlox, wondered what the swayback would think of three riders, and didn't hang around to see.

I held onto Poppy and started back for Laurel. The smoke was too thick, but Laurel found me. The riderless nag limped by, heading straight for the fire. Was the poor creature dumb, or was this a case of horsey suicide?

I knew I would never get up on my trusty mount again without a saddle or a fence, and I didn't even try. I took the reins from Laurel and dragged the horse ahead. He thought this was fine. He couldn't see where he was going and was happy for me to try.

The path ahead was getting worse, just like Orchid had said. There were scattered rocks and boulders, treacherous ravines, unexpected obstacles and twists. If the horses couldn't take level ground, how were they going to handle this? Maybe the horses were a bad idea. Maybe we'd be better off on walking, even if it was rough ahead . . .

I turned and looked back at the fire. My mouth went dry at the sight. I'd checked only seconds before, and now the flames had gained another twenty, thirty yards. I tried to work it out in my head. The fire was x and we were y. That's seven times two and carry your six, and I made a "D" in every math class I ever had. Even if I'd been as smart as Margery Sweet who had dimples on her knees and sat two seats ahead, we were totally and thoroughly fucked, done in and out of luck, because headlights suddenly burst through the flames, Michael Galiano's babyshit Lincoln and the black one after that, both slightly scorched and Pirelli tires afire, transmissions scraping on the ground, trunks wide open and bumpers falling off, two cars ready for scrap but apparently intact, both heading straight for Wiley's strumpet caravan . . .

21

Poppy gave a high-pitched, glass-breaking scream, a scream straight out of *Mars Needs Chickens*, 1953.

Laurel said, "Shit-shit-shit!" which is what Laurel says when she's under lots of stress.

I said, "Goddamn-look out-get down-jump!" or words to that effect.

Everything happened at once. It didn't but I'm pretty sure it did and it was too late to think, too late to blink, too late for anything at all. Michael's lights sizzled in my eyes and hurt my head, swung to the right and pinned Iris, Phlox and Orchid in their glare. The antique horse kicked its heels, gave a spastic leap and tossed its riders in the air.

Orchid disappeared. Phlox did a double twist and landed on her back. Iris rolled and came up on her knees, staring at the lights, her features melting in the blinding flare of white. The car came at her, howling through the night. Iris froze, Iris couldn't move, Iris was transfixed . . .

Iris didn't have a chance, but God was sure she did. The driver didn't see the rock and if he did he couldn't stop. It was a very big rock, rooted firmly in the ground. It ripped the car's belly from the front to the crotch, gutted the Lincoln like a trout. The big car came to a sudden, bone-jarring halt. Everything inside kept moving, a quirky law of physics that can turn you into Spam, that can turn you into soup in a second and a half.

The doors flew open, and four chunky guys staggered out. One fell flat and broke his nose. A big guy kicked him in the groin. The big guy couldn't stand a sloppy attitude. I recognized Carl at once. We had almost met in our frolic through the woods.

Carl left the guy alone, walked quickly to the rear and peered in. Reached in and eased Michael out of the back. Michael was pissed and slightly stunned. He yelled at Carl like Carl was the cause of all this, and Carl backed off. Michael yells at Carl, Carl kicks a guy, the guy goes home and kicks his dog.

Everything happens at once, I believe I said that once before. Three things happened while the babyshit Lincoln was goring itself on a rock:

The other Lincoln jerked to the left, avoided a collision and skidded to a stop. Two more guys got out and ran to the car up front. Carl slapped one and kicked the other in the butt . . .

Iris hadn't moved. She was close enough to kiss the bumper, close enough to count bugs on the Idaho plates. Iris passed out. Phlox came out of nowhere, Zinnia at her side. Zinnia lifted Iris up. Phlox hoisted the girl on her shoulder and hauled her off into the dark. Michael yelled for them to stop. He pulled out a large ugly pistol and fired three shots in the air. Phlox didn't care, Phlox was already out of sight. Zinnia paused to throw a rock. Orchid was out there somewhere, I heard her dog yap. Two ancient horses trotted by, but I didn't see a Spudette anywhere . . .

All this took about thirty-two seconds, and the other thing that happened was Laurel said, "Get *down* here, you stupid fuck, they can *see* you up there!"

Okay, not a bad idea. I squatted like a frog and followed her into a shallow ravine. It was full of loose rocks of every size, but we were safe from the lights of the car. The sky was blood-red but it was dark down there. I could make out Laurel's shapely rear, and I kept my eye on that.

Someone fired a round of shots. I stopped and climbed a boulder, stretched and looked over the side.

"Moss, get off of that thing right now," Laurel said, but I was already there.

It was a frightening thing to see. The heat burned my face, and the sound was like the Big Bartender was about to close the world and kick everybody out. Michael and his crew were spectral silhou-

ettes against a raging wall of flame, a curtain of fire that licked the
sky. It was truly awesome, a real and very costly special effect, a
background for Wagner, only Wagner takes a long time to sing. We'd
all be charcoal puppies long before the fat lady could get her number
out . . .

It was like watching TV from four rooms away, with the house
on fire and the sound turned down. I couldn't understand what they
were doing up there, I could hardly see a thing. Michael was angry,
stalking about, waving his arms and jabbing at the woods, the woods
to the north where the girls had disappeared. His hoods weren't
happy in their work. They were scared of Carl, they didn't like fire,
they didn't want to be there at all. I watched the scene two or three
times. Michael would threaten them and send them off into the
dark—they'd run and fire their weapons, dart around in circles and
hurry back to the cars.

It didn't make any sense to them, and it didn't make a bit of sense
to me.

Okay, I thought, what the hell is going on here? The world is on
fire and Michael Galiano is chasing after tarts. Does Michael need
a girl? Michael doesn't need a girl, Michael can get about any girl
he wants . . .

"Something's wrong here," I told Laurel, "something isn't right.
Michael is up there and—Laurel?"

I turned and she was gone. I saw her hunched down, running
back south, back toward the trailers. Terrific. Exactly where we didn't
want to be.

I muttered obscenities and ran to catch up. Jesus, everything had
happened so fast. It had been maybe six, eight minutes since Phlox
and I had shared a literary moment at Vinnie's horse corral. It
seemed like forever, or possibly an hour and a half. I hoped everyone was all right. Iris, Zinnia, Poppy and Aster, and the lovely
Phlox herself . . .

It suddenly struck me that Poppy wasn't with us anymore, and I
felt real dumb about that, because I couldn't remember when she'd
left. The lights burned my eyes and Poppy screamed and I'm certain
that the horse disappeared, and I couldn't place Poppy after that.

Damn it, *everyone* was missing, everyone was somewhere else.
Daisy and Columbine were missing and all the Spudettes and I had
to assume that I was missing too. I tried to remember a zip code,

my last-known address. Wiley Moss came to mind, a very promising start, but there was little after that.

Laurel, as ever, ran like a girl, and I caught up with her fast.

"What is it with you," I said, grabbing her arm and turning her around, "are you nuts? You can't go back there."

"Hell I can't. I can go anywhere I want to, Moss, don't you tell me I can't."

She drew back her arm and shook me off. Her chin stuck out in defiance, but I was looking at her eyes.

"Daisy's not back here, Laurel. There's no use looking for her here."

"You don't know, you don't know that."

"Okay, I don't. I got an idea she's not. If she was, she'd have the good sense to get out of here quick. I don't know if you noticed, there's a raging inferno climbing up the hill. Daisy's got fairly good sense, and she might react to that. I know I am, that's what I'm doing, I'm reacting right now."

"She could be hurt, Wiley. She might be lyin' in a trailer, hurt and severely maimed."

"Huh-unh. Forget it." The pouty lip didn't work on me at all, I'd seen this show before. "Listen to yourself. Ten minutes ago you said Michael had her in his car. Now you got her maimed in a trailer somewhere. Hey, why don't you go and ask? Run back and ask Michael if he's seen her anywhere."

Laurel rolled her eyes. "Well that is a dumb idea, I surely can't do that."

"What's Michael doing, Laurel? Why is he chasing Spudettes, you want to tell me that?"

"I don't know. How would I know? How would I know that?"

She was quick, she hardly blinked. Still, I caught her on a little-known technique. It's used by spies both here and overseas. One sentence is fine. Two is okay, three means you're lying through your teeth. I hear this works every time.

"No. You do know, Laurel, I can tell you do. Damn it, you're doing it to me again, I am getting awful tired of this."

"Okay."

"Okay what?"

"You're getting tired of bitching at me, babe, just stop. Don't do it anymore. Start doing something else." She had a little soot on her nose, a very saucy effect. I didn't let it get to me at all.

"That is a real familiar tactic with you. You want to throw me off, you toss in something that doesn't make sense. Your aim is to sow disorder and confusion in my head."

"Lord, I doubt I could handle a job like that."

"What's that supposed to mean? Is that a put-down, is that a smart remark?"

"Now how would I know, hon? In Psychology II, we got about as far as Wreaking Havoc, I remember some of that."

"Okay, I think that's a put-down, I think that's what it is."

"You're the one's got a big art degree, why don't you tell me."

"That is definitely a put-down, Laurel, and I do not appreciate that."

"Got a degree in *art* is what he's got . . ."

"What's that?"

"I said, that big degree you got's in a—*Jesus, Wiley!*"

Her eyes went wide and her face got suddenly bright. A sound like six tornadoes went *WHUUUMP!* and the fire leaped up like something had sucked it in the air, leaped like a snake about to strike, stretched in a bloody arc of red above our heads and struck the ground again.

I grabbed Laurel's hand, turned around and ran. Stopped, ran back the other way. There was no place to go now, no place to hide. The fire was all around us, the flames were everywhere, we had about a minute, a minute and a half . . .

I pulled Laurel down to the ground and held her close. She made little sounds against my neck. I could smell the hair sizzle on my arms, feel the awful heat on my face. I wanted to tell Laurel something, something real nice but there wasn't any time. You want to say something, don't wait around until you're caught up in a fire.

Goddamn it, I thought, we have already done this tonight. Once is enough and twice doesn't seem right. I've got a lot of things to do, I've got a lot of stuff to see. And even if I didn't, even if I couldn't think of anything at all, I wouldn't want to go right now. I could get bored a real long time, okay? I could go sit in a chair. I could sit around for years in a fairly comfortable chair and I'd never say, "Okay, fine, I got nothing else to do, that's it, I want to die." You think I'm going to say that? Don't hold your breath, you think I'm going to say that. No fucking way I am going to say that . . .

A tree exploded overhead and a flaming branch crashed to the ground. Laurel cried out as hot embers twisted through the air. I noticed my shoe was on fire. I stomped on it, kicked it in the dirt but it wouldn't go out. I reached down and yanked it off and peeled the sock off too.

"Wiley Moss, you put that shoe on right now," Laurel cried out, "you can't walk around out here without a shoe, you're going to catch on fire."

"For Christ's sake, Laurel, get with it, I'm already on fire. Hold on to me, it'll all be over and we'll have a better life."

"Huh-unh, I don't want to, Wiley, I don't *want* a better life!"

"Nobody wants to, hon, just hold on tight."

Laurel screamed and tried to break free. Something hot fell on my back. Something hot licked at my pants. Something went *honk!* Something went *honk! honk!* again.

Laurel pounded on my chest and broke free. The car roared out of a shrieking wall of flame and nearly ran us down. It jerked to a stop, skidded on the charred and burning ground. A door flew open and Angela DeMarco said, "Don't just stand there, dummy, get the fuck in!"

No one had to ask me twice. I picked Laurel up and shoved her in, squeezed in behind her and bounced in Angela's lap.

"Not up here, you idiot," Angela shouted, "in the back!"

I squeezed out again and Angela slammed the door. I grabbed the other handle, howled and left a layer of skin behind. Someone opened up from inside. I jumped in and yanked the door shut, fell into a tangle of arms and legs, cutoffs and collarbones, T-shirts that stuck out to here.

The car lurched and took off. I said, "Hi there," and slammed against the floor.

"Oh, my Looooord—!"

Laurel squealed with laughter, clapped her hands with joy, climbed the front seat and spilled over in the back. The long-lost Daisy was found, and so was Columbine. Everyone bawled, then everyone hugged. The scene was intense. I was in the way and I was hugged quite a bit. I wound up in the lap of the lovely Columbine. A slightly taller version of Laurel, same hair and different eyes, a little gaunt, maybe, but I could live with that.

The car bounced and shook and threw us all to one side. Everyone shouted, everyone complained. Angela told us to shut the fuck up, and so everybody did.

Angelo was driving, I didn't have to ask. I'd know that hair oil anywhere. We were racing through smoke, through the edge of the fire which was howling to our left. The windows were shut, but the smoke got in anyhow.

"Drive straight," Angela told her brother, "don't jerk around, stay in the middle of the road."

"There isn't any road," Angelo said, "you see a road, I don't see a road, what are you talkin' about?"

"Then stay on whatever it is. Don't get off and don't bounce around. Don't steer all over the place, don't get off to the side."

"You wanna drive? You wanna fuckin' drive? Fine, you can fuckin' drive."

"I am not going to drive, *you* are going to drive, and you're going to—look out, you stupid shit, you almost hit a tree!"

With little warning at all, Angela started pounding on her brother, doubling up her fists, pummeling him about the head and neck. Angelo DeMarco was difficult to hit. He didn't have a neck, and his head was protected by Lucky Tiger, 1943. Angela could land a solid blow, but they tended to quickly slide away. Angelo tried to fight back, gripping the wheel with his left hand and fighting with the right. One hand didn't help a lot.

While the twins beat away at one another, the scene outside was a raging holocaust. The grass, the trees, the very air was on fire. Clumps of flaming wood and debris fell on the roof. Cinders rained down from the sky. Angelo turned the wipers on. This worked fine until the wipers caught fire.

"We're going to die in here," Daisy cried, "we're all going to fry!"

"We are not going to fry," Columbine told her. "Jesus'll see to that."

"Jesus knows what kind of life I've led, I doubt he's going to care."

"He cares, darling. He cares about us all. Saints, businessmen and whores, they're all the same to him."

Daisy sniffed. "You think?"

"You could be a Hitler or a serial killer, he'd love you just the same. You could be a banker like that nice Mr. Hinkers comes in from Salt Lake or somewhere? The one's got the anna-tomical teddy bear? You could be that bitch what's-her-name runs the convenience store?"

"Miz Earl."

"No, now not Miz Earl, the other one's got some kinda Mes'can name . . ."

"Shut it *down!*" Angela turned around and glared. "I do not want to hear this, okay?" She stabbed a finger at Laurel. "You're in charge. Further aggravation is on your head."

Laurel looked appalled. "Me? Well why the hell me, I'd like to know."

Angela didn't answer. Angela turned around and told Angelo to slow the hell down. Columbine and Daisy sank back in their seats. Laurel gave them both a hug. I peered out the window and watched a moose go by, a large, ungainly beast with an oversized nose and frightened little eyes. Angelo didn't see the moose, and we could all be grateful for that.

"*Oh, my God!*" Angela sat up straight and gripped the dash. "I'll kill him, I'll kill that sorry son of a bitch! Angelo, stop the car."

"What?"

"I said *stop* the car. Stop it right now."

Angelo shook his head. "Are you nuts? No way. No way I am stopping the car."

"You're stopping. You're stopping right now."

"I am not stopping, Angela. I am not stopping the car."

Angela reached down under the dash, and came up with a short, ugly sawed-off shotgun and poked it in Angelo's face.

"I'd like you to stop, I'd like you to stop the car."

"Fine. That's what I'm doing, I'm stopping right now."

Angelo stopped. Angela got out and took the weapon with her. Smoke poured in and Angelo closed the door fast.

"What's she doing," I said, "what's this all about?"

"Shut the fuck up," Angelo said. He leaned over and hit the glove compartment and pulled out a black automatic, a very large Colt .45.

"Shit," Angelo said, "nothing but shit, what kinda life is this?"

He got out and sighed and closed the door. I watched him walk off in the smoke and disappear. He was wearing the very same pin-stripe suit, white shirt and polka-dot tie he was wearing when we met by the lake. I recall we had a talk about meece, nature, and animal sex, and after a while we watched Rocco bleed to death.

"Wiley, get up in front," Laurel said.

"Do what?"

Laurel gripped my arm. "Get up and drive and get us the hell out of here."

I stared at her. "I can't do that. I'd—we'd be leaving them here."

"Right. That is the *idea*, Wiley, okay? Get up there and *drive.*"

"Laurel, I'm not sure where you're going with this—"

"Goddamn it, Wiley Moss, just do it!"

I looked in Laurel's eyes. I'd seen Laurel scared and I'd seen her mad before, but I'd never seen her quite like this. I couldn't begin to guess all her emotions, but certainly there was terror, doubt and desperation there. That, and something more frightening, something I didn't expect to see, something big as life and cold as death itself: a bright red touch of homicide.

I said, "You know what you'd be doing, you'd be leaving them here, you really want to do that? These people just saved our hides, Laurel." I nodded at Daisy and Columbine. "Theirs too."

"I know what I'm doing, Wiley. Okay?" The sudden calm, the total confidence I saw in her face and in her eyes, was scarier than what I'd seen before. "You going to do it, or what? I can't drive, but Daisy can."

"Huh-unh," I said, "no I'm not. They don't come back in about—half a minute, I'll get us out of here. We're not going to roast, I promise you that. Not after all we've—"

She slapped me hard across the face. Not your standard Bette Davis slap, where you stand there kind of stunned, and maybe lose your cigarette, but a real jaw burner that nearly knocked me flat.

"Don't you ever even speak to me again," Laurel said. "You're a—you're a *Midwest* person, and you're not our kind."

"Laurel, now you don't mean that."

"Try me. Just lay a hand on me and you'll—oh, shit, hon, oh my God, look at that!"

The shotgun coughed twice before I could even turn around. The smoke blew away and the flames leaped high and there was the babyshit Lincoln impaled on a pinnacle of rock, its headlights poking at the dark and smoky sky. One of Michael's hoods was down. Everyone scattered, and someone fired back. Angela stood her ground and blasted everything in sight. Carl raised up, spotted Angelo and took a quick shot. Angelo yelped and tumbled on his back.

Angela screamed in fury and fired off a killing barrage. Michael dived behind the black car. Angela saw him and got off three shots. The headlights shattered and the trunk blew off. The car was already a mess and the shotgun didn't help. The windows were spidered and the heat had blistered off the paint. The Lincoln looked like a rhino with a bad skin disease.

Gunfire came from the safety of the car. Angela took another shot and backed off. Angelo was limping, dragging himself along. I knew it was a bad idea but I got out and ran through the smoke and helped her get him to the car. Angelo fell in the front seat and got behind the wheel, stripped a few gears and took off.

"Son of a bitch, Michael," Angela screamed, "you are dead, you are fucking *dead,* man!"

Angelo gripped the steering wheel, and plowed through the smoke. A stray shot pinged off our car. Daisy and Columbine yelled and we drove into a wall of fire. I could feel the terrible heat. It gnawed at the roof and it wanted inside. The fire was behind us, then, and we were safe—for maybe ten seconds, then Angelo plunged into a wall of flame again.

"You don't mind me asking," I said, "you got a destination, anywhere special in mind?"

"Out of here, dumbshit, what do you think?" Angela didn't look at me, she didn't turn around.

"Out of here."

"Right."

"Like a road maybe, the kind real people use, something like that."

"You're quick, Moss. I like that in a man."

"No," Laurel said, "you can't, there's a whole bunch of girls out there, we got to *find* 'em, we can't just leave 'em here!"

Angela threw back her head and laughed. "Are you nuts? I'm going to hang around fucking ground zero, I'm hunting down hookers all over Idaho? Get real, babe. I am *out* of here."

Laurel started screaming and swinging at Angela. I didn't want to do it, but I pulled her off and held her back. Columbine hit me in the face and Daisy grabbed my crotch. Angelo moaned, and hunched against the wheel, Evel Knievel with a bad attitude, bouncing over boulders, dashing through flaming ravines.

I like to wrestle women, but only under certain conditions, and seldom ever three at a time. I was losing the battle fast, then Angela let out a whoop that stopped Laurel, Columbine and Daisy in their tracks.

"We made it," she shouted, "we got us a road!" She pounded on the dash, something she liked to do a lot. "Burn, Michael, burn to a crisp, you lousy son of a bitch!"

Daisy loosed her hold on me a minute and I looked out the back. The world was still on fire. I could see the pall of smoke, the stark skeletons of trees, dead black shadows against a red sky. And nearly lost in this great inferno, this mighty cremation that had eaten Vinnieland, one feeble glow, one single headlight, probing its way through the thickening veil of smoke, maybe fifty yards behind.

"You don't want to hear this," I said, "but I can't help that. A Lincoln's a good car value, they make those suckers to last . . ."

22

Daisy was crying.

She was scrooched up in the seat like a scared little kid. Her hair was scorched on the ends and the Maybelline was running out her eyes.

Laurel said, "There, there, hon," but it didn't seem to do a lot of good. Columbine said she had to throw up or pee, but she wasn't sure which.

"You better find a place to stop," Laurel said. "I've got me two real sick girls back here."

"I better do what?" Angela glanced around briefly and gave her a look. "You are flat-out bonkers, lady. I got Michael Galiano and a carload of full-time killers on my tail. I'm going to stop, I'm going to stop right here, that's what you think I'm going to do?"

"A little compassion, a little thought for others, that isn't going to kill you, Angela."

"Hah! Wanna bet?"

I said, "I don't think they're back there anymore. I don't see any light."

"Fuck what you think, Moss. You're a hired artist, I don't believe this is your area of expertise. I got an art question, I'll ask."

"Well excuse me."

"Fine. You're excused. Shut up and leave me alone, I've got things to do. I need any help I'll ask."

"She needs any help, she'll ask," Angelo said.

"You shut up too. How's your leg?"

"I been shot, how you think it is? You got a shot leg, you're asking how it is? Somebody's got a shot leg, they're going to say, 'Hey, the leg's great, the leg's fine?'"

"I'm asking, Angelo, it's okay if I ask?"

"No, it's not okay you ask. Fuck you, Angela, it isn't okay if you ask."

"This is how you talk to your sister, this is how you talk to me? I thank the blessed Jesus that Mother's dead, Angelo, she doesn't have to hear this."

"Don't start, don't start with Mother."

"Make me."

"What?"

"Make me stop. Go ahead, try it. Make me stop, Angelo. Go ahead and make me stop."

"Fuck you, Angela."

"Fine. Now it's fuck you to your sister again. How can you have a nasty thought like that? You know what that is, you have a thought like that about your sister, you know what God's gonna think about that? How's the leg, it hurt real bad or what?"

"The leg's not bad. I'm bleeding to death, what do you care? I'm bleeding to death, I got what—I got a minute and a half, what do you care?"

This wouldn't stop, but I didn't have to listen, I could maybe listen to something else. I leaned back in the seat. A Lincoln is bigger than a Geo but the backseat isn't built for four. A salesman's going to tell you it is, but it isn't built for four. Four little kids, it's okay, but not three long-legged women, and a guy who mostly wears a large.

Laurel was cleaning Daisy's face with a Kleenex she'd scared up somewhere. I was squeezed in close to Columbine. Ordinarily this would be fine, but these weren't ordinary times.

"Listen," I said, "you feeling better now?"

Columbine said, "I am feeling like shit, and I'm scared out of my pants, Mr. Moss."

"I don't blame you," I said, giving a little thought to that, "and you don't have to call me Mr. Moss."

A tear ran down her cheek and she laid her head against my chest.

"Lord, all those poor girls back there. I hope it was merciful, I hope they burned to death real quick."

"Now you don't know they did, they might be just fine."

Columbine sniffed. "You're just being kind, you don't have to do that."

"No, now they could. Strange things happen in a fire, I saw a show on that. These people were out in a national park. A fire came up and they were trapped. They thought they were goners, but the fire swept right on by, left them in the middle and they came out just fine."

"You mean that?"

"Sure I do. Those girls, they could just as easy been caught in an incident similar to that."

"Really?"

"It's entirely possible," I said.

I didn't believe that shit for a minute, and I wished I hadn't ever brought it up. Zinnia and Poppy and Iris and Phlox weren't *fine*. Columbine knew better and so did everybody else.

For lack of a finish to this, I said, "Listen, you got the time? They stole my wallet and my watch. I don't have a personal possession of any kind."

"Me neither," Columbine said. She gave a little sniff and her thigh pressed close to mine. We were packed in tight, but I had an idea there was something more than body pressure here. Even under dire circumstance, in the midst of personal distress, I felt this woman was beginning to care for me a lot.

I turned and looked out the back. I guessed it had been maybe six, eight minutes since we'd bounced onto the highway and left the single beam of Michael's car behind. The sky glowed red but I couldn't see anything else. That Lincoln was scorched, gutted and shot up pretty good. Even a top-flight car with regular maintenance would be lucky to be in one piece after that. They might have made it out, but I strongly doubted that. More likely than not, they were back there with the hapless Spudettes, consumed by smoke and fire.

Daisy began to sob. She had never really quit.

Laurel said, "There, there," again, and kept a wary eye on me and Columbine.

Angelo drove, and Angela supervised. Nothing happened for a minute and a half, then Angela said, *"Jesus Christ, what's that!"*

Everybody sat up, everybody was rapt. They came straight at us in a blaze of phosphorescent white, in a dazzle of blue lights, red lights, pink lights, yellow lights, every kind of light there was. They howled and they screamed, they hooted and they wailed. They passed us going sixty, eighty, ninety, ninety-five, giant red hosers, hook and ladders two blocks long, every local, yokel, state, and county cop, every EMS, every chopper in the state of Idaho.

And, forgetting for the moment that I was a victim of this holocaust myself, that people I was fond of, and people that I didn't like at all, had perished back there in the flames of Vinnieland, I could feel that *whuka-whuka-whuka* in my belly, that thrill of disaster, that hunger, that need, for a tragedy that's happening to somebody else, and not you . . .

Then, suddenly, everything was gone, nothing but the lights in the distance and a faraway whine, nothing but the darkness and the highway ahead.

"I don't know you ever heard of this or not," Angela said, "but you're supposed to *pull over to the side,* you see emergency vehicles on the road. You don't keep driving, asshole, you *pull over to the side!*"

Angelo shrugged. "Yeah, fine. That's a swell idea, you stupid bitch, I wish I'd thought of that. I pull over to the side, some cop drives up, he says, 'Hey, what do you know about the fire back there, what's your name? You got a license, you got a registration, pal? And by the way, how come your car's full of holes, how come you don't have any fuckin' paint? Where you people been driving, Kuwait?' I'm going to stop, I'm going to talk about that? Uh-huh, that's what I'm going to do, all right."

"That is exactly the point," Angela said, "like you are always missing the point. You *don't* stop, you don't pull over, the cop sees you don't stop, *then* he pulls you over, right? That's when he—" Angela sat up straight. "Pull over. Stop. Pull over right now."

"What, I'm pulling off the road, there's nothing there, what's the matter with you?"

"Pull *off* the fucking road, Angelo. Stop—the—car—right—now!"

Angelo muttered to himself, but he did what he was told. He'd been doing that forever and he couldn't stop now.

Angela slammed the door and stomped around the car. Angelo

slid over, moaning about his leg. Angela slid in, ground a few gears and took off with a jerk, slowed at once and took a hard right.

Angelo was wrong. There was something to see up ahead, something only Angela saw, and not anybody else. The dirt road was scarcely wider than the car. A rusty sign maybe twenty years old was nailed up to a tree. The sign said: PRIVAT EEP OUT. If Angela wanted to disappear, she had picked a good place. Anyone driving down the highway would miss the road entirely, even if they were looking real close. The trees closed in overhead and the branches sagged down. Ten yards up the road, we were lost in a tangle of limbs and vines.

Angela doused the lights, handed the shotgun to her brother, got out and walked behind the car. I watched her through the back. Just like in the movies, she ripped off the sign and tossed it in the brush. Then she tore off a low-hanging branch and swept out our tracks. This wasn't hard to do; no one had passed this way in some time.

Great, I thought, so what do we do now? Camp out in the woods? Eat marmots and bugs?

Angela got back in the car. She drove very slowly and used the parking lights.

"Excuse me," I said, "you mind sharing your thoughts with us? What are we doing now?"

"We're camping in the woods for a while. We're maybe eating bugs. That okay with you?"

"I don't like it," Columbine said, "it's real spooky in here."

"Just shut up," Angela said. "I need any help from the backseat crowd I'll let you know."

"Yeah," Angelo piped in, "just shut up like she said."

It was a small hunting shack, one room, maybe ten by ten, fifty yards down the twisting road. A rusted skillet hung on the wall. Sitting on a lopsided table was a burned-out coffeepot. In the corner was a three-legged chair. Two collapsed cots. Insects and animals had eaten the canvas and left the wood to rot. Shelves on the wall had held food at one time. The rusty circles of cans were still there.

Angelo had kicked in the sagging door, forgetting for the moment that someone had shot him in the leg. As soon as he remembered, he bit his lip and squeezed his eyes shut, and tears ran down his face.

"Dumb son of a bitch," Angela said, and Angelo limped off in a huff.

I looked at a wasp's nest just above the door. Yellow mud dauber, *Sceliphron coementarium.* Abdomen joined to thorax in the typical fashion of its kind. I pretended not to hear the DeMarco twins. They fought like cats and dogs, but you don't interfere with family quarrels. Families like to kill and maim their own, and they don't care for comments, or help from outside.

"Okay," Angela said, "here's the way it's going to be. We're here for the night. We'll get back on the highway when it's light."

She looked at me, then at Laurel, Daisy and Columbine. Laurel was standing by the hood, holding Daisy close. Columbine was sitting cross-legged on the ground. She had promised to throw up and she did. She was holding her head in her hands like she might have a go at it again.

"Sleeping arrangements. Moss, you and Laurel and Columbine in the house. Angelo'll be in the front seat of the car. Daisy'll stay in the back with me."

"Huh-unh, no way." Daisy looked alarmed. She pulled away from Laurel and shook her head. "I don't—I don't want to do that, I want to stay with her!"

"Daisy stays with me," Laurel said. She gave Angela a look. "What you want her with you for, Angela? What've you got in mind?"

Angela grinned. "You're kidding, right?" The grin faded fast. "Daisy stays with me so the rest of you behave. You want to run off and leave her, fine. But I'd be real pissed off at Daisy if you did."

"It's cold and it's going to get colder," I said, "we need to build a fire."

Angela's eyes went flat. "Don't you ever say 'fire' to me, Moss. I don't want to hear it. You want to say 'fire,' you say it to yourself. You say it to yourself, you better not be where I can hear. There's blankets in the trunk. Two girls and a guy, you can cuddle up nice. It'll be just like church camp, you can have a lot of fun."

"Goddamn, you are pushin' it, Angela . . ."

Laurel came at her, flailing her fists in the air. Angelo raised the shotgun, racked in a shell. Angela jerked the pistol from her belt, brought it up and aimed it at Laurel's head. Laurel stopped in her tracks. Angela swept the weapon around to me, then back to Laurel again.

"In the house. Now. Daisy, get your ass in the car."

Daisy whimpered. When Daisy whimpered, she sounded pitiful, like a newborn puppy. Laurel took her hand, walked her off behind the car, talked to her awhile and came back.

"I never liked you, Angela," she said. "I hope you realize that."

"Good," Angela said, "now haul it out of here."

Columbine dragged herself up and followed Laurel to the house. She still looked sick. I wasn't even sure she'd heard our dramatic interlude. If she did, she surely didn't care.

I started after them, and Angela called me back. "Not you, Moss, I want to talk to you."

I stood there and waited while she got more blankets from the trunk. Angelo sat on the porch. He had torn off one pant leg and wrapped it just below the knee. He looked like a short little kid who'd gotten in a playground fight with a lot of bigger guys.

"How's it holding up?" I said.

"Lead went through the calf. Lots of bleeding, but no big deal."

It had been a real big deal before, but I didn't mention that.

"Fine, I'm glad you're okay." I glanced over his shoulder to make sure his sister couldn't hear. "You want to tell me something, you want to tell me why I'm supposed to keep pretending we never met, I never saw you before, what the hell is this?"

Angelo looked right at me. "You never saw me before because you didn't, asshole."

"I didn't."

"That's right, you didn't. You remember that, okay?"

"You and me, we weren't down at the lake. We didn't see Rocco, we didn't see a bunch of meece."

"Moose. There ain't any such thing as meece, I fucking told you that before. And no, nothing ever happened like whatever you were saying, there, whatever that was. I'd keep that in mind if I was you."

"Fine. That's what I'll do."

"That's good. What that is, that's the smart thing to do. A guy, he knows the smart thing to do, he's going to be okay. You got it now, right?"

"Right. I think I got it now."

"That's fine. I'm glad you got it now." Angelo gave me a wink, picked up his shotgun, picked up himself and limped away.

I said, "I'd like you to know I'm sorry about the meece."

Angelo turned. "Huh? What'd you say?"

"It's not real pleasant to think about, but hey, we got to face life. Life is real and we've got to just look it in the eye sometimes. What you got back there, you got a herd of meeceburgers extra well done, you got meece chuck roast, you got meece barbecue—"

Angelo's eyes went wide. "Hey, you cut that out."

"—What you want to do, you want to think how they're up in meece heaven now. They're happy, they're doing just fine. Everybody's got silly looking legs, they got a big ugly snout. Their hair isn't burning, their eyes aren't falling out—"

Angelo started to shake. "They're—fine. They'd of took off in the lake, they're just *fine* . . ."

"Uh-huh, right."

I walked toward the woods and I didn't look back. Angelo came after me, thrashing through the brush, and I knew he had the shotgun in his little stubby hands, and a .45 concealed on his person somewhere.

"I've got some business to do down here," I called out, "you want to come and watch, that's fine. I wouldn't if I were you."

Angelo stopped. "They're all fine. They made it to the lake and they're—*fine!*"

"Hey," I said, "that's what you got to do, you got to hold the good thought. Put that bad stuff right out of your mind . . ."

23

"Moss? You talk to me, Moss. You hear me, you do it right now . . ."
I didn't answer, I kept perfectly still. Angela was twenty yards away up the hill. I was sitting on a rock behind a tree. I couldn't see her and she couldn't see me. She'd been there eight or ten seconds and her patience was wearing thin. When people don't do what she tells them to do, Angela tends to take offense.

It was no big surprise when light flashed through the trees and sound ripped the night. The first round clipped a branch high over-head and whined off in the woods. The second and the third dropped off to the right.

"Ten seconds," Angela called out. "Ten seconds, and then I'm cutting loose with random and erratic gunplay. It's dark and the odds are good I'll miss. But if fate steps in, we could have a tragic accident. You feeling lucky or what?"

"Where's your brother," I said, "is he anywhere close?"

"You're lucky I was here. Angelo was real intent on coming after you."

"I doubt he could make it. The terrain's not right for those wingtip shoes."

"Moss?"

"What?"

"What the fuck are you doing down there?"

"Come on down and look."

Angela muttered to herself. "That's dirty talk, and I won't put up with that. You coming up or not?"

"He's not coming down?"

"He's over by the car, and I've got the shotgun here. Goddamn it, it's been a long night, I am tired of talking to you."

"All right."

"All right, what?"

"All right, I'm coming up. Don't shoot, I'm completely unarmed."

"Well, hell, I guess I know that."

I went up slow. When the other party has a gun, slow is better than fast.

She was standing in the dark with the shotgun crooked in one arm. She held the pistol at her side, pointed at the ground.

"That was a real dumb trick. I want to know what you said set him off like that. I thought he was having a fatal heart attack."

"I told him he ought to quit using that greasy shit on his hair. I told him the girls don't go for that at all."

"You told him more than that."

"Listen, I was in mortal fear at the time. I don't remember what."

Angela looked as if she'd tasted something bad. "Move it, all right? Get over by the house."

She waved her pistol to show me the way. She was as weary as I was, as beat as everyone else. She walked with her shoulders in a slump, and the lines ran deep around her eyes and the corners of her mouth.

I looked past her to the car. Angelo was leaning on the hood, looking as mean as a guy like Angelo could. I thought I could see Daisy's shadow inside.

"What you want to scare her for?" I said. "Let her stay with Laurel, okay? You got all the guns, no one's going anywhere."

"How about you just shut the fuck up? How about I want some advice, you'll be the first to know?"

"You got it," I said. "Wiley Moss is here for you, though. Don't forget that. If I can help in any way."

"Jesus Christ," Angela said.

I was sitting on a log. She was sitting on a broken cane chair. The shotgun was propped against the chair, and the pistol was in her right hand, resting in her lap. No big surprise there; the surprise was she hadn't sent me right off to bed. She'd set me down and offered me a drink, a flask of good brandy she found in her jacket somewhere. All I could see was her pale white skin, the slash of her lips, a fleck of moonlight on her hair.

She looked real fine in the dark. No big deal, Angela looked terrific in the light.

Maybe romance was in the air, how would I know? I was unfamiliar with the mobster way of life. Maybe when a lady takes a shot at a guy, maybe that's a first date, you kind of take it from there. Or maybe she was way ahead on the brandy, and I was the only guy in town.

"I would really like to know what happened back there," I said, when we'd passed the flask around. "I'd like to know what that was all about. I don't mean to intrude, you understand. I'd like to know, right? But you don't want to get into this, you don't want to talk about it, fine."

"I don't want to talk about it."

"Fine."

"It's none of your business, Moss."

"Fine."

"And don't say that again."

"What?"

"Don't say *fine*. I don't want to hear it, I don't like *fine.*"

"All right."

"Good. *All right* I can handle. Don't say *fine.*"

"I'm not saying it."

"Good. Just don't say *fine*. I can't handle that." She took a deep slug of the brandy and passed the flask to me. It tasted like fire going down, and the warm spread everywhere. I watched her as our fingers touched, and I thought about going for the gun. A little geometry in the head. Two degrees right, carry your six. If I reached for the weapon and missed, she'd shoot me in the crotch. The bullet would go out my ass, and on through Idaho. It seemed like a bad idea.

"You can say it's not my business, Angela, but I can argue that it is. A bunch of people got killed back there, and most of them didn't know why. One of them could've been me."

"But it wasn't you, right? So what are you complaining about?"

"Like I said, a lot of those girls are dead, and they never had a chance to—"

"I *said* I don't want to talk about it, Moss. I have to fucking tell you again?"

"No. I guess not."

"I don't want to talk about it at *all.*"

"Okay."

"Okay."

Angela took another drink. I was used to the dark and I could almost see her eyes.

"Jesus, you saw what happened, why are you asking me? Vinnie's dead. That son of a bitch shot him, my brother is fucking *dead.*"

I looked at her. "That was a shot? It looked like a nuclear strike to me."

"Yeah, well Vinnie kept a lot of stuff in the cellar."

"What kind of stuff?"

"Stuff that—tends to explode." Angela closed one eye in thought. "Shotgun shells. 12-gauge and 16. Might've been some 17s and 18s, too. There was ammo for .32s, .38s, .44s and .45s. What else they make? Fifties? I think he had some .62s. He had a Henry and a Remington .22. He had a Winchester .44-40. An AK-47. A Colt .45. A Gatling gun. He had a Mauser and an Uzi and a Smith & Wesson that belonged to Jesse James. He had a Schmeisser and a Sharps. I know he had an M-1. He might've had an M-2. What he had was your basic hunting needs, that's what he had down there."

"Vinnie liked to hunt a lot?"

"He didn't hunt at all. What Vinnie didn't like, he didn't like to run out." Angela made a face. "Shoulda kept his fuckin' arsenal *up*stairs, maybe he'd have stopped Michael cold. Goddamn it, Moss, if I'd have been there with him—"

Angela stopped, stared at me as if she'd forgotten I was there. "This is none of your business." She looked at the flask, turned it upside down. "I don't want to talk to you."

"All right."

"Good. I don't like you, Moss, you aware of that? I don't like you, I don't want to talk to you at all, and I wasn't there because Vinnie changed his mind. Right? Vinnie said, 'Angel, go up and find Bobby and bring him back. Stop him and bring him back here.' I

said, 'Vinnie, stop him from doing what?' And he said, 'Go an' tell
Bobby not to set fire to the artist and the whore.' 'Jesus,' I said, 'are
you losing it, Vinnie, you're burning people up? What the fuck's the
matter with you?'

"Vinnie says, 'Hey, I got my reasons, go bring the fuckin' Indian
back.' "

"That tape he did of me and Zinnia, he might've been pissed
about that—"

Hold it, Wiley . . .

Only hold it won't cut it when you've blabbed it right out. I
could've kicked myself in the butt. I knew, from Angela's startled
look, that she didn't know what I was talking about, that she'd never
heard about any tapes at all.

You can't take anything back, you've got to live with what you've
got. Angela started going "What! What! What!" and nearly jumped
out of her chair, giving me that spooky lizard eye.

She still had the gun and she'd been drinking quite a bit, so I
gave her the story in abbreviated form, leaving out words that might
tend to alarm, words like "dumbfuck," "nutcase," "moron," and
the very abusive "potatohead," words that Michael used to describe
the DeMarco clan, plus Bobby, Rocco, Nix and others he considered
just short of gravel in the evolutionary plan.

Angela seemed to get the drift even in digest form, that Michael
did not respect Vinnie the way that Michael should. I added that I,
personally, did not share any of these feelings, and did not hold a
grudge against Vinnie, just because he'd kicked me a lot, and sent
Bobby Bad Eye to set me on fire.

"Michael never liked Vinnie," Angela said, "you don't have to
tell me that. He didn't like the DeMarcos because his father trusted
our old man more than he trusted anyone in the Galiano family,
even his own son. Michael never got over that. None of the Galiano
bastards did."

Angela looked past me. The dim light caught her face, and I saw
a glint of pain and anger in her eyes.

"Shit, I'll bet Vinnie knew, I'll bet somebody tipped him off that
Michael was coming back. He didn't send me off to stop Bobby, he
wanted me out of the way so I wouldn't get hit."

She paused, and stared at her hands. "When the shooting started,
I turned back to help. Angelo said we better go and get Bobby, like

Vinnie said to do. Which is bullshit, and Angelo knew it, Angelo was scared. He's been like that forever, he was chickenshit when we were kids.

"Okay, so maybe I'm holding back for Angelo, maybe I'm holding back for me. Vinnie's got five or six guys down there, Michael can't get to him as long as he's holed up in the house. If I go back, Angelo's going to go with me, I don't care if he's scared or not. Even if I drive down there we're not going to make it to the lodge, Michael's bunch is there and they're going to cut us off.

"What I'm thinking, I'm thinking Bobby's heard the shooting, Bobby's on the way back. Bobby can get through to Vinnie better than I can. Only, we don't run into Bobby, Bobby isn't on the road coming back. Where fucking Bobby is, his Jeep is parked under the trees, he is dumping out cans of gasoline, he is setting your trailer on fire, like nothing else is happening anywhere."

Angela patted her pockets, just to make sure there wasn't another bottle there. "I'm saying, I'm saying to myself, I'm saying, hey, maybe I'm slow, but I get this feeling that if Bobby's not headin' back to rescue Vinnie, he's got a good reason, okay? Like maybe the son-of-a-bitchin' Indian isn't working for the DeMarcos anymore."

"You mean Michael, he'd gone over to them?"

Angela looked pained. "What did I say? Did I say I'm thinking the son of a bitch isn't working for the DeMarcos anymore? Is this what I'm saying, you hear me saying this?"

"I think that's what you said."

"Right. This is what I said. I said, I think Bobby Bad Eye's found a position elsewhere. At which point I fire him on the spot, I rap him on the skull with this—" She slapped the barrel of her pistol into her open palm. "I don't know if I whacked him out or not. I'm hoping maybe not. I'm hoping he woke up in time to enjoy the fire."

"I thanked you for getting us out of there, Angela. You don't mind if I thank you again."

"Hey, don't bother." Angela shook her head. "I am still trying to figure that one out. Maybe I got a good gene from mamma, maybe I don't have any sense. Once you do a good deed, it's too late to take it back.

"Anyway, I sent Angelo up to check the roads, see if Michael had anybody else coming in. This is what I told him—what I did was send him off to get him out of the way, same as Vinnie did for me, so I could go and try to help Vinnie, and maybe shoot Michael in the ass. Ever since I was eight and Michael was twelve, this is what I want to do. Shoot Michael in the ass."

"I had two girlfriends when I was eight. This was back in Cincinnati. Mary Ellen Skimmertz wanted to be a model. Peggy Blutt, her best friend, wanted to be CEO of a major banking firm. Neither one did, as far as I know."

Angela gave me a puzzled look. "What do I care, Moss? Why do I give a shit?"

"I don't guess you do."

"Right. Get in the house with your floozies. We got a big day ahead."

"I've got a question. No, I've got two."

"I don't want to hear 'em."

"Why did Michael Galiano decide to go after Vinnie?"

"I told you. He didn't *like* Vinnie. Vinnie didn't like him."

"Okay, but why then? Why did he come and see Vinnie, *then* come back to do him in?"

"Ask him."

"What?"

"You run into Michael, ask him that."

"That doesn't sound like a good idea."

"Right. Get in the house. Stay there. Don't wander off."

Angela stood. I stayed where I was. "Why did Michael stop in the middle of a forest fire to chase the Spudettes? Does that make sense? I don't think it makes any sense at all."

Angela was gone and I was talking to the night. I looked at the car and saw a match flare up as Angelo lit a cigar. He was leaning on the hood. I could see his chubby little face and his little gecko eyes, then the match went out, and all I could see was an orange glow hanging in the air, maybe four-feet-nine, maybe five-feet-two . . .

24

" I hope you weren't worried," I said, "I'm not hurt at all, I'm just fine. What happened is, I had a talk with Angelo and he got sore and I ran down the hill. Then Angela took a few shots, but they all went over my head."

"Me and Columbine were watching out the door," Laurel said. "I bet her two dollars he'd blow your ass off. She said she didn't think he would."

"I'm glad I could furnish a little entertainment. There's not much to do around here."

"That's the damn truth."

Laurel sat cross-legged on her blanket. Columbine was sleeping, curled up a few feet away. Moonlight slipped through the boarded-up window. Columbine was wearing a T-shirt that came down to her thighs and it was clear there was nothing under that. The light turned her long legs a buttery shade of gold. I looked at her every chance I could, but I couldn't look much because Laurel would catch me every time I did.

"What you ought to do," Laurel said, "is leave those people alone, and spend your time thinking how to get us of here. I am worried sick about Daisy spending the night in that car. She is scared to death, Wiley. She won't sleep a wink, I'll tell you that."

"I don't think she'll come to any harm, I think she'll be fine."

"You do."

"Yes I do."

"You think she'll be fine."

"I think that's what I said. I think I said she'd—"

"Well I am greatly relieved to hear that, Wiley Moss, I cannot tell you what a weight you have taken off my mind. I think I'd be a fucking nervous wreck without your sage advice."

"Laurel—"

"No, I am *grateful,* all right? My tiny female mind is just drained of all worry and concern. Lord, it is such a blessing to have a great big ol' man tell you everything'll be all right."

"Okay."

"*Okay?* Okay what? Is *Daisy* okay? Am *I* okay? Am I going to get a minute of sleep, knowing my best friend is being—being bisexually fondled in the backseat of a car?"

"The word 'bisexual' implies that a person is—"

"I know what it implies, you Midwestern shit. You think a whore can't use a *Webster's Collegiate Dictionary?* What the hell you *think* they're doing in there?"

I could not for the life of me bring this vision to mind, Angelo and Angela sharing Daisy's charms, but I kept this opinion to myself. Contradicting Laurel was not the road to harmony and peace.

Instead, I lay down beside her, careful to avoid any carnal intent, any lusty advance, careful not to grab at any parts. Soon, this tactic paid off, and she snuggled in close and rested her head on my arm. Finally, she gave me a sisterly kiss, sniffed at my face, and looked up at the dark.

"I wish I had a date that'd buy me a drink. I guess I can't cut it any more."

"I don't think you're Angela's type. I don't know who that would be. Maybe Attila the Hun. Possibly Al Capone."

"I bet she likes Daisy. I bet she likes Daisy just fine."

"No she doesn't, Laurel. She's not after Daisy, get that out of your mind."

Laurel made another throaty sound that might have meant anything at all.

I heard some kind of bird, but I couldn't tell what. Just outside there was a common house cricket, *Acheta domesticus,* looking for romance. Getting laid in the insect world is very much like it is for us. Sometimes it's easy, and sometimes it's not.

I told Laurel everything Angela said to me, everything I could recall about Vinnie and Michael and Bobby Bad Eye, who did what to who and why. Laurel gave a snort now and then, little grunts and sounds that said anything Angela told me was likely a lie, that Angela could not be trusted, that, basically, Angela was full of shit.

"And you bought that, Wiley? That woman lies through her teeth, that woman is full of shit."

"I didn't say I bought it, I said that's what she said. I don't know what happened back there, I don't have any idea. Some of what she said makes sense, Laurel. Some of it could've happened like she said."

"Huh!" Laurel had an arsenal of *huhs!, hahs!* and other sounds of disbelief.

"So which is the part you like best? Tell me the part that makes *sense.*"

"I don't know if any of it does, I just said it might."

"Hah!"

"Quit saying that, please. That's a sound, Laurel, it doesn't mean anything at all."

"It does to me. It means a woman plies you with brandy, you don't much care who it is, you're going to buy anything she says."

"Oh, for Christ's sake . . ."

"Uh-huh. Right. That's a good answer, that tells me a lot. What else you all do on your date, she let you get in her—"

She felt me moving and tried to get away, but I rolled over quickly and grabbed her by the shoulders and pinned her back down.

"Listen," I said, "I'll tell you again, you try and get it right. I don't know if Angela's full of shit or not. If she isn't full, she's likely halfway to the top. Someone's got a gun, they can tell you most anything they like."

"Someone's holding me against my will doesn't have my complete attention, Moss."

"Oh my God, look at me." I jerked my hands away and let her go. "Some evil force overcame me, Laurel, I completely lost my head. I've been fighting that bondage shit all my life. It started out with magazines . . ."

Laurel tried not to laugh. "Hon, I'd say we are both overwrought, okay?" She brushed her head against my chest. "You think we could lie back down?"

"Good," I said, "that's what we ought to do."

She scooted up in my arms again, and slid one leg over mine.

"You and me do better horizontal, Wiley Moss, you ever notice that?"

"Once or twice, yes."

"It might be we lack a certain depth. Sometimes that works out fine."

"Sometimes it does. There's a lot to be said for a shallow relationship. You got enough shallow, you avoid a lot of problems in life."

I looked at her from half an inch away. I could smell her warm breath, I could see a strip of light across her mouth. She moved and the light kissed her eyes. This seemed a good idea, and I kissed her eyes twice.

"I meant exactly what I said, Laurel. I hope I made that real clear. I don't know if anything Angela said is true. What I think, is, there's likely a lot that Angela doesn't know herself, stuff she thinks she knows—and maybe that's mixed up with the stuff she made up.

"And you know what bothers me a lot? If all or even some of this came out of Angela's head, she drank more brandy than I thought. You know what I mean? Would you try to sell me a story like that? Michael Galiano shows up to hit Vinnie. Bobby, Vinnie's right-hand goon, happens to be away from the house, setting fire to *us*. And hey, guess what? Angela's not at home, either. She and her ugly twin are out looking for Bobby Bad Eye. It's like there's a director on the sidelines somewhere, right? He's telling the actors what to do, showing the cameras where to go. That, and before the show begins, Rocco and Nix hit the dust in a rash of *hunting* accidents.

"And Michael, Michael's got a forest fire climbing up his ass, but Michael doesn't care, Michael's out chasing Spudettes. My God, Laurel, who wrote this shit?"

"I don't know, but I wish I wasn't in it. I'd just as soon be Julia Roberts, and you're this stud millionaire comes into town and buys me clothes and stuff."

Laurel reached over and pressed a finger to my lips. "There isn't any use talking, babe. I don't see it's going to do us any good to guess about stuff we don't know anything about. I am worn to a nub and I expect you are too."

"Yeah, right. Like I'm going to drop off to sleep here in the Idaho Holiday Inn."

"If you can't go to sleep, just lie there and close your eyes."

"You're not my real mother. I don't have to listen to you."

"No, but you have to shut up, you have to do that."

"If I had some kind of incentive—"

"Wiley Moss!" She reached out and slapped my hand away. "You ought to be ashamed. We are not by ourselves in here."

I had a comment on that, but I kept it to myself.

I think I maybe slept, but I didn't sleep long. The tail-end of a sound was still there when I opened up my eyes. A coon, maybe, or a herd of marmots outside. A covey of meece, or possibly a single Angelo.

I couldn't get Angela off my mind. Laurel was right. We could talk all night and still not know if anything—or everything—Angela said was true. And if it wasn't, what the hell was? What really *did* happen out there?

When Laurel's breath was slow and even, I eased my arm from under her head. It was numb, of course, completely paralyzed. No big deal, the American male is used to that. None of us grow into manhood without a bad case of gangrene. I remembered those agonizing dates in ninth grade with Sarah Lutt. I would spend the first feature snaking an arm around her seat, and you didn't dare move it after that. Move a hair, move an inch, make a try for the mythic Lutt breasts and Burt, Bud and Biggo Lutt would hear about it and kick you in the nuts.

Columbine moaned in her sleep. I turned to take a look and my heart skipped a beat. That T-shirt had worked its way up to her waist, and those extra-fine legs and that silky hipbone were caught in the happy moonlight. And oh, my Lord, there was the cutest caterpillar inching up Columbine's tummy, making its way up the road from Wonderland.

Columbine opened up one sleepy eye and gave me a lazy little smile, and said, "Hi there, Wiley Moss."

And I said, "Hi there, Columbine."

Laurel said, "I'd think real hard about this if I was you."

I rolled back over and she was looking at me in the dark, and her blue eyes didn't blink at all.

"There isn't any reason I can't say hello to someone, without you getting uptight."

"Yeah, there is, hon, I can think of eight or ten. You like me to write 'em down?"

"No, I wouldn't," I said, "and I don't feel a person should sound like they're asleep if they're not."

Laurel reached out and poked me in the chest. "You want to answer me something? Just what in hell do you imagine that woman's got between her legs I haven't got between mine? They are *all* the same, Wiley. With minor, nearly indistinct differences, they are all just exactly alike."

"I know that."

"Huh-unh. I don't think you do. I'd be real surprised if you did."

She turned over then and went to sleep, or it seemed as if she did. And I knew that she was right, that female equipment was very much alike on a universal scale, that I couldn't argue that. But I also knew there was no way to really be sure, to be absolutely perfectly sure, without a thorough program of research, a long-term study on a very extensive scale, a program that starts off with minor revelations like a cold numb arm around the lovely Sarah Lutt, and continues, if you're lucky, till you're dead.

And I made a mental note to ask her the question that men ask women all the time—the one where they get this real vacant look and a silly little smile, and say, "It doesn't matter, hon, about size or shape, or silly stuff like that, all men are pretty much alike, and you're fine the way you are."

So if she's going to lie, and you *know* this is what she's going to do, then why in hell shouldn't I?

25

When I woke, the room was thick with morning shadow. An inch from my nose, a column of ants marched up the wooden wall. They might have been red but they could have been black. It was too dark to tell what kind.

Laurel and Columbine were dead to the world, curled up in tight little balls against the chill dawn air. I couldn't see any private parts, so I got up and went outside.

The sun was runny-egg yellow behind the trees, and the sky was an ugly shade of bruise. The beat-up, scorch-bubble bullet-hole Lincoln was gone. In its place was a '93 Buick Skylark, possibly maroon, with Arizona plates. On the hood there were franchise sacks from McDonalds, KFC, Taco Bell and a local barbecue.

I could smell this feast from thirty feet away. The various families of grease were nearly visible in the air—vile, rancid, gamy and stale. This topped off with evil tomatoes, lettuce long-deceased, the bouquet of mayo, 1968. The reek of burned meat and primeval fries.

My body was confused. Juices flowed up, but they also flowed down. I hadn't eaten anything at all in some time. The food smelled awful, the food smelled fine. Your mind is a fussy eater. Your stomach, however, has all the taste of a barnyard swine.

"Dig in, Moss. Breakfast's on the house, courtesy of me. You need anything, there's mouthwash and toilet paper in the car."

I hadn't seen her when I walked out on the porch. She was leaning up against the house, legs crossed at the ankles, arms across her chest. This is the way you're supposed to lean when you're leaning out West.

"I'd stay out of food service," I said. "That isn't what your average diner likes to hear."

"Oh, yeah?" Angela grinned, raised her shades and showed me her frosty lizard eyes. "You don't like the menu, Moss, you can sniff around for bugs, you can chase a fucking bear."

"The menu's just fine. Mother used to cook like this all the time."

"I'm glad to hear that. I am greatly relieved. Because if you weren't happy, Moss, I'd have to go back and get you something else."

You could say she was in rare form, but for Angela, it wasn't rare at all.

I walked to the car, and I could feel her eyes on my back. It was flat irritating that she looked so fine. The rest of us were grubby, unkempt and bleary-eyed. We had bad breath and we reeked of smoke and sweat. Angela had clearly been to town, or at least a country store. She had cleaned herself up, bought new clothes and abandoned her derelict car. She looked slick and lean and tall. Foxy little nose and shiny midnight hair that flowed down her shoulders like a dark waterfall. New red blouse and new skintight jeans. And, sometime during the night, I suspected she'd eaten a very nice meal— the kind that comes on a plate, instead of a greasy paper sack.

I swallowed my pride, then swallowed a Big Mac whole. On the ground was a Styrofoam chest full of ice, Pepsis, Cokes, Sprites and Big Reds. I looked on the ground then searched the hood again for what I clearly couldn't see.

"No coffee, right?"

"Coffee's not good for you, Moss."

"Now I didn't know that."

"See, that's something you didn't know, now you know that. Life is a learning experience, Moss. This is how we grow and enhance our daily lives."

I reached down in the cold water and pulled out a Sprite.

"Where's Daisy? I don't see her in the car."

"Daisy's not in the car."

"That's what I said, Angela, Daisy's not in the car."

"Over there." She nodded toward the trees by the road. "She's got a coupla blankets, she's sleeping just fine."

"So where's Angelo?"

"Angelo's around."

"And where might that be?"

Angela gave me a look. "You're getting on my nerves a little, Moss. Finish up your breakfast, go and sit down."

I didn't want to sit. I drank my Sprite and got another and walked around the car. I looked at the tires. They weren't real old and they weren't real new. A few little dents in the fenders, a hubcap from some other car. I walked around the back. Without bending down, I could see that the screws that held the plates were red with rust, but the metal was shiny inside the grooves themselves. Someone had taken the old plates off, and then put the new ones on. I was pleased with this nice piece of work. If you watch the cop shows, you can learn to do this kind of thing yourself.

So Angela left us in the night, ditched the death car and stole one she liked. I remembered something Zinnia had said, that Angela liked to steal a lot—which was why they shipped her off to Idaho with Vinnie and Angelo.

Angela was watching me, she hadn't really stopped. She still looked lovely, but she couldn't help that. Beauty's not even skin deep, it's not even deep as that. It's about mascara and makeup deep is what it is. You can see a woman with a cheerleader smile, a woman who changes her underwear. This woman could be cunning as a snake, she could have a shitty outlook on life.

I folded up my Sprite in one hand. It's always good to know you can still crush aluminum cans.

"I want to talk to you," I said, and took a few steps toward the house. "I won't take much of your time."

"Forget it. I don't want to talk to you." Angela slid her hand to the butt of the gun in her belt. "What I want you to do, I want you to hold it right there."

I stopped. It seemed the right thing to do.

"Fine. Okay. Not another word out of me. Just let me say this. We talked about a great many things last night. I want to thank you for the brandy, it was nice of you to share. What we didn't talk about is now. I was brought to Idaho against my will. Since then I have been caught up in your personal family strife, and you can't say that's any fault of mine.

"You saved my life and I'm grateful for that. Fine, I'm thinking, it's over, I'm out of this shit. Only now I see I'm not. I'm still being held against my will, and so are Laurel, Daisy and Columbine. I'm not going to ask you why, that's an intrusion on your personal life. I don't *care* why, okay? Whatever's happened here or at the lodge, I'll be glad to put it out of my mind. There. It's gone. It's out of my head right now. What I'd like you to do is let us off somewhere. A couple of bucks for the bus would be nice. Okay, never mind the bus fare, fine. We can walk, there's no problem there. Let's put all this behind us and get on with our lives."

Angela looked at me. "You through, that's it?"

"Yes, I am."

"Good. Go sit down."

"I beg your pardon?"

"Go sit down, Moss, and don't fucking talk to me again."

Angela turned and walked off. She walked down the road a few yards, then Angelo stepped out of the brush. Angelo looked rumpled but he'd washed his face and shaved. He held the shotgun loosely in his arm, and listened while Angela talked.

"That was a real fine speech, Wiley Moss. Darrel Joe Murk won the civics prize in fifth grade, and he wasn't half as good as that."

Columbine was standing beside me looking sleepy and tall, running her hands through her hair. I like it when a woman does that.

"I don't think it did a lot of good, but I thought I'd give it a try."

"Angela's real hard to please. I guess you've noticed that."

Yes, I told her, I certainly had. I looked past Columbine then and movement caught my eye. Laurel appeared, and I knew she'd been standing there, just inside the door.

"Hi," I said, "you sleep okay? I don't guess anybody did. Stay away from the food if you can. It's not real—"

Laurel gave me a chilling look, jerked her head around so fast that her hair whipped the air. She clenched her fists at her sides and stalked off toward the road, toward Daisy's grove of trees.

"What'd *I* do? Every time I start talking, everybody walks off."

"Well you got bad breath, but I guess we all do." Columbine laid a hand on my arm and gave me a weary smile. "Laurel is real concerned, Wiley Moss. She's got a lot on her mind right now."

"Yeah, well so do I." I looked at Columbine. "You don't mind me asking, you think *she* thinks there's something going on with you and me?"

Columbine grinned. "Is there? What do you think it might be?"

"Eat a taco if you have to. That barbecue smells funny to me."

I left her and walked through the brush toward Daisy and Laurel. Possibly a bad idea, but there's nothing new in that. Angela looked up once, then went on talking to her very lovely twin.

"Hi, Wiley, you doin' okay, hon?" Daisy tried her best to show me a cheery smile. She had sleep creases in her face, and leaves stuck in her tangled hair.

"Hi, Daisy. Laurel, can I talk to you?"

"No. Get out of here."

"Laurel!" Daisy bit her lip. "That is not nice at all!"

Laurel rolled her eyes. She stood and walked off and leaned against a tree. She didn't look at me.

"What is it, Moss? I got things to do."

"What? You got to take a squirrel count, you all tied up with that? What the hell's the matter with you?"

"What is the matter with *you*, Moss?" Laurel's blue eyes turned black. "Standin' there asking that bitch why she doesn't let us go. My God, I think you've lost your mind!"

"Listen," I said, "I am not entirely dense. I didn't think I'd get far, I didn't feel she'd fall for that, but I figured I ought to try."

"Uh-huh. Right. You sure did fine."

"Laurel, we both know what's in Angela's head." I moved in front of her a little so Daisy couldn't read my face. "There's Rocco and Nix and that little mob war back there. I didn't see any reason to not bring it out. She knows it and we know it too. I wanted to try and work it out."

"Jesus, Wiley." Laurel stared at me, less anger in her eyes than pain and despair. "She isn't going to work anything *out.* Why do you think I been carrying on about getting us out of here? That's the only way we're going to be around for the new fall shows."

"I don't think so. I don't think Angela wants to do that. I think all she wants to do is put a lot of miles between herself and Michael Galiano."

"You don't think she'll do what?"

"Huh? What are we talking about?"

"You don't think she'll do what? Say it. Say it out loud, Wiley Moss."

"I don't think she'd—do that."

"Whack us out."

"Yeah, that."

"She wouldn't. He would."

"Who, Angelo?"

"Angelo's a wuss. But he'll do anything his sister tells him to."

I looked past Laurel. The woods were getting brighter. The sun was rising up above the trees, and I thought my breakfast might be rising up too.

"Okay. Let's not walk around it. If she's going to do something, how come we're still here? How come we're camping out, she's filling us with junk food, why's she doing that? See, this is what I'm thinking, what I'm thinking is, if she's going to do something, how about here? This is a real good place, you ask me."

Laurel took a breath and looked away. "I can't answer that, Wiley. I really don't know. I don't have any idea."

"Okay. Then I don't see why you can't—"

I stopped, then, saw that distant gaze, that faraway stare, that moony, slack-eyed, totally deliberate look that said "pay no attention to me, I am not even here . . ."

It hit me right between the eyes, shook me down to my knees. I grabbed her shoulders and shook her hard. I shook her till her eyes bugged out.

"Goddamn it, you are doing it to me, Laurel. You have done it to me from the start and you are doing it to me again!"

"Wiley . . ." Laurel shook her head and tried to break free. "Wiley, you let me go, you stop doing that!"

"You said the same thing. You said it three times. 'I can't answer, I don't know, I don't have any idea.' You did it to me before. You say the same thing three times, you are telling an outright lie. That's a verified fact, everybody knows that. You are—"

The thing I was looking for rose up where I could see it, rose up and took my breath away. I stared at Laurel and my heart nearly stopped.

"Oh my God, you know, don't you? You *know* what Angela's up to, *you know what's happening here!*"

Laurel opened her mouth, but nothing came out. It didn't have to. The answer was there, I could see it in her eyes.

"Okay," Angela yelled, "ten minutes, everybody, we're moving

out of here. You gotta do your business, girls to me, boys to Angelo.
I guess that's you, Wiley Moss."

Laurel broke free. I didn't even watch her go. The thought of
performing a physical act with Angelo lurking nearby, swept every
other thought from my mind . . .

26

No one had very much to say.

Daisy sniffed and Laurel said, "There, there, hon," and Columbine went to sleep again.

Laurel sat on one side, and I sat on the other. This was as far away from me as she could get. If I couldn't trust her, fine, she would never speak to me again. I had caught her and she knew it. We had done this before and we were doing it again.

I watched the lovely scenery go by. The signs said 93 South. The Salmon River was on the right. There were mountains, trees and high, white clouds. Postcards everywhere you looked. We passed a little town called Ellis in a second and a half.

Columbine opened her eyes and said, "Listen, y'all, maybe we could sing? I find a songfest passes the time real well."

"Forget it," Angela said.

"Well why not? What is wrong with that?"

"I said forget it. Shut the fuck up."

That took care of that. We didn't get to sing, but we all understood that life isn't fair for everyone.

"Sportsmen go for steelhead on the Salmon River," Daisy said. "The steelhead population's made a nice comeback in recent years. Whitewater trips are available as well. It's real exciting, I hear."

"I'll bet," I said.

"They call the Salmon the 'River of No Return.'"

"Why's that?"

"Now I don't really know. I guess you maybe get there and can't get back again."

"I'd think twice about a trip like that."

The car was fine if you liked four people in the back. There is little demand for backseats in this wonderful country of ours. Even the welfare folk have their very own cars. If I was a cop, I'd stop anyone who had people in the back. A guy's got people in the back, the guy's going to rob a bank, he's going to hit a jewelry store.

Angelo drove. Angela sat with her back against the passenger door, the shotgun resting in her lap. She had the A/C on high, and a window down besides. This was because we smelled worse than we had the night before—everyone but Angela, of course. Everyone smelled like wood-smoke and sweat. There were feet and body odors, odors of tacos and Macs. One of us, I couldn't say who, was punishing the others with a silent but deadly attack. At this rate, I thought, it wouldn't take long for us to smell like a bus.

"Somebody let one in here," Angelo said. "It better not happen again."

I said, "How do we know it isn't you?"

" 'Cause I been taught better, that's why. You're supposed to hold it till you can safely release it somewhere."

"I never heard you were supposed to hold it, I didn't know that."

"Jesus, where'd you grow up?"

"Defiance County, Ohio. We were outdoors a lot, so it didn't really matter if you held it or not."

Angelo shook his head. "I never heard of that. I never heard of anyplace you weren't supposed to hold it back."

"You can't see it now, but directly back northwest? That's Taylor Mountain, 9,690 feet tall."

"Daisy, shut the fuck up," Angela said.

The town we stopped in was Challis. Home of the North Custer Historical Museum of Indian, ranching and mining artifacts, the

Challis National Forest, and somebody's restaurant out on the edge of town.

Laurel, Columbine, Daisy and I didn't get to go in. Angela and Angelo did. We were guided, one at a time, to the restrooms behind the place and back, and the twins had pistols in their belts at all times. I didn't think they'd shoot us with tourists all about, but there's only one way to find out.

There were plates from many states. There were bumper stickers on many of the RVs and cars. One said: I'VE BEEN TO BOISE AND BACK. Another said: I ♥ POTATOES.

One, on a '93 Aerostar van, read: ASK ME ABOUT VLAD THE IMPALER.

I wanted to wait and get a look at the driver, but Angelo wouldn't buy that.

The sign outside said: KC—SIRLOIN—NY STRIP. What we got in the car were burgers and fries, bad iced tea, and our choice of a Hershey's with almonds or without.

"Wiley, what you got to do is get their guns," Laurel said. "That's the only chance we've got. Grab their guns and drive them somewhere and dump 'em out."

I hesitated, hamburger poised, iced tea balanced in my lap.

"Are we speaking again? Am I to understand that?"

"No, we're not speaking again, I am *talking* to you, Wiley Moss. We are sure not speaking, and don't you even think about that."

"Okay."

"Well, are you going to do it?"

"Do what?"

"What was I talking about? You got to get their guns. She gets back here you got to take her, Moss. You got to wrench that thing away, take her unawares."

"Oh, Jesus!" Daisy moaned and covered up her face.

"Stop it," Laurel told her, "that isn't going to help. Moss, I know an Oriental hold Zinnia showed me one time. Do it just right and the victim's paralyzed for life. Me an' Daisy'll grab Angelo while you get the bitch unarmed."

"You've got a little dab of mayo, babe, right there," Columbine said. She touched a finger to my lips, then gently stuck it in her mouth.

"I don't think that's real important right now, you don't mind."
Laurel gave Columbine a chilling look. Columbine fed me a fry.

"I haven't been sitting here counting the trees," I said. "I've
thought a whole lot about what you're talking about. Any way you
cut it, someone's going to hurt, and very likely killed. She never takes
her eyes off me, Laurel. You know what that weapon'd do back here?
It'd be real ugly, that's what. There'll be a better time. We're going
to have to wait for that."

"When'll that be? When they line us up against a fucking wall?"

"God, Laurel, don't *say* that!" Daisy broke into tears, and Laurel
said, "There, there, hon," and we were pretty much back to step
one.

I never did see the driver with the odd bumper sticker on his van.
For a while, I watched Angelo DeMarco lean against the hood. He
had a pistol in his belt and a jacket over that. While we were stopped,
the shotgun stayed in the trunk.

The sun beat down on Angelo's nearly bald head, turning it a
strawberry red. Hair oil trickled down his neck in an oily little stream.
Rivulets of sweat joined in, and the River of No Return flowed to
Dirty Collar Land.

Another thing I saw while I watched was Angela on the phone.
There were pay phones attached to the restaurant's outside wall.
Angela would stay inside, in there with the nice A/C, then she'd
come out and try her call again. She tried it eight times. She was
getting irritated, something that she did extremely well. Meanwhile,
Angelo was steaming, drowning in his juices in the Idaho sun.

Finally, Angela got her call through. She walked back to the car,
a spring in her step, a little smile on her face, a little smirk, a little
grin, a nasty little simper, possibly a sneer. Whatever it was, I didn't
care for it at all. Angela angry is one thing. Angela happy is something
else again.

Highway 93 turned into 75. Somewhere between Clayton and
Sunbeam, Daisy informed me that the Salmon River had hooked off
to the south. She showed me Castle Peak, altitude 11,820 feet. I

told her I could see it just fine, which wasn't true at all. Every mountain looked the same to me.

I laid my head on Columbine's breast and nodded off to sleep. First, I looked down her collar just to kind of check her out.

I dreamed I had a date with Laurel, Sharon Stone and the lovely Claire de Mer. We were in a chic restaurant somewhere in D.C. The theme of the place was Billy's Gas & Auto Repair. We all ordered steaks. They brought us potatoes instead. The waiter was Nix. Someone shot him in the head, and Nix and potatoes were scattered everywhere. Daisy started bawling and she wasn't even there.

When I woke up again we were somewhere else, which looked like everywhere we'd been. Mountains, trees, sky and lots of air.

"Hey, where are we?"

"Almost there," Angela said.

"And where would that be?"

"None of your business, Moss. Sit back. Shut the fuck up. Go back to sleep."

I don't know what happened but it did . . .

Maybe I didn't want to shut the fuck up, maybe I was tired of doing that . . . maybe I was pissed at not getting any steak . . . maybe I shouldn't eat Hershey bars with nuts . . . whatever it was, I simply didn't give a shit, something snapped, something flipped, something went off like a bomb inside my head . . .

I stared past Angela DeMarco with a horrid, stricken look, a look of unadulterated fear, the kind when you're having a cardiac attack, the kind of look you get when Godzilla's stomping Tokyo flat . . . I looked past Angela and tore at my hair and yelled *"OH MY GOD, WHAT'S THAT!"*

What happens, then, you catch the other person off guard, they turn around and look and you take them unawares, you grab their weapon and then you knock 'em flat.

This is your standard "Look Behind You" ploy. It's based on simple human nature, the fact that very few of us really have a good reaction time. And, nine times out of ten, this is just what happens, it goes down exactly like that . . .

27

What you want to do if you possibly can, you want to get hit in a different place than the place where they hit you once before. This isn't what I did, but I would have if I could.

Laurel said, "How you feeling, Wiley, you doing okay?"

And I said, "Feel . . . lye . . . shid, how'you?"

There was that familiar cold rag and the water running down into my eyes. It felt bad and good and I pushed her hand away. Tried to sit up and then fell back again.

"God, Laurel, what did she hit me with, a semi-truck?"

"She hit you with that 12-gauge, hon. You went down like a rock. You been out for some time."

I shut my eyes against the pain, pressed my hands flat and forced myself to sit. Everything ached, every muscle, every tendon, every joint. Everything hurt real bad. I felt as if I might have been folded up twice and stuffed inside a trunk.

"I expect you're kinda sore," Laurel said. "Angelo stuffed you in the trunk."

"Whoever owned that Buick had dogs. They must've kept dogs back there."

"I wouldn't think they'd do that," Laurel said. "You lock up a dog in there, that dog couldn't breathe at all."

"You're right, they probably wouldn't do that."

I was laying on a bed. Laurel was sitting by my side. A semi-bare room with powder-blue walls, a water-spot ceiling overhead. I could see a lamp and a chair. A battered chest of drawers. A primal TV with rabbit ears and several pounds of foil. Everything there had been scorned by Goodwill.

"Okay, I'll say it. Where the hell am I, what are we doing here?"

Laurel leaned over and kissed me on the cheek. Her hair smelled clean and I knew she'd found a tub.

"We're upstairs at Tommy Gee's, hon. That's north of Ketchum, I don't know how far. The room isn't big but we got our own bath."

"Tommy Gee's. And what's that?"

"It's just a place, Wiley."

"What kind of place?"

Laurel stood up. "I'm running you a nice hot bath. You get in and soak, you're going to feel fine. I got your clothes in the washer downstairs."

"Laurel . . ."

Laurel was up and gone. I sat on the bed and let everything throb then I made myself stand. Nausea knocked me down again. The second time I didn't hardly fall. I seemed to be naked. I hadn't noticed that. A window was above the chest of drawers, but it was permanently shut. The glass was painted black. I looked inside the chest. The drawer was lined with papers from Boise and Idaho Falls. I noticed that Ike had been elected president.

In the bottom drawer, I found half a pack of matches. The cover was Day-Glo pink. Cursive silver type read:

TOMMY GEE'S TOTALLY NUDE
DOMINO PARLOR
& FAMILY ENTERTAINMENT
PARK

I tried hard to think about that. I couldn't bring anything to mind. I turned the cover over and inspected the other side. No phone number, no address. It simply said:

"IF YOU FOUND US
BE SURE AND COME AGAIN"

I put the matches back in the drawer. Steam was coming from under the bathroom door, and I walked my poor body to the tub.

"I would've told you," she said, "you didn't have to go snoopin' around, Wiley Moss, there wasn't any call for that."

"I didn't snoop around. I found some matches in a drawer. Finding something, that's not the same as snooping, something's just laying around."

She sat on the edge of the tub. We had fried chicken and a local brand of beer. Laurel looked slick and tan in her clean cutoffs, cut off up to here. Her hair was fine as spider silk, fine as fairy gold.

"What it is, it's a domino parlor, just like it says. That's exactly what it is."

"Guys play dominoes."

"Right. They play dominoes, they play Forty-Two sometimes."

"They play dominoes with totally naked girls."

"No, they do not."

"They don't."

"You can watch the girls dance, but if you want 'em to play, now that's an extra charge."

"A naked girl comes over, you play dominoes."

Laurel looked pained. "Is that what I said? Is your hearing okay, is that what I said? You want a chicken leg? I got a leg and a breast."

"I'll take the breast. I like the white meat, I don't like the dark. When I was a kid, the grown-ups told us the dark meat was best, that they saved it for the children, they wouldn't keep any for themselves. I didn't fall for that shit, but I still got the rear end and the thigh. Who's Tommy Gee?"

"I was awful proud of you, babe. That was a real brave thing to do."

"No, it wasn't, Laurel. What it was was real dumb."

She leaned down and granted me another greasy kiss. "You tried, Wiley Moss. You tried, and that's what counts."

"Huh-unh. Something doesn't work, you don't say it counts. Why does it count? Something doesn't work, it doesn't count, it doesn't count at all."

"So when do you think you'll try again?"

"What?" I dropped my chicken in the tub. "What are we talking about? I hope we're not talking what I think we're talking about."

"You got to try, Wiley. You got to get us *out* of here."

"I did try, Laurel. You asked me to do it and I did. It didn't work out too good, as far as I can tell. I got hit hard. I was dumped in a trunk where a bunch of dogs had been."

"You don't know that. You don't know there were dogs back there."

I sat up in the tub. I fished the chicken out and threw it on the floor. "You want to help get us out of here? Fine. Quit playing games with me, Laurel. Play it straight and tell me what you know about this mess. Let's start off with the fat guy, right? And don't bother making something up, because I'll know it if you do."

I could hear the gears turning, hear the whirring in her head. I could see the shifty cast in her baby-blue eyes as she spun me a whopper, a big fat lie, a bedtime story for the mentally impaired.

"Don't," I told her, "don't even think about it. You are not going to do this to me, so don't even try."

She looked at me a very long time. She seemed very sad and very tired. Her shoulders slumped. She looked as if someone had punctured her balloon and let the air out.

"I have not been totally honest with you, hon, I guess you know that. I did not lie simply to deceive. That is not my nature, my mamma didn't raise me like that. I hid the truth because I was scared for Daisy's life."

"This is about the fat guy, right?"

Laurel didn't answer. She ran a hand across her eyes. "Daisy— Daisy's sweet as she can be and she's my very best friend, but Daisy's . . . I'm looking for a word so you'll see what I'm trying to say. Daisy is—Daisy is *dumb*, Wiley. That's the word I'm searching for, dumb. Daisy is flat-out dumb."

My fingers were wrinkled and the water in the tub was getting cold. My parts were retreating back into the Bat Cave, looking for a place to keep warm. Still, I didn't dare move. If I moved, I was sure I would snap Laurel's tenuous thread to reality and ordinary life.

"Rocco had a thing for Daisy. It wasn't two ways, she couldn't *stand* him. He'd been driving her nuts for some time."

"When I first got here," I said, "she wanted to go back to her trailer. Rocco made her stay in the car and go with him."

"The staff's not supposed to mess with the girls, but you can guess how much they worried 'bout *that*. If pussy's free and a man don't have to walk far, isn't nothing going to keep him away too long. Daisy never complained. Rocco was a son of a bitch, and she knew what he'd do if she did.

"Rocco got around quite a bit, because Bobby had stuff for him to do. Stuff Bobby Bad Eye was doing for Vinnie, or maybe for himself some, too. Rocco came back from Tucson or Denver, I don't remember which. He brought a bunch of pictures and a stack of videos. He put on the videos and made Daisy watch, and Jesus, they must've been bad because they just about flipped Daisy out. He'd done this before but this time the stuff was really sick. It wasn't a film like you rent—someone had shot it in a bedroom or in a hotel. Daisy said she hadn't even *heard* of anything like that, and Daisy's seen some pretty kinky shit in her time."

"She didn't tell you what?"

"Lord, no." Laurel made a little shiver with her shoulders, a gesture that told me a lot. "She'd have bad dreams and wake up scared and wouldn't sleep again all night.

"Maybe it all would've worked itself out if Daisy hadn't done what she did. Here's where the dumb comes in, okay? Daisy was so scared of Rocco she figured she'd *protect* herself by taking something of his and hiding it somewhere. Boy, is this a good idea or what? This is a *bad* idea, this is what it is. She was afraid to steal a video because he only had three or four. So she took a couple of black-and-white pictures, thinking how he's got lots of these."

Laurel rolled her eyes. "She showed me one of the shots and I 'bout threw up. There were men dressed up like women, and women dressed up like men. There were some that I couldn't tell which. In one of the shots, there was a South American mammal I could not identify.

"One of these guys . . . okay, one of these guys is the fat guy you're always nagging me about. Only when I *see* this guy I almost drop my teeth, because he isn't just a guy, he's a really famous guy, a guy you've seen on the cover of *Time,* you've seen him everywhere.

"Daisy doesn't notice this, of course—a national figure to Daisy is Barney or Mr. Spock. But I knew who he was all right, and I'm thinking, holy shit, Daisy, you don't want to get tangled up with this dude, hon."

I waited. Laurel picked something off her lip and gave it a critical eye.

"Okay, so?"

"So what?"

"So who *is* the guy, who is the *fat guy*, Laurel, you didn't say who the fat guy is."

Laurel looked pained. "Well of course I didn't, Wiley, I can't tell you that."

"Why the hell not?"

"Because I can't, that's all. I'd be breaking a confidence, if I did. I mean, you and me are one, in a shallow sort of way, we got an immoral thing going that binds us pretty close. But let's face it, hon, under duress you'd likely spill everything you know. And no one'd blame you if you did."

I stared at Laurel. "That's it, you think you're going to stop right there, this is all I get to hear? Huh-unh, no way, you can't do that, you can't just tell a person something, you get to the part that really counts and you stop right there."

"Why not?"

"Because you can't, that's all. You're not telling me anything, Laurel, you've left about everything out. Did Rocco *know* she'd stolen the pictures, did he ever find out? Does this have something to do with Rocco turning up dead? When did all this happen, how long before I got here? See, everything you've said, you haven't said a thing."

"I told you it's a confidence, hon. I've likely said too much as it is."

"No, goddamn it, you haven't done that, you have *never* done that. What you've done, what you always do, is leave me in the fucking middle somewhere, and I'm getting tired of that. Rocco's dead, all right? But Daisy's still scared. Daisy's got pictures of the fat guy with a mammal, and the fat guy shows up in Michael Galiano's car. You see the fat guy and *you* start freaking out. There's a big mob fight and Michael is chasing Spudettes. I want some answers, Laurel, and I want them right now. And don't you try that vow of secrecy shit, I am not buying that."

Laurel leaned over and looked in the tub. "Lord, Wiley, did you know your genital parts have completely disappeared somewhere?"

"Never mind that. It's cold in here, and my parts'll come back."

"I hope you're right, hon. And you be sure and let me know when . . ."

28

"Hey, Moss, you don't look bad for a man stuck his head where it didn't belong," Angela said. "You want some ice for that, it's in the fridge. Laurel, the man wants some ice, there's plenty in the fridge."

"The man wants some ice, he can get it for himself." Laurel was sitting at a table in the kitchen of Tommy Gee's. Daisy and Columbine muttered hello. Laurel pretended I wasn't there. I had put her on the spot upstairs, and Laurel didn't care for that at all. I was totally invisible now, and this would go on for some time.

Angela showed me a nasty grin. "My, I hope we aren't having discord and strife." Her lizard eyes sparkled with delight. "I just hate it when people can't get along. It ruins my whole day."

Angela speared a blob of bloody red steak and shoved it in her mouth. That cow was slightly wounded, it surely wasn't dead.

A man in the kitchen was slapping more meat on the grill. It sizzled as it hit and sent great gouts of smoke into the air.

"That was a real dumb trick. You don't want to do that again." Angela poked the air with her fork. "I came real close to blowing your fucking head off, friend."

"You would've messed that Buick up good."

"I don't guess you'd know it if I did."

"There's that."

"Damn right it is."

"How you want your steak, pal? I got one with your name on it here."

The man in the kitchen was swinging a twelve-ounce T-bone in the air. He wore a white apron that came up to his chin.

"Medium well," I said. "What I really like is just past medium, right before you get to medium well, right there in between somewhere."

The guy gave me a look.

"Mr. Moss is a hired artist," Angela said.

"Oh, right," the guy said, and dumped my steak on the fire.

"This is Tommy Gee, Moss. He runs the place here."

"Pleasure, Moss."

"Same here," I said. He nodded me to join him and I did.

He was medium to medium tall. Right there in between. Slightly balding hair combed straight back on his head. Blue eyes that danced and a shit-eating grin.

"Thought you'd like to supervise. You seem to have some set ideas about meat."

"I'll bet you used to be in law. I bet you had a practice somewhere."

"What makes you think that?"

"I don't know, you just look that way to me."

"I'd watch my mouth if I were you."

"You don't need to take offense."

"None taken, pal. How's that look to you?"

"Another half minute, then do the other side."

Tommy Gee muttered to himself, and poked at the meat with his fork.

The kitchen was cavernous and dark. The heat in the room was intense. Two ancient ranges and a flat and greasy grill. Old brick walls and worn linoleum floors. The fan in the wall churned against the sluggish air. The blades were weighed down with fat from 1949. The walls, the floors, every black and murky surface was thick with ancient muck. You could send young health inspectors here to school. All the violations were laid out for students to see.

"You make yourself at home," Tommy said. "Enjoy yourself. Have a good time. Don't bother anyone. Don't touch the girls."

I said, "What girls are that? Don't touch who?"

He slid my steak onto a plate. "My girls, asshole. The girls that work for me. They're performers, professionals just like you and me. Some of 'em got a dance degree. Don't go grabbing their tits, don't poke their private parts."

"All right, I can handle that."

"Good. You have a good time. It's all on me. Any kind of beer you like. No hard stuff, that's for the payin' customers. Don't talk to them, and don't wander off anywhere."

He saw that got a rise and gave me a shitty grin. "Angela says you're a guest for a while. Guests stay in the confines, they don't walk off somewhere, they don't if they got any sense. Enjoy the steak, okay? I never made one for an artist before."

"It's a first for us both," I said.

One thing you can count on. Bad taste never goes out of style.

For his Totally Nude Domino Parlor, Tommy Gee had chosen the auto parts motif. Radiators, fan belts, bumpers and grilles. Headlights, tail lights, spark plugs and tires, mufflers and shocks from many lands. They hung from the ceiling and covered the walls, remnants of Nissans, Cadillacs and Cords. Reos and Geos, Hondas and Fords.

And if that were not enough, and I'm certain that it is, this sacred shrine, this holy place of the highway and the wheel, echoed with the hymns of rock and roll, with the dirge of country song. Blue lights, green lights, pink lights and red, sparkled and glittered, shimmered and flashed across the chrome and steel and glass. Here, the worshippers gathered to gaze on naked flesh, at innies and outies and peachy little mounds, gathered to stare at these unclad beauties named Impulse, Legend, Blazer and Dart. Here, lost in this dark and musty land, men came to watch with constipated lust and secret desire, came here to pray to that awesome trinity, the spirit of life, the three basic food groups, tap beer, gash, and the red Corvette, circa 1959.

White trim, white leather, black top . . .

It was nearly six and the men were drifting in, drinking in the cool, blinking in the dark. There were dominoes at every table, though I never saw a game, never saw a single play. The girls were skinny or slightly overweight, pale white creatures of the night. Not a one could match the clear-eyed, rosy look of the average Spudette.

The very thought of those bouncy, happy-go-lucky tarts sent a lump to my throat. Aster, Iris, Zinnia and Phlox! It didn't seem fair, it didn't seem right that they'd perished in the very prime of life.

A girl pranced by on six-inch heels. She wore an ankle bracelet and a smile. I watched her dance, and when she was finished, she wasn't near as skinny as I'd thought. I decided she looked real fine. If I watched her every day and I drank enough beer, we'd be married in the fall.

"She's okay, huh? That's Prelude. She's been here 'bout a month, really draws the dudes in."

"I'll bet."

The guy was maybe 385, no neck, no fat and a flat-top cut. Barrel chest and little BB eyes. He took my tiny hand and gave it a very gentle squeeze.

"I'm Bosco. You're the bug art guy. I'm not supposed to let you get out."

"Word gets around," I said. "I'm Wiley Moss."

I'd seen him, of course, the instant I walked in the room from the back. There was only one door that I could see. All I had to do was knock Bosco on his ass and I was free. Maybe an Oriental hold that would fell him like a tree. Maybe a howitzer, maybe a 155.

Bosco leaned down and placed a giant paw on my chest. "I used to mount the lepidoptera. I bet I've seen your work somewhere. Shit, I had about five hundred of the suckers mounted on my wall. This was in Angola, I was working out some time for aggravatin' assault, and a phony dismembering charge which I didn't do at all.

"Louisiana's got a lot of butterflies. I had everything from the common monarchs, *Danaus plexippus,* up through the fuckin' moths. I had a lovely hairstreak, the one that seems to mirror the depths of the sea? I had a zebra swallowtail and the spicebush too. I had me a black, a *Papilio polyxenes,* biggest mother you ever saw. You won't do nothing dumb, will you, Mr. Moss? If you do, I'm supposed to rip an organ out."

"I did a series on the swallowtails in the the *National Geographic.* If you'd like, I could send you an original color plate."

"No shit?"

"No shit, Bosco. I'll send you the entire Smithsonian collection if you'll let me out of this place."

Bosco grinned. "You're joshin' me, Mr. Moss."

"Yes, I am."

"I thought as much. You art guys are really into fancy and wit."

"We can't help it," I said.

Prelude was doing her thing on stage one. I watched her in the mirror behind the bar. The bartender was a naked girl in Reebok running shoes. She had carrot red hair, upstairs and down. A "HI, I'M MUSTANG" sticker was pasted to her breast.

Behind the bar, mounted in K mart frames, were full-color pictures of Tommy Gee dancers from the present and the past. There was Fastback, Hardtop, Low Rider, several Cougars and Sevilles. One of the Sevilles looked familiar. I leaned across the bar and saw it was the lean and lanky Phlox. Different hair, but you couldn't miss the legs. The incredible legs said Phlox.

You sweet and lovely woman, I thought, where are you now? Lost in the ruin of Vinnieland, last week's burger, stuck on a grill.

My eyes moved past a chubby Corolla, past a Maxima who'd truly earned her name. Past a wide-eyed blonde called Civic, a name that didn't really have a ring.

Stop. Two rows over, one up. Standing there together in suggestive embrace. "Shadow" Dodge and "Victoria" Crown. Laurel and Daisy, the flashbulb turning their eyeballs red.

"Well I'll be," I said.

And Daisy said, "I wouldn't mention this to her if I was you. She's not too fond of looking back."

A double-take, and there was the present-day Daisy at my side.

"When was all this? You both look good."

Daisy blushed, and I recalled that I had never seen her fully unclothed.

"Two years, I guess. We didn't last long. There's nothing but scumballs come in a place like this. You're not going to meet your hunters and your sportsmen in here, like we did in Spudettes. You take a guy fishes with an artificial fly, a guy like that he'll smoke a pipe, he's got a wife and kids back home, he'll keep himself clean."

"I used to fish a lot when I was a kid. All we had, though, was a bamboo pole and a cork, we didn't have a fly."

"Most of the guys I met in Spudettes, they preferred the dry fly. I found them to be a gentler sort. Your wet-fly dudes tend to be a more aggressive breed. Assholes who want to sell you stock. Wiley, are you going to get us out of here? I am scared to death."

I looked at Daisy in the semi-pink dark. Hard rock blasted through the room, shaking the hubcaps on the wall. Everyone cheered as Blazer shook her apparatus at the gaping throng at twice the speed of sound.

"I don't know what to tell you," I said. "My last cool move didn't get off the ground. I'm looking for something more subtle next time."

I didn't look at Daisy, I looked in the mirror at Blazer, Pillsbury flesh under blue and yellow lights.

"I haven't known what these people are up to since the day I got here. I take that back, before that. If I knew a little more, if someone'd clue me in, I might be more help. Laurel's told me some, but you know how she is. Getting anything out of her's like pulling teeth—"

I knew what might happen and it did. I was trying to get past Laurel, to break something loose, come in another way, and the moment I did, I wished I hadn't tried.

Daisy went berserk. Her eyes rolled back and her mouth went out of synch. The bartender gave me a look. I steered Daisy over to a table, set her down gently and took her hands in mine.

"Listen, whatever I said I'm sorry, okay? I didn't mean to get you upset."

"You didn't? No shit?" Daisy couldn't stop shaking. Her lips started twitching like Marilyn Monroe and her eyes began to blink.

"You didn't want to get me *upset?* What the hell did you want me to *do,* Wiley Moss? Jesus, what did Laurel tell you, what did that crazy bitch say!"

"She just—told me stuff is all. I don't recall exactly what."

"What did she *say,* Moss? You better talk to me."

Now that I'd stepped right in it, I didn't know where to go. Where I wanted to go was back, but it was too late for that.

"She might have mentioned Rocco. She brought you up a few times. Okay, there was Vinnie and the twins, of course. I think, I believe a fat guy was mentioned once or twice."

"Oh my *God . . .*" All the color drained from Daisy's face. She was pale as Blazer's tummy, white as Prelude's thighs.

"She . . . mentioned . . . a fat person."

"A fat guy, yes, I'm real sure she did."

"And who else?"

"Like I said, Rocco came up a few times."

"In what way?"

"In a very negative way, as I recall. Like this dude was not a nice guy. That he didn't exactly treat you too well. No big surprise, I didn't care for him myself."

"And she *talked* to you about this—fat guy."

"Yes she did."

"And what did she say? Goddamn it, Wiley, you started this shit, you *answer* me!"

"I did, and I really wish I hadn't, Daisy. I can see this bothers you a lot. Maybe you'd like to talk to Laurel, then we could all sit down and—"

"*I am talking to you!*" Daisy's eyes filled with tears. They ran down her cheeks in a Maybelline path, and stained the dominoes.

"I know she cares for you, Wiley, but Laurel had *no business* sharing this stuff with you. What she did, she broke a confidence, and that scares the shit out of me, and makes me mad besides. This man? This fat person she is talking about? Well he is possibly the most dangerous and evil human being alive. There is no telling how many women that monster has secretly abducted and shipped off to slavery in many foreign climes."

Daisy leaned in close. "You know what a sheik lives out in a tent, what he'll pay for a lovely person like me? A lot, that's what. Money means nothing to them. They can buy a carload of virgins with what they got in their pockets at the time. Okay, that virgin stuff's crap, but those mothers aren't aware of that.

"Say what you will about Rocco, Wiley, and he was a son of a bitch first class. But if it hadn't been for him, me and a bunch of Spudettes, we'd be in some godforsaken desert like Kuwait or France right now."

I stared at Daisy. "You're telling me the fat guy's a slaver? This is what he does, he sells women overseas?"

Daisy thrust her chin out like a rock. "You're the one talked to Miss Big Mouth. What the hell you think he did?"

I had an answer but it never got out. At that very instant, Chocolate Armageddon and the Spitballs reached a manic peak of sound that burst eardrums far and wide. Strobe lights pulsed in a weird unearthly hue, as Blazer plopped down in a dinette chair, and displayed her awesome charms for everyone to see. The crowd gasped for breath, stunned, shaken, blinded once again by the secret of everlasting life.

And, just an instant after *that*, Bobby Bad Eye walked in the door, his ears and his nose scorched black, every single hair burned off his head. Staggering behind him, lizard eyes blazing in the alien dark, wrapped up like a mummy in half a mile of sheets, was Vinnie "Spuds" DeMarco, back from Halloween, back from the dead, back from the fiery hills of Vinnieland . . .

29

What an awesome event, what a stunner and a half! The stink of fire and flesh, the lights of pink and bloody-red. With the clash of rock and roll, our heroes rise from the horror of crispy critter hell to live again.

Daisy and I were struck dumb, frozen in our seats. No one else seemed to notice, no one seemed to care. All eyes were locked on Blazer, who had suddenly slid from her dinette chair and was having a spasm or a fit, humping like a snake in a bed of fire ants, writhing on the floor.

Bosco proved his worth at once. Bosco didn't hesitate. He picked up Vinnie and Bobby, tucked one under each Herculean arm, and headed for the kitchen door.

Vinnie yelled "Muthuh-fucka!" or words to that effect. Bobby didn't bother to protest.

There must have been a button, some kind of alarm. Before Bosco got halfway to the door, Tommy Gee and Angela burst into the room. Bosco stopped, and set his cargo down. Vinnie took a swing at him and missed.

Tommy Gee stared, dropped his jaw in wonder, but halfway kept his cool. Angela was something else again. In a quarter of a second, a rash of emotions blurred across her face. Fear, anger, sorrow and regret. Rage and relief, shock and disbelief. One going this way, one going that, each one tugging at the rest. All this happened in a flash, then Angela ran to her brother, arms outstretched, dark eyes brimming with tears.

"Oh, Vinnie, thank Jesus, you're alive!" she cried out, and threw her hands around his neck.

"Get her off me," Vinnie screamed, *"goddamn it, I haven't got any fuckin' skin!"*

Angela backed away, backed away or staggered, her eyes wide open, her fingers clasped against her face.

Tommy Gee jerked a thumb at Bosco. "Get him inna back, get him outta here." He looked around to see if his carnal enterprise had been disturbed in any way. Satisfied, he jabbed a finger at Daisy and at me. "You. Outta here. *Now."*

"In a minute," I said, "I've still got a beer."

"Take it with you, pal. Lift your ass off of that chair."

Prelude slouched up beside me and slid something fuzzy down my arm.

"Want to do some dominoes, hon? Twenty bucks here. Forty and we get us a table in the back."

I nearly dropped my glass.

Daisy said, "He don't want to play dominoes, dear, but he appreciates you wantin' to share."

Prelude sighed. Her eyes met mine. They said I was all she'd ever wanted out of life.

Daisy took my glass and set it down. "You know how to play dominoes, Moss?"

"No I don't. Does she?"

"You bet she does. But not near as good as me."

"What kinda family I got, you want to tell me that? You wanna tell me, I'm listening, go ahead. I'm all ears, or whatever fuckin' ears I got left. *You* tell *me* what kind of family Vinnie DeMarco's got, I'm lyin' in a holocaust, I'm frying like bacon in a pan."

"Vinnie—"

"Shut up! I am talking to you, you ain't talking to me."

Vinnie lashed out, waving a mummied hand. Angela looked at him and stared. Her brother was a fearsome sight to see as he stomped about the kitchen, moving in the jerky, stiff-legged style every mummy learns. As he walked he unraveled, trailing strips of sheeting that smelled like soot, bacon and Bactine.

Everyone was frightened of Vinnie. Vinnie was a scary-looking guy. Nobody knew what was under those sheets, nobody cared to find out. And, if the visual effects weren't enough, it was clear that Vinnie was unsettled at best, pissed off, nutso, slightly out of synch, not entirely mentally intact. The mood in the kitchen was gloomy, fearsome and dark. However, the undercurrent was chaotic and intense.

"What you want to do now," Angela said, "is stop that stomping around and lie down and get some rest, we can talk about this some other time. And I'd like to get a doctor to look at those burns, Tommy knows a real good man."

"Don't you talk nice to me," Vinnie said, "I won't put up with that."

"I will talk nice to you if I like. You are my only living brother, Vincent, and I got a right to be nice. I'm sorry, Angelo, I didn't mean that."

Angelo raised a weary hand and dropped it back. He had gone unnoticed for most of his life and he'd learned to handle that.

"Him," Vinnie said, suddenly coming to a halt and stabbing a finger at Bobby Bad Eye. "*He* didn't leave me roasting my butt back there. He came and got me out. He ain't even family, he's a fuckin' Injun, he come and got me out. Didn't nobody else do that, he come and got me out. Where the hell were you, little sister? Where were you when that asshole Michael's burning my house down, I'm *dying* in there."

"There was a *lot* of confusion, you don't even know what was going on," Angela said. "Nobody left you to die, Vincent, everybody did what they could."

Vinnie looked right at me. I could see a tiny mask of darkened skin, I could see the lizard eyes.

"You, art guy. You got that son of a bitch Michael Galiano to thank for still being alive. You know that? Bobby would've barbecued your ass like I told him to do, if he hadn't had to come back for me. Right, Bobby? You're my man, aren't you, Bobby boy?"

"Yes, sir, Mr. DeMarco," Bobby said. "I'm your number-one guy."

"Damn straight." Vinnie stumbled over his sheets, turned to take us all in. "Anyone isn't for Vinnie, then they're maybe for somebody else. Anybody here, they're for some other guy, they're not for Vinnie Spuds?"

"For Christ's sake, there is no one against you, Vincent." Angela looked him right in the eye. "Everyone's for you, don't start acting like that."

"Yeah. Okay. That's the way it's gotta be."

The more Vinnie talked, the more obvious it became that the fire which had damaged a lot of Vinnie's parts had greatly overheated his head. Vinnie wasn't all there, he was walking a very thin line. Sometimes he was Don Corleone. Sometimes he drifted right into Daffy Duck.

One thing Vinnie didn't know, and most everybody did, was what had really happened back there. He didn't know what Angela and Bobby were doing while he was under fire. Angela knew about Bobby, and Bobby knew about her, and we all knew both of them were lying, even if we didn't know why. Neither of them looked at each other, not at any time. Neither of the two were dumb enough to discuss their problems there.

Daisy, Columbine and Laurel concentrated on the floor. Angela showed a great interest in her hands. Bobby looked intently at times gone by, and Tommy Gee looked at a stove. Tommy didn't know a thing, but he could see that nearly everybody did. No one looked at anybody else, and I looked at the wall. If Vinnie hadn't been goofy at the time, he might have wondered why everyone was heavy into Zen.

"I'm going to get that son of a bitch," Vinnie said, to no one at all. "Michael's betrayed us, so Michael's gotta pay. He isn't like his father, Johnny Thumbs was nothing like that, Johnny Thumbs had respect, Johnny Galiano was a stand-up guy. Johnny Thumbs, he had to whack a guy out, you knew he'd do it right. He wouldn't do something that didn't show respect, he wouldn't try and burn a guy out. What is *with* this bastard, I'd like to know that, somebody want to tell me that? He's burning down my house, he's tryin' to *kill* me, for Christ's sake. What the fuck did *I* do, I'd like to know that!"

Vinnie got tangled in his mummy outfit and nearly fell.

"We can do that," Angela said, "we can get the son of a bitch, but first we got to straighten things out, you've got to get a little rest—"

"Fuck rest!" Vinnie swung at Angela and missed. "I haven't got time to rest, this mother is trying to wipe me out!"

"We'll get him, Vincent."

"I'll kill him. I'll kill his fuckin' dog."

"I don't know if he's got a dog. I don't know I ever heard the Galianos talk about a dog."

"He hasn't got a dog, you don't think he's gotta dog? I'll *buy* him a dog, *then* I'll kill his fuckin' dog."

"We could do that." Angela tried to look perfectly calm. "You want to, we could do that."

"I don't know what kinda dog, I don't know from dogs. Anybody know about a dog? What I want, I want to get a dog that burns. I want to get a dog that's gonna burn real good. I wanna getta— getta—"

Vinnie came to a halt. He blinked, and stared about the room. A quick inventory: what he might be doing, approximately where, and who he might be.

"What is with this, what're the whores doing here? They're supposed to be working, what're they doing here?"

Angela cleared her throat. Daisy and Columbine pretended they were anybody else. Laurel came to her feet, stood so quickly that her dinette chair, a mate to the one that Blazer was using at that very same moment in time, tumbled and skidded across the floor.

"You got no right, talking to us like that, that's a shameful thing to say. You owe your employees some courtesy and manners, Mr. Vinnie DeMarco, you don't badmouth 'em and you don't beat on them like you did on Zinnia, and you don't go around settin' trailers on fire—"

"What is this, what's happening to me?" Vinnie spread his arms in despair. "I got the Galianos on my back, I got a whore she's mouthing off at me. I got a whore, she's standing here telling me what to do."

Laurel's eyes caught fire. "You want to tell me what happened to those other girls that worked their hearts out for you? You hang around to help 'em, or you run off and save your godless gangster self?"

Vinnie stared. "Get 'em out of here. Get 'em all *out* of here." He came at Laurel, flailing his mummy arms about. Bobby stepped in to hold him back.

"Get them all out of here," Vinnie yelled. "Just family. No whores. No one but family in here!"

Tommy Gee moved quickly, deftly herding Columbine, Laurel

and Daisy out of Vinnie's path. Vinnie swung at him and missed. So far, he was swinging like the Mets, he hadn't hit anything at all.

"Fuckin' pervert. Girls prancing around with their whatsits hanging out. I'm going to close this mother down."

Bobby got Vinnie in a chair, wrapped him up tightly in his mummy outfit which was totally unraveled by now. I got a glimpse of raw, red flesh, blisters the size of Morgan silver dollars, and quickly looked away.

We could still hear Vinnie raving, as Tommy hurried us up the back stairs. Tommy Gee was in a fury. You could see the static in his cobalt eyes.

"Guinea son of a bitch. Talking to me like that. Hey, the guy's nothing. He's nothing but a sawed-off little shit. No I take that back. He isn't that big. If he grew another foot, a foot and a half, he'd be a sawed-off little shit."

Columbine said, "I hope he doesn't hear you talking like that, I think he's pretty mad."

"Mad?" Tommy Gee threw up his hands. "I could care, the little bastard's mad? Chicago trash is what he is. Show me a wop from Chicago, I'll you show a sack full of trash."

"There's some real nice people in Chicago," Daisy said. "I've got an aunt there and she's got her own store."

"You got an aunt in Chicago? She's trash. I don't even know her, your aunt is fucking trash."

Daisy started bawling. No one tried to shut her up.

"Guy probably thinks he owns the place. Dumb son of a bitch, probably don't know any better than that."

"I'd watch that kind of talk I was you." Laurel shot him a warning glance.

"Hey, you think I care? I look like I care? I look like I care to you?"

"What about family entertainment?" I said.

"What about what?"

"It says on the matches, TOMMY GEE'S TOTALLY NUDE DOMINO PARLOR & FAMILY ENTERTAINMENT PARK. Where's the family entertainment? I don't guess I saw that."

"We got a cage out back," Tommy said. "We got a badger, we

maybe got a squirrel. I don't know about the squirrel, the squirrel is maybe dead."

"Oh, Lord," Daisy said, "don't tell me that."

"I don't know what kind of daddy'd bring their kid to a place like this," Columbine said. "I simply can't imagine that."

"A daddy likes to look at naked girls," Tommy said, "what do you think? Who else is comin' here?"

Laurel didn't want to talk. Somehow, even in the chaos of The Mummy's grand entrance, she'd found out Daisy and I had talked, which completely pissed her off. That, and the fact that Tommy Gee had locked Daisy and Columbine up in a room by themselves, she didn't care for that.

"If I didn't have to pry every word out of you, I wouldn't have to go asking anybody else," I told her. "That's what I have to do. I want to know anything, I've got to go and dig it out."

"I have always been open and up front with you. Don't you *ever* say I haven't, Wiley Moss, I will not stand for that."

This was one of seventeen ways to tell Laurel was mad. She would clamp her teeth shut, and talk without opening her mouth.

"Is this up front like selling lovely virgins overseas? I don't believe you ever brought that up, I think I might remember that."

"I didn't, because it isn't real true."

"Daisy says it's true."

"Some of it isn't and some of it is."

"Which part is which?"

"I'm not at liberty to go into that."

"Oh, for Christ's sake, Laurel. Are you lying or Daisy? Or how about both? Is the fat guy selling girls to France and Kuwait, or is he fucking sloths on video?"

"I never said it was a sloth."

"You said a South American mammal. That's what I thought it might be."

"That isn't the only mammal they've got. They've got other mammals down there. Besides, a sloth is real disgusting, Moss."

"Well, excuse me. I didn't do the video. I didn't sell anybody to a sheik."

"I don't want to talk about this."

"I'll bet."

"I wasn't lying to you."

"Okay. Who was?"

I tried to get angry at Laurel, but I couldn't bring it off. She was pouty and enchanting, mean and bad-tempered, pretty and cross. I loved her yellow cornsilk hair and her nasty mouth, and her tan drove me nuts. I cared for her a lot, and I couldn't help that.

"Daisy was scared," Laurel said, "you got her real upset. You hit her with that fat guy stuff and she 'bout peed in her socks. She made stuff up on the spot. The videos I've been talking about? That's tied in with the slaver operation, I maybe didn't mention that. See, it isn't just the fat guy with mammals and stuff. Rocco knew better than that, he knew it was something pretty big. What they do, they use the videos as a sales and marketing device. Kind of tantalize your horny foreign dude. Get him to order a couple of girls, where he might've just only bought one."

"My God, that's awful!"

"Damn right it is." Laurel shivered, holding her arms real tight against her breasts. "It's just another goddamn way to use the female person for unbridled lust. It's been going on since before recorded time."

"Yeah, I guess it has."

"You know it has, Wiley. Isn't any guess to it."

"Listen, why did Tommy Gee say what he did? About Vinnie thinking he owned the place?"

Laurel frowned. "Where the hell did that come from? You got a mind like a chicken, Moss. You can't stay in any one place."

Laurel rolled her eyes. "What Tommy ought to do is keep his mouth shut. Vinnie doesn't know it, but he doesn't own half of this place like he did. Angela did a little two-step shuffle and screwed him out of his share. Same as she did on the moose taco deal."

I looked at her. "What moose taco deal is that? There isn't any taco deal, you already told me that. You said it's nothing but token meece back there—"

"Not that one, silly. The *real* one. Only it isn't moose, it's horse. They got a place near Missoula, Montana. They'll buy any nag you bring in, dead or alive, long as it isn't stiff. That's where Mario's Sicilian Moose Tacos come from. I bet you've heard of them, they're all over the West."

"You know very well I haven't, Laurel. How come you never mentioned this before?"

"I don't guess you ever asked."

"And Angelo runs this taco thing, right?"

"Are you serious?" Laurel looked horrified. "Angelo doesn't know anything about it. That man couldn't piss on the ground if Angela didn't draw a map. And don't you *ever* say a thing about this."

"I wouldn't dream of it. Last thing on my mind. If it isn't any trouble, you like to tell me what else I don't know? I'm certain there's a lot of stuff we missed."

"Whatever it is, it can wait. I'm getting me some shut-eye now."

Laurel plopped down on the bed and turned her face to the wall. "If I were you," she said, "I'd spend my idle time thinking how to get my lovely self free. Something where I'm not killed first would be nice."

"Laurel?"

She answered with her phony heavy breath. I'd been through this before, and knew I couldn't bluff her out. I turned on the black-and-white TV without the sound. Someone had reruns of *I Love Lucy,* and I couldn't handle that. There was ballroom dancing on PBS. I had watched this several times before. They have a new contest every day or so. Dancers come from near and far. The men look a little strange to me. Most of the women look fine. You dance about twenty-two hours every day, a woman does that, she's got thighs strong as steel. With thighs like that, she could kill a man if she tried.

"Laurel, you asleep or what?"

"Goddamn it, what?"

"Michael doesn't know the DeMarcos are into this stuff on their own, I know that. I mean; it stands to reason that he doesn't, or Angela and Vinnie wouldn't be here."

"You've got an insight that won't quit, Moss. It's flat uncanny is what it is. Of course he doesn't know. If he did, he'd have whacked 'em both out long ago."

"As opposed to right now. Is that why's he's pissed off, or is this just the fat guy thing?"

"Go to sleep, Moss."

"You know Tommy Gee long?"

Laurel didn't answer for a while. "What do you care?"

"I thought you maybe had something going one time."

"And why did you maybe think that?"

"Miss 'Crown' Victoria. In a titillating pose with the lovely 'Shadow' Dodge, they're grinning and they're naked, the flashbulb's popping in their eyes . . ."

Laurel sat up. "He's still got that picture on the wall."

"You look real nice."

"I don't care to talk about this."

"That's a big surprise."

"Wiley, what is that shit on TV?"

"Ballroom dancing. I watch it all the time."

She looked at a tango for a while. She watched the swirling skirts, and the black and white thighs.

"Uh-huh. You're hell on cultural events."

"I used to dance a lot myself, only nothing like that. The girls in Cincinnati, they've mostly got legs like—"

A car door slammed, then another after that. I got up and went to the window and pressed my face against the glass. I had scraped a little paint off the window when we first got upstairs. What I wanted to see was if the badger and the squirrel were still there.

There was still a lot of midsummer light. I got there in time to see them jump in the car and take off, leaving a plume of dust behind.

"It's Vinnie and Bobby," I said. "They left in a car. It might have been a Volvo, I can't be sure of that."

Laurel gave me a weary look. "Vinnie and Bobby drove off in a car."

"That's what I said."

"What am I supposed to do about that?"

"I don't know, Laurel, I just thought I'd mention the fact."

"Good. Can I go to sleep now?"

Laurel turned over again. I looked at her ever-lovely self for a while, then I watched the TV. I couldn't pay attention, my mind was on Vinnie and Bobby Bad Eye. Where were they going, down to the corner store? Where can a scorched Indian and an gangster mummy go?

Maybe they were headed for a major burn center. They've got stuff there you can't get at the local drug store. There's a fine burn center in Galveston, Texas, one of the best around. They've got a lot of great hospitals, but it's not my favorite town, considering my daddy was foully murdered there. Something like that, it's going to bias you a while.

I left on the TV because I like the light. I could hear all the noise from downstairs, hear the drunks, hear the stomping and the cheers. I could feel every deep bass note, like a big heart pounding in the floor. I closed my eyes, and let the TV flash against my lids. I listened to the beat and I made up a story in my head. The story featured Prelude and Blazer, and some naked girls I'd never met before.

Things were going well, things were going fine. And then we were rudely interrupted by a special effect I hadn't included in my fantasy at all, a sound I had heard the night before, and hoped to God that I'd never hear again, the gutsy, terrifying roar of a shotgun, the icy chatter of automatic fire . . .

30

"Oh God, Wiley, get me out of here, get me out of here *now*, oh shit, honey, I don't want to die!"

Laurel wasn't sleepy anymore, and she liked me just fine. She leaped off the bed, grabbed me and held on tight. A bullet ripped through the floor, struck the ceiling and shattered a fiberboard tile. Pink insulation fluttered down upon our heads.

"If that's asbestos, we're inhalin' certain death. It's illegal to use that stuff anymore."

"Get a hold of yourself," I said, "stay out of the middle of the floor."

I pulled her to the door. It was chaos downstairs. The customers were scared and they were mad. They sounded like a herd of frightened meece. More gunfire, and the smell of cordite seeped up through the floor. I opened the door and looked out. Tommy Gee hadn't bothered to lock us in. These people showed us little respect, and they weren't afraid of us at all.

The stairwell was dark. Someone fired a pistol, then everything was quiet.

It has to be Michael, I thought, who else? Angela thought the place was safe, but Angela hasn't gotten anything right for some time . . .

The stairs split off at the landing—one set went to the kitchen, the other to the front. I led us quickly to the left, the way we'd come in. There had to be a door in the kitchen where they brought stuff in the back.

Laurel stopped, jerked away from me and stared. "Daisy and Columbine. Oh, Jesus, I flat forgot!"

"I did too," I said, "hold it right here," and I ran back up the stairs. I remembered they were two doors down. Both doors were open and no one was there.

"No one's there," I said, "they're gone." A shout from downstairs. It might have been a gangster, it was really hard to tell. "Laurel, we've got to get out of here. Right now."

"Huh-unh. We got to find those girls."

"I think they're just fine. We'll check in the kitchen, I'll bet they're down there."

She tried to pull away but I held on and got her down the stairs. I opened the door to the kitchen. The door to the big room was three feet away. Michael and his hoods. Someone could walk in and find us standing there.

I led us toward the back, putting the big stoves between us and the door. There had to be a way outside. Even a joint like Tommy Gee's would have a service door.

There were cases of beer stacked eight feet high, cartons of toilet paper, totally naked napkins in a vivid shade of pink, barrels of coronary lard.

"Look back there," I told Laurel. "I'll check the other end. Don't fool around, we don't have a lot of time—"

"Oh, shit, Wiley, get over here!"

Laurel backed off and sagged against a tower of beer. The door we were searching for was just down the hall, but she wasn't looking there. I came up behind her and there was Tommy Gee, sprawled on his back with his arms spread wide. His left leg was twisted underneath the right, and something was wrong with his head. I moved around to get more light and I was sorry that I did. What was wrong with his head was he mostly didn't have it anymore. What he had was maybe half, from the nose on down, and the rest was splattered everywhere.

Tommy Gee's underdone steak began to crawl up my throat and I grabbed Laurel's arm and pushed her down the hall. I reached for the door and it opened by itself. We all looked surprised. One of

Michael's hoods was standing in the door with a shotgun dangling at his side.

Laurel screamed.

The hood said, "Son of a bitch!"

One hand was on the trigger, the other was shoving the sawed-off barrel in my face. I didn't have any time to think, so I kicked him in the crotch.

He gagged and folded like a sack. The shotgun clattered to the floor.

"Hey, you!" someone said, and charged up the back steps, someone running like a rhino in heat, someone in a black gangster suit with his nose squashed flat, someone with a dumb little chauffer's hat atop his head.

I snatched up the shotgun and aimed it at Carl's tiny eyes. Carl said, "Put that down, you little fuck, you ain't about to use that."

"Yes I am," I said. Carl had a sudden insight and dived for cover as I squeezed off a shot.

The sound ripped the night. Someone shouted outside and lead whined past my head. I yelled at Laurel and turned around and ran. There was no place to go. Back upstairs was no good, and out front was worse than that.

"Shit-shit-shit," Laurel said, and we burst through the door and into Dominoland.

The music blared. Strobe lights flashed off the auto parts wall. Customers and strippers crouched up by the bar. Two of Michael's crew were standing guard. They'd heard all the shots and they were ready when we came out the door.

I fired in the air just over their heads, jacking in shells as quickly as I could. A shotgun has no discretion at all. If I tried to hit hoods, I'd maim half the perverts in the state of Idaho.

The hoods were impressed. They both hit the floor. No one's more deadly than a frightened bastard with a gun. I backed off, covering Laurel, watching the guys on the floor. We were almost home free. All we had to worry about was Carl and his pals. Maybe they'd rush us from the kitchen, maybe they'd circle around from outside.

Then what? I wondered. If we got by that, which I didn't think we would, then we didn't have a car. We never had a car, we were always in somebody's car, we never had a car to call our own.

"Wileeeey, look out—!"

I didn't need the warning, I saw him from the corner of my eye. The door that led upstairs jerked open and Michael Galiano stepped out, Michael looking cool, Michael looking sharp, Michael looking fine in a three-piece suit from Milano, or maybe Paris, France. Not a wrinkle, not a stain. Snow-white shirt and a very nice tie. He wasn't in a hurry, and he wasn't scared of me at all. He drew his silver pistol from his pocket, and showed me a happy mobster smile.

I fired one shot and I knew I was off, that I was too far to the right. I took out a mirror, blew up a hubcap from a '49 Ford, and, purely by accident, hit Michael Galiano himself.

Michael looked stunned. He stared at his arm in disbelief and the pistol dropped from his hand. I couldn't believe I'd hit him either, and I turned around and ran.

Bosco was sitting on the floor, leaning against the wall. He was covered in blood, every inch of his enormous body was a murky shade of red. I remembered the very first chatter of automatic fire, and I knew he'd absorbed a great deal of that himself. Someone had stitched him up and down, someone didn't want to stop. His mouth was wide open and his face was belly white.

"You ain't supposed to be leaving," he said. "I'm not supposed to let you in or out—"

"Keep your eyes open," I said, "you're doing real fine."

Someone started shooting, and knocked out a bank of colored lights. No time to waste, no time to check the way out. For the second time in a matter of minutes, Laurel and I went through a door with no idea what was on the other side.

Okay, so we had an idea and we were right. Gunfire blazed from behind a row of cars. I yelled at Laurel and didn't stop. I pumped in shells and kept firing until the weapon ran out, then I tossed the gun away, and dived behind a Chevy truck. A '96, or maybe a '95. Blue or maybe black.

Laurel gave me a frantic wave and ducked off to the right. I fell on my face, picked myself up. Someone was shooting, but they couldn't see us, and the lead went wild.

Cars. We were always out of cars. Now we had a parking lot full, and not a one would do us any good. No one with an IQ over six would park at this place and leave their doors unlocked, leave their keys inside. If you wouldn't do that at your grandmother's house, then you wouldn't do it here.

We had to do something, but I couldn't say what.

"Laurel, what I think we'd better do, I think we'd better—*Laurel?*"

I suddenly noticed that Laurel wasn't there. My heart nearly stopped. I could hear them coming up behind me in their wingtip gangster shoes, I could hear them breathing hard, I could hear them spreading out.

Goddamn it, Laurel, where are you!

Someone saw me. White light flashed and glass exploded on my back. The next shot was close and I felt it burn my pants. There was no use looking for Laurel, no place to go. I ran out of the lot, out into the open, out onto an asphalt road.

Lead sang by my head. Hell, how could they miss? How many other guys peeing in their pants were jogging in the middle of the night?

I saw them clearly then, and they clearly saw me. One kept running, and the other went down on his knees.

Oh great, a gangster who watches the cop shows, that's all I need . . .

He was back there, taking his time, squeezing one off. This was the one that would get me, this was the one that would surely do me in . . .

Headlights bounced off the road, licked up all the colors, burned everything bright. The guy tried to run, tried to get up off his knees. The car hit him with a flat and meaty sound, the same sound a buffalo makes when its parachute fails and it plummets to the ground.

The marksman soared through the air. His partner, running just behind me, gave up and headed for the ditch.

The car squealed to a stop, turned halfway around. The door popped open and someone yelled, "Hey, hon, get the fuck in!"

I threw myself inside, let the door shut itself. Laurel took off, peeling rubber from the tires. A bullet spanged off the roof. Laurel slammed her foot through the floor and we were gone.

I tried to quit shaking but I found I couldn't stop. I thought I might have to throw up.

"Nice car," I said, "what moron left his keys in here? I can't believe anyone'd be as dumb as that."

"Michael did," she said.

"Michael what?"

"Michael left his keys in the car. Michael Galiano isn't used to thinking someone's going to steal his car. Michael gets out, Michael leaves the keys. Michael's thinking, no one's going to steal a Galiano car."

"Oh, Jesus," I said, "I think I maybe shot him back there, Laurel, and now we took his car. If he wasn't already, I bet he's really pissed off now . . ."

31

The sign said KETCHUM but we didn't go there.

Ketchum was for tourists and skiers, Laurel said, at the big Sun Valley resorts. Michael had connections everywhere; he'd send out word on the car and the plates, and they'd bottle us up in there.

Instead, we were somewhere in the Sawtooth National Forest, on a road the pioneers had hacked out the day before. It was easy to see why very few made it as far as Oregon.

It was sometime in the middle of the night. We drove a long way and I don't believe we talked. I kept an eye open for bears. After a while, Laurel got tired and I took the wheel. It was a very nice car, a Chrysler Fifth Avenue, I don't know the year. Michael was partial to Lincolns, but he was burning up Lincolns pretty fast, and was driving whatever he could get.

Two things happened as the sun came up to sear my eyes. I came out of the woods onto Highway 20, which told me very little at all. The second thing that happened is I ran out of gas. I had maybe eighteen seconds to think about this, and Fate led me into a roadside park.

Laurel woke up and said, "Shit, Wiley, you could've found a station somewhere. I expect this lapse of yours will cost us our lives."

"Laurel, there weren't any places to stop. Those animals live in the forest, they don't have any cars. Besides, if we *had* a service station, how do you suggest I pay for gas, charge it to the mob?"

Laurel rolled her eyes. "Jesus, Wiley, you're about as dumb as a newborn bird. You don't want to ever leave home without some 'fuck you' cash."

With that, she slipped off both her Nikes, scratched around inside, and came up with two worn twenty-dollar bills.

"See? Don't say I never gave you anything, hon. I mean, besides *that . . .*"

Even worn and bleary-eyed, running from gangsters all night, Laurel looked fine. Okay, a brush and a shower and some makeup wouldn't hurt. Still, Laurel came as close to earthly beauty as any woman could who got her fashion tips from biker magazines.

"You've given me an awful lot, just being with you," I said. "I certainly can't complain."

"That is so sweet," Laurel said. She kissed me on the cheek and pressed her hand against my chest. "Wiley, what are we going to do, you got any idea at all? I hate to promote a negative attitude, but we are up the fucking creek, hon."

"In a way we are," I told her, "in another way we're not. We've still got problems but we're basically free. We've got to stay clear of Angela, and Michael Galiano's bunch. We need to call the cops. We need to get something to eat. Something to eat sounds really good to me. There might be a restaurant just down the road. Someone'll pull in here to pee, and they'll give us a lift real soon.

"You find a place to eat, you're going to find a service station too. We'll get some law enforcement out here, and you and I'll have sausage and scrambled eggs. Butter and toast and jelly. Coffee and some fresh orange juice. I'm going to have the juice, even if they don't have it fresh, I could use a little juice, I'm running out of 'C.' I'd guess it probably does, but I hope the place we stop doesn't have those jellies in little foil sacks where you can't pry it out. Man, I hate that. How much trouble would it be, is that a big deal, you put some jelly on the table in a jar like the way it used to be. Is this a big deal, this is asking too much? You like your scrambled eggs with cheddar cheese? You can't get it on the road, but I grate in a lot of cheddar cheese, I'm making eggs at home. I'd like to fix it for you some time, we ever get a chance, I think you'd like it a lot. We could—Laurel? Laurel, you okay?"

Laurel had dropped off to sleep. Her breath was soft against my neck, and her silky hair brushed my face. The morning sun glared straight in my eyes but I didn't want to move, I wanted her to stay like that. It seemed to me the best moments in my life were very similar to this. I was with someone that I cared for at the time. Maybe we were messing around a little, maybe we weren't doing anything at all.

And that was the thing right there. The not doing anything at all was the part that seemed to linger in my mind. You didn't have to do a thing, you didn't have to think of anything to say. Maybe you'd end up being close, and maybe you'd both go on your way. But right then and there, everything was fine. Which makes you wonder why anyone'd want to do anything else, why you wouldn't want to do that all the time.

You wouldn't, because if you could, you'd get tired of it and you'd want to start doing something else . . .

I woke up sweating and semi-paralyzed. The windows were closed and the car was steaming hot. I couldn't see the sun but it had to be noon or after that. I looked at Laurel. Her head was face down in my lap and her hair was soaking wet. I opened the door and tried to lift her up. She sagged in my arms and said, "Whasa-whasa-whuh?"

"Laurel, we both went to sleep," I told her. "I'm surprised we didn't suffocate in here. It happens all the time. People leave their dogs locked up and go shopping in the mall. When they come back to their cars— You going to be all right?"

"No I'm not, Wiley, I am having a stroke of some kind. But thanks for asking, babe."

We dragged ourselves out, stretched our legs and breathed a lot of air. The roadside park wasn't empty anymore. Two big semis were parked up ahead. A Ford pickup and a red Tercel were just behind our car.

Laurel fanned herself. I walked past the cars to look for a water fountain or a soft drink machine, and they didn't have anything at all. They had little dinky restrooms and a kids' playground. There were two kids playing on the swings.

Parked just behind the Tercel was a white RV. On the front it said, CHARLIE & FREIDA DUCKMAN, TRAVELIN' ON. A man was leaning on the RV door. He was short and squarely built, as if he'd come out of a box and still retained the shape. Everything about the man was blue, blue and brand-new, blue Nikes and socks, blue shorts and blue polo shirt with an animal on the top. He spotted me and started my way. He walked as if life was full of purpose, the top half of his body well ahead of the rest, apparently gravity-free. His hair, his nose, his chin, every feature seemed to buck a strong wind. He looked to me like the Indian on the hood of those early Pontiacs.

"Say," the man said, striding right at me and holding out his hand, "I saw you two sleeping in your car. I was just coming back to knock soundly on the glass. Doing the figures in my head, I calculated the cubic air remaining in that Buick Park Avenue. I came up with four point seven minutes tops. Four point eight, you and the missus would likely be dead."

"Thanks," I said. "I'm grateful for your help."

"I'm Charlie Duckman, you likely guessed that from the sign. That's our motto, Freida and me. 'Travelin' On.' It's a way of life with me. 'Course Freida throws up every time I start the car, but she's a trooper, that ol' gal of mine."

Duckman looked past his RV to the swings. "Those two sprites are my grandkids. We've got 'em for the summer. Say, that wife of yours is a looker, and I mean no disrespect in any way."

"None taken," I said. "Look, could you give us a ride down the road? I hate to ask but the car's out of gas."

"Do what?" Duckman looked me over with his Pontiac eyes. "No way, boy. I wouldn't pick up a stranger on a bet. You know why? I *know* better, that's why. I'm a former agent of the F.B.I., recently retired. I can see you're surprised. Don't think anything about it, they teach us to blend right in."

"My God," I said, and my heart skipped a beat, "this is really fine! A lawman is just the man I need. What's happening here, and you'll find this hard to believe, we're fleeing from a Mafia don and his men. They set a major forest fire, and killed a bunch of people right here in Idaho. God knows how many they've murdered out of state. Last night we engaged them in a fierce gunfight at a naked domino bar. Several of the killings took place right there.

I don't know where the gang is now, but I expect they're in pursuit."

Duckman gave me a sour look, like he'd tasted something bad. "Have you got a hearing problem, son? What part did you miss? I am a *former* agent of the F.B.I. You recall me saying that? Me and Freida travel about and see the sights. I don't do that shit anymore. I thought I made myself clear."

I was stunned by Duckman's attitude. "I give you a tip on a major crime ring and that's it? What kind of lawman are you, anyway?"

"The retired kind, mister. Clean out your ears."

"Jesus, you won't even give us a ride."

"Not on your life. Your wife's a real cutie, but you don't look respectable to me."

"Wiley, will you come *on?*" Laurel made a little speaker with her hands. She was perched on the fender of a semi up ahead. "Bradley D.'s goin' to give us a ride, if you'll quit standing around."

At that moment, Bradley D. himself appeared, stepping down from his truck. He looked at Laurel's long legs golden in the sun, then he looked at me, and his face said Laurel had neglected to mention she was traveling with a friend.

"Have a nice day," I told Duckman. "Fuck you, pal."

"Same to you, son. Only a mental defective's going to run out of gas. You might want to think about that."

Bradley D. was a skinny asshole with Coke-bottle glasses and a bad attitude. What he had in mind was a quickie with Laurel at the next truck stop. Since he couldn't do that, he lost interest real fast. He took us maybe thirteen miles, said that's it, honey, and roared off in the west.

It wasn't a very good ride. On one side of 20 was BOB'S MARMOT CITY & RATTLESNAKE FARM. On the other was a mom-and-pop store with a mom and not a pop. Mom's name was Flo, and she was maybe ninety-three. There were two gas pumps but there wasn't any gas. There also wasn't any phone. Laurel and I bought cold ham sandwiches and swallowed them whole. Laurel used the restroom and Flo didn't much care for that. We bought Big Reds and walked back out in the sun.

"That was sure fun," Laurel said, "what do you want to do next?"

"Bob's Marmot City. They've maybe got a phone. Give me some money. If you want, you can stay over here."

"Forget it," Laurel said. "Those marmots have got to be more fun than Flo."

Bob was a scrawny old man in dirty coveralls. No shirt, no shoes, no teeth, just a lot of stringy hair.

Bob didn't have a phone.

Bob said he had to feed the snakes. Go look at the marmots for a while, and he'd drive us down the road.

All of the marmots were dead. They were dead, stuffed, and posed in panoramas depicting the story of the West. Railroad marmots laid track up a Styrofoam hill. Gold-miner marmots panned nuggets in a creek.

Most impressive of all was the Battle of the Little Big Horn. Hundreds of marmots were frozen in action across the battlefield. Each soldier or Indian was dressed in authentic costume. The Indians wore feathers from the native birds of Idaho. Some marmots writhed on the ground, tiny arrows in their chests. Some carried rifles that shot puffs of white cotton smoke. A very fine roadside display. It deserved consideration for attention to detail, as well as its most ambitious scope.

"This is really something," I said. "I've never seen a marmot show before."

"Fine," Laurel said. "Maybe we'll get real lucky and not run into one again."

"Laurel, someone spent a great deal of time on that, it was really well done."

"It was rodents in little suits, Wiley, okay? I want to see a rodent in a suit I got fucking Mickey Mouse. Will you get me out of here?"

We walked back out into the withering heat. A hand-lettered sign said the creatures we had seen were yellow-bellied marmots, *Marmota flaviventris,* along with specimens of the larger, grayer hoary marmot, *Marmota caligata,* a variety that preferred higher ground. I wondered which variety Nix had tried to serve us that night, moments before someone shot him in the head.

"You buy anything across the road," Bob said, " 'fore you come over here?"

"Sandwiches and drinks," I told him, "why you want to know that?"

Bob made a face. "That bitch uses tainted meat when she can. Tried to poison me a number of times in forty years. I finally got wise and moved out."

"Well I wish we'd come here first," Laurel said. "I don't like the sound of that."

Bob spat on the ground. "You can take in the snakes if you like. They're mostly your western diamondbacks. I also got some copperheads and two or three kings. I feed them all mice. Most people don't much like to watch that. Ones who do are lawyers and kids in junior high. You owe me three bucks each. That's for the marmot show, I throw the snakes in free. So what did you think?"

"I doubt there's another show like it anywhere," Laurel said.

"Well, I appreciate that." He looked Laurel up and down. "I'd say Flo used to be pretty as you but that'd be a lie. That woman was asshole ugly from the start. You want to wait here, I'll go and start the truck."

Bob said he'd take us as far as Mountain Home. He had to get snake wire there, and he assured us the town had a great many phones. I told him that would be fine. He said he'd show Laurel the john. I said I'd go look at a snake, I hadn't seen one in a while.

The snakes were still choking down mice and I didn't hang around. I wandered out back of Marmot City. I looked at the sky and the trees and the grass for a minute and a half. I thought about Giselle. I thought about the lovely Claire de Mer and a girl I knew in Cleveland one time. I could not recall her name. I was sure she would not remember mine.

Mostly, I thought how this mess would be over real soon. I thought about a bath and a good night's sleep and nobody shooting at me anymore. These are some of your really basic needs, these are things you ought to have. Bob would drive us into town and we would find a good meal, then we would find us a nice motel. Laurel's forty bucks wouldn't go real far, but I could find a phone and call my good buddy Phil.

Before we did that, we'd find the law. Mountain Home was small, but they'd have some cops around. Sane, rational people who would listen to what we had to say. These would not be people like Charlie Duckman, former agent of the F.B.I. These stalwart lawmen would sound the alarm, round up a posse, send out an APB. In only moments, every cop in the West would be on Michael's trail.

Just thinking about this, I felt light and free. Like you feel when you've got maybe, what, six or eight bowling balls, you've got these balls in a sack, you're hauling them around for three days? And then you just *drop* that sack, and you don't have to do it anymore?

This is how I felt, that I had this stuff I was carrying around, I didn't have to do it anymore. I didn't have to do it, I didn't have to *think* about it now. If God would get me out of Idaho I would never even think about mobsters or meece, I would put it all behind me, I would never let it cross my mind again.

Someone'd say, hey, all the shit that happened, you couldn't do that, you couldn't get it out of your head. Listen, I'm pretty sure I could. I could go through life and never wonder who knocked off Rocco and Nix. Why Michael Galiano wanted Vinnie Spuds dead. Why he chased the Spudettes through a raging forest fire. Who's side Bobby was on, and what was going on in Angela's head.

I would not even wonder how Daisy, Columbine, Vinnie and Bobby, Angela and Angelo, *everybody* in the goddamn place, somehow managed to be *out* of Tommy Gee's when Michael and his mobsters showed up. Everyone but Tommy and Bosco and Laurel and me, who somehow didn't get the word. I wouldn't even wonder, I wouldn't even think about that.

One other thing I would put out of my mind. I would no longer wonder who the fat guy was, and what the hell that was all about. I wouldn't care if it was semi-virgins or porno pix, or a carnal need for sloths. I wouldn't even think about that.

Laurel. Laurel I would not be able to forget. I didn't want to and I wouldn't even try. We could talk about that when everything was over, though I'm not sure what we'd say. A shallow affair is a whole lot easier than love, I guess I know about that. But even just fucking around is a tender and fragile thing at best.

Another thing I wouldn't forget. I wouldn't forget the Spudettes, or what happened to them out there. And when they caught Michael and his hoods? That wouldn't bring Zinnia back, or Aster or Iris or anyone else. Justice is one thing. Making things right, that's something else again. The bastard who killed my daddy in Texas is very likely dead, and so what? There's not a whole lot of satisfaction in that . . .

"That bathroom they got, it smells like marmots in there. Lord, I just about threw up."

"I don't think that'd be a marmot smell," I said. "Those marmots are dead. What you might've smelled is snakes. Was it dry, a kind of dry and musty smell?"

"No, it was not dry and musty, is that what I said?" Laurel did the thing with her eyes. Smolder is the word that comes to mind. "What I said is it smells like *marmots* in there. Would it help if I said it again?"

"Let's not talk about this, all right?"

"Fine."

"Let's put this aside."

"Okay, fine."

"Good. All right. Bob says it's not far to Mountain Home. He says they've got some good spots to spend the night. You know what else he said? He said Idaho's time zone splits down the middle of the state. *Sideways.* Can you believe that? Not up and down like it's normal to do. Sideways, horizontal. I'm talking straight across."

"I knew that."

"Well I certainly didn't. I never heard of such a thing. Anyplace else, your time zone's going up and down. It's not going horizontal, it's going up and—*huuuuh!*"

He wasn't there and then he was, and he hit me in the jaw and knocked me flat. I looked up at Carl. Carl looked down at me and grinned.

"Anything I hate, it's a guy takes a shot at me, I ain't even met the guy before, I don't know who the fuck he is. A guy does that, a guy don't have no respect for me at all."

"Okay," I said. "I can understand that. It's happened to me a couple of times, you're a little pissed off, you're a little upset, I don't blame you for that—"

"Moss, just shut the fuck up."

Angela appeared from behind a cage of snakes. "Don't even listen to this guy, this guy'll drive you nuts. This is the guy, the guy that draws bugs."

"Oh, right," Carl said.

He gave a little shrug, like okay, he got it now, that explained a whole lot . . .

32

No big four-door this time, this time they had us in a van. There wasn't any carpet, nothing but a rusty metal floor. I'm guessing a stolen delivery van. It smelled like hardware to me. My family's been in hardware since 1847, I'd know that smell anywhere—lumber, rope, hammers and nails. You wouldn't think it, but nails have got a smell.

"Angela, I am real surprised at you," I said. "You hear a whole lot about loyalty and family in the mob. As far as I can see, you people have a moral code as shaky as anybody else."

"Jesus," Angela said, "will you listen to this? I gotta listen to this?"

"What you want to do," Carl said, "you want to keep your mouth shut, this is what you want to do."

"Can I ask a question?"

"Moss, you hear the man? Shut the fuck *up.*"

This from Angela, who stood back and watched while Carl bound us hand and foot. He used a lot of duct tape, which does the job quick.

"It's just one question, that's it. I won't ask anything else."

"Don't." Carl stuck his big finger in my face.

"What happened to Bob?"

"Bob who?"

"Don't give me 'Bob who.' Bob, the old guy that runs the place. What'd you do to him?"

"I don't like you any, you aware of that?"

"Yes, I am."

"Good. What I want, I want you to be aware of this, I don't want you thinking somethin' else."

The door slammed shut. Moments after that, Carl took off with a jerk. That physical law I never can recall slammed us hard against the back.

"Laurel, I think they did something to Bob. I don't feel this bozo would leave a lot of tracks."

Laurel let out a breath. "I expect you're right, and I hope he didn't suffer any pain. But you know what? Bob and I never got close. I am *real* concerned about these assholes whacking me."

"You think that's what they'll do?"

"Don't you?"

"I don't have any doubts at all. I just didn't want to worry you."

"Wiley, that's nice. I appreciate that." She scooted over some and put her face next to mine. The van was noisy and they couldn't hear us talk.

"I was thinking back there at Marmot City, Laurel. I was thinking it was over and we were out of this, and I wondered about you and me."

"You did, huh?"

"Yes I did. I wondered if we'd be together after this. We know very little about each other, scarcely anything at all. My friend Phil Greenburg, Phil's in D.C., Phil says a deep understanding of your lover's inner self is what tears a relationship apart. You and me, we've used each other with hardly any meaning or intent, and I'd say that's a start."

Laurel closed her eyes and gave me a soft and very lingering kiss. The kiss turned into a grin and a silly little laugh.

"An insect artist and an outdoor whore. I don't see how we could miss. Why, a combination like that . . ."

Laurel's smile faded. Tears suddenly filled her eyes.

"Shit, Wiley, I'm not fooling anyone, I'm sure not fooling me. I cannot *handle* this. There isn't going *be* any us. You and me and Daisy and Columbine, all those girls that burned up back there. When this is all over, isn't anyone going to be alive!"

"There's a lot of things might've been that won't ever be."

"See, that's what I'm trying to say. There's a lot things that won't ever—"

"You know what one of them is, Laurel, you know what's going through my head? That I had to go through this crap, and I don't have the least idea why."

She tried to look away, to pretend I wasn't there. She knew where I was going, and she didn't care to make the trip again.

"I have seen that lie in your eyes so many times I can't count it any more. That morning, after we all camped out? That really got to me, that shook me up good. I remember exactly what I said. I said, 'My God, Laurel, you *know* what's happening, you *know* what's going on here.'

"You've got that very same look right now. You're doing it again, and I'm thinking, Christ, this mobster is hauling us off, he's going to drop us in a well, and I won't ever know why. I won't ever know because *Laurel's* going to *lie* right up to the end. I am leaving this world as dumb as when I came in!"

Laurel didn't answer. She lay with her head next to mine, with her hair in my face, with the tears streaming down, but she wouldn't say a thing.

"That's it, that's the way it's going to be? I get whacked by a goof with his nose squashed in, and you won't *bother* to tell me why? Is it just me, or does this seem fucking ridiculous to you?"

Laurel tried a little sniff, a little pout. "I am real scared, Wiley, all right? I don't feel it's right you should jump on me in adverse conditions such as this."

"You don't."

"No, Wiley, I don't. And I'm not sure I could share a carnal life with a person who doesn't trust me any more than that."

That really pissed me off. If I hadn't been sweating like a pig, I think I would've gotten pretty hot.

"Well you know what?" I said. "We are lucky in that respect. Other couples find fault with one another over time. You and me, we're not going to *last* long enough to do that."

"Oh, Jesus, Wiley, I know we're not . . ."

Laurel's lips began to tremble and she squeezed her eyes shut. I cuddled up close and a tear fell in my nose.

"Hon, we shouldn't be fighting, not now."

"Okay, let's not."

"I care for you, I think you know that."

"I care for you too. I care for you a lot. So you want to come clean, Laurel? You want to talk straight just once while you've still got the time?"

"Fuck you, Wiley Moss. I will not put up with that."

"Right. And the same to you, hon . . ."

I slept for a while and my head bounced on the floor. My arms and my legs went numb. My breath smelled bad and the sweat ran in my eyes. My face had a lump where Carl had hit me on the jaw.

Laurel's mouth sagged open in her sleep. Her cheeks went limp and her hair stuck to her face. I wasn't mad at Laurel anymore, I was totally disgusted with myself, because I knew, the moment I opened my eyes, how Angela and Carl had tracked us down. Someone spotted our car and turned us in. I couldn't say who—people like Michael can get the word around. And who was there to lend Carl a hand? "Hey, that girl was a looker. She and the guy hitched a ride on a truck."

And the first place you come to is Flo's, and right across the highway, Bob's Marmot City and Rattlesnake Farm.

Why couldn't I run out of gas on some deserted road?

Why couldn't Duckman live in Orlando with the other old farts?

Fate kicks us in the ass now and then. And sometimes the bitch puts in some overtime.

The road got worse and then it got bad.

We bounced around the floor and we yelled a great deal. What it's like, it's like a guy puts his bowling balls in the dryer, he's down at the corner laundromat? This is what it's like, you're a bowling ball and the guy is doing that.

Carl enjoyed this a lot. We'd come to a very rough spot, and Carl would step on the gas and he'd turn around and grin. Angela didn't say a word, Angela was holding on tight.

———————

Everything comes to an end. This is good news maybe six, seven percent of the time. The rest of the time it's not. Carl stopped and slid the door back, picked us up and dropped us on the ground.

I spit up rocks and said, "Goddamn it, watch it!" and Carl kicked me in the head.

"Carl, just cut them loose and get 'em out of here, okay? You're supposed to be working, you're not supposed to be having any fun."

"I can do both," Carl said, "it's all the same to me."

Angela looked bored with all this. She looked a little tired. "Well do it, then, quit screwing around."

The knife felt cold against my skin. The tape came off and the blood rushed back, and I didn't want to lie there, I didn't want to give him any pleasure in that. I stood too fast and I fell down on my face.

Carl got a laugh out of that. Carl enjoyed that a lot.

"You know what?" Laurel said. "I don't think I ever heard a soul say anything good about you."

"I sure like your tits," Carl said. "They really look nice."

Laurel stared. She didn't have an answer for that.

They put it in a little toolshed. There wasn't any light, but we could see through the cracks. The van was parked near a broad, flat river, green water turning dark on a late afternoon working up to a long summer night. Rugged canyon walls plunged straight into the river, colorful bands of stone worn slick by the water and a million years of time.

On the way to the shed, we passed a log house, perched on a steep rock shelf above the river, in a grove of tall pines. There were people on the porch, and they looked up and watched us as we passed.

"I don't think there's much in here you can hurt yourselves with," Carl said. "If there is, well go right ahead."

"Thanks," I said, "we'll be as careful as we can."

"That's the Snake River out there. There's sturgeon in it eight feet long. One like that'll weigh a hundred and fifty pounds. They can live for maybe sixty, seventy years. Shit, there's bigger ones than that. They caught one once weighed fifteen hundred pounds."

"Where was that, here?"

"No, it wasn't here, did I say it's here? It's somewhere else it's not here. They got a picture in a folder, I seen it somewhere. They got a picture of the fish, it don't even look like a fish, it looks like a fuckin' crocodile."

"I'd like to see that."

"Oh, yeah?" Carl grinned. "Who gives a shit?"

Carl stomped out and slammed the door. Laurel walked up and gave it a solid kick.

"Well I really need that. Some clown's going to kill me, I got to hear a nature lecture first."

"We don't know that's what they're going to do. They've had a lot of chances and they haven't done it yet."

"So you think what? You think they're going to let us go?"

"No. I think we're going to end up dead."

"Then why in hell you say something like that?"

"Because I don't feel negative talk is conducive to a healthy attitude. Even if you're doomed, the person who keeps up a cheerful outlook is going to do better in the end."

Laurel gave me a look. "Man, you are really full of shit, you know what?"

"There's that," I said.

33

Without a watch I couldn't tell the time. but the light hadn't faded outside. My eyes were full of grit. I had a headache that wouldn't quit. One of those pounders like you see in an ad, where they draw little hammers, the hammers are hitting this guy, so you know he's hurting bad.

Laurel sat against the far wall. She'd found a rusty nail and she was scratching her name on the floor.

"There's an old garden hose back there. I could hang myself with that. That'd really piss 'em off."

"I bet it would," I said.

Laurel didn't look up. "I don't want you mad at me, Wiley. Not at a time like this."

"I'm not mad at you at all."

"Yeah, I think you are, too. You feel I haven't been honest with you, and I have to say you're right. On occasion, I've stretched the truth some, and I've left some things out. I'm sorry, I regret doing that, and you're right—it doesn't make sense to hide stuff, when we're not going to make it out of here."

"What I thought, I thought you didn't trust me, and that hurt more than the lies, because I thought we were getting kind of close."

Laurel showed me a very weary smile. "That was pretty good superficial lovin', if I do say so myself."

"It was more than that. Nobody's had a better pointless romance.

Okay, I take that back. Clark Gable, Claudette Colbert, 1934. *It Happened One Night.*"

"Did they fuck as good as us?"

"Absolutely not. They didn't even do it back then. They drank champagne and they dressed up a lot."

I reached out and took her hand. "Laurel, if you don't feel like it, you don't have to say a thing. I thought it mattered, but I don't guess anything's important anymore."

Laurel sighed. "I am real mixed up now, hon. I thought I had a hold on this, but Jesus—Angela getting hooked up with Michael, that's thrown me some. I can't make sense out of that.

"Michael's been using Vinnie for a front, I don't have to tell you that. What he's doing, I don't guess I mentioned that, he's got this major dope operation, stuff comes in from Seattle and Vancouver all the time. I think it's sealed up in cheap Asiatic souvenirs. They truck it into Idaho and ship it out from here. I mean, shit, can you think of a better place? Everybody's looking in Florida and down in Texas, and they're bringing the stuff in here? To Idaho? Who's going to figure there's *any*thing's going on here?"

I thought about that, and it made a lot of sense. "And Vinnie's lodge, what did they do, they have a cocaine lab there or what?"

Laurel made a face. "No, they didn't have a lab. Can you see the potatoheads runnin' a lab? Vinnie and Rocco? And Nix? You got a picture of that? Huh-unh, Michael bought the place for next to nothin' when it went broke a few years back. He used the lodge for a—what? A transfer point, somethin' like that. A guy, he'd come in as a tourist, he'd leave a package for someone, he maybe spends the night and takes off. Another guy comes in, *he* picks up the dope and takes it somewhere else. This is a great vacation spot, right? There's maybe four or five people staying there every *week?* Anybody watching the place'd know something fishy's going on, but who's going to bother doing that? So some straight dude with a carload of kids drops by, the place is full up. Sorry, we're booked for the season, pal."

Laurel stopped a moment. Someone laughed at the cabin, and everybody else joined in. Everyone but us was having fun.

"Vinnie didn't have a thing to do with Michael's operation, hon. Vinnie's job was to mind his own business, keep out of the way. He wasn't supposed to even *talk* to anyone that stayed in those cabins. The guards they had around the place? He wasn't supposed to talk to them. This pissed him off, right? Vinnie has a lot of his old man's pride, he doesn't go for this at all. Michael's set up Vinnie and the lovely twins up for life, but Vinnie's not happy with that. Michael lets him run the Spudettes, that's it, he won't let him mess with anything else."

Laurel made a face. " 'Serving the American Sportsman's Needs.' Shit, I don't mind whoring too much, but I sure hate looking like a fool."

"The moose taco business and Tommy Gee's. Michael didn't know about that, of course, or Angela wouldn't have gotten near the place."

"Lord no, he didn't." Laurel rolled her eyes. "He didn't, but he damn sure found out. Somebody tipped him after that fire. Or Carl sweet-talked it out of someone, Carl's awful good at that. Michael kept Vinnie on a tight leash, Wiley. If he'd had any idea Vinnie and Angela had gone into business for themselves, he'd have come down on 'em a whole lot sooner than he did."

"Right," I said, "only that wasn't the reason he came after Vinnie. That had something to do with the fat guy, and you've always had trouble with that, you don't like to get into that."

Laurel gave me a fiery look. *"You're* having trouble with the goddamn fat guy, Wiley, I'm not. I told you everything I know, all right? You got some kinda fixation on the dude, you're going to have to work it out."

I looked at her maybe a full half-minute. Half a minute is a very long time, you look a person right in the eye, they look right back and they don't react at all. Laurel was very good at that, but Laurel was under stress. That cool, bullshit demeanor was still intact, but she was tired, scared out of her wits.

"Okay, right," I said. "I think I got it straight. You stop me, now, babe, if I get off the track. Rocco had the fat guy on tape. The fat guy, the fat guy's fucking people and lower forms of life. Daisy says he's also shipping cuties overseas. You say the cuties are on the tapes, too. We've got a porno tape, we've got a sales video. Abdul sees the tapes. He buys two girls instead of one, okay, he buys three.

"Meanwhile, Michael is running dope through Idaho, hidden in tacky souvenirs. This is why the fat guy's in the car with Michael that night. The fat guy's working with Michael, he's into dope too.

The fat guy's got a piece of Michael's action, Michael's got a little stock in slaves and video. So far so good?

"Michael and the fat guy leave Vinnie's that night. Later, Michael comes back. Only this time, Michael is really pissed. Michael isn't happy so he blows Vinnie Spuds all to shit. Why, though? Why that particular night? I don't know, I don't have any idea. Did Michael kill Rocco and Nix? What for? And if he didn't do it, who did?

"If it isn't any trouble, Laurel, while you're dreaming up answers to the rest of this crap, could you tell me what Angela wants with Daisy and Columbine? You haven't ever bothered to let me in on that. And Michael, why did he chase the Spudettes? Why are Michael and Angela the very best of friends? What's Bobby up to, where does *he* stand? Can dolphins talk to each other, or is that another scam? If God's everywhere, where does he go when he gets some time off? If I'd listened to my family, I'd be in Ohio right now. I'd have a house, I'd have a dog, I'd have a hardware store. I'd have a wife and a kid by now. Okay, strike that, I want to think about that.

"You see what I'm saying? There aren't any 'maybes' in my life anymore. I'm going to die right here in fucking Idaho. Jesus, Laurel, I'm going to die in a state that's got a *horizontal* time zone . . ."

More laughter from the house. I heard a glass clink. They were sure having fun over there.

Laurel said, "Are you through, is that it?"

"I don't know. It's all I can think of right now."

She took a deep breath. "I don't know if the fat guy's into dope. Michael is, I don't know any more than that. I don't have any idea why he did Vinnie in. You want a good guess, I'd say he learned Vinnie had some rackets on the sly. Maybe he tried to scare Vinnie, knocking off Rocco and Nix. Only Vinnie's too dumb to ever figure that out.

"Michael would whack the Spudettes because they were there, okay? Because he was closing Vinnie down. Your bigtime mobsters don't like a lot of loose ends, hon. A man like Michael doesn't have any soul. Killing off a bunch of whores, that isn't anything to him.

"You want to know why Michael and Angela are big buddies now? I thought you watched the cop shows, Moss. Crime is the same as your ordinary business enterprise. Whoever's winning, that's who's side you're on."

"Winning *what*, Laurel? Like, getting the best of Vinnie Spuds?

Vinnie isn't worth the trouble. A guy like Michael, he's got better things to do."

"I don't *know* that, Wiley." Laurel ran a hand across her face. "You think I know the secrets of the entire universe, but I don't, all right? I just know a little bitty part."

Laurel stopped, gave me a deep and searching look. Reached out and took my hand, changed her mind and drew it back.

"I told you I stretched the truth some, I said I left some stuff out. The part I left out was Daisy, Wiley, because it wasn't my secret to tell. I told you they might use force sometime and you'd talk, and you kinda laughed at that. Shit, honey, it's nothing to laugh about. Everybody talks, and you break a lot sooner than you'd ever dream you would."

She held my hand again, and this time she didn't let go.

"Daisy isn't—who you think she is. Daisy isn't her name, and don't ask me what it is. She comes from a real rich family back East. I'm not talking your ordinary rich, I'm talking 'bout folks who piss on the Rockefellers, right?

"Rich doesn't always mean happy, I don't have to tell you that. Daisy was a troubled child, and she ran away from home when she was barely fifteen. That was five years ago and she's been gone since. She wanted to go back home, but she was in the life then, and couldn't face her family again. Besides, the work seemed to suit her just fine and she didn't want to quit. I can tell you for sure, there's plenty of rich girls has trodden that same path before.

"By the time she really *wanted* to go, she was working for Vinnie, and Vinnie doesn't let his girls out. It wasn't long after we got here from Tommy's, Angela found out who Daisy really was. I'm thinking it was Rocco found her out first. I think he got her drugged or flat scared her to death, or likely maybe both.

"Rocco passed on what he knew to Angela. Something like that, he knew he couldn't handle it himself. Angela paid him off, or promised him a cut he'd never get. I think Angela had a feeling things'd turn to shit for her and Vinnie someday. If they did, she could use Daisy to get herself out.

"Daisy told me what she said, she put it to her straight, and she scared that girl half to death. You got two choices, she said. I get you out of here, I take you back home. Your old man's grateful, I trade you for a couple of million bucks. Your other choice is, I give you to Rocco for good. You think he's been rough on you before, you haven't seen anything yet. A week with that freako I tell him go ahead, you'll wish you were fucking dead."

There were fine beads of sweat on Laurel's cheeks and on her upper lip. "What do you think Daisy did? You know what she did. She was scared of Rocco, and she stole those pictures to keep him off her back. Rocco found her out in about a minute and a half. The son of a bitch would've killed her on the spot, only Angela wouldn't like that. Rocco knew what Angela would do if her ace in the hole turned up dead."

"And she told you all this."

"Yes, she told me all this, she's my very best friend. I've known who she was since we worked together at Tommy Gee's, maybe a year before that."

"So when trouble did start, Angela ran right to her nest egg. She got Daisy out. She also got Columbine, though. I don't get that."

Laurel looked away, but not quite fast enough. "I don't know why, I don't know the answer to that."

"Sure you do, Laurel. You've got an answer for everything in the fucking universe."

"I said I *don't*, goddamn it!" I was startled by the sudden explosion of anger, and I knew it wasn't all for me.

"There's—something between those two and I don't know what it is. I never have. You see 'em together, you wouldn't think they even know each other. They sure as hell do, though, I'll tell you that."

A thin slice of late evening sun slanted through a crack and burnished Laurel's hair with gold.

"Columbine's here because Daisy told Angela she could threaten all she liked, she wasn't going anywhere without her. That's what she said. Angela didn't have a lot of time to argue, with half the state on fire."

Laurel showed me a little lopsided smile. *"I'm* here, hon, because Angela wanted a little insurance on the side. Daisy didn't behave, she'd do both me and Columbine in."

I thought about that. "And I'm here for what? Make sure *you* stay in line? If you don't behave she'll whack me?"

"Get real, Wiley." Laurel looked pained. "You're here because you're shit out of luck. What you should've done, you shoulda stayed away from art."

"Thanks, it's a little late for that. Laurel, when they come in here, you toss that garden hose at them, I'll hit 'em low. They'll get tangled up, I'll go for a weapon and gun a few down."

"Wiley—"

"Hey, I know it's risky, but I'd rather do that than just sit here and wait. At least we can—"

It struck me, then, hit me like a bowling ball, you don't get a real good grip and the ball falls on your foot.

"Laurel, what are we *thinking* about? If Angela's making a couple of million bucks off Daisy, what's the big deal? Her old man isn't going to pay to get Daisy back dead. And if Daisy's okay, we're all okay, right? Angela won't risk hurting Daisy's friends. Hey, we're going to be just— Laurel? Laurel, you're looking at me funny, stop doing that, I don't like you doing that—"

"Oh, shit, Wiley. Hold me, will you? Hold me good, hon!"

Laurel's face twisted out of shape. Everything seemed to come apart. She came into my arms and her whole body shook. I could feel hot tears on my neck.

"Laurel, what is it, what's wrong? Get hold of yourself, everything's going to be fine—"

Okay, not what she wanted to hear, there was something wrong with that. Something caught fire in her eyes, something went wrong inside her head.

"You stupid fuck!" She doubled up her fists and started pounding on my head.

"STUPID . . . MIDWESTERN . . . FUCK!"

Laurel screamed and shook. Her hair flailed about like a whip. She got her legs in gear and tried to kick me in the crotch. I tried to hold her off but she hit me like a woman gone berserk. I knew she couldn't help it, I knew she couldn't stop. I didn't want to hit her back. I don't think you ought to hit a woman, even if she's nuts.

"I don't know what's gotten into you," I yelled, "but I wish to hell you'd stop. I think we ought to talk about this."

"STUPID . . . ASSHOLE . . . MIDWESTERN . . . FU—"

The door of the shed flew open. Light flooded in and Carl blocked it out. He plucked Laurel up with one hand, held her by the neck and slapped her in the face. Not a big slap, Carl didn't have to do that, Carl was very large. Laurel made a little sound and he dropped her on the ground. Picked her up and slapped her again. Stepped to the door and tossed her outside. Tossed her away like a used-up match or an empty paper cup.

"You son of a bitch!" I said, and came in swinging at his head. Carl looked annoyed. He took the blow on his arm, grinned and grabbed my nose.

Jesus, that hurt, it hurt a whole lot. A guy grabs your nose, it isn't just your nose, your nose has got nerves that go everywhere at once. You feel it in your toes and you feel it in your gut.

"All right, Carl, that'll be fine . . ."

Carl gave me one last twist and let go. Michael was standing by the shed, Angela by his side. She was wearing a bright sundress, holding a drink in her hand. Blood dripped off my nose and I wiped it on my shirt. I helped Laurel up. Her mouth hung open and her eyes were out of whack.

"You're something else, Moss, you know that?" Angela shook her head in disgust. "Michael, is this guy something else or what?"

Michael didn't look at her, he looked right at me. He was dressed in pale linen slacks, a white silk shirt and no tie, fawn-colored loafers without any socks.

"You took a shot at me, pal. I don't much care for that."

He held up his arm and showed me a neat white bandage, just above his wrist. He had a very hairy wrist and a Rolex watch.

"It looks okay to me," I said. "You might want to get a tetanus shot."

"You think?"

"I don't think it ever hurts, something like that."

Michael smiled. I had never seen him in the daylight, I'd never seen him close. His eyes were dead black, black without any whites at all. Stick a flounder in the freezer in 1946. Take it out and have a look, this is Michael Galiano, his eyes are going to look like this.

Laurel trembled by my side, Laurel held on tight. Michael looked at Carl. Carl turned and walked down toward the van. Three of Michael's hoods were there, and Angelo was squatting on the ground. The river was already dark. The sun was dropping behind the canyon wall, and the light turned everybody red.

"I don't need this, you know? This guy shoots me, you bring the guy here, you bring the guy and the broad, why the fuck you bring 'em here?"

He turned his cold eyes on me, glanced at Laurel, then back to Angela again.

"Michael, I just—"

"Fuck that. Fuck you, okay? This is fucking aggravating, I haven't got time for this shit, you think I got nothing else to do?"

Little white circles appeared below Angela's eyes. She licked her lips and kept her mouth shut.

"Wiley," Laurel said, "I think I'm going to throw up."

"Don't." Michael wagged a finger in her face. "You're not doing that, I don't like it, someone's doing that. Bobby, get your ass out here, it's getting fucking dark."

Michael scarcely raised his voice. Bobby Bad Eye appeared on the porch by the house. He was wearing old jeans and a white T-shirt. Hey, why not, I thought, everybody else is here. Everyone but Vinnie, Vinnie wasn't there.

"Where's Vinnie," I said, "is Vinnie here or what?"

Michael said, "You play a lot of golf?"

"I do but not a lot."

"Vinnie's not playing. Vinnie didn't make the cut."

"Oh. Right."

"Any more questions?"

"No I guess not."

"Bobby, let's get this show on the road, I'm supposed to be in fucking L.A. right now."

Bobby waved. Bobby walked back in the house. When he came back out, he had a guy with him, a very fat guy in boxer shorts. The guy's hands were taped behind his back, and his mouth was taped shut. He was crying and he'd messed up his shorts. His legs were shaky and he had a lot of trouble standing up. Bobby kicked him off the porch and he landed on his face. The hoods enjoyed this a lot. Carl didn't laugh. Angelo looked at something else.

Bobby stepped back in the house. He came out with two tall women in T-shirts and shorts. I looked at them and stared. My mind went totally blank. I closed down shop, shut everything out. You can't see something, then something isn't there . . .

Laurel saw them too. A sound started low in her throat, grew into a scream, rose past it through a howl, through a shriek, to an unearthly wail. She tried to get away and I wrapped my arms around her and held onto her tight. She kicked and she clawed but I wouldn't let her loose, I wouldn't let her go.

Daisy and Columbine turned and saw their friend. Their eyes above the tape were wide with fright, eyes like scared little kids who knew their nightmares were real, eyes like animals, wild and terrified, cornered by the light.

Bobby marched them down to the river, kicking the fat man, pushing him along, the fat man crying all the time, Daisy and Columbine out of it now, too numb, too freaking paralyzed, to do anything at all. At the river he shoved them to their knees, lined them in a row, went to the fat man and held his shoulders down, pressed a big pistol to his neck. The fat man jerked and went down and the weapon hardly made a sound. Bobby moved to Daisy and the gun made a little noise again, and he went to Columbine and quickly put a bullet in her head. Daisy twitched once, and Columbine lay perfectly still.

Laurel screamed and wouldn't stop, and the sound echoed off the canyon walls, and down the dark river, and I've never heard anything like it, not anything at all, not ever in my life . . .

34

Michael turned on Laurel in a fury, fury in the tight white corners of his mouth, in the set of his jaw, fury in the black marble rattlesnake eyes.

"Shut her up . . . *Shut—her—up—right—now!*"

He reached behind his back, whipped out the silver pistol and aimed it right at Laurel's head.

"Listen," I said, "she can't help it, Goddamn it, she's real upset. You'd be screaming too."

I turned half around, holding Laurel close. If he shot at her now he'd hit me in the back.

Michael glared. "Get away from her. Move over there."

"Huh-unh, I can't do that."

Laurel kept screaming, Laurel couldn't stop. I held on tight and she kicked me in the shins and waved her arms about.

Michael looked cool in his pale linen pants, in his shoes with no socks, in his summer gangster shirt. He was cool but he was pissed. He didn't care for screaming, screaming seemed to bother him a lot.

"Shit," Michael said.

He dropped his hand to his side. He looked down the river. It was getting too dark to see faces anymore. No one moved, everyone was very still. Laurel wasn't screaming anymore, she was gasping for breath, she was shaking in my arms.

Michael muttered something to himself, jerked quickly around and faced Angela.

"You do it. You take care of this."

"What?" Angela blinked. "Do—take care of what?"

"What the fuck you think, do what? You brought them here, I don't know 'em, I don't need 'em, okay? You should've taken care of this, Angela. You didn't, so do it, finish it now."

Angela got it. It took her a second but she got it, and even in the dark of the river I could see the color drain from her face, I could see her stagger back like she'd hit a solid wall.

"I don't—think I want to, Michael. I mean, I could, but I—don't want to right now, is that all right with you?"

Michael laughed aloud. "You don't *want* to? I tell you something, you say to me, I don't *want* to?"

"Michael—"

"It don't bother you, I'm in a fucking forest fire, you're shooting at *me*, I'm burning up in there, you and your fat ass brother, you're shooting at my car, this is okay, you're fucking shooting at me. I ask you nice to shoot somebody else, you don't *want* to. You don't want to shoot these fucking clowns, it's okay to shoot me."

"Michael, we got all that straight between us, we talked about that, okay? We got that settled, now don't you start on me."

"I didn't talk. You talked, all the talking came from you."

Angela glared. "Don't you say we didn't talk, we had a *talk.*"

"Do it, Angela—"

"You son of a bitch!" Angela clenched her fists in anger. "I got you what you wanted, I saved your sorry ass, Michael Galiano, you think about that."

"I'm thinking," Michael said. "Thanks for all your fucking help."

He raised his arm and shot her. The night turned flashbulb-white. The bullet hit Angela like a fist, turned her around and knocked her off her feet. Before she hit the ground, Michael swung the weapon on me . . .

I was halfway there when the shot whined a foot above my head. I hit him at the knees, took him down, heard the breath explode from his lungs as he struck the ground hard. He still had the gun. He tried to club me in the head and I punched him in the face. The gun fell away. I hit him again and I heard the bone snap in his nose.

Michael yelled and the blood poured into his mouth. I grabbed his hair and pounded his head on the ground. He spat a red glob in my face. Man, I hated that. I tried to pull away. His right came up out of nowhere and clipped me on the jaw. I fell on my back and he was on me like a cat. He hammered me with both hands, shaking his head, tossing blood about. I held up my right to keep him off, brought down my left and punched him in the nuts.

Michael howled and fell away, rolled on the ground, and struggled to his knees. I went in low and kicked out at his head. Michael grabbed my foot, gave a quick twist and tossed me to the ground. I came up in a crouch. We faced each other in a ritual stance. *West Side Story* without any music, in darkest Idaho.

Someone down the beach said "Son of a bitch!" Someone else ran. Someone fired a shot. Someone said "Shit!" and yellow fire blossomed in the night.

Michael came at me, shaking his head and spitting blood. I called Laurel's name, couldn't find her in the dark. Michael's eyes were black in the black-black night. His shirt was in tatters, an off-the-shoulder rag.

Another shot somewhere, another bright light. Michael came at me, hit me in the chest and I hit him in the neck. He kicked at me and missed. A gangster loafer went sailing through the dark. I grabbed Michael and Michael grabbed me back. We grappled and we grabbed. We stood toe to toe, and we beat on each other for a while.

"You crime lords aren't as tough as you think," I told him. "I'll bet you never tangled with an artist in your life."

"Fuck you," Michael said, just the reply you might expect.

"Talk's cheap," I said, and he hit me in the mouth.

I hit him in the gut, he hit me in the head. I hit him in the eye and he howled and grabbed his face, turned around and ran and stumbled in the dark.

I jumped on his back, pounded on his head. He bucked and threw me off. I got to my feet, went back at him, swung at him and missed. The lights came on and struck me blind, sizzled in my eyeballs, sliced through my head.

I stopped, threw up my hands before my face. Michael stumbled back.

A car door opened. Someone stepped out and stood behind the lights.

"You got a left, Mikey," the guy said. "I seen a better right."

"*Joey*. . . ?" Michael stared. "What—what are you doing, what're you doing here?"

Joey shrugged. Joey was big and he had a big shrug.

"You better oughta ask Uncle Sal, Mikey, don't be asking me."

"Sal's here?"

"He just wants to talk to you, Mikey."

"I didn't call him, I got nothing to talk about. He's got no business coming here."

"Hey, Mikey." Joey showed him an easy smile. "The old guy wants to talk, talk to the man, okay?"

Michael didn't move. Joey looked at me. "I don't know him, who's this supposed to be?"

"He's an art guy," Michael said.

"Yeah? No shit?"

Joey led us out of the light. A man who looked like Joey sat in the driver's seat. He didn't look at Michael, he didn't look at me.

The back door was open. Inside was a skinny old guy in a yellow polo shirt, a shirt three sizes too big, a horsey on the front. Black pants and lace-up shoes. Black socks with little white dogs. Pit bulls or poodles, I couldn't tell which. Seventy, maybe seventy-five. Thinning white hair, combed straight back. Wide broken nose. A mouth that hadn't smiled since 1946. Cloudy gray eyes. Eyes like water in a sewer. When the drain backs up, this is the color that starts filling up the sink.

I'd never seen the man before, but I knew the man sitting to his right. It was Vinnie "Spuds" DeMarco, Vinnie in half a mile of gauze, Vinnie's lizard eyes poking through his mummy suit. And even though Michael had told us he was dead, he didn't look very dead to me. The look on Michael's face said this was a big surprise to him.

"Hey, Michael," Vinnie said, "you look like shit, you look as bad as me."

"Nobody looks as bad as you," Michael said. "I've run over dogs looked better than you. Fuckin' dog's been lying in the street for a week, the dog's looking better than you."

"Shut up, the both of you . . ."

Vinnie and Michael shut up. The man was old and frail, but the man had the magic in his awful offal eyes.

"Good to see you, Uncle Sal. I knew you were coming, I'd of put on somethin' nice."

"No dirty talk. I don't want to hear no 'fuck' or no 'doo-doo,' I don't want to hear nothing like that, either one of you. My wife, God rest her, she rode in this car for thirty years. The woman was a saint. She never heard a filthy word in her life, she don't want to hear one now, *I* don't want to hear nothing now. I'm sitting in the car, I'm sitting here all the way from Chicago, I got hemorrhoids the size of cantaloupes, I don't want to hear no dirty talk, I don't need nothing like that . . ."

No one said a word. The old man blinked. He looked at Michael and Vinnie, then he looked at me.

"Who's that, what's he doing here?"

"He's an art guy, Uncle Sal," Vinnie said.

"He's a what?"

"I've got a friend down there, sir, I'm a little concerned, I need to get back—"

"Shut up." Uncle Sal had a voice like gravel in a can. He studied me a minute, wasn't sure what I might be, gave it up and turned away.

"Michael, we got some kinda problem here, I don't know what, I don't know, maybe you can tell me. People are coming to me, they're calling me up, they are telling me things that I don't want to hear. These things I am hearing, they are very disturbing to me. People tell me stuff I say, hey, don't tell me nothing, I don't want to hear this from you. Something like this, I want to hear it from the nephew I love and respect since the day he was born. I want to hear these things from him, from the son of Johnny 'Thumbs' himself, this is what I want to hear."

Michael made a face. "Hey, Sal, what is this?" He waved his hands like he was chasing off flies. "This is some kinda, what? Where are you going with this—"

"Don't, Michael . . ."

Uncle Sal held him with his sad, septic eyes. "You lie to me, Michael, you show the family disrespect, you show disrespect to me. A lie comes outta your mouth, you're spitting on your father's grave, you're hawking up a big one, you got a whole mouthful of stuff, you're standing there you're spitting on his grave, sure as you were there instead of where you are now, which is some kinda state I never heard of before I got here."

Uncle Sal leaned back in his seat. He didn't look at Michael anymore.

"Get in the car, Michael. Joey, get Michael a towel or something, he's got stuff on him, I don't want nothing on the seats."

Michael jerked up straight. He stared at Sal, then turned on Joey, his eyes full of fire. "Who's running the family, Joey? I'm missing something here or what? Last time I looked it was me."

"You need to talk to him, Mikey . . ."

"You didn't answer. I ask you a question, you don't answer me."

Joey looked down at his feet. Michael looked at him, saw something there, then quickly glanced away. Wherever he was looking, it was somewhere else, it wasn't Idaho. Joey put his hand on Michael's shoulder. He leaned in close, said something no one else could hear. Whatever it was, it was something Michael clearly understood, something that left no doubt at all, because he'd known it and believed it all his life. He didn't look at Joey anymore. He got in the front seat of the car.

"Who was it?" Michael said. He didn't turn around, he didn't look back. "Who talked to you, Sal?"

"What's it matter? It don't matter who."

"It fucking matters to me."

"Hey. What did I say? No dirty talk in here . . ."

"Salvatore?" Joey leaned in the open door and nodded toward the front of the car.

I turned around and looked. The driver was out of the car now, standing by the hood. Bobby Bad Eye was struggling up the slope from the river, squinting against the lights. His face was cut and bruised, his features dark with blood. One shoulder dropped, and one hand clutched his side. Every time he took a step, pain raced across his features, clouded his single eye.

Bobby held Carl by the back of his collar. Carl looked a lot worse than Bobby Bad Eye. His face was raw burger, hold the onions, hold the fries. His hands dangled loosely by his sides. Bobby gave Carl a shove, and Carl collapsed on the ground.

Sal made the effort to pull himself erect. He looked at Carl on the ground.

"This guy worked for Charlie Catelli in Gary, I seen him up there. Runnin' over people, something like that. I think it was '87 or '88." He looked at Michael with sorrow and disgust. "Charlie Catelli was garbage. You work for a guy he's garbage, the stink rubs off on you. You can wash all you want, you can use a lot of soap, it don't matter any, the stink rubs off on you. A guy like that, he reflects on the guy who hires him, Michael. This was something we taught you, you ought to know that."

Sal looked at Joey. He didn't nod, he didn't say a thing. Joey leaned down and stuck a gun in Carl's ear. Joey's hand was so big you could hardly see the gun. Carl looked up with his hamburger face and said, "Whuuuh?" Carl didn't know where he was. Joey pulled the trigger and Carl didn't care.

Michael kept his eyes to the front. Carl wasn't his problem anymore, he had problems of his own.

"Bobby, you don't look good," Sal said. "You want a towel? Joey could get you a towel."

"I'm all right," Bobby said.

"I think you're maybe a stand-up guy, Bobby. For a guy that's not white, he ain't even civilized, I think you're okay. Vinnie wants you to know he isn't dumb, you didn't pull nothing on him. He knows you messed up a couple times, you maybe made a buck behind his back. Vinnie says you did him a favor, he's overlooking that."

"Yes, sir. And I want you and Vinnie to know I appreciate that and—"

"Shut up." Sal raised a bony hand. "A guy keeps talking, a guy don't know when to quit, this is a guy he maybe ought to take a rest. You want to look down, you'll see what I'm talking about."

Bobby didn't look down. He didn't look anywhere at all.

"Get me outta here, Joey. I see another mountain and a tree I'm going nuts."

Joey started to close the door. Uncle Sal stopped him and looked at me. "This guy he's a what? You told me what, I forgot."

"He's an art guy," Vinnie said.

Uncle Sal frowned. "The guy's been standing here, he hears a whole lot, he sees us whack a guy. Joey . . . ?"

"He's okay," Vinnie said. "The guy's an artist, the guy draws bugs. A guy like that, who's he going to talk to, who's he going to know?"

Uncle Sal thought about that. "Get me outta this place, I'm freezing out here."

"Vinnie? Back at the lodge, I mean before it burned down? You had a bunch of trout in a tank? All the fish were naked, but one had a little red shirt and little jeans. It was breathing real hard, I don't think it cared for Western wear—"

Vinnie looked stunned. Sal looked annoyed. "What? What's that, what's he talkin' about?"

The driver took off and left us in a plume of dust. In half a minute it was quiet. The lights disappeared, and Bobby and I were standing in the dark.

"You hurt pretty bad? You look shot up."

"What do you think, what's it look like to you?"

"Good. I'm going down there and find Laurel. Then I'm going to bury those poor girls you murdered, you savage son of a bitch. If you're not dead by then, I'm coming back up here and kick you to death."

"You are, huh?"

"You're damn right I am."

"Fine. Have at it, white man—"

Bobby's good eye looked funny, and his head rolled back and he dropped to the ground. I bent down and touched his throat. He was breathing real hard but he didn't look good. I got up and ran past the house to the river. I called Laurel's name, but there was nothing but the darkness and the silence down there . . .

39

It took half the night to reach Cottonwood, Idaho. The trip was 220 something miles, which is no big deal when you're out in the West, but I didn't want to speed since the car was semi-hot. Bobby had stolen it late the day before at a family restaurant.

The highlight of the trip came at one A.M., when we stopped for gas at Riggins and crossed the Pacific time zone. The zone cuts Idaho in half from east to west. At Riggins, it turns abruptly north, makes a long loop up the Salmon to the Snake, and runs back south again. This kind of shit must drive the locals nuts.

I picked up a pamphlet when I filled up with gas. Before it was Riggins, Riggins was called Gouge-Eye. The pamphlet didn't say why.

We checked into the motel a little after five. I told the very tired lady it was Laurel and me, I didn't mention anyone else.

Bobby looked bad. Carl had shot him twice, once in the thigh and once in the side. The thigh wound was minor, but the hole in his side was fairly deep and he'd lost a lot of blood. We got him inside, and Bobby came to for a moment and gave me a number to call.

It was quiet in Cottonwood, and the morning was pleasantly cool. Clouds hung low over Washington state, which is just past Lewiston and the Snake. I found a convenience store two blocks down, and used the booth outside. The doctor answered on the second ring. I told him I was calling for Bobby Bad Eye. A moment's hesitation and he told me how much. A cash call only, no plastic or a check.

We were in Cottonwood because it sits on the border of the Nez Perce Indian Reservation on Highway 95. Bobby said he wasn't welcome there, but he thought he might die. If he did, it'd be okay if we dropped off his body inside. *I* was there because I wanted to get as far from the shootout as I could. I didn't know shit about the state of Idaho, and Bobby Bad Eye did.

Bobby was asleep. He didn't look scary any more, he looked a little dead. His dark skin was white and his cheeks were hollow pits. I told Laurel the doctor was coming and he said his name was Smith. Laurel said she doubted that was it.

"I wish you'd gotten me a Pepsi, I don't much care for Cokes. And I'd rather have a Mounds than a Mars."

"They didn't have Mounds. All they had was Mars and Almond Joy."

"Why didn't you get me one of them?"

"You didn't say Almond Joy, you said a Mounds. A Mounds isn't like an Almond Joy. A Mounds is dark chocolate and coconuts. An Almond Joy's got—"

"I know what it's got, I am not feeble-minded, hon. An Almond Joy and a Mounds are sister candy bars. They're not alike, but they are."

"Sister candy bars."

"That's right. Mounds and Almond Joy. Wiley, if the son of a bitch croaks, I want him out of here. I don't care for him alive, I'm not going to like him any dead."

"Why don't you lie down awhile and watch the TV? I'll get you up when the doctor gets here."

Laurel made a face. "Lie down where? That's not even a queen-size bed. I doubt it'll handle any more."

I looked at the bed across from Bobby's where Daisy and Columbine were zonked out under the spread. They breathed now and then, but they hadn't moved an inch since we'd pulled in at five. They'd been through a lot, and they needed all the rest they could get.

"I'm scared, Wiley. I don't like being here, and I don't like being here with him. I got a funny feeling 'bout this."

"Look at him," I said. "What's he going to do?"

"He's an Indian, Wiley. They are closer to the earth than you and me. He could be lying in a coma and call up a—a spirit from ancient times. He could bring an evil presence in here."

"Bobby Bad Eye would scare the shit out of an evil presence. I think we're okay."

Laurel didn't answer. She gave me a look that said she wasn't buying that.

She sat in a straight-back chair, she didn't go to bed. The ceiling had leaked for some time. It had those stains like dirty brown clouds. I saw a motorcycle and a horse. Richard Nixon talking to a dog.

Dr. Smith was a sleazeball, a nervous little guy with dirty nails and bad teeth. Dandruff and cheap whiskey breath. If you run in Bobby's crowd, you can find these people everywhere. They will patch you up or hide you out, sell you an Uzi or some coke. Some of them will quickly sell you out.

This one gave Bobby a bandage and some pills. He told me Bobby needed blood, and the bullet was too deep for him to take it out. Bobby might make it without proper care, and then he might not. He said we owed him five hundred bucks.

I went in the bathroom and got Bobby's money belt and counted out the bills. Bobby's belt was a convenience we hadn't counted on. Laurel found it when we got him in the car. Nine tightly-packed stacks of Franklins, fifty bills in each. Forty-five grand, which helped a lot with gas and candy bars.

Laurel said she couldn't sleep but she did. She slept on the floor curled up in ball. The first hint of morning leaked through the blinds. Sometimes a car whined by.

I thought about the car outside. I'd rubbed a little dirt on the plates. I hoped this would thwart the local law if they had the time to look for stolen cars.

There seemed to be some irony in this. It hadn't been long since all I wanted was the highway patrol, the F.B.I. and every cop in Idaho. Now, all I wanted was out. I didn't want to talk about Vinnie or meece or Michael and Uncle Sal. I didn't want to talk about the problem on the Snake, and all the dead bodies back there. Sometimes, the law is understanding. Sometimes, if you're among the living, they tend to blame you for the people who are not.

I woke up freezing to death. The A/C rattled in the wall and I couldn't turn it off. Bobby's watch said twenty after ten. Bobby himself said, "What time is it? Some thief stole my watch."

I went quickly to him. "I did," I said. "It's twenty after ten. How are you feeling, can I get you anything?"

Bobby said it was much too hot in the room, and some water would suit him fine.

"I guess I got to thank you for hauling me out. You could've left me there, I wouldn't much blame you for that."

"Let's get something straight," I said. "I don't give a shit about you, I want to be clear about that. I mostly did it because you didn't shoot Daisy and Columbine. That, and you said you knew a place to go. I figured you did, and I didn't mind using you for that. Only, all the way up here I thought about what you did to me, and what you did to everybody else. I thought about Billy, at Billy's Gas & Auto Repair. I thought about that, and I thought about my date with Claire de Mer. I wished I had the guts to stop and dump you in the road. I still wish I did, but I don't."

"Yeah, I kind of figured that."

He tried to turn his head and glance at the other bed. The pain hit him hard and he moaned and held his breath.

"You okay?"

"What do you think?"

"I'd say you're not. You want a pill you can have it. I gave you a couple last night. If you want to know about them, they're all right. Their ears are going to ring for a while, and you scared them half to death. You like to tell me why you didn't do it, Bobby? I mean, besides the fact that you're a really caring guy."

Bobby gave me a sour look. "White guys always gotta know why. I never saw a white guy, didn't have to work it all out, didn't have to know why. I didn't want to, okay? The girls were all right. The fat guy was a prick. I should've shot him twice."

"You kill the fat guy, you don't shoot the girls. You work for

Vinnie, you work for his sister sometimes. You work for Michael and Uncle Sal. What do you do, make up the rules as you go along?"

"In this business, you look out for yourself. Organized crime's got its drawbacks, Mr. Moss."

Bobby stopped to catch his breath. His face was beading up with sweat. I couldn't tell which eye looked worse, the good one or the bad.

"That stuff you said, that's crap. I never worked for anyone but Vinnie, I got a personal pride. I'm up there setting fire to you like Vinnie said. Michael shows up, he's been there once, he's back again, this time he's shooting up everything in sight. I go back and help Vinnie and I'm dead. I don't see any sense in that. Angela shows up and hits me in the head. When I wake up everything's burning, I go down the hill and take a look. Vinnie isn't dead but he's burned real bad. Vinnie's pissed off because Angela went and left him there. 'If she's running, I know where she's going,' Vinnie says. 'She's hauling her ass to Tommy Gee's.'"

"Vinnie didn't send her to tell you to stop, he changed his mind, he didn't want to burn me up?"

Bobby looked annoyed. "Who told you that? Shit, I guess I know who told you that."

"What did Angela want with the girls, Bobby? She wanted them a hell of a lot to risk her life in that fire."

Bobby forced a painful grin. "Maybe she's a caring kind of person like me."

"Bobby, what did she want the girls *for*? Angela and Michael have a big shoot-out, but she ends up giving the girls to *him*. Michael wants the girls and the fat guy dead. *What the hell for?*"

Bobby didn't answer. He closed his good eye and his mouth fell open and a tremor shook him from head to foot. A terrible rattle came out of his chest, a deep and hollow sound, a sound an awful lot like death. I counted to three. Bobby took a breath, then another after that. In a minute he was sleeping with an outlaw smile on his face.

"I'm going out for a while," I told Laurel, "if I knock four times that's me."

She opened her eyes, gave me a sleepy little kiss. "I care for you a lot, Wiley Moss. You and me, we going to make something out of this or what?"

"I wouldn't mind," I said, "as long as it's shallow with a lot of mindless sex."

"You know how to turn a girl's head, I'll say that."

At noon I got a bus into Lewiston, which is fifty-something miles away. I changed a few hundred dollar bills at a bank and a couple of grocery stores. I got the Boise papers and ate the biggest steak in town.

Startling events had occurred, and no one was sure just exactly how they fit. The big forest fire had left several dead bodies and burned-out cars. None of the bodies had been identified. I didn't want to think about that.

There had been a big shootout at Tommy Gee's Totally Nude Domino Parlor and Family Entertainment Park. Several known felons from out of state were dead. Also deceased were Thomas "Smiley" Gee, and Billy Joe Bosco who was shot at least eighty-seven times.

Finally, discovered too late for a detailed account, was a "possible gangland killing" on the Snake. Again, none of the victims had been identified. One had had his head blown away, at least two mobsters had severe sturgeon bites. One of the victims was a woman and the paper said she'd been shot twice—once in the shoulder and once in the head. Interesting, I thought, since Michael had only shot Angela once. Laurel could probably shed some light on this, but I decided not to ask.

Columbine was crying.

Bobby looked dead.

Laurel and Daisy were nowhere in sight.

"What do you mean, gone," I said, loud enough to wake the possibly dead. "Gone *where?*"

"I haven't done a thing, Wiley Moss, so don't you yell at me, I can't handle that."

"I'm sorry," I said, and held her to my chest. "I'm a little upset. I can't imagine why she'd go and do something like this. Everything was fine, she was fine when I left. Did she say anything, you have any idea what got into her head?"

Columbine sniffed. "I don't have a single thought left. All I've got is confusion and sorrow, Wiley. Those girls meant everything to me. They didn't even wake me up, they didn't even say good-bye. I think I deserve a lot better than that. Here, I guess you better read this."

Columbine handed me a note. It was all wrinkled up, written on a sack from the store down the street.

Dear Wiley,

Well I expect you are real upset with me but I have to do what's right and that is to get Daisy out of here before she has a full-blown nervous attack. I don't expect you to understand, hon, but I owe her a lot because she's done a lot for me, I don't know if I can ever pay her back but I know I've got to try. It has been real nice knowing you in an intimate and personal way, and I hope the winds of Fate, which operate in ways you and I can never fully comprehend, will sometime waft you back my way.

Sincerely yours,

Laurel

"Well, great," I said, "just what is this supposed to mean? She could have waited until I got back, there wasn't any reason for something like this."

"Reason isn't always clear to us, Wiley. God doesn't wholly reveal his plan to those down on the mortal plane . . ."

"Don't you start, okay? I've got about all the cosmic shit I can take right now. I brought some stuff to eat. There's sandwiches and chips and some root beers in there."

"I'm not real hungry right now, but thank you just the same."

I looked at Bobby and he still looked dead. I went to the bathroom and came back out and Columbine had eaten her sandwich and half a bag of chips. Bobby was awake. I brought him some water and he drank about an ounce and said he didn't want a pill.

"It don't even hurt anymore," he told me. "Your body doesn't hurt, that means your time is near. I had a lot of money. I guess you got your hands on that."

"Yes, I did. You want it back, that's fine with me."

"You doing a joke of some kind, it doesn't work with me. Give it to the Nez Perce. They got a tribal headquarters up at Lapwai, that isn't far from here. What I think you'll do, I think you'll keep it for yourself."

"Uh-huh, that's what you'd think, all right, that's the working of the criminal mind. I know where that money comes from, Bobby. It comes from illicit enterprise. You said you never cheated Vinnie, but I'm not buying that. You knew what Michael was up to, even if Vinnie didn't. This is cash you skimmed off of coke or illegal video, or those poor girls the fat guy shipped overseas. You think I want money comes from that? I don't make a lot in art, but I can sleep at night."

Bobby looked at me and stared. He choked and coughed and spat and his face turned ethnic red.

"Whuhda—what are you smoking, Mr. Moss, what the shit is this? What's with the coke and who's going overseas, what are we talking about here?"

"Fine," I said, "you don't want to do this, that's okay with me. You're headed for the Happy Hunting Ground, I'd get myself straight if I were you."

"Might be a good idea," Bobby said.

"Damn right it is."

"You want straight, you've got it. I've got nothing to hide, I've got nothing else to do. First I got to tell you, Mr. Moss, you're the whitest guy I ever saw. It's no big surprise that you don't know shit about anything at all. Angela and Michael? They been fucking on the side for some time. He's using her, she's using him.

"I never heard of this dope and video crap. Michael told the Galianos he's running a string of gambling joints. What he did, he used the family money to make big bucks in Western real estate. Michael makes a million profit on a hundred grand, he sends the family fifty percent. Not fifty percent of the million, half the hundred grand. The family's happy, they think they're makin' a mint.

"Angela knows about this, it's her job to see Vinnie stays asleep. Meanwhile, she's using her cut to squeeze Vinnie out of Tommy Gee's and that moose taco deal, which Michael doesn't know they've got."

I looked at Columbine. Her face was a ghostly shade of TV blue. The guy on the game show had just won a two-week trip to Idaho.

"You're telling me the video thing, all that other stuff, Laurel and Daisy made it up?"

"Don't take my word for it, white man, ask 'em yourself."

"Well I can't do that."

"Why not?"

"Bobby, none of this makes any sense. Michael's buying real estate, someone's knocking everybody off. So what's going on, and *where does the goddamn fat guy come in?*"

Bobby started shaking and coughing up death, a terrible sound that sent a shiver up my back.

"Can I have some water? I'm not feeling real good."

I gave him some water. Maybe half an ounce.

"The fat guy's Abner O. Zzann. He built half of California and a whole lot of everything else. Zzann is stopping at the lodge one night. He's going to meet Michael, Michael sent him there. Zzann is the guy who's made Michael rich. The family thinks the lodge is a front for Michael's gambling operation, that Michael maybe launders money there. Michael doesn't use the place for shit. Some of his guys stay there when they're traveling for Michael, that's it."

"That's it?"

"That's it. Michael got a kick out of that. Vinnie and his sister and his brother just sitting in the place, doing nothing at all. Like dummies you dress up in a store, in case somebody walks by."

Bobby paused for breath. Thought a minute, decided not to die.

"I was out of town. I'd have been there, this never would've happened but it did. This Zzann guy gets pretty drunk. He tells Nix to get him a girl, he knows there's a bunch of girls there. Nix doesn't know what to do. Nix has got a minus IQ. He goes to Rocco and Rocco says no. Zzann gives the guy a couple hundred bucks, says 'that's for one whore, how much for two?'"

Holy shit . . .

My stomach tightened in a knot. I knew where we were going with this, I knew exactly where we'd been. I could see it unfolding like a pizza nightmare where you wake up with the sweats. Only this time it's real and it's not a dream at all, I'm in a fucking horror show . . .

"Right," Bobby said. Bobby wasn't dead yet, he could still read a face. "That's it, only that's not the end. Zzann starts bragging at the country club he knows this Mafia don, this gangster's got lots of pretty whores. Zzann is a guy who shouldn't drink. Word gets to Michael and Michael knows the family ever hears about this, Michael's had it, Michael's dead. They hear about the whores, they'll hear about the real estate deals.

"I don't even know about this, Rocco's too scared to talk to me. Michael gets nervous, Michael makes a big mistake. He doesn't come to me, he doesn't talk to Rocco or Nix. What he does, he tells Carl to go out and whack 'em both out. Fine. Only Michael gets to thinking, he better whack the girls out too, wrap everything up. Only, guess what? Rocco and Nix are dead, they're sleeping in the family rock pile. And Zzann was too drunk to remember what the girls looked like.

"Michael has to go and tell Angela what happened, and get her to help. Angela is pissed, but she's in too deep to back out. Michael drives in one night, he says he wants to have a drink with Vinnie, have a good time. The reason he's there is he's brought the fat guy around, he's got Zzann in the car. Angela slips Michael some ID shots of all the Spudettes. Michael shows the pictures to Zzann. He picks out the two Rocco brought to his room, and Michael knows who he's got to get."

"Daisy and Columbine."

"Right. Michael tells Angela he'll come back later in the night and take the girls. Angela doesn't like that, but Michael doesn't care. 'Don't worry,' he says, 'we'll do it real quiet. In and out, everyone'll think the whores just ran off.' "

"Only it didn't work out that way."

Bobby shook his head. "You think Michael Galiano's that dumb? Michael knows he's got to cover his ass, he can't leave any loose ends. What if Daisy and Columbine saw Abner Zzann's picture somewhere? This Zzann's got his picture everywhere. What if they told the other girls about their night with the big millionaire?

"Michael thinks about this, and he thinks about the family getting word some way that Rocco and Nix got whacked down here. What kind of operation has Michael got running his people are getting killed? There's only one thing he can do. He's got to wipe out the whole Idaho deal—Vinnie, Angela, the Spudettes. Tell the family another mob tried to muscle in, and he's taken care of that."

I tried to imagine what went through the mind of a man like

Michael Galiano. A man with the heart of a wolf, and ice cold Jell-O in his veins. Lemon or maybe lime.

"And you knew this," I said, "you know what Michael was up to all the time and you didn't do a goddamn thing!"

"Huh?" Bobby looked hurt. I'd hurt a man's feelings and the man was nearly dead. "No, I didn't know it, what kind of a guy you think I am?

"Okay, I knew something was up, but I didn't know what. I didn't know about the girls until Vinnie and I got to Tommy Gee's. Vinnie didn't get it, Vinnie was burned like a brisket, he was too pissed off to see straight at the time . . ."

Bobby told me the rest, the rest of it wasn't real hard. I probably could've finished it myself if Bobby dropped dead. Angela didn't trust Michael. She felt he might toss her away as soon as he got the girls. If she could get them first, she could squirrel them away somewhere and hold them over Michael's head, make sure he didn't cut her out. That's where she was going when Michael showed up and started shooting everyone in sight. Angela was quick—she knew right away their love affair was over, she wouldn't get out of there alive.

When Bobby showed up with Vinnie at Tommy Gee's, Angela panicked. Bobby saw Daisy and Columbine and knew something fishy was going on. Angela had to think fast. When they got a minute alone, she let Bobby in on the deal to buy herself some time.

"Angela figured she'd screw everybody," Bobby said, "and come up smellin' fine. She'd called up Michael on the car phone a couple of times, shaking him up a little, holding the girls over his head. Now, at Tommy's she's getting cold feet. She's scared what Michael might do, he catches up with her, she knows what kind of guy he is.

"So what does she do? She calls him up again. Says she sneaked down to use the phone, tells her it's *me,* the fuckin' Indian, it's me that's got the girls, I said I'd kill her if she didn't go along. Michael's to come to Tommy Gee's and get her out, but he's got to come in swinging, because Bobby Bad Eye's got his own people there.

"She said she'd shot at him back at the lodge because he broke his word and whacked Vinnie, but she could maybe live with that. She didn't have the girls when that happened, *I* did. I forced my

way into her car and made her drive to Tommy Gee's, made her
stop and make a bunch of phony calls.

"She was outside in the car with Daisy and Columbine when
Michael and his people got there. He's supposed to go in and kill
me and Vinnie and anybody else isn't a customer or a girl. She's
saved Daisy and Columbine, she's in the clear."

"Only you weren't there," I said. "I saw you and Vinnie take
off."

"Naw, I wasn't there. I knew better'n that. I got us in the—
Whuuug! Guuuukh! Guuuukh!"

Pain nearly shook Bobby out of his skin. He made a sound in his
throat, a sound so frightening and grim, Columbine nearly looked
up, nearly looked away from her show.

"I—got—got Vinnie outta there— She didn't know that, right?
Thought we—was all asleep. Michael was pissed about that, he was—
comin' apart at the seams . . ."

I was there, and "pissed off" scarcely described Michael's feelings
at the time, but I didn't want to get into that.

Once more, Bobby stopped to get his breath. He clutched at his
side, tried to grab the pain and pluck it out, but the pain knew it
had him, and it wouldn't go away. I'd mentioned the hospital twice
and he'd swung at me and missed, there was no using going over
that.

"You need to rest, take a break a while?"

"I'm dying, you want me to take a break? That's what dying is,
white man. Dying is taking a break."

"Right," I said, "no break. You got Vinnie out. You went to
Michael's place on the Snake. How did you know it was there, you
ever been there before?"

Bobby showed me a sly and happy grin. Crazy Horse had the
same grin at the Little Big Horn.

"No, I didn't know, I didn't know shit. Sal knew, though. Sal
had been down there, Sal knew where it was."

"Sal did."

"I called Sal the minute me and Vinnie got clear of the fire. I told
him Michael was fucking him, I didn't know how. Sal says go to the
cabin, he's flying right down. I leave Vinnie at Ketchum, Sal picks
him up there. I told Michael I've knocked Vinnie off, I've done him
a favor, I want to work for him."

"You what?" Something wasn't right about that. "Sal didn't fly down here, they drove him in a car."

Bobby let out a breath. "Naw, he didn't fly, he's in a rental car. He's a gangster, Mr. Moss. Your big time gangster's going to lie. A man runs a family like the Galianos, he wants to stay alive, twenty-four hours a day, the guy's gotta lie."

Bobby grinned again. "You know what's funny, you wanta hear the kicker to this? *I* turned Michael in. Angela covered her ass three ways, *Angela* turned him in. I think a couple guys worked for Michael, they turned him in. I think the lines to Chicago were all tied up, people turning Michael in."

Bobby closed his good eye and licked his dry lips. "I done a lot of bad shit in my life, Mr. Moss, there isn't any taking that back. But I'll tell you what, I've always been straight with a guy, I've always done my job with professional pride, and I never stole more than you'd normally expect from a man you're working for."

"You've got to be proud," I said.

"Fucking right, white man. A guy can go out of life smiling if he's done the best he can . . ."

36

Bobby got dead around eight.

I waited until it got dark, then I took him out and put him in the trunk. Columbine was all upset. She didn't like Bobby, but she said he couldn't help who he'd been, that he'd surely do better the next time around.

"This life is strewn with your karmic potholes, Wiley. You can fall in one of those, or your soul can have a flat. A lot of things can happen on the road to astral bliss."

"I think Bobby might've dropped a transmission somewhere. He might've cracked a block. Listen, I've got to drive him to the reservation, that was his last request. When I get back, we'll figure out what to do next. I know one thing for sure, we're going to leave this dump behind."

"I'll go along with that," she said. "I'm sure not getting any good vibes here."

We were sitting on the bed. Columbine shivered a little, her shoulders tucked in and the spread held tight around her back. I had managed to turn the A/C down to hurricane strength, but it was still too cold in there.

"You have any idea what you might want to do, Columbine? Somewhere you want to go, you have family anywhere?"

"There isn't anyone, Wiley, no one at all. I told you, those girls meant everything to me, that's all the family I had."

She looked up then and I took her face in my hands and I kissed her tears away. Then I kissed the corners of her mouth, and the little tuft of hair above her cheek. It felt so fine to hold this slim and lovely woman in my arms, to sniff the sweet scent a woman hides behind her neck, the salty beads of sweat, the cheap perfume and the drugstore shampoo.

As I held her close, as I peeked down her neck where her shirt pooched out, I thought what a wonder, what a miracle it is, that even in a time of sorrow and grief, of sadness and regret, we never lose sight of lust and deviation and desire, of the basic needs that define our way of life.

"I don't understand it, Wiley, I don't know to this day just why those people were doing that stuff, why they were being so mean. All I know is I was scared."

"Doing what stuff, Columbine, what do you mean?"

She laid her head on my chest. "You know. Taking us off in the car like that? I said, 'why, why do they want to do that?' And Daisy said we just had to be quiet, not to do or say a thing, do everything they said. Do that, she said, and she figured we'd come out all right."

I looked at her. "Daisy said that? She said you'd come out all right?"

"Uh-huh. She said, 'Columbine. I think it's going to be all right, I think we're going to be okay.' Well, I began to have doubts when that Indian dragged us down to the river. What I thought was, he was going to blow my head off."

"I guess that would—give you a start," I said. I had never thought Columbine was smart as a whip. Shameful to say, I'd never really looked that far until now.

"Daisy and Laurel going off like that. I don't know what I did to offend, but you shouldn't do people that way, you know? That's not the thing to do."

"I can't explain it," I said, "it's an unfeeling act, but I'm sure they just got a little scared. I guess we've all been going through that."

"And what about you, Wiley Moss?"

"What about me, Columbine?"

"You going away and leave me too, like everybody else?"

Her hand trailed down my neck and down my chest and then down after that.

"Not on your life," I said, "don't you even think about it, I'm not going anywhere."

"You and me came close a couple times. I know you were thinking on it too."

"Yes I was," I said. "I was thinking like that."

She gave me a sleepy little smile, and her hair fell down about her eyes. "I think the good Lord above or the creator of your choice has meant for us to be. I think there's feelings that we got to work out."

"I think you're right, Columbine. I definitely think you're—"

Columbine sat up straight, held both my hands and looked me in the eye.

"What *I* think, Wiley, is all the damn time we were going through troubles, and didn't know what might happen to us next, I felt like I was flat being left out. Sometimes they'd act like, I don't know what, like I wasn't even there, like I—"

Columbine pulled away and buried her face in her hands. "Oh, Lord, listen, to me, I don't even know what I'm *talking* about anymore. I don't know what's right and what's wrong, I just know I cared for those girls and they didn't *treat* me right!"

She laid her cheek next to mine and a tear trailed down her face. "Is that what you're going to do, you're just goin' to leave and not say anything, and not ever come back?"

"No, now don't you say that, I told you that I'm not. I said I'd—"

Columbine gave a little moan and put her arms around my neck and kissed me hard. I kissed her back and she squirmed in close, and I thought to myself, I thought, Bobby's not in a hurry, Bobby's not going anywhere, Bobby's doing fine . . .

Huh-unh, no way, this isn't going to work, I can't think fun and romance with a dead Indian in the car, this isn't going to cut it at all . . .

I gained some control, sat up and peeled her off.

"Sit tight," I said. "I got to go do this, I'll be back in a minute and a half."

"You better," she said, and leaned up and kissed me on the neck.

I peeked through the blinds and the SWAT team wasn't there. I checked out the parking lot and hurried out to Bobby's stolen car.

Idaho was cool and it looked like rain over Washington state and I didn't really care.

It wasn't one of your long, wordy ceremonies where everyone starts nodding off. I stopped twenty yards inside the reservation and dumped him in a ditch.

"Lord," I said, "we commit this gangster to the deep," and I got out fast and burned rubber, and hurried back to Columbine.

Columbine wasn't there.

Columbine left a note. She wrote it in the dust in the mirror by the door.

OVER TO THE CONVEENUNCE
STORE. RIGHT BACK SOON.

Right below that she drew a little heart.

I sat down to wait. I didn't sit on Bobby's bed, I sat in the straight-back chair. The TV was on and a guy was giving the news. Trouble here and trouble overseas, trouble right here in Idaho. He switched to a remote, a dark and woodsy scene. I looked at the screen and then looked at it again. Phlox was there in a pink jumpsuit. She was still lean and lanky and her legs were still long.

"If I'd of had to sit in that lake with those meece another *minute*," Phlox said, "I'd of been ravished for sure. One of those *bleep!* didn't give a *bleep!* if I was the proper species or not!"

The newscaster pretended this was fun. She didn't care for Phlox at all. A lot of Spudettes were bunched up behind Phlox. I couldn't tell if it was all of them or not. Sprinkled among them were some very large guys in their rescue suits and hard hats. Each had a smile on his face, and a lovely strumpet at his side. The smiles said rescue work had never been as much fun as this.

At ten I walked down to the convenience store. At eleven, I knew that she wasn't coming back. It occurred to me I ought to check the money that I'd hidden in the john. The money wasn't there. Forty-five grand, minus three-hundred bucks I'd taken out for pocket money, gas and Mars bars.

Did Laurel and Daisy take it, or sweet Columbine? What difference did it make, it was gone, it wasn't there. The Nez Perce were out a big bundle, screwed by the white man again.

These and other questions would remain unanswered in my life. Was there really an Abner O. Zzann, or did Bobby make him up? Maybe there were videos and dope. Maybe there were slave girls doing it with sheiks. Secret mammal love in the steamy Amazon.

Everybody made up everything else, how would I know? Lies from Daisy and Columbine. Plenty of lies from Angela and Vinnie Spuds. *Untold* lies from Laurel. Jesus, you couldn't beat Laurel, Laurel topped them all. Laurel told so many lies she couldn't keep them straight, she needed a goddamn memory bank . . .

I wondered if Flo knew mayhem had occurred at BOB'S MARMOT CITY & RATTLESNAKE FARM?

I wondered if Angelo lived through the shootout on the Snake? I wondered if anybody cared?

I wondered if my former love, Giselle, was in Texas with Chicken Man, Stirling R. LaFrance?

I wondered if Claire de Mer was fucking my best friend Phil?

I wondered if Bosco and I could have ever been friends?

I wondered how I'd get out of Idaho with two hundred dollars and forty-eight cents?

Plenty of questions and not a single clue, not a hint, not an answer in the bunch. A brain full of cells named Louie, Huey, Goofy and Daffy Duck. Slap-happy neurons, enigmas in drag, Stooges with bad haircuts. All this crap just bouncing about in dizzy orbits in my head . . .

. . . And just when I'm certain that the light's wimping out, that the batteries are shot, something appears and peeks over the edge, slips and tries to catch itself, falls on its tail like a bucket full of lead . . .

It hits me and it shakes me like a gerbil in a malted milk machine.

My body does the gut-gripping, heart-stopping shit and nearly brings me to my knees.

Because there it is and I see it, and I know it has to be. Because Columbine's dumb, but she's not as dumb as that. She didn't know why she was in our crazy caravan, because Daisy and Laurel kept it from her, they couldn't ever tell her that. Laurel's note said she had to get Daisy away because I owe her a lot . . . she's done a lot for me . . . I don't know if I can ever pay her back. . . .

Right, Laurel, it's pretty damn safe to say that.

Abner Zzann was so drunk that night he didn't know who he was with. Columbine and Laurel look a lot alike if you haven't seem them together too much, that struck me from the start. If you're drunk on your ass, if you're Abner O. Zzann, if you don't really care . . .

It was Laurel and Daisy Nix took to Zzann, not Daisy and Columbine. And when Zzann picked Columbine out of Angela's pictures, what's Daisy going to say? "Listen, you got the wrong girl, the one you want to whack is my very best friend. . . ."

Laurel and Daisy could have straightened this out, but what if they had? If Angela or Michael had believed them, how would that have helped Columbine? They would have killed her anyway, and Laurel and Daisy too. Michael didn't care who was guilty or innocent, he was closing down shop, all Michael wanted was to wipe the slate clean.

The TV lady said cloudy in the evening, sunny tomorrow and the day after that. Fine if you're a marmot or you've got an RV with the A/C on and the fridge full of beer . . .

I'm sorry, Laurel, and Daisy, that goes for you as well. I'm glad it's over and I'm glad it worked out the way it did . . . but that doesn't change what you've got to be thinking, what's got to be going through your head . . . I know you've got to wonder if you might have missed a fine, noble, goddamn lofty or tricky way out of all this, without feeling guilty, embarrassed and dead . . .

I don't have an answer and I wish to hell I did.

BOISE, IDAHO

A Native American male, approximately 45 years old, was discovered late Tuesday morning just inside the Nez Perce Indian Reservation southeast of Lewiston. Shot twice, once in the thigh and once in the side, the victim was rushed by emergency vehicle to a hospital in Lewiston.

"He was barely alive," stated EMS attendant Garley Fine. "We didn't get any pulse, we thought he was dead for some time."

After four days in intensive care, the victim regained consciousness and identified himself as the Reverend Heavy-Iron-Bear of Altus, Oklahoma.

"I was collecting for the church," Reverend Heavy-Iron-Bear said. "Never you mind which one. I was robbed of a considerable amount of cash while attacked by a number of armed, white racists, which is about what you'd expect those m—r f—s to do."

Reverend Heavy-Iron-Bear was released at noon today, against medical advice.

37

Fuck you, Angela, Vinnie and Michael and Uncle Sal . . .

38

Fuck you, Bobby Bad Eye, and the meece you rode in on, pal . . .